PRAISE

THE DARWIN ELEVATOR

"The best part about alien stories is their mystery, and Jason Hough understands that like no other. Full of compelling characters and thick with tension, *The Darwin Elevator* delivers both despair and hope, along with a gigantic dose of wonder. It's a brilliant debut, and Hough can take my money whenever he writes anything from now on."

KEVIN HEARNE, *New York Times* bestselling author
of The Iron Druid Chronicles

"Claustrophobic, intense, and satisfying... I couldn't put this book down. *The Darwin Elevator* depicts a terrifying world, suspends it from a delicate thread, and forces you to read with held breath as you anticipate the inevitable fall."

HUGH HOWEY, *New York Times* bestselling author of *Wool*

"Jason Hough writes with irresistible energy and gritty realism. He puts his characters through hell, blending a convincing plot with heart-stopping action and moments of raw terror as the world goes crazy in the shadow of unfathomable alien intentions."

SARA CREASY, author of the Philip K. Dick
Award–nominated *Song of Scarabaeus*

"A thrilling story right from the first page. This book plugs straight into the fight-or-flight part of your brain."

TED KOSMATKA, author of *The Games*

"Deliciously complex and satisfying... The story unfolds with just the right balance of high adventure, espionage, humor and emotional truth... As soon as you finish, you'll want more."

ALSO AVAILABLE FROM JASON M. HOUGH AND TITAN BOOKS

THE DIRE EARTH CYCLE
The Darwin Elevator
The Plague Forge (September 2013)

EXODUS
THE
TOWERS

BOOK TWO OF THE DIRE EARTH CYCLE

JASON M. HOUGH

TITAN BOOKS

The Exodus Towers
Print edition ISBN: 9781781167656
E-book edition ISBN: 9781781167663

Published by Titan Books
A division of Titan Publishing Group Ltd.
144 Southwark Street, London SE1 0UP

First edition August 2013

1 3 5 7 9 10 8 6 4 2

The Exodus Towers is a work of fiction. Names, characters, places, and incidents are the products of the author's imagination or are used fictitiously. Any resemblance to actual events, locales, or persons, living or dead, is purely coincidental.

Jason M. Hough asserts the moral right to be identified as the author of this work.

This edition published by arrangement with Del Rey, an imprint of The Random House Publishing Group, a division of Random House, Inc.

This book contains an excerpt from the forthcoming book *The Plague Forge* by Jason M. Hough. This excerpt has been set for this edition only and may not reflect the final content of the forthcoming edition.

A CIP catalogue record for this title is available from the British Library.

Printed and bound by CPI Group (UK) Ltd, Croydon, CR0 4YY

For Kip, who lived twice
and didn't make a big stink about it

THE CLEAR

AURA'S EDGE
(No Man's Land)

THE AURA

LYONS

THE MAZE

Stadium

THE DARWIN
SPACE ELEVATOR

Rancid Creek

NIGHTCLIFF
FORTRESS

Clarke's Café

PLATZ
DESALINATION
PLANTS

Temple Sulam

EAST POINT

Skyler's Hangar

THE
GARDENS

OLD
AIRPORT

Prumble's
Garage

THE
NARROWS

OLD
DOWNTOWN

HIDDEN
VALLEY

DARWIN, AUSTRALIA
circa 2283

0   2 km.

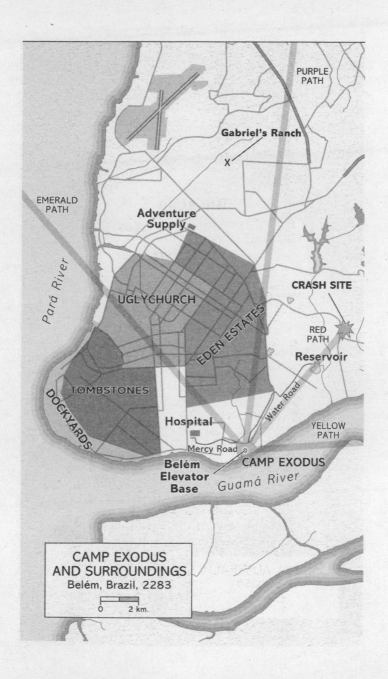

PURPLE
PATH

Gabriel's Ranch

X

EMERALD
PATH

Pará River

Adventure
Supply

UGLYCHURCH

EDEN ESTATES

CRASH SITE

RED
PATH

Reservoir

TOMBSTONES

DOCKYARDS

Hospital

Water Road

YELLOW
PATH

Mercy Road

Belém
Elevator
Base

CAMP EXODUS

Guamá River

CAMP EXODUS
AND SURROUNDINGS
Belém, Brazil, 2283

0   2 km.

If a heathen on the ladder
Raise your gun high.

Take his place, make it matter
This is our time.

Lyric by ~/funk, Cape Town, 2270,
inscribed into the *Testament of the Ladder* by Sister Haley, 2281

Builders? That's a laugh.
All they did was drop a cable and a nasty bug.
You want to call someone a builder,
I say look at Neil Platz.

Skadz, Darwin, Australia, 2280

EXODUS THE

TOWERS

1

BELÉM, BRAZIL

27.APR.2283

The girl danced for an audience of ghosts.

She twirled in a slow, graceful motion, sending ripples through the pristine white dress that draped her lithe form. Her outstretched arms glided through the humid air with a poise and balance Skyler had not seen in many years.

She'd yet to notice him. She was a mirage under the bright sun, and he'd tucked himself in the shadows at the edge of the secluded square. Her focus lay entirely on movement and footing. The cobblestones beneath her bare feet were cracked and uneven, like everything in Belém. Aside from Skyler's motionless form, two skeletal corpses lay in one corner of the courtyard, locked in an infinite embrace, grass sprouting up through their hollow rib cages. She paid no attention to them, either. Ghosts, all.

The looted remains of boutique shops hid the square from the wide avenue beyond. Skyler had only stepped in to find a defensible, quiet place to prepare his midday meal. If that had been one minute ago or ten he couldn't say. For now he stood, whisper quiet, beneath a stucco awning that gave some respite from alternating bouts of glaring sunshine and torrential rain.

Pillars, once white and elegant, supported the partial ceiling. They were nearly encased in flowering vines now, just like the walls and surrounding rooftops. Even the statue that stood watch over the woman had succumbed to the embrace of the rainforest's green, tentacular limbs. In a few decades the whole city would be engulfed, Skyler thought. Just like everywhere else.

Except Darwin, of course. A different scourge consumed that place.

He leaned against the nearest pillar, wholly absorbed in the fluid motions being performed. The girl was not beautiful, not in the classic sense. Not like Tania. She had short auburn hair that flared as dramatically as her dress, but it was dirty and matted. Her deeply tanned skin showed traces of scars on the forearms. When her skirt billowed on the more enthusiastic turns, Skyler could see welts and scrapes on her toned legs. Despite her exquisite movements and dancer's figure, she was a survivor.

She was an immune.

Moving with great care, Skyler slipped a handheld radio from his belt. He kept it switched off when scouting, lest the frequent anxious calls from base camp give away his presence to the forbidding wilderness around him. On any other day he'd wait until his return to camp to give an account of his findings, but the sighting of an immune was worth breaking that pattern, he thought.

Skyler thumbed the power switch.

"—it's *urgent!*" boomed a frenetic voice from the speaker. In one heartbeat the serenity of the courtyard vanished.

Skyler had had the volume on maximum during an earlier downpour and forgotten later to dial it back. The crass sound echoed off the walls, sending a trio of parakeets fluttering from the tangle under the awning. The girl stumbled and caught herself. Her eyes found Skyler and widened.

He started to raise his hands, a universal sign of noble intentions, but he'd scarcely leaned away from the pillar when the girl turned and ran.

"Camp Exodus to Skyler. Come in!" Karl's voice blared from the radio.

Skyler's hand flew to the device, knocking it loose. It fell to the ground in a plastic clatter. He knelt, snatched it up, and wheeled the volume to zero, all in one motion.

When he glanced back up, the courtyard was empty. "Wait!" he called out. She'd darted into an open archway on the opposite side of the square, and he ran toward it, not bothering to swing his machine gun off his shoulder.

He rounded the corner into the arched tunnel and almost had his head blown off.

The crack from the handgun blotted out all other sound. The bullet passed so close to his earlobe he felt a tickle. Skyler skidded to a stop and dove back the way he'd come, only just rounding the corner again when another shot rang out, sending chunks of cobblestone into the air mere centimeters from his feet.

"Cease fire!" he shouted, barely hearing himself over the high-pitched whine in his head.

And she did. The yard fell silent again.

"I mean no harm," he called out. "Just . . . relax."

No answer came. Cautiously, he poked his head around the corner, enough to clear one eye. The hall beyond was empty. "Dammit," he muttered, and bounced to his feet. He ran ahead, his machine gun instinctively in hand now, pointed at the ground five meters in front of him. He slapped the flashlight attached to the barrel and bathed the hall in a pale blue beam, warming to white a second later as the bulb came to full strength.

Her bare feet left obvious tracks in the grimy tile floor. She'd taken a turn, then another, moved around a thick root that had wormed up through a crack, and jumped a spate of broken glass. Skyler repeated her route, wondering absently how long she'd lived here, and how many times previously she'd danced in the noonday sun without a care in the world.

Often, till I came along, he thought.

At the end of the hall he came to a bedroom. Her flowing white dress lay in a heap in the doorjamb, a portion of the skirt hooked by a nasty splinter that jutted from the wooden frame. She'd shrugged out of the garment and left it like the meaningless trinket it was.

The window on the far wall had been thrown open, and he could see the wide, churning waters of the Rio Pará beyond.

In another corner he saw a green bedroll, upright and neatly tied in a circular bundle. A lantern sat on the floor next to it.

His ears still rang from the woman's failed attempt to shoot him in the face. She could be screaming taunts at him from outside and he doubted he'd hear it. Nevertheless he chanced a look out the window.

The young woman was sprinting across a parking lot toward a row of cottages that fronted the swift river. She was naked save for a pair of hiking boots on her feet. In one hand dangled her pistol, and she clutched a heavy olive-green backpack in the other. As he watched she shimmied the full bag over one shoulder, then the other, before disappearing from view.

Not once did she look back.

Skyler sighed. "I'm the least of your worries, dear."

Remembering the radio, he switched it on and immediately heard Karl's frantic voice.

"—in now. *Urgent!*"

"What? What?!" Skyler growled into the mic. Everything was *urgent*. The word had no meaning anymore. "You just scared off—"

"Skyler, thank God. Some colonists are missing, along with a tower."

He closed his eyes and willed himself to relax. "They stole it?"

"No. God, no. They were working on the reservoir perimeter and reported hearing something in the rainforest. They've made no contact since."

"What did they hear?"

"The leader said it sounded like a choir."

"A choir. As in singing?"

"Those were his words."

Skyler pinched his nose between his eyes to stem a coming headache. "Did they mention if they ate some wild mushrooms, or wandered too far from their aura tower, or anything like that?"

"I know how it sounds," Karl said, "but this is a reliable group that has been building that perimeter barricade for two weeks."

"Okay, okay," Skyler said. "I'll head over there. How long ago did they go silent?"

"Two hours."

Skyler swore. "And you're just telling me now?"

"You had your radio off!"

Skyler glanced at the device. "Fair enough. All right then, uh, send a team to meet me there. People who can shoot—"

Karl spoke over him. "Sorry, friend. Tania doesn't want to risk another tower."

"Oh, for fuck's sake." His frustration with the frugal use of the aura towers fell on deaf ears, unless he spoke to Tania alone, a scenario that happened rarely in the last two months. She kept to orbit mostly, after an initial wondrous week of exploring the bizarre alien towers. The logistics of survival took precedence, and Skyler couldn't begrudge that. Still, a weekly visit might be nice, for the colony's morale as much as his.

"If they were moving," Karl added, "and something happened to them, the tower could be adrift."

Skyler grunted. If true, the tower might reach a river or pond. No one had yet tried to send a tower into deep water. They were as likely to explode in world-consuming hellfire as they were to simply float, sink, or stop. As such, Camp Exodus ratified a decree, put forth by Tania, that the towers should be kept away from any water deeper than ten centimeters. For his part, Skyler had chuckled at the arbitrary number and counted himself among the few "no" votes. Now was the time to experiment, he thought. In private Tania chastised him, if gently. "Your survival doesn't depend on the aura, Skyler." A fair point. He still voted no.

"Skyler?" Karl asked.

"Give me their last coordinates," he said, "and I'll see what I can find."

The base camp leader rattled off the numbers.

Skyler spread out his map on the floor of the bedroom. From his breast pocket he pulled a pen that included a convenient ruler along the side. He traced a route through the city from his current position. "I'm all the way over on the west side of town, near the hospital. I'll go northeast until I hit Water Road, and follow from there."

"That's a hell of a hike. Please, hurry."

"Oh, I plan to," he said.

He drew a mark on the group's last known position. Then he

traced a circle around the area he currently occupied and wrote IMMUNE in bold letters above it.

The dancer would have to wait.

Outside on the street, Skyler picked up his duffel bag and glanced east in the direction of the reservoir. He turned south instead.

The sack weighed heavily on his shoulder. He'd filled it that morning, in the dingy back room of a touristy gift shop, with eight hundred palm-sized packets of water purification tablets. Iodine and something else, a vitamin he suspected, but the Portuguese label offered no specifics. The partially collapsed store had little else to be scavenged. Shelves of snacks were long rotted, save for a few Preservall-laden candy bars, which he'd bagged. The toiletries he left behind, knowing the hotel found close to base camp had a stockroom full of such things.

He walked one block south and then another east until he reached Mercy Road, so cleverly named by the colonists because it led to the nearest medical facility to the Elevator base, a few kilometers west. The aura "road" twisted and turned down many of Belém's original streets, but all that mattered to the colonists was the trail of Builder towers placed along the path, providing safe passage to those bringing supplies back to camp.

In less than a minute he heard the hum of a truck coming down the street. Skyler waved and the driver pulled to a stop. After a terse explanation, Skyler hoisted his bag onto the flatbed and shoved it under a stack of folded mattress frames bound for the camp. Then he smacked the passenger door twice and gave a friendly wave to the tense driver.

Skyler had to remind himself of the peril being undertaken by anyone working the aura road. Stray too far from a tower and you might never return. If you did, the chances were good it would be in a psychotic, primal rage.

Orange traffic cones had been placed in rough circles around the towers that linked the Elevator to the hospital, indicating their safe zones, but the markers didn't always stay put. A stiff wet-season storm could wash them away if they were placed carelessly, a situation that happened with surprising regularity considering the stakes involved.

Word of strange sounds and a missing crew had undoubtedly spread, which could only add another dimension to the fear among the colonists.

As soon as the truck moved off, Skyler jogged south down an alley. He crossed the next street diagonally to a row of mansions near the waterfront. His aim was a large house tucked behind a three-meter-high wall. A week earlier he'd explored the place after hearing the faint hum of electricity coming from somewhere within. He'd found some portions of the villa had power, likely coming from a small thorium reactor buried far below, a luxury all the mansion owners along the avenue pooled their money for, no doubt.

Skyler jogged down the crumbling driveway, hopping over clumps of wild grass that knifed through the bricks. He hoisted open a garage door at the end of the path and found his discovery still sitting within, practically begging him to hop on.

The motorcycle would have been expensive a decade ago, and even now, despite five-odd years of neglect, it looked like it had never been touched. Sleek red paint covered the carbon-fiber portions, surrounded by either polished chrome or brushed aluminum arranged as much for aesthetics as functionality.

Unlike the other five bikes in the long garage, this one had knobby tires and ample ground clearance. The others were all low-slung, built for racing just like the row of sports cars that shared the space. Useless on the cluttered roads of Belém, so full of cracks, sinkholes, weeds, and worse.

Skyler ran a hand along the bulging pack at the center of the bike's frame. "I'll call you Takai," he said with sincerity. The bike had an Italian pedigree, but he didn't think it would mind.

Tucked within that central red shell were the important parts: a fully charged Zigg ultracap and a powerful electric motor.

He yanked the charging cable from the receptacle on the side of the bike and tossed it aside. Depleted when he found it, the gauge cluster showed a full cap now, and Skyler grinned from ear to ear. One small Zigg could run a bike like this for a thousand kilometers, easily.

A helmet rested on a nearby workbench, but Skyler ignored it. He needed his senses more than he needed the protection it offered. He did, however, grab the pair of sunglasses that lay next to it. Wiping away the dust, he studied the reddish lenses and then slipped the pair over his nose. Driver's glasses, in good condition. He smiled again.

Outside, he flew down the driveway, taking the bumps and dips in stride, swelling with juvenile delight at the high-pitched whine of the motor-and-cap combination. Out on the main road, Skyler twisted the handle to full acceleration and nearly fell off as the motorcycle came to life, its front wheel lifting off the ground as it surged forward.

As he weaved his way through the streets of Belém, the speedometer kissing 100 kilometers per hour in some stretches, he thought of Samantha. She would kill to ride a bike like this. Over the years they'd brought a few back to Darwin, but the price offered always outweighed her desire to keep one.

The thought of her dampened his mood.

Flying past the vine-choked buildings of Belém, Skyler wondered if Samantha was having anywhere near as much fun, wherever she was.

2

DARWIN, AUSTRALIA

27.APR.2283

The fist caught Samantha squarely on the temple.

A solid blow, and she might have fallen had she not expected it. Fallen and lost.

Instead she let the guard's punch assist her in a shift of position, her weight moving to her left leg. She pushed with that leg and brought her right arm around in a vicious uppercut to the guard's abdomen. Air rushed from the man's mouth in a gasp.

A few of the onlookers groaned in sympathetic pain.

Fueled by their reaction, Sam pressed the advantage. A left jab, again to the midsection. Then a right hook that caught the poor bastard on his jaw and produced a loud, sharp crack.

He spun a half turn, his eyes rolling back in his head, and toppled to the floor. Just like that, Sam's first bout ended.

Shaking the sting from her knuckles, she walked over to the guard and leaned over him. "Can you stand?"

He coughed in response. Then the Nightcliff goon turned his head and spat blood onto the dusty concrete floor. "Damn well try," he muttered.

Sam extended her hand and he took it. Conversations

embroiled the room as bets changed hands. Fistfuls of stamped notes here, a half bottle of cider there, and all the bravado and excuses that went with such things.

"That was fun," she said, rolling her head from side to side. "Who's next?"

"Take a break," someone replied, handing her a labeled bottle of vodka, quarter-full. "No one fights twice in a row. That's a rule."

She shrugged. "Advantage, me."

Another bout started and the fifty-or-so gathered Nightcliff personnel returned their attentions to the fight, bets, and drinks. She pushed through the crowd, noting the icy stares of potential opponents as she passed. Each wore their thirst for revenge like a badge.

Her handler waited at the back of the room near the only door, billy club resting across his knees. His face betrayed a hint of admiration as Samantha handed him the bottle.

Sam had learned his last name, Vaughn, from the handwritten label on his helmet. She'd yet to learn his first. A field of even stubble grew on his face, framing a wide nose and narrow eyes. The brown hair atop his head he kept shaved as close as his young beard. "I'll eat like a king this week thanks to you," he said.

"Told you," she replied, taking the spot on the wall next to him. "Should've brought me here sooner."

"No kidding." He took a polite sip from the bottle and offered it back.

"That's yours. I need my wits."

He grunted. "Well, I'm on duty, so I guess we're both staying dry." He handed the bottle to his right instead, and the spectator there took it without hesitation.

As much as she hated to admit it, she was warming up to the bloke. He'd become her target for seduction on the first night of her imprisonment. The look in his eyes the first time he'd brought her food marked him as possible prey. A way out if she played her cards right.

Seduction had never been her strong suit, though. She knew from past experience that being too overt usually killed her chances, and that most of the men who sought her company liked her for her toughness and robust curves, not for her feminine wiles. So she'd skipped the batting of eyes and licking of lips bullshit, and taken a more subtle strategy: tough talk, opportune lack of modesty, and what she hoped came across as a genuine interest in his miserable, mundane life.

A month on and all she'd managed to do was get Vaughn to admit her into the informal boxing club that met once a week in the mess. Still, she counted this as a big milestone in her escape. She was out of her cell, step one in any prison break.

Next on her list was finding Kelly. Vaughn occasionally answered her inquiries about the woman, with reluctance. Blackfield had ordered the two of them held separately, he'd told her. No contact whatsoever. Kelly was doing okay after a short hunger strike, kept in a similar cell to Sam's but on the other side of the fortress. That's all he claimed to know.

Remembering her gambit, Sam began to tug at the collar of her tank top. Men loved a wet shirt—she knew enough about seduction to know that—but the bout had ended quickly. In hindsight it might have been a good idea to drag it on just to get her white shirt nice and sweat-soaked. She settled for stretching the collar in and out to fan herself, giving Vaughn an eyeful with each pull should he bother to glance.

All you have to do is ask, you idiot, she thought, *and we'll be rolling between the sheets. A good time for both of us, though the last time you'll ever see me. I'll make it worth your while.*

The crowd erupted as another match ended. Someone was dragged from the makeshift ring, feetfirst.

"My turn, jailbird," came a rough voice nearby.

Sam stood to face her next opponent. The swarthy giant of a man stood a few centimeters taller than her and had a bushy beard that came down to his chest. Faded tattoos laced his neck and arms. "I'm not sure if that's drink in your beard," she said, "or drool."

He glanced down at her chest, then back. "Bit of both. C'mon, prisoner. If your owner don't mind . . ."

Vaughn gave the slightest of nods, and folded his arms. Sam knew where his wager would fall.

They walked to the center of the crowd, where an open space formed the boxing ring. Samantha flexed her hands and then did a few quick jumps off her toes. The resulting bounce of her breasts caught the attention of half the room, though if Vaughn saw from his place at the back, she had no idea.

Her opponent noticed, though. *He* licked his lips. "Nice big targets," he said with a drunken grin.

"Sorry, mate," Samantha said. "If I can't hit below the belt, you have to stay away from the twins."

Laughs went up from the audience.

The big man tilted his head to one side, looking genuinely wounded. "Christ, woman. Wasn't gonna *punch* them. . . ."

Vaughn guided her by the arm through Nightcliff's dreary yard.

He hadn't bothered to cuff her, a good sign, in her view. Still, he kept his black baton in hand. He would put up a hell of a fight if she picked one, and besides, there was still the issue of Kelly. *Patience.*

"I'll find you something to put on that eye," he said after a time.

"Don't bother. It's not that bad."

"It's purple."

Samantha sighed and gave a terse nod. Her skull pounded. She had to keep her right eye closed for fear it might bulge right out of her head.

He led her between buildings and through narrow, fenced-in spaces. Clouds kept an otherwise bright moon from providing much illumination, but it was enough that Vaughn didn't bother with his flashlight. Their wet footfalls almost drowned out the loading work going on at the climber port.

She took a chance and feigned a stumble. Righting herself, she groaned and stepped wide.

"You okay?" he asked.

"A little dizzy. It's fading." After a second she tried to rest her head on his shoulder, but her height made the position awkward, so she simply leaned on him.

Vaughn caught the hint and slipped an arm around her waist.

Perfect, she thought. *A nice romantic stroll.*

"So," she said, "what's the news outside?"

Vaughn shrugged. "I don't pay it much attention."

"You must have heard something."

He fell quiet for a dozen steps. She imagined he must have orders not to share any news with her. The fact that he now wrestled with that she took as a very good sign indeed.

"I heard," Samantha said, "they tricked Russell into going to Africa, then dropped a bomb on his fleet."

"Wasn't a bomb," Vaughn said. "They pushed an old satellite out of orbit, or something."

"And missed? Well, obviously." Russell had paid two visits to Samantha, peppering her with flirtatious small talk and vague threats. Mercifully he'd stopped coming a few weeks ago, finally convinced she did not know the whereabouts of the "traitors."

"Still took out a bunch of the scavenger planes Russell brought along." Vaughn let that settle. He knew of her past, knew she might have had friends out there. "They also tried to drop a satellite on Nightcliff, but missed. The thing fell outside the aura over in Old Downtown, took a few landmarks with it."

Two misses? Skyler's new friends either had horrible aim or Vaughn had things wrong. Sam couldn't see what they'd gain by nuking Nightcliff anyway. Even if the alien cord of the Elevator survived, the infrastructure would be annihilated beyond hope of repair. No, it must have been a warning shot. Blackfield might not comprehend it, but she saw the angles.

"Water plants are on strike," the guard went on, opening up. "Platz people over there, you know. They're the only ones who can work all that machinery."

"A strike, eh? What do they want?"

He hesitated. "Doesn't matter. Blackfield is sending in a few squads to put an end to it."

"That's our Russell. Way of the gun."

"He's got no other choice."

"Give them what they want?"

Vaughn tightened his lips. "No," he said. "No, that he can't do."

"They must be asking a lot," she said.

"I'm not supposed to talk about it."

There it was. A line, and Vaughn was tightroping it. Another week, she thought, and he'd be telling her all about it in the afterglow of a good romp.

"What else, then? How are the Orbitals handling their new generalissimo?"

He paused and let go of her. For a split second she thought she'd gone too far, but he made a twirling motion with his index finger. Sam turned her back to him and clasped her hands behind her back. She held them low, against her buttocks, so that he couldn't avoid incidental contact in order to replace the handcuffs. Some small part of her didn't mind the brush of fingers there.

For the first time since she'd attempted this tactic, he didn't jerk her hands to the small of her back. In fact, he took longer than usual getting the cuffs on.

Shackled again, he led her back into the brig. A pair of guards on patrol wandered by them and grunted their hellos to Vaughn. The cuffs were a show for them, she realized. Vaughn didn't want them to know he'd broken protocol. She knew, though, which meant they shared a secret now. *Not long now,* she thought, *and you'll be snared in the web*.

The low jailhouse building butted against Nightcliff's north wall. She heard waves crashing on the rocks beyond, as reliable as a beating heart. Unfortunately that calming sound didn't reach her windowless cell. Nothing reached there except cold meals and her mirthless guards. Vaughn at night, an ass named Saul during the day. She called him Paul, just to piss him off, which was easy enough to do.

Vaughn guided her back into her makeshift cell in the makeshift prison. The bars had been welded together from rebar and old pipes. It worked well enough. The bed, a flimsy foam mattress that left her feet hanging, lay upright against the back wall. Someone had swept the place while they were gone. Probably searched for contraband, too, not that she had any.

"See you tomorrow," Vaughn said after the cuffs came off. He closed and locked the gate behind him.

"You were telling me the news," she said to his back.

"Tomorrow," he repeated.

Samantha folded her arms and leaned against the wall by the door. "Vaughn . . ."

He paused.

"C'mon, man," she said. "You don't know what it's like, trapped in here, no way to know—"

"We're both trapped in here, Sam."

The words tripped her. His voice held more than a hint of wrath. Not for her, she thought. "So talk to me, then. What's the harm?"

"I have orders."

She snorted a laugh. "Hell . . . Orders. I'm not going to squawk."

The guard stood in the outer doorway, half-in, half-out. Without looking back, he said, "Food's scarce. The traitors took the farms, I heard, and Nightcliff's reserves are either used or spoiled. So Russell needs the roofers to share theirs, but no one is playing along and he doesn't have enough manpower to force the issue."

Sam swallowed and kept quiet. *The traitors took the farms.* The words almost brought tears to her eyes. If Skyler were sitting here, she'd crush him with a hug. Stealing the farm platforms, what a damn brilliant move.

The guard sighed. "Water plants are on strike. The bloody scavengers are on strike."

"Hey! I was a scavenger, you know."

"Everyone wants a part of Russell's pie," he said, ignoring her, "before they'll throw in with him. That's what I hear, anyway. . . ."

"And Russell's not the sharing sort."

Vaughn laughed at that. "No, no he is not. Besides, all he cares about anymore is finding the runaways. He hardly ever comes down here now. See you tomorrow, Sam."

"Night."

Half an hour later a kid came in and handed her breakfast through the bars. Inside the parcel she found an ice pack, still frozen.

Samantha lay down on the thin mattress, ignoring her aching arms and knuckles, and placed the frozen block against her swollen eye.

"Another week and I'll come for you, Kelly," she whispered to the ceiling. "One more bloody week."

She drifted off to sleep as the sun rose over Darwin.

Not that she could see it.

3

BELÉM, BRAZIL

27.APR.2283

At the reservoir Skyler decided to ditch the bike.

Rain had begun to fall in large, irregular drops and when the paved portion of the road ended he found that even the knobby tires on the motorcycle had trouble keeping their grip. Worse, tall grass choked the land around the square, man-made lake.

He slowed enough to keep from killing himself, and upon reaching the lake he dismounted and sought a dry place for the motorcycle. A worthy candidate came in the form of an office behind the deserted purification facility, and Skyler tucked the bike inside, harboring selfish hope that it might still be here the next time he needed it. The colony, being populated entirely of Orbitals, had a strong "community property" bent. Teams of technicians and scientists worked out here frequently, trying to get the machinery back online. After two months, the colony still had no way to purify large quantities of water, a situation now at the top of the priority list.

He set the motorcycle's key on top of the back tire, gave the machine one more appreciative look, and left. Outside again, he traced a path around the water's edge. Swelled by months of near-constant rainfall, the water nevertheless gave Skyler pause. If he stuck his arm in up to the elbow, he doubted he'd be able to see his fingers in the greenish brown murk.

At the far side of the lake, he turned north and trudged across the wide field that buffered the water from the rainforest. Rain began to fall in a steady thrum. Skyler stopped in the tall grass and knelt. He'd taken to keeping a wide-brimmed bushman's hat on his back, and flipped it up onto his head. The dark brown leather reeked when wet, but it kept the rain at bay.

The reservoir, despite being less than a kilometer outside the city, was completely surrounded by thick rainforest. Belém's eastern edge transitioned from slum to forest so abruptly that Skyler had been initially reminded of Aura's Edge in Darwin. On one side dense slums and concrete buildings were packed in with a density that rivaled the Maze. Walk a few paces east across a street or creek and the rainforest took over. He guessed some sort of conservation law had been in place here before the disease came, designed to protect the resource that brought in wealthy would-be adventurers from everywhere else. Unlike many cities, Belém had grown up instead of out.

From his position, Skyler heard no choir. The mild storm, thwacking against both his hat and the endless green canopy, would likely cover up any such sound, if it even existed. He had his doubts. More likely the missing colonists all ate the same tainted food.

A thorough scan of the horizon produced no hint of an aura tower above the treetops. This came as no surprise, as the mobile work crews were usually assigned the smaller towers, the assumption being that the tall towers were "better" and thus more valuable. Skyler knew of no evidence for this, but he had long given up arguing such trivial points.

He moved on. A perimeter road, almost consumed by the regrowth, marked the border between the clearing and the imposing tree line. A crude barricade, less than half complete, was being erected along the meter-wide path, more to keep local wildlife out than subhumans. Skyler walked to the endpoint of the improvised fence and took in the surroundings. The work had stopped at a sharp corner in the perimeter, and from there a wider dirt road forked off and plunged straight into the dark heart of the rainforest. The canopy stretched over the trail from one side to the other, forming a natural tunnel filled with weak green light. The ceiling of broad leaves also served to keep the dirt below mostly dry.

Dry enough to still hold evidence of an aura tower's passage, at least.

Despite being small, the aura tower still left a wide, smooth trail in the muddy path. Though the towers seemed to float above the ground when they moved, the "cushion" field they created still smoothed out the rougher parts of the ground beneath. A clean series of footprints trailed in the wake, spaced at a walking pace. Skyler concluded that the missing team must have been calm and in control when they left. The accepted practice for moving with an aura tower was to keep one person on each side of it, ready to nudge it should the thing start to drift. Once in motion the towers would keep moving, and thus they were prone to stray if not kept under constant watch. But they could just as easily become tangled or stalled if they collided with anything of significant bulk or height, thus the need for spotters ahead and behind the alien objects.

Beyond the four guides, anyone else in a party tended to stay out in front, ready to warn the others if a course correction might be needed.

In a low voice, Skyler spoke into his radio. "I'm at the point where they left the perimeter. Looks like they went into the rainforest here. Going to follow."

A few seconds passed before Karl replied. "You made good time. Any sign of the alleged choir?"

"Negative," Skyler said. "But I did pass a simply *lovely* string quartet."

"Keep in touch, you prick," Karl replied, chuckling.

Skyler clung to the edge of the path, where a carpet of fallen leaves served to keep his boots from sinking into the hungry organic mulch beneath. Flush tree limbs made a cathedral ceiling above him, thick with flowers and birds and strangler vines. Emerald-tinged light filtered down in tiny patches, and the air smelled of fresh rain mixed with old decay.

The path had once been a narrow road. Chunks of blacktop poked through in places where the relentless rain had eroded everything to the hardpan and beyond. Mother Nature had already won this war, and Skyler thought even the hint of a path here would disappear in another five years, giving way to ferns, roots, and strangler vines.

Ahead, as the road crested at a low rise, Skyler saw a break in the canopy and a wisp of rising smoke. The acrid smell of flame hit him an instant later.

A memory tugged at him of his descent on that first climber down to Belém. There'd been smoke northeast of the Elevator base, debris from the climber destroyed in orbit earlier that same day. But that had been months ago, and rain had fallen almost daily since. Surely those flames had long since been banished.

Campfire then?

He readied his new weapon, a compact machine gun scavenged a week earlier from the basement of a Belém police station. Skyler left the path and worked his way parallel to it through the forest. Years of wet dead leaves softened his footfalls. Even just a few meters off the road the forest became dark as night. Almost no vegetation grew this low to the rainforest floor, with so little sunlight available, but vines hanging from the branches above still forced him to take a winding path. It took every ounce of self-control to keep his machete sheathed against his leg instead of slicing back and forth across the tangle all around him. Such a sound carried, even in rain this heavy.

At the crest of the rise he paused to study the scene before him.

The path made its way through a ruined village, long succumbed to the unchecked forest growth. Vines as thick as Skyler's arm snaked their way through every opening. Tall grass sprouted in damp clumps from the fractured soil.

A body lay just inside the perimeter of the small town, facedown in a puddle of brown water. Skyler dropped to a crouch and brought up the rifle scope to his eye, clicking off the holographic target in order to clear the view.

Other than the body, the village looked empty. He could not see the far side through the misty rain, however. Near the corpse, white smoke rose from the wall of a tiny wooden shack. Flames licked out from an object lodged there, too small to discern at this distance.

He let a moment pass before creeping down the rise. A backpack lay discarded just off the path, ten meters from the body. Stepping over it, Skyler raised his gun again and crept forward.

It was a woman. A colonist, from the clothing. He could see the rash on her neck clear enough, but walked to her anyway and used his boot to nudge her onto her back.

Facedown in the dirt, that's no way to go. Skyler kept walking.

The meager fire came from a flare. It struggled to burn the moldy, rotten wood of the structure. Someone had fired the thing straight into the building, either in self-defense or a botched attempt to launch it into the sky above. The glowing fuel within the yellow shell sizzled under the falling water.

Two more bodies lay near the center of town. One still held the ankle of the other in a viselike grip, and both had the rash. SUBS affected people differently, and a propensity for either fight or flight often manifested first. In Skyler's experience, the fighters survived more often—assuming their brain wasn't crushed by the infection.

"That's three," he muttered to himself, glancing left and right. "Where are the rest of you?"

He found the aura tower on the far side of town, resting against a low building of rotten wooden walls. Some planks had snapped where the tower's hard edge collided, and only vines now held the flimsy single-room structure together.

The stillness of the tower's idle state gave Skyler a chill. He wondered if the thing would move an inch, or look any different, should a billion years pass. In the wan light he could just make out the strange, overlapping geometric patterns that laced the surface of the alien object.

He stepped around a Land Rover parked near the small home. Weeds and wild grasses burst through every seam in the rusted body panels. A power coupling was still attached to the recharge port on the rear flank, though the cord had all but disintegrated.

Someone—*something*—nearby coughed.

Skyler jumped at the hacking noise, which carried through the static of rainfall like glass shattering in a silent room. The sound came from within the damaged hovel, still five meters away behind the hulking form of the aura tower.

Without a second thought he clicked his holo-sight back on and brought his newfound gun to a ready position. Stepping sideways, he moved in a slow arc around the crumbling shack.

"Someone there?" he called.

Another cough came in response, muffled this time.

"You can come out, I won't hurt you."

In a span of five seconds, the rain dwindled to a sprinkle, and then stopped completely. Only residual runoff could be heard, clacking against the forest floor from the lush canopy that ringed the village.

Still moving sideways, Skyler continued his curved path until he'd come around to the back of the building. There were gaps, once filled by a door and window, now rimmed with pale yellow vines, like maggots clogging a wound. The room within remained shrouded in total darkness.

Skyler paused long enough to click on the flashlight slung below the barrel of his weapon. The strong LED beam had limited impact outdoors, but it was enough to cast the interior in pale white.

Having already announced himself, Skyler strode to the window frame with little concern for the plodding, crunching sounds his boots made.

Two meters from the opening the creature leapt out at him.

He fired on pure instinct, the bullet leaving a coin-sized red splotch in the center of the being's forehead. Only after it slumped to the ground did he allow himself to exhale. He quelled the urge to put another round in its back, and swept the room with his light instead.

Another body slumped against the wall. A man, his throat torn out in a bloody mess that made Skyler's stomach clench. No rash marked the poor bastard's neck, which meant he'd managed to stick close enough to the aura tower to survive, for a time. Too bad his comrades hadn't.

Five of the six accounted for, Skyler backed away from the building and walked a wide circle around the edge of town. Made up of perhaps fifty small structures, the tiny village turned out to be otherwise devoid of life. He crisscrossed from building to building and found nothing larger than a two-meter-long snake, which he happily left alone.

Satisfied there was no immediate danger, he returned to the aura tower and sat near it. A full hour passed in quiet solitude. He ate some dried mango, a staple of the fledgling Belém colony, and a Preservall-packaged granola bar, something he'd pocketed earlier in the day. It tasted like almonds and honey, not bad if he ignored the chemical aftertaste the preservative gave. Two long draws from his canteen washed down the midmorning meal, and he took his time refilling the stainless steel bottle with rainwater dripping from a plate-sized leaf, allowing the carbon filter in the canteen's lid ample opportunity to purify the cool liquid.

The sixth member of the doomed group never materialized. Skyler had no trouble imagining the man or woman lying dead in the tangled undergrowth, vibrant rash proudly worn on their once-human neck. Or maybe they were a survivor, doomed to a life as a subhuman, and even now were stumbling through the rainforest in search of a meal or shelter like any other primal creature.

Whatever their fate, he doubted they would ever be found. Certainly they posed no danger to him anymore.

He lifted his radio and spoke. "Karl, Skyler. I've got bad news."

When Karl responded, Skyler painted the scene for him. He knew the stoic man well enough not to sugarcoat any of it.

"The Mercy Road team brought back a bunch of stretchers," Karl said, sounding numb. "We'll send a team back out there tomorrow to recover the bodies and their gear."

"Suits me," Skyler said.

"Can you bring the tower in?"

"Sure," he said. "See you soon. Over."

Ten minutes later, as he packed his gear in the shadow of the aura tower, Skyler heard singing.

Not singing, he decided.

No, this was a chorus of primal humming. He knew the sound well enough: subhumans, and a lot of them. The sound was distant still, coming from the northeast, by his estimation.

He listened for a full minute. The voices were just on the edge of his hearing, fading in and out. There was, he realized with dread, an unmistakable rhythm to their hum.

"Perfect," he said to himself. "Every time I figure you bastards out, you change again."

Kneeling in the mud, Skyler set to work disconnecting the flashlight attached to the barrel of his gun. He slipped it into his backpack and pulled out a plastic green case. Willing himself to remain calm, he thumbed the latches and opened the hard-shell box, revealing a grenade launcher within.

He'd yet to fire it. The weapon had been recovered the same day he found the gun itself, in the munitions locker of a Belém police precinct. Normally he would test any equipment before taking it into a dangerous situation, but with only five rounds of ammunition, he'd erred on the side of conservation. The flashlight would do him little good in the outdoors, though, so he took the risk and slid the launcher module into position until it snapped into place.

Skyler slipped his backpack on again and pulled the shoulder straps as tight as they would go. Satisfied it wouldn't jostle about, he focused on the sound and began to walk toward it.

4

MELVILLE STATION

27.APR.2283

"Remove your clothing," Zane Platz said, "and lie facedown on the floor. Please."

Tania held her breath and watched, uncomfortable with the order but unable to deny the wisdom of it.

The new arrivals glanced at one another. Their surprise and discomfort at the order came through the video feed with surprising clarity, by way of nothing more than their body language. Some of them must have recognized Zane's voice, too, which only added to their confusion.

Tim suggested the strip-down tactic after the first batch of colonists came aboard, one month earlier. With them, the order had been to simply sit on their hands and wait to be searched. The process took far too long, she thought. More important, after studying the video they'd found a correlation between those who obeyed eagerly and those who were spies.

A request to remove one's clothing, Tim suggested, would be even more telling. The idea surprised her coming from the young man. Or, man, rather. She'd learned over dinner recently that he was a year older than her, despite his boyish looks. It was the freckles, Tania decided, that seemed to radiate youthful innocence.

One of the forty individuals began to disrobe without hesitation.

Zane put one hand over the microphone. "Spy," he said.

"Yup," Tim replied from behind. "That one, too," he added, pointing. "Too eager to comply. See?"

Tania grinned and shook her head at the same time, as if she'd lost a friendly bet. She wrote quick descriptions of the two on a pad of graph paper, marking their rough position within the larger group. By the time she looked back up, all of the candidates sent from Darwin were in the process of undressing. A few already lay naked on the deck of the curved room. Only then did she find she could exhale.

That first moment, when the fresh arrivals walked out of their capsule, terrified her. Up until that instant, all she could picture was a stream of well-armed Nightcliff guards rushing forth from the makeshift shuttle. Or worse, no one at all, but instead a bomb with a red ribbon tied around it. *Russell Blackfield is toying with us,* she thought. He needs the food, yes, but not enough to set aside his wounded ego. Sooner or later he will try something, something more ambitious than a handful of informants. At least this second shipment contained no overt surprises.

There was still the matter of interviewing the newcomers. They'd be photographed, too, the images sent up to Black Level and down to Camp Exodus so existing members could look for people they recognize, vouch for them. She promised herself she would apologize personally to all the legitimate colonists. Tim's technique for rooting out spies might be effective, but she wanted to make sure the others realized they were leaving indignity like this behind.

Of course, she had more to apologize for. Leaving in the first place, taking the farms. The innocent scavengers and crews who'd died when the farm platform came down in Africa. These crimes weighed on her, as if she bore the corpse of her former self on her back.

"Are we ready?" Zane asked.

"Ready," Tim said.

"I'd feel better if Skyler were here," Tania said. "We're not as good at judging people."

"There's too much to do down below. . . ."

"I know, I'm just . . ." Tania let the sentence die and handed Tim the graph paper. "Take the team in, and be careful."

He took it and offered her a reassuring grin. Then he vanished through the door of the tiny security office.

A section of hallway one level over had been designated for "colonist processing," if for no other reason than it had lockable doors at both ends, and an access tube up to the cargo bay. Tania felt strongly that no one should be in direct contact with an arriving group until they could ascertain that none carried concealed weapons. As with the first shipment a month ago, Russell appeared to be exercising some restraint once again, if the nude bodies on the monitor said anything.

"We're at the door." Tim's voice, over the handheld.

Zane replied, "It's still clear, son."

On the screen, the door at the far end of the room opened, and Tim entered with the processing team, a group that consisted of seven other fighters trained by Kelly Adelaide months earlier. Most had either a military or law enforcement background.

The process went smoothly. The fresh colonists were escorted in groups to cabins that lined the hub hallway beyond. Each would be interviewed later, the spies or miscreants sent back at the earliest opportunity.

Soon only the two men marked as spies remained. Tim returned with four of his team in tow. The suspected Nightcliff agents' bags and clothing were searched, and then Tim gave them a short speech. "Sorry, going to need to hold you two for a while."

Slumped shoulders and heads hung low, the two men walked between an escort of guards toward their improvised cells. They weren't stupid.

"I wonder how many more we'll find," Zane said, "in the interviews."

"Your guess is as good as mine," Tania replied, standing. She dreaded this but saw no other choice. So much work had yet to be done on the ground, not to mention the myriad of tasks being neglected on the farm platforms.

Before she reached the door of the security office, the comm activated and Karl's face appeared.

"I'll take it," Zane said. "Hello, Karl."

"Zane. Is Tania around?"

"Right here," Tania said, stepping back into the room. "How about some good news?"

Karl grimaced.

Oh, hell, Tania thought.

"Just talked to Skyler. He found the reservoir team. Looks like they let their tower get away from them somehow. All are lost, I'm afraid."

Tania slumped into her seat, her eyes never leaving Karl's sad, exhausted face. "Go ahead without me, Zane," she said flatly. Her focus went to Karl. "Tell me what happened."

She closed her eyes as Karl recounted the story. Memories of Hawaii, of battle and the crumpled bodies that resulted, helped her picture what Skyler found out there. More than anything, she wished a role could be found for him here, in orbit, next to her.

His immunity still meant too much, though. Despite the aura towers, Skyler's unique attribute and his ability to find things made him ideal for scouting and mapping the city. If anything he could help even more down below by training others to scavenge. They had two years, a bit less now, to get Camp Exodus running smoothly before the Builders' schedule indicated another event would occur.

Schedule. The concept still boggled her mind, even though the math worked. For reasons she figured she'd never understand, each Builder event arrived after a specific fraction of time from the last. First the Darwin Elevator arrives, then almost twelve years pass and the SUBS virus begins its relentless march across the planet from somewhere in Africa. A bit less than five years later Tania spots the next ship, the one that brought the Belém Elevator and the strange aura towers. Forty-two percent of the time elapsed between prior events. If that pattern holds, in just about two years something new will happen.

She shuddered. On most days two years seemed like a luxurious amount of time to her. Sometimes, though, it seemed like a blink of the eye. She had to resist the urge not to rush things. They'd only get one chance to start over, of that she felt sure.

"How's it going up there?" Karl asked, breaking her train of thought.

She sighed. "So far, so good. Only a few obvious spies this time."

"A welcome change, I guess."

"Tim is processing them now. Anyone able-bodied we will send down to you as soon as we can."

Karl nodded. "I do have some good news. We've got a climber loaded with a partial shipment of water and air. The crane just hoisted it onto the cord, and it should begin the climb in about ten minutes."

"That is great to hear," Tania said. Other than a few test shipments, no significant delivery of air or water had occurred since they arrived above Belém. She'd already moved all noncritical personnel down to the surface and closed off empty portions of the station. Recyclers were few and far between on Platz-built stations, as the design specifications relied heavily on the promise of resupply via the space elevator. "Cheaper that way," Neil used to say.

Karl glanced at the watch on his wrist. "Twelve hours, give or take, and you'll have it."

Under any other circumstances, Tania would have called for celebration. Her mind returned to the dead colonists instead. "About the lost team. We're not going to . . . leave them out there, are we?"

"I'll take a group out there tomorrow," Karl said. "Recover the bodies and give them a proper burial."

"And the tower?"

A flash of disapproval crossed his face. "Relax. Skyler's handling it," he said.

"I'm sorry," she said. "The loss is heartbreaking. I shouldn't be bothering you about the tower. It's just—"

Karl held up a hand. His attention had shifted away from the camera. She heard a faint noise through the speaker. It sounded like an argument.

"Just a second, Tania, there's shouting outside."

"What's going on?"

Karl stepped away from the camera, out of view. "A sub at the perimeter, maybe? Hold on."

Her view now consisted of the wall behind Karl's seat. The corner of a map of Belém filled the left side of the screen. She heard a rustling sound and then saw light as Karl opened the door, off camera.

"Who are you people?" Karl barked, his voice faint but unmistakable.

A second later a form flashed across the image: Karl, falling. His shoulder smacked against the table and knocked the camera on its side.

Tania stood, tilting her head to match the angle. "What's happening? Karl?!"

A gloved hand came into view, straight to the camera.

The image went black.

5

BELÉM, BRAZIL

27.APR.2283

Ten steps into the rainforest, Skyler came to a steep embankment that dropped two meters down to a narrow stream. Rivulets of water traced miniature caves and waterfalls into the earthen wall. He hopped down and crouched by the water. The rhythmic sound of subhuman humming danced at the edge of his senses, as the dense foliage confused and baffled the noise. He forced himself to pause in order to ascertain the source's direction and let his eyes readjust to the twilight darkness of the world below the treetops.

Satisfied he had the right vector, Skyler moved ahead. As the sound grew ever louder, he took care to step over any fresh-fallen twig or leaf in his path that might otherwise crack beneath his boot.

The trees here were tall, forming a ceiling above that blocked almost all hint of the sky. Raindrops fell in irregular places as they percolated through the maze of broad leaves and smooth branches. Insects small and large buzzed around his face, an annoyance he'd grown accustomed to since arriving in Belém.

A chill swept over him. With so little sunlight, the air here had a surprising bite. Skyler zipped his vest all the way to the top and did his best to ignore the tingle from his earlobes and nose.

After fifty meters, the chorus of crooning subhumans became unmistakable. The farther Skyler crept, the more voices he estimated were part of the inhuman choir. They came from left, right, and center. After a dozen more steps, a growing fear slowed his pace to a crawl. He'd stepped over countless roots and vines, ducked under as many low branches. Retreat would be slow, should he need to run. Part of him said to go back now, report the subhuman tribe, and come back with twenty armed colonists.

Yet the strange noise pulled him. He couldn't deny that, and he had to know what the miserable beings were doing out here, in the middle of nowhere, deep in the Amazon rainforest, singing softly in a babble of meaningless sounds.

Skyler slowed further when he came to realize a thick mist enveloped the forest ahead. He thought it might be smoke at first, but no odor accompanied the haze. Against every instinct save curiosity, he took another step. Then another. Before long the still mist surrounded him, and visibility fell to five meters or less.

"Stupid, stupid," he whispered, even as he took another step.

Individual subhuman voices stood out against the thrum now. The sounds came from the left and right, but not from ahead, he realized. It was as if the beings were formed in a line, and he'd just crossed it. He glanced left and tried to peer through the heavy mist. Just at the edge of his vision he thought he saw a human form, swaying on its feet as if in a trance. To the right he saw the same, or thought he did. The cloud made it hard to trust his eyes.

Only then did it occur to him that there were no trees here. None upright, anyway. Fallen trunks of shattered wood littered the ground around him, some still tucked in the embrace of strangler figs. He stepped around the huge stump of a kapok tree. The smooth, fleshy base ended in a violent mess of splinters. Another nearby had been uprooted completely. The chill he'd felt before vanished, replaced by humid warmth that grew with each step.

The mist cleared slightly, if only for an instant, and Skyler realized he'd walked into a wide ravine with curved walls. The ground beneath him sloped gradually downward.

Not ten steps later a wall of earth loomed ahead of him, and then he saw the mouth of the cave. Or, more aptly, the tunnel, for this huge circular opening was clearly not a natural formation.

Skyler knew then, with sudden certainty, where he was.

Something had crashed here. It didn't take much imagination to guess what. The proximity to the Elevator, the ring of chanting subhumans lining the site . . .

He'd found one of Tania's five mystery shell ships. Of this he had no doubt. The objects had trailed in behind the Belém Elevator's construction vessel, and then she'd lost track of them. In truth, no one had given the objects much thought since then. Not that he was aware of, anyway.

Swallowing a growing dread, Skyler crept forward, gun constantly sweeping the fog ahead of him until he reached the mouth of the tunnel.

Faced with that black opening, tall as a two-story home, and no backup, Skyler finally stopped. He stood there, caught between the sane choice of returning to get help and the intoxicating urge to see what lay within.

A vision hit him. The colonists, huddled around the comm, a dozen people speaking at once and as many more coming through the speaker, as they debated the proper course of action to explore the crash site. If it even was a crash site. A slew of other theories were offered. Fair or not, the mental image resonated.

"Yeah," Skyler said to himself, "enough of debate and consensus."

He set to work on his gun again, taking care to keep noise to a minimum. The grenade launcher came off, the flashlight taking its place once again. Backpack re-slung over his shoulders, he took a few tentative steps into the darkness. He glanced back with each step, waiting until he could see little of the ground outside before turning on the flashlight. The last thing he needed right now was for a slew of subhumans to spot him and come charging in.

Root systems from the trees above the tunnel dangled from the ceiling, charred and gnarled. The air had an overpowering smoke scent to it. Exposed rocks dotted the curved wall of the circular passage, some cleaved in half, signs of slag from the heat of whatever had forged this cavity. Water trailed down the center of the floor, eroding a jagged path into the darkness.

When the trickle of runoff began to widen into a pool, Skyler knew the back of the tunnel loomed. The diameter of the cavity began to shrink as well, and the heat became stifling. Without taking his eyes off the dark passage, he reached and unzipped his vest. Moisture and sweat trickled down his neck and sides.

Two steps later he caught the first hints of a shape in the gloom. The light from his gun struggled to illuminate the form at first, as if it were somehow absorbing the beam. Each step brought more clarity, and Skyler was up to his knees in water when he finally had a clear view.

A shell ship, just as he thought. Perhaps ten meters long, miniature compared to those above Belém and Darwin. It rested on the bottom of the tunnel, a portion of it submerged in the pool of runoff. How the Builders' vessel had forged this cave so much wider than its own girth, Skyler had no idea.

The tapered end wasn't quite circular, he realized, but ovoid. The very tip of it folded inward on itself in a sharp beveled edge, not unlike the corners of the aura towers. He stepped to one side, staying behind the hulking black form, to study the length of it. Much of the fuselage lay submerged in the rainwater, obscured by steam where the cold pool met balmy air.

His beam caught a gap in the center of the vessel, as if part of the shell had torn off. The gap spanned three meters left to right and went clear over the top of the vessel.

Knee-high in cold water, Skyler froze up. He dared not draw a breath.

Something lurked within.

6

BELÉM, BRAZIL

27.APR.2283

Despite the intense heat, Skyler shook all over. It took a conscious effort to suck in a breath. His heart raced unchecked.

Contact. My God, like this. Contact.

After a time the shiver abated. His breathing returned to something akin to normal, his hammering heart slowed.

Skyler swallowed. "Hello?" he said. It came out in a croak, and he coughed. "Hello?" he repeated. No response from within the vessel. No movement, either. Yet he thought he heard something. Breathing.

Yes, breathing.

Fighting every instinct he had, Skyler waded forward toward the hole in the ship. He kept to the edge of the tunnel as best he could. The deeper he went into the water, the more the humid mist clinging to its surface obscured his view. Yet he found he couldn't move any closer to the fuselage of the ship.

The water came halfway up his abdomen before he finally got a clear view inside the hole. A hexagonal pillar rested in the center, perhaps a half-meter high, topped with a myriad of irregular protrusions, the tallest no longer than Skyler's hand.

The surface of the object resembled the aura towers: matte black with geometric indents layered across. As he took in the sight, the barest hint of red light pulsed within those patterns, tracing impossibly thin lines in a wave across the surface.

Movement caught Skyler's eye.

At the base of the pillar, something stirred. He took a step back on reflex, and in that small movement lost what little clarity he'd gained by approaching the ship. Mouth dry, eyes itching from the strain, Skyler leaned in toward the ship even as he backed away.

Hands gripped the base of the pillar. Human hands, if only in shape. The skin had been replaced, or covered, in that same black material.

Frozen with pure fear, able only to move his eyes, Skyler glanced along the being's arms. Near the shoulder the black material became fractured, like broken glass tattooed onto pale skin.

On the neck he saw the subhuman rash.

The creature was on its knees, legs bent all the way, perfectly still. It was naked, most of the body still exposed, pale where grime and bruises didn't mar the skin. A woman, he realized.

Her face, though, had become partially enveloped by the Builder material. Even as Skyler watched, one of the sub's ears vanished underneath the material. In the span of ten seconds the other patches of skin still visible on its head were obscured.

The sound of breathing stopped, then.

Skyler stepped back, unable to quell his instincts any longer. His foot slipped on debris hidden below the water's surface, and he stumbled before righting himself.

The splash he made broke the intense silence.

He heard an alien noise. Like breathing, but coming in sharp bursts. Glancing back to the cavity in the ship, he saw the woman again.

Her head turned, until she faced him. That same red glow rippled across the surface of her alien skin, coalescing where her eyes and mouth should be, before fading.

Skyler turned and fled.

He waded through the water in a panic, until his knees were free of the liquid and he could run. He stumbled twice, landing hard on his elbow once. If it hurt, he had no idea. Every neuron in his brain screamed *Run, RUN*.

Boots heavy, fluid sloshing with each awkward step, Skyler flew from the tunnel and back into the gray mist outside.

Subhuman wails rose all around him. He had enough sense to ready his weapon, and he surged forward, not wishing to slow down and allow himself to be surrounded.

A human shape formed in the mist ahead. Skyler fired without thinking, and the creature dropped. He did not break stride, even as he heard snarling from left and right.

He dodged shattered stumps and fallen trees, using the angle at which they lay to tell him which way was out. When he reached the stream he leapt across, took a sharp right turn, and followed the water. Skyler had no idea whether he had the direction right. He just ran. *Figure it out later*.

After a time he chanced a quick glance over his shoulder, then slowed to a stop when he realized he'd outrun them.

"The hell I did," he muttered. Never in the last five years had he outrun a sub over any significant distance. They stopped short, for some reason. Baffled, he took a knee and waited for five long minutes. When his breathing and heart rate returned to normal, and no subhumans came loping out from the undergrowth, he stood and forced himself to relax.

Suit yourselves, he thought, and started walking. He let his feet guide him where they may, his mind wholly consumed with the image of that . . . *thing* . . . inside the shell ship. Patterns of red light pulsing through the microscopic lines of its skin, converging where its eyes should have been. He replayed the scene over and over, hoping it would become less terrifying. The fact that it didn't only served to scare him more.

After a few hours of wandering he found himself back at the tiny village where the abandoned aura tower still waited, lodged into the side of a shack. The sun sat low in the western sky, kissing both horizon below and rainclouds above.

Halfway through securing a small home to make camp in, Skyler swore. He'd never reported his findings.

"Karl, come in," he said after fumbling with the radio. "Hello? I need a team sent out here at dawn; it's urgent. Full kit. We have a problem. Please acknowledge."

Silence.

Skyler smacked the radio with his palm, tried again, and found the same result. Either his device had failed, or Karl's had. He tried a quick search of the dead colonists' bodies, but if any had carried their radio out here, it had been lost in the confusion of their demise.

He had no other option but to camp here and return at dawn, and went about securing a small outlying building to serve as shelter. Satisfied he wouldn't be surprised in the night, he ate a quick meal and cocooned himself in a blanket on the gritty tile floor.

Drifting off, beneath the insects, frogs, and other wildlife, Skyler thought he could hear the chanting again. It lulled him to a dreamless sleep.

He woke in a foul mood.

The sun blazed, already well above the horizon. Clouds huddled in angry clumps, scattered evenly across the sky, allowing long periods of sunlight to fall. Not even noon and the day promised uncomfortable heat. At least in Darwin the ocean breeze provided some respite.

After washing his face and swishing the staleness from his mouth, he heated a military-style packaged meal over a small flame. "Pork in rice," the Aussie army package boasted like a dare. With some hot sauce it might have had enough flavor to excite a taste bud or two, but Skyler ate the mush just the same. Calories were calories, and it sure beat munching on another goddamn mango.

Sweating through breakfast, slapping his neck when insects landed there, Skyler mentally plotted his course. His duty to return the aura tower prevented him from reclaiming his motorcycle, so he saw no need to return via the reservoir and Water Road. Besides, he thought it best to keep the bike secret as long as he could. Instead he decided to take a shorter path to Belém's edge, then return to camp via the straight and wide city streets, which were somewhat easier to navigate with a giant alien device.

Skyler took some time cleaning up the camp. He found the breakaway colonists' backpacks and piled them neatly together under an awning. With no way to carry them all, Skyler figured they were safe enough after he draped a parka over them. Next he searched the bodies, finding only a few useful items: a pocketknife, a flashlight, and two compasses. *Bloody amateurs.* He made a mental note to prescribe a standard kit for any "away team" traveling beyond the established perimeter. The adventure travel store he'd found three weeks back would provide all the gear necessary and could be emptied out with one well-staffed mission.

He tried and failed again to contact Karl with his radio, then dashed the useless thing against a brick wall.

Belatedly he remembered it might be Karl's radio on the fritz.

By the time he'd dislodged the aura tower and started to guide it back toward the Elevator, Skyler had begun to dread the colony's reaction to what he'd found. They would probably debate it for a week, if not two.

So it had been with every topic in the last two months. He imagined that even the sighting of an actual Builder would be unlikely to change that.

Back during those first few exciting days he'd pictured himself in lockstep with Tania, working side by side with intelligent, highly motivated scientists and techs. Good people making good decisions, all under a clearly defined goal of building a colony worthy of the price they'd all paid to leave.

Bollocks.

Skyler paused to take a drink of water. The liquid came out warm and tasted of minerals. He twisted the bulky cap back onto his canteen, but the threads didn't line up. He tried again, gritting his teeth. The cap slipped again, and Skyler threw it in frustration before catching himself. He stood there in the muddy road, breathing evenly and unclenching his fists, until the emotion passed.

"Let it go," he whispered to himself. "They're doing the best they can."

The truth was, most of the colonists in Belém hadn't asked to leave their previous situation, in orbit around the Darwin

Elevator. Tania had taken them when she detached Black Level. There'd been no time to explain, and most thought it was simply a temporary measure to escape the heavy-handed guards of Nightcliff. In the afterglow of their escape, they were seduced by the news of a fresh elevator. Another gift from the Builders.

And then came the aura towers. The scientists were in nirvana, for a time.

Less than two weeks later, the grumbling started. Scratching out an existence was hard enough. Add to that the grueling work of loading climbers to get supplies on the cord before the farms began to fail. With astonishing speed, questions were raised about societal structure. Who put Tania in charge? When will we have an election, a constitution? Who gets to live in orbit? Who is this dirty scavenger from Darwin and why isn't he out finding us some meat?

Most Orbitals were used to buying their survival.

Rock bottom was reached, in Skyler's opinion, when the first shuttle load of colonists arrived from Darwin. Tania and the others had really botched this part. Skyler found himself shaking his head even now, two weeks on.

Blackfield sent over an even mix of Cro-Magnon rejects from Nightcliff security and coughing swagmen from some forgotten corner of the Maze. The ones who showed any intelligence at all were so obviously spies that Skyler found himself chuckling about it right in front of them. "Back inside, mate, and give Russell our regards."

Sam had not been among them, nor Kelly, despite his request to Tania that they be asked for by name. Blackfield claimed he was trying to track them down, and Skyler could practically see the smirk surely on his face while making that claim.

Slogging through the mud and broken concrete, he guided the device roughly in line with the road, fine-tuning its pace until he could walk beside it without exhausting himself. The queer creaking sound made by a moving tower still raised the hairs on his forearms, but he found it somehow comforting. The constantly shifting form of the tower's base, as it altered its shape to track the ground beneath it, mesmerized him. Informal tests done at base camp implied the towers could deform over and around objects about thirty centimeters high, and climb inclines as steep as twenty degrees. At least, that was the maximum slope they had available to try.

Remarkably, the towers required human contact, the firm press of an ungloved hand, to be set in motion. The implication rattled many in the camp, that the Builders had somehow "keyed" the objects to humans. It meant their actions were specifically targeted at us, and not just a random event. So the theory went, anyway. Skyler thought they were jumping to conclusions, and besides, what difference did it make?

He heard the scream just before impact.

The creature plowed into him and they both went sprawling into the mud of the road, Skyler falling backward, his hands pinned down, gun slung over his shoulder. The subhuman hit him squarely in the abdomen, wrapping strong arms around him. They tumbled and rolled, down the sloped road back toward the village.

Mud filled Skyler's mouth and nose. He gasped and spat, blinking his eyes. Kicking wildly, he yanked his arms straight upward, freeing them even as he rolled. The tumble ended with Skyler on his back, the sub clawing at him. Skyler threw a blind punch, cuffing the animal on its ear. It held on, so he hit it again, and then once more, before it finally fell away and scrambled for a better position.

Skyler rolled in the opposite direction, using one hand to push himself to a crouch and the other to wipe the mud from his eyes. He cleared his vision enough to see the sub—a woman—bounding toward him again. No time to ready his gun, Skyler dipped his shoulder low and let the creature topple over his back. He jerked upright at the same time, raising his shoulder, sending the creature in a full flip straight into a thorny, gnarled bush.

It shrieked and flailed, which only served to entangle it further.

Skyler spat more mud from his mouth, feeling the grit between his teeth. He brought his gun to bear and unleashed two rounds into the creature's torso.

A tech from Belém, the clothing implied. The sixth member of the missing team.

"There you are," Skyler muttered, between gasps. Everyone present and accounted for, finally.

When the creature drew its last breath, Skyler slung his weapon again and washed the mud from his face with water from the canteen. The earthen taste in his mouth took some time to cleanse, ample opportunity to come down from the adrenaline high.

Wits gathered, he jogged back to the still-moving aura tower, giving it a small course correction as the road turned.

7

BELÉM, BRAZIL

28.APR.2283

Skyler kept a slow pace on the way back to base camp. Mock conversations played out in his mind about how to explain what he'd seen. The colonists were scientists for the most part, and would ask him endless questions.

The truth was he had no idea what he'd seen. A subhuman, he thought, being—transformed? Enveloped? Armored? Hell, he might have it reversed. What if the ship was creating them? Clones, or something.

He shook his head. Speculation accomplished little, and he could leave that to campfire chats among the colonists. As soon as Tania and the others voted to do so, he'd take a team back there and figure out what new toy the Builders had sent.

At the city outskirts he guided the alien tower over a short bridge that spanned a man-made tributary. Despite years of neglect, runoff still raced toward the Rio Pará. He nudged the tower around a derelict Toyota. The tall mass glided as if it weighed no more than Skyler himself.

He'd spent more time than he cared to admit pondering the point of the devices. Their usefulness was obvious: movable pockets of precious aura to fend off SUBS. His immunity didn't lessen an appreciation for the gift.

But why? Usefulness aside, what were the bloody Builders up to? He shook his head again. More speculation. A pointless topic to ponder. Everyone at base camp had theories, from plausible to crazy and everything in between.

Someone had suggested that perhaps the Builders had intended to colonize Earth, had sent their construction vessels, but had themselves died along the way. That or the project lost funding, someone had joked. Skyler had barked a hearty laugh at that. "What a terrifying thought," he'd said, "that they're just as fucked-up as we are."

Across the bridge he found himself in Belém's vast outer slum. Kilometer after kilometer of shanty homes, hopeless churches, and the occasional grouping of shops and taverns. All abandoned, all in some state of embalmment by the unchecked growth of the rainforest. Skeletal corpses littered the ground with such number that they became as mundane as trees.

Skyler pulled the tourist's map from his breast pocket, along with a permanent pen. Once he found his bearings, he began to walk again and make abbreviated notes. A pharmacy he noted with "rx." Taverns and liquor stores got a little happy face. A circle around the marking meant he'd gone inside and found it to contain useful things. An X meant nothing worthwhile remained. The map had around fifty such markings already, all within a few kilometers of the Elevator. He'd barely explored the city at all yet.

For an instant his eyes lingered on the mark he'd made the day before. IMMUNE. The vision of that young woman, white dress billowing about her perfect legs, clouded his mind's eye. He pictured her naked backside as she ran from him across the field. A longing stirred within him and he mentally slapped himself back to reality.

He drew a little monster wherever he encountered a subhuman. In the month since touchdown, only a handful had been encountered, until yesterday. The bizarre scene at that crash site explained their absence across the rest of the region. He drew a bold circle around the rough location of the crashed shell ship.

A chill coursed through his body and Skyler paused. He let the tower drift on and ducked into the shadow of a single-room home made of lashed-together aluminum siding. For a long minute he stood there, studying the surrounding homes. Nothing moved, save the occasional lizard sprinting across a wall, or birds darting from tree to electric pole.

He'd been deep in thought, and sensed something, heard something perhaps. The moment passed. With nothing else to go on, he readied his weapon just in case and jogged to catch up to the aura tower.

Halfway there he heard the faint sound again. A *wump wump wump,* scarcely loud enough to be heard over the constant background of birds, insects, and countless drips of runoff water.

A machine gun. A big one, at that. Not like the weapons some of the colonists carried.

He pushed the tower around a corner in the road to get a view south, toward the space elevator.

Sunlight caught the thin cord like a strand of spider silk. Skyler followed it to the ground and saw birds. Hundreds of them, streaming from the trees that surrounded base camp.

He started to run.

Some stupid sense of duty kept him from abandoning the aura tower altogether.

He pushed and guided it through the uneven grid of streets, around abandoned vehicles and the occasional tree sprouting right through the road.

The gunfire had stopped. Or at least he hadn't heard any more over his own labored breathing.

With the aura tower in tow it took almost an hour to weave his way through the city before he found familiar terrain. The Elevator had implanted near a tributary that fed into the Rio Guamá, on the city's southern edge. A university campus to the west were the nearest buildings of any real size, ringed by a two-meter-high stucco wall that had been white half a decade ago. Vines blanketed the surface now.

Skyler slowed the tower as he passed the campus entrance.

There were tire tracks in the mottled road. Fresh ones, from multiple vehicles.

Baffled and concerned, he let the massive object amble along on its own while he kept it within arm's reach. He moved around to its side, keeping it to his left and the stucco wall on his right.

At the edge of the wall, base camp came into view. He saw the sign first, hand painted on a plank of wood. CAMP EXODUS. One of the colonists had made it of their own accord and nailed it to a fence post. In a colony where every little decision required hours of pointless debate, Skyler reveled in the fact that the name had been coined on a whim and stuck. It wasn't the greatest name, not by a long shot, but he could only imagine what sort of stupid blandness a consensus would have arrived at. A hundred tents of varying size and color dominated the mottled field beyond, interrupted here and there by shipping containers that constituted the communal buildings—meeting hall, mess, and storage.

The aura towers were interspersed throughout all of these, arranged now in concentric circles, with the smallest ones at the outside.

In between these towers and his position, a dozen or more military and police vehicles were parked, forming an inverted wedge around the landward part of the colony. At least two had gunners manning turrets, sweeping back and forth in slow arcs.

Skyler counted roughly twenty men and women, in matching black uniforms, fanned out across the line, weapons in hand. Beyond them, colonists were standing in clumps, hands raised. Some of the black-clad intruders were barking orders at them, too far away for Skyler to hear the words.

Nightcliff? No. Impossible. Unlikely that they could have found the colony, and even more ridiculous that they could get so many fresh ground vehicles halfway across the globe. *Who then?*

He realized with sudden panic that he was standing in the open, a few steps out from the cover of the wall. The aura tower he'd brought back now drifted slowly east in blissful, uncaring ignorance of its surroundings. Its path, Skyler realized, would take it straight into the side of an armored personnel carrier.

The scene gripped him. He knew he should back away, find

cover, and watch, but the ambling tower's collision course was like watching a car wreck in slow motion. Two of the militant intruders sat atop the vehicle, their posture relaxed, their focus on the colony. Skyler thought of shouting a warning but found he couldn't. He knew the tower would halt its own progress, but the men sitting there might not. They'd just see a giant black obelisk bearing down on them—

One of the intruders, a dark-skinned man, finally turned enough to see the shape looming, a second before impact. He shouted something and leapt from the roof of the massive truck. His partner dove off the other side, an instant before the tower reached them.

The aura tower hit the side of the vehicle, rocking it slightly before coming to a rest.

A moment of confusion passed. The closer man had come up on all fours, looking at the huge shape. Others from the group called out. Some of the militants were running over to investigate.

The man on the ground, though, stared directly at Skyler.

He rocked back onto his knees and raised an assault rifle.

Skyler took a gamble with his life. He turned and ran, rather than taking cover. Bullets hissed over his head even as the crackle from the gun reached him. The man was firing from the hip, a shot that only worked in movies and sensories.

A chorus of alarmed shouts followed. Skyler figured the man would correct his position and take a more calculated shot next, so he grasped a thick vine that ran horizontally along the old university wall and used it to propel himself up and over the barricade.

He landed hard in a courtyard on the other side, in knee-high wild grass. A plan formed on pure instinct: Move west, into the city. Disappear.

Weaving through the old campus at a full sprint, Skyler reached the wall on the western side in less than a minute, the shouts at his back growing dimmer with each second. He spotted a section of wall that had partially collapsed, and hurdled it without breaking stride. The ground beyond was muddy and he slipped on it, tumbling and rolling. Old wounds complained, a din he knew he could shove from his mind. He'd be a mess in the morning, assuming he survived that long.

A quick glance back proved inconclusive. He heard activity but saw nothing. Looking west, he scanned the low buildings along the city edge, looking for a good place to go to ground.

Behind him came the sound of bulky tires crushing rock and soil, and the high-pitched hum of electric motors.

Shit.

He began to run again. A snap decision made, he raced toward the wide river and the dockyards that lined it.

The realization hit him as he reached the dockyard: The newcomers must be immunes.

They'd arrived in that hodgepodge armada of combat vehicles without any aura towers to protect them. No other explanation made sense. There were deep implications his brain desperately wanted to analyze, but the roar of tires on the tortured road behind him renewed his focus.

Skyler raced through an open gate and down a steeply sloped asphalt road that led to trampled shore. The murky Rio Guamá stretched more than a kilometer wide here, still swelled by the rainy season. A line of trees on the horizon marked the far shore, too far to swim. On this, the northern side, long wooden docks stretched out fifty meters over the water, as far as Skyler could see. Two- and three-story warehouses, all broken windows and weathered walls, backed the crumbling structures.

Corpses of watercraft filled the spaces between docks. Many were cargo ships and flat barges, faded logos of international produce companies still visible on their sides. The rest were smaller, recreational, likely borne down the fast river over the years only to snag here on the piers. Amassed around the boats were islands of trash, dead trees, and other debris. The smell of mold, dead fish, and rotting vegetation permeated everything and churned his stomach.

Skyler slowed when his feet met the wooden slats of the dock. Many of the boards were black and rotten, and he guessed the massive vehicle chasing him would fall right through. He chanced a glance back and saw the beast careening down the ramp he'd just traversed. Knobby tires under an angular black shell of riveted steel. An anti-riot car, he guessed. It looked like it had been painted black recently, with hints of an FNSP logo—national police—underneath. A shielded turret topped the vehicle, and Skyler could see someone's helmet behind the slotted plate. The gunner struggled to keep his aim as the vehicle careened down the ramp.

Skyler angled toward a gap between warehouses just as the buzz from the chain gun shattered the quiet of the shore. Shards of rotten wood filled the air around him. Skyler covered the sides of his face with both arms and high-stepped the last few meters until he'd safely moved behind the building.

His heart raced, blood pulsing in his ears. His breaths came in short bursts as the rush of the narrow escape swelled through him. Skyler vaulted himself over a stack of blue plastic fruit crates and kept running, angling toward the wall of the next building over. He came to an open door and took a glance in, only to find it a horrible rotting mess. Rats were everywhere, bolting for shelter when he stepped into view. The smell of the place forced him to cover his mouth and nose. He moved on, rushing around the back of the building, dancing around abandoned skid-steers and electric forklifts.

Shrieking tires and anxious shouts were heard behind him. They'd stopped short of driving onto the dock then, killing Skyler's hopes for a farcical end to the chase. He let his pace dip so that he could get his breathing under control. Everything stank, worse than even Darwin's choked shoreline. The odor brought tears to his eyes.

He jumped over a corpse, a dockworker judging by the faded coveralls. Nothing but bone and some gray skin with matted hair underneath the brittle clothing now. Bodies were everywhere in the urban places Skyler had visited, but once in a while he saw one that still disturbed him. They were a hard reminder of the billions that died in the first months of the disease.

He heard footsteps somewhere behind, and took the next corner to put himself between buildings again, facing the brownish river now. Guessing his pursuers would flank him from both ends, he stopped and lay down on the grimy wood. A hard three-count later, he rolled back around the wall with his gun at the ready.

The man pursuing him was looking down, stepping around the decayed body of the dockworker.

Skyler lined up the red dot of his holo-sight on the man's chest and squeezed off two rounds. The gun's sight made his aim virtually flawless, and the poor fellow collapsed on top of the body that already lay there. *One more to the tally.*

A pang of regret gripped him for shooting a fellow immune, something he'd never done before. The sound of approaching footsteps meant he would have to repeat the performance if he didn't get away. So Skyler set aside his instinctual urge to search the body, stood, and ran.

Moving quickly again, he dashed along the backside of the warehouses, scaling one chain-link fence and ducking through a gap in another. Near the end of the dockyard he heard shouts off to his left, over a series of ragged grunts.

Then came a familiar wail.

Subhumans.

He never thought their presence would be so welcome.

Against a backdrop of shouting and gunfire, Skyler left the dockyard and bolted straight into the dense slums of Belém, head thick with confusion and numbing fear.

8

MELVILLE STATION

29.APR.2283

Tania could not look Zane Platz in the eye.

He sat across the metal table from her, drumming his fingers like his older brother had sometimes done. Between them lay the comm, their link to the ground, theoretically. Nothing had come across in forty-eight hours.

They should be celebrating. The first climber to rise from Belém with a significant shipment of air and water was supposed to have arrived hours ago, a critical milestone in the colony's survival. But the climber never left the ground. Instead Tania had seen Karl thrown violently across the screen, then a hand deactivating the camera. Five seconds later a simple message filled the screen: "Connection lost."

"Something has to be done, Tania," Zane said, in a quiet and pitiful voice.

People, Karl had said, not subhumans. *People*. It couldn't have been a mistake.

"Tania . . ."

She kept her eyes on the comm. "What did he mean, 'Who are you *people?*' What people?"

Zane ran a hand over his tired face. "We've been over this many times."

"Suppose Blackfield snuck an aircraft in and has taken over? They could be on their way up."

"The controller still shows red. The climber is attached, but it hasn't left Belém."

Tania grimaced. "What other explanation is there?"

Zane broke eye contact at that. He stared at the table in front of him, a vein visibly pulsing at his temple. After a moment he pinched the bridge of his nose and winced. "I should have a lie-down."

Tania studied him. His face contorted in pain for a few seconds, then he seemed to relax. "Okay. We can talk later," she started.

"My headache can wait," he grumbled. "This decision can't."

"Maybe it's the Builders," Tim said. He leaned against the wall by the closed conference room door, a steaming cup of tea in his hand. "Maybe they look like us, like people."

Zane did a half turn in his chair. "You're worse than she is."

"I'm just saying—"

"Tania," Zane said, gathering himself, "we can't continue to sit here and speculate endlessly. It's been two months since we had a solid shipment of consumables. We'll have to evacuate soon. Crops are starting to brown—"

"I know," she said.

"Something's gone wrong down there, and we need to act—"

"I know, dammit!" She looked up at him, finally. Met his eyes, saw the thick black bags under them. She saw his fear, his yearning to fix things, but most of all she saw his plea for someone, anyone, to make a decision. Zane had spent his whole life leaving the decisions to his deceased brother, Neil. In many ways she had, too, and she wondered if Zane saw the same plea in her eyes. She turned back to the screen. "The climber controls show red. We can't send anyone down to investigate, or rescue them, or anything else."

Zane and Tim both stared at her with glum expressions.

"Worse," she added, "we can't evacuate."

"Not to Belém," Tim whispered.

A long silence followed. Until now, no one had voiced that

option. Tania forced herself not to speak until she could control her voice. "Returning to the Darwin Elevator is a last resort, agreed?"

"Personally, I'd rather suffocate," Zane said.

"Hear, hear," said Tim.

Unable to stare at the comm any longer, Tania stood and paced the back wall of the room. Tim's posture by the door made her feel trapped.

Think, think.

More than anything she wished she could talk to Skyler. Increasingly gruff attitude aside, he still had a certain knack for laying out stark options in a clear manner. Somehow it made things easier. Taking a deep breath, Tania decided to try the technique herself.

"Let's assume for now that Nightcliff has taken over the ground colony below us."

"We don't know—"

"Would you just listen for a moment, please?"

Zane closed his mouth and gave a slow nod. Despite his words, she caught a glimmer of relief in his eyes.

"Nightcliff holds the ground. Fine. Let's get Blackfield on the comm, then, and find a way to resolve this. We still hold the farms."

"You'd think he would have contacted us by now," Zane mused.

"If they hold the Elevator base, the air, and the water," Tim said, "we're in no position to negotiate."

"We have to try," Tania said. "It's the only logical action at this point. Unless you have other ideas?"

Neither man offered a suggestion.

"Okay, settled," Tania said. "Tim, see if you can get us a connection, and patch it through here, please."

"You got it," he replied.

A half hour later, Tania found herself looking at Russell Blackfield. He looked like he always did. His blond hair was uncombed and close-cropped, and stubble shadowed his face. His eyes perpetually gave the impression that he was about to spar and wanted to win.

"A video feed this time," he said with a grin. "How lucky for me."

She made a conscious effort to keep her face blank. They'd spoken only three times since she'd tried to kill him, and she'd avoided video in those calls lest he see the fear and uncertainty in her face. This time she decided it was worth the risk, so that she could study his expression as well.

"Hello, Russell."

The man nodded. "Nice to see you, too. I'd forgotten what a lovely woman you are."

Tania fought to keep a wave of revulsion behind her mask. Dark memories of a dank cell below Nightcliff, two foul-smelling guards scrubbing her naked body as she stared at herself in the wall-sized mirror, retreating within, knowing somewhere in a deep corner of her mind that Blackfield watched from the other side. She'd refused to acknowledge it, and sat there in numb stillness with no effort to cover herself. The lack of struggle had been seen as an invitation to continue. A shudder rippled through her.

"Talkative as ever," Russell added.

"We need to discuss the situation here," she said, surprised at her own words.

His eyes dipped for a moment, and he shifted his weight in his seat. "Was our second delivery of slaves—*pardonnez moi,* volunteers—not up to snuff?"

Tania kept her eyes on the screen, but in the corner of her field of view she could see Zane Platz. His eyebrows went up, and she knew they shared the same thought: *Russell doesn't know.* He doesn't know about the silenced colony, he doesn't even know where they are. The tone of his voice told her this with absolute certainty.

"The new colonists will do fine," she lied. "We're still placing them."

"Oh, colonists. What an interesting word to use, as it implies a colony."

Dammit.

A sarcastic grin stretched across his face. "Let me know when you're ready for more."

Tania drew a breath. "About that. We would like to change the parameters of the next shipment."

"Want a few whores this time? We've got plenty of them. Nothing keeps a bunch of cooped-up men happy like a few loose tarts."

She refused to be baited. "No, thanks."

"Handling the needs of the men yourself?"

If not for their predicament, she would have ended the call right then. She would let Darwin starve, just to avoid ever speaking to this man again. If only . . . if only the colony wasn't offline. If only supply shipments were coming in at a reliable pace. If only they'd had more time to think this whole endeavor through. *If only Skyler would rescue me again so Russell didn't have to,* she thought, lamely.

Tania wanted to slap herself for that. She felt weak and helpless, and despised that feeling even more than she despised the man on the screen in front of her.

There were no other options though. Time was not on their side, either. Something had to be done. "No people this time, Russell. We'd like you to deliver two standard shipments of air and water."

Russell's laughter came through the speaker so loud that Tania winced.

Across the table, Zane had his hands over his face. He was shaking his head.

What? Tania mouthed, but Zane didn't see.

"Wow," Russell said, his chuckling finally under control. "Bad move, sweetheart. You admit to me that you're all about to die. Unless we help, of course."

Tania's hesitation gave him his answer, and Russell pounced.

"Now I have *you* over the barrel," he said. "God, the visual that gives me."

He pretended to daydream for a few seconds, and Tania could only watch.

"Sorry," Russell said, "I was in another place there for a second. Air and water, eh? Tell you what, love, I will trade you . . . oh, let's see . . . twenty standard shipments, for the return of the farm platforms." He folded his arms in satisfaction, leaned into the camera, and smiled.

She held his gaze for a few seconds, aware of the stunned silence coming from Zane and Tim. "Two. We just need two shipments."

"But I need all the bloody farm platforms, and not dropped on my head this time, please. Twenty shipments in exchange is my very generous offer."

There were nineteen farm platforms, and they represented the Belém colony's only leverage against Darwin. To give them up, she knew, would either make Belém dependent on Darwin or force the abandonment of the colony's other two space stations. Neither scenario could be allowed.

Tania exhaled, slowly, through her nose. "Nine shipments, for nine platforms."

"Deal," he said, without hesitation.

Zane stood, red-faced. She'd never seen him angry before. "Hold please," she said, and tapped the corresponding icon on the screen. When Russell's face vanished behind a red overlay, she met Zane's eyes. "What?"

"What the hell are you doing?" he barked.

"Buying us time."

"You're giving away our leverage!"

"Less than half of it," Tania said. "They'll still need us. We'll probably get fewer people now, but considering the quality of the first two shipments, I don't think a deluge of spies and vagrants is what we need right now."

Zane grimaced. "We should have discussed this first."

If Skyler had been in the room, Tania expected he would chuckle at that. "Everything's a discussion now," he'd said to her in frustration a few days ago.

Tania gathered herself. "If the two of you are going to sit off camera every time we have to deal with Darwin, I'm going to take that as permission to act on our behalf." The words tumbled out before she could think to soften them.

Tim stopped leaning against the wall. His hands went to his sides and he glanced at Zane, then back. "Come on, Tania, it's not like that. You're just . . . the face of things."

"Just a pretty face?"

"I didn't mean that, you know I didn't. Er, that didn't come out right. Pretty, obviously, but . . . can I start over?"

"Tania," Zane said, "you put too much burden on yourself. This . . . Camp Exodus, Melville Station, all the farms, this was Neil's plan. We all followed it, we all knew the risks and knew what we were leaving behind. You don't have to redeem yourself."

"There's plenty of people here who didn't ask to come."

"Correct me if I'm wrong," Zane said, "but no one has yet requested to go back to Darwin with the food shipments, despite the blanket approval to do so."

Tania checked herself. Anger had risen so quickly she'd failed to recognize it, and had let it sneak out. "You're right," she said. "I'm sorry."

Zane cleared his throat. "Still, you make a good point. Major decisions should be put to a vote, as a general rule. That being said, sometimes it's better to show decisive strength. Neil knew this."

"He was the master at it," Tania pointed out.

"And you may be right," Zane went on, nodding. "We're overburdened dealing with all these farms. Picking and packaging the food, the logistics of shipping ninety-five percent of it to Darwin. We have as many people working on that as they're sending us, so what's the point?"

"My thoughts, exactly," Tania said.

Tim cleared his throat. His cheeks were still red from his earlier flub. "Nine shipments of air and water will last us months, a big chunk of the two-year plan. And half the remaining platforms will still be enough to feed us all, many times over, for years after that. I say we proceed."

Zane took a breath, then nodded.

Tania tapped the hold icon again, and made her deal with the devil.

9

DARWIN, AUSTRALIA

29.APR.2283

Russell Blackfield prowled across the rooftop, back and forth, barely able to contain his glee.

"I should call Alex first," he said to himself. Gloating would feel so good.

Ten minutes earlier, before Tania came begging, he'd been slumped over his desk, beset by problem after bloody problem. A strike across the bay at the water plants. Confusion and lack of cooperation from the remaining space stations. Scavenger crews refusing to fly. Whispers of more rioting from the hungry mouths of Darwin. Rumors of the missing farm platforms sparking turf wars among the rooftop garden communes. From his vantage point high above Nightcliff's yard, Russell could see a handful of smoke plumes rising off the skyscrapers that surrounded his fortress.

It all came back to food. *And I've just solved that.* "Thank me later!" he shouted at the city below him. "Ungrateful sods!"

All he wanted to do was get back to orbit, away from this miserable mess. The farms would come back soon. Not all, but enough to placate the miserable masses. He'd be the hero again and could focus on the most important issue: wrapping his hands around that gorgeous woman's Indian neck and—

"Mr. Blackfield?"

Russell spun at the voice. Kip Osmak stood in the doorway that led downstairs to the office, stringy gray hair framing his skeletal face. He might be, Russell mused, the ugliest secretary in the history of mankind.

"You're supposed to bow," Russell said.

"I . . . what—"

"I'm joking, you moron."

Kip nodded. "Sir."

After a few seconds of silence, Russell spread his hands. "Well? The fuck do you want?"

"Mr. Grillo is here to see you," Kip said flatly.

"What the hell does he want? Is he at the gate?"

Kip stepped aside.

Grillo stood in the stairwell behind him. He stepped forward onto the roof, gingerly, as if afraid to get his shoes dirty.

The slumlord stood well short of two meters tall, his stature so slight that Russell thought he could pick him up with one hand. He wore narrow glasses low on his nose, and kept his black hair slick and combed back. A neat gray suit covered his thin frame, over a black turtleneck sweater. Russell had no idea how the man didn't faint from the heat. How this slim and prim man built an empire of thugs and pushers across Darwin's eastern quarter was an even bigger mystery.

"Greetings," Russell said.

"Your grace," Grillo said, with a respectful if sarcastic bow.

"Very funny," Russell said. "Kip, shut the door behind you."

Once the secretary clicked the door closed, Grillo stepped farther out, avoiding the puddles, until he reached the roof's edge. He looked over the press of buildings beyond Nightcliff's wall, ignoring Russell's gaze.

They'd spoken by comm, briefly, after the fiasco in Africa. Russell had made a point not to apologize for the loss of aircraft, many of which Grillo had provided. The last thing he wanted was to admit any debt to the man. Instead he'd given him a scavenger list.

"Fantastic view," Grillo muttered.

"I've got a busy day and a climber ride at six. Are you here to deliver the tracking device personally?"

"Your request has top priority," Grillo said. "Scavenger resources are somewhat limited. We will find a working sample soon."

Just ask me to apologize, man. Left unsaid was the fact that the independent crews, working out of the old airport, refused to cooperate with Russell after the immunes' hangar had been searched and looted. He desperately wanted to take a few truckloads of regulars over there and clean house, if only he had some pilots to take their places. "Well," Russell said. "What then?"

Grillo studied the city for a moment longer. "No fires to the east," he said.

The comment surprised Russell. He glanced in that direction, and then studied the rest of the horizon. Sure enough, all of the buildings showing evidence of violence were south, and west.

East, Grillo's territory, looked the very picture of business as usual. Russell struggled to see the point. "You run a tight ship, I'll give you that."

Grillo replied with a thin smile. *Smug son of a bitch.*

"Are you here for an apology?" Russell asked.

The short man cocked an eyebrow at that.

"Fine. I'm sorry," Russell said. "I apologize for your aircraft lost during our chase of the traitor, Tania—"

"Apology unnecessary," Grillo said, waving a hand as if the air held a stench. "That endeavor was worth its risks. And, no, that's not why I'm here."

The measured way he spoke unnerved Russell. "Why, then?"

"I'd like to show you something," Grillo said. "Perhaps you could spare a few hours."

"Show me what?"

"A solution," the man said with total sincerity.

Russell's assumption that Grillo had flown to Nightcliff proved wrong. The man had walked, through the Maze, with just two bodyguards. His turf, after all.

So Russell commandeered an idle water hauler from

Nightcliff's yard, and in less than half an hour they were airborne, heading east.

The cramped cabin had not been made for casual passengers, and Russell found himself sitting in a foldout hot seat across from Grillo. Their bodyguards filled the four remaining spots, save for the cockpit, where a bitter Platz company pilot guided the aircraft over Rancid Creek, then the Maze, toward the old football stadium where Grillo ran his scavenger crews. The pilot's daughter had made the mistake of shacking up with one of Nightcliff's workers, and thus became the perfect motivator to keep her father from striking like the rest of the Platz workers across the bay. The girl would remain confined to her lover's quarters until the storm passed. "Anything other than total enthusiasm from you," Russell told the pilot a month earlier, "and I'll start visiting the little whore myself."

He'd been a model of reliability ever since.

Grillo stared out the open side of the cabin, watching his territory drift by below. The wind swirling into the cabin failed to ruffle even one hair on the slickster's head. His expression held no hint of the ruthless overlord everyone claimed him to be. No, Russell thought, he looked upon the crumbling buildings like a concerned father.

Not just concerned, he decided. Proud.

"Solution to what?" Russell shouted over the roar of wind.

Grillo took a few seconds before removing his attention from the ground below. He fixed his gaze on Russell and leaned in. "Riots. Disease. Hunger. Warring neighborhoods. Unruly, ungrateful citizens who ultimately only care about one thing."

"Saving their own asses?"

"No," Grillo said with sadness. "Whom to blame for their misfortune."

Russell's mouth snapped shut with a click.

"We no longer live in a world where Neil Platz can shoulder the burden of scapegoat."

The aircraft banked, circled, and began to descend.

"Scapegoat," Russell said. "I suppose that's my job now?"

Grillo tilted his head to one side and back, so that he could study Russell through his narrow glasses. "The line between scapegoat and savior is a thin one, Mr. Blackfield."

Whatever you've got to show me, Russell thought, *it better be fucking incredible after this sermon.* "Wise words," he said.

The aircraft set down in the center of the playing field. The vast space that once held green grass and painted boundaries had long ago been stripped down to bare concrete. Makeshift houses and tents covered the stands where roaring fans once cheered. Despite their ramshackle materials, Russell couldn't help but notice the orderly layout. Laundry hung from wires between the gaps, and wisps of smoke rose through ductwork chimneys.

Only two other aircraft were parked on the improvised airfield. Seven had been destroyed in Africa thanks to Tania's lie. Russell knew the loss had depleted Grillo's fleet, yet somehow the sight of two lonely planes made the impact a tangible thing.

A fleet of trucks and vans waited for them, parked in a perfect line at the edge of the landing zone. Men and women in plainclothes sat on the bumpers or atop the roofs, weapons resting across their knees or strapped across their chest. They watched as Russell and the others stepped down from the idling aircraft.

Through some silent order, the foot soldiers sprang into action. Drivers jumped into their seats, sparking up their electronics to warm the vehicle's ultracaps. Others moved to stand in the truck's empty beds, leaning over the driver's cabs, rifles at the ready.

Russell couldn't help but harbor some envy. If only his men reacted with such efficiency at the simple flick of a hand.

Grillo led them to a nondescript truck near the center of the line. If the vehicle held any special feature—armor plating, or some hidden weapon—Russell couldn't see it. The crime boss might have chosen it at random, for all Russell knew. It fit his personality, at least.

"Old McMillan's, in Coconut Grove," Grillo said to the driver.

With only a second to spare, Russell managed to find a handhold. The truck's motors whined as it surged forward, spearheading the group as the others fell in behind.

The driver took them out a huge gate at the far end of the field, and in less than a minute the line of vehicles snaked through the slums Grillo owned. Men, women, and children alike came out to watch the caravan roll by. Their complacent faces filled the windows above the narrow streets, too.

Russell kept quiet. Coconut Grove was near Nightcliff. Why Grillo hadn't gone straight there from the fortress confused him, until he realized the obvious difference: Grillo didn't have a small army with him when he met Russell at Nightcliff.

Yet he could have lined all these vehicles up outside the fortress gate. Rolling through the Maze, Russell thought he understood. Grillo wanted him to see this. Calm streets, faces filled not with fear or dismay but with quiet respect.

In Coconut Grove, a portion of Darwin that butted against Nightcliff's southern edge, the buildings were much taller. Offices and luxury apartments before the disease came, the once-gleaming structures were called home by many multinational aerospace and tech companies that had flocked to Darwin during the heyday of the space elevator. Some had been abandoned before completion, their upper floors just framing and scaffolds. These made the best gardens, with potted plants and trees stretching all the way up the open grid of steel beams.

One, Russell saw, had a few spot fires burning near the lowest floors of the garden.

If Russell's intelligence was up to date, Grillo had little sway in this area. Barreling down the center of the street, at the tip of a fleet of vehicles carrying armed civilians, Russell didn't need any more hints to guess the purpose of Grillo's theatrics.

He played along, regardless. "What are we doing here?"

"Attempting to impress you," Grillo said.

Russell grinned, despite himself. "I've been to orbit. Fought in orbit, shagged in orbit. Saw the Builders' turd of a spacecraft."

"There's fondness in your voice," Grillo said. "I've heard you spend most of your time up there now."

True enough, Russell thought. He shrugged.

"Hold your judgment," Grillo added. He leaned around the truck's cab and spoke to the driver again. "Proceed," he simply said.

Russell heard a noise above. He glanced up, fighting the noon sun, and saw two aircraft swooping in over the skyscrapers. They were in formation, side by side. As Russell watched, one banked and separated while the other matched the same direction the ground vehicles were on.

The truck slowed and turned. Russell glanced down in time to see other vehicles in the line surge forward on either side. They approached the same building the aircraft had and surrounded it.

Grillo's people leapt from the backs of their vehicles before they even stopped. They took down two lackwit guards at the barricaded entrance and swarmed inside before the bodies even hit the ground.

Russell took a quick glance backward, expecting to see the remaining portion of Grillo's force moving in behind. His eyebrows shot up when he saw the truth: They were moving on a building across the street, using the same tactics.

Grillo hadn't budged. He stood firm, on the bed of the truck, both hands resting on top of the cab. Five minutes passed, marked by sporadic gunfire from within the building. The aircraft above circled the two buildings. Twice Russell thought he heard machine-gun fire from them, but they were too high up for him to be sure.

"I would have gone in with them," Russell said, hoping to sound casual.

Grillo frowned. "We all have our specialties. Yours is fighting."

"What's yours?"

"I make friends."

Russell snorted a laugh. He doubted many residents in these buildings would be friendly now.

Grillo turned and stepped lightly from the back of the truck bed. His bodyguards stayed behind. Russell followed, ordering his two men to wait in the truck as well. He fell in next to Grillo, expecting they would enter one of the buildings. Instead Grillo moved with calm confidence to the center of the street, placed his hands behind his back, and waited. Unsure what to do, Russell stood next to him. He shifted from foot to foot, feeling exposed in the middle of the wide avenue, out in the squalor and anarchy of Darwin.

"In hindsight," Grillo said, "I should have had you wear a

disguise of some sort. Your presence adds some complexity."

"Give me a gun and I'll go inside where the action is."

"The real action is out here, Mr. Blackfield. Ah, as you now will see."

A group of Grillo's people came out of the building to their right. They prodded an Asian man ahead. Three other prisoners were shuffled off to the side and held there. All four of the captives shared the same bewildered expression.

The man, an elder, was ushered toward the center of the street. His eyes grew even wider when he recognized Russell.

Before anyone could speak, another group came out from the building to the left. Two burly men were led forward. One held a hand to his forehead, and Russell could see a trickle of blood coming down his wrist and forearm.

These two scowled when they saw Russell, and their expressions turned to raw hatred when they saw the Asian man held across from them.

Grillo moved to stand between the two parties. He held out a hand toward each, motioning downward, willing them to be calm.

"You are Shane Killen and Ben Paston," the crime lord said to the two men on his left. "You claim ownership and control of the building called Phoenix, and its inhabitants."

"Who the hell are you?" one asked in a thick New Zealander accent.

"I go by Grillo in most circles," the short man said.

The two men exchanged a glance, faces flushed. Their eyes both darted to Russell, then back.

Grillo ignored them for the moment and turned to the Asian on his right. He spoke to the man in accented Chinese. The man's anger melted away as Grillo spoke. "May I continue in English?" Grillo asked, and received a nod.

The fighting had stopped, and a strange serenity fell over the wide street. Russell saw faces in the shadows, people gathering in the alleyways, watching.

"If you're going to kill us, get it over with," the one called Shane Killen said.

"On the contrary, Mr. Killen, I'm here to hire you."

The word tripped everyone present, including Russell.

Shane's eyes narrowed as he recovered his composure. "Meaning what?"

"I've a job for you," Grillo said. "For all of you. It's a simple one, one you're already extremely good at: growing food."

"We do this already," the Chinese man said.

"Not lately. Not enough," Grillo said. Russell marveled at how he kept his voice calm, even when calling someone a liar. "You see, gentlemen, rumors have spread like SUBS through this city of a problem with the farms above. Such chatter has brought panic to certain districts—"

Except yours, Russell added mentally.

"—and has led to a situation humanity cannot afford right now. You fight each other. You fend off the poor who live on these streets, forcing them to fight among themselves. The problem cascades across the entire city. Worst of all, you hoard your food even as you burn the other's."

The Chinese man cast his eyes down to the cracked pavement, shamed. The two Kiwis remained steadfast, if not defiant.

"Unity is required," Grillo said in a new tone of unmistakable authority, without raising his voice.

"You want us to work with *him*?" Shane said.

"No," Grillo said. "You're going to work for Darwin. You're going to set aside your petty squabbles, your outdated sense of ownership and entitlement. You're going to grow food, more of it than you thought possible, and you're going to share it."

"Or what?"

Grillo tilted his head, the same way he had with Russell when they stood atop Nightcliff. "Or nothing," he said. "I'll leave you to your vertical kingdom, and devote all of my energy, resources, and *friends* to the buildings that surround yours."

Another group came out of the Phoenix building. Shane and Ben both turned to watch as a gaggle of women and children were ushered outside.

"Ah," Grillo said. "Your wives and families. I've invited them to visit my home over in Lyons." With a simple gesture, Grillo's people prodded the terrified group toward a pair of waiting vans.

Shane stepped toward Grillo. "You lay a damn finger on them—"

"Please," the slumlord said. "They're to be my guests until our new business arrangement is fully up and running."

For a span of ten seconds Shane stared down Grillo, his nostrils flaring. His partner, Ben, reached out and gripped the man on his shoulder. "Give us a minute, Grillo," he said.

They stepped away and began a quiet, animated chat.

"All right," Russell said. "I'm impressed. But this is two buildings out of a thousand."

"Dominoes," Grillo said.

"Even you don't have enough people to enforce such deals across the city."

Grillo offered a quizzical look. "No? Mr. Li, how many people reside in your commune?"

The Chinese man had been watching his own family, who still stood near the entrance of his building. "Four thousand."

"A similar count across the street, I'd guess." Grillo looked at Russell with total sincerity. "You see? I've just added eight thousand people to my sphere of influence, and it's not even lunchtime."

Russell bristled. "Li, give us a moment," he said. When the man moved out of earshot, Russell stepped close to Grillo, using his height advantage to full effect. "I'm not going to let you take over my city."

Grillo shook his head. "Let's not pretend you exercise any authority out here. You've left these people to their own devices for years." He raised a hand to quell Russell's objection. "Who can blame you? You have enough problems to deal with."

"Get to the damn point, Grillo."

"Under centralized, coordinated leadership, this city can flourish. I can make that happen, with your . . . blessing."

"Or without, it seems."

Grillo shook his head. "You still don't understand."

"Stop talking like a Platz, then, and get to the point."

The man nodded. "Under the flag of Nightcliff, I can bring order and prosperity to this city. They will *sing* our names."

"Or?"

"Or," Grillo said, "I could fan a shit storm beyond anything you can imagine."

Russell clenched his fists.

"Raise a hand against me," Grillo said, "and no less than six snipers will compete to put the first bullet through your brain."

"I don't like being threatened," Russell growled.

"No one does. This is an excellent deal for you, Blackfield. I'm offering to take over the headache this city gives you and allow you to focus on bigger issues."

"And all I have to do is, what, turn a blind eye to your conquest of the roofers?"

"A bit more than that," Grillo said. "Without your explicit mandate, this won't work."

"Mandate."

"Make me your prefect of Nightcliff, with full confidence to do whatever is required to bring the city under control. I'll give you regular reports, and you'll still have full authority, while being able to spend your time in orbit, settling matters there."

The words percolated through Russell's mind. He craved a healthy gulp of vodka.

"Six months," Grillo said. "If you give me that, I'll give you Darwin on a silver platter."

"Starting when?"

Grillo extended a hand. "About an hour ago."

By the time the firm handshake ended, Russell found himself considering ways to root the ambitious prick from his inevitable hold on Darwin. Three months, he thought, should be enough for Grillo's strategy to become a bullet train with no brakes, and then he could be tossed over Nightcliff's north wall and no one need know any more about it.

Really, was it any different than allowing Kip Osmak to handle the day-to-day operations at the climber port? A good leader delegates. Russell had read that, somewhere. Maybe Neil Platz had said it, in one speech or another.

And in the meantime, Russell could get down to the business of finding Tania Sharma and her band of merry misfits.

Later that day, he called everyone of importance to his office in Nightcliff and introduced them to the new prefect. Their shocked expressions told him what they thought of the arrangement, but they weren't people whose opinions mattered much.

By sunset Russell found himself on board a climber. He felt the weight of Darwin's problems fade as his altitude increased, and understood then why all the world's elite had fled the city as well, five years ago, rather than deal with the aftermath of SUBS. He'd stuck it out then, taken the reins and done what had to be done.

No matter what anyone said, Russell had earned his place at the top of the food chain, and it was high time he enjoyed the perks that came along with it.

10

BELÉM, BRAZIL

30.APR.2283

A snake slithered over his left leg, then under his right.

Skyler guessed from the weight that it must be as thick as his arm. Confirmation would require looking, and he had no intention of moving a muscle. The creature took so long to finish its languid journey that he imagined it being more than five meters in length.

Only when he felt the tail tickle his right ankle did he allow himself to breathe. He'd fallen asleep, stupidly, in the undergrowth east of the Elevator and base camp. The last two days had left him exhausted. The tenacious immunes were stubborn to the point of insanity and had chased him through the city for six hours. When they finally gave up, Skyler collapsed in the first place he found to sleep: on the couch inside a psychiatric office. Offices were less likely to be tombs for the first victims of SUBS as most people forgot about work when the end came, and that had proved true here. He'd dusted off the plush leather couch, lain down, and listened to the river through a broken window. A pack of dogs woke him three times, baying and snarling at one another as they roamed their masterless world.

In the morning he'd begun to walk, each step a conscious effort, his mind clouded with scenarios and theories as to what was going on inside Camp Exodus. An organized group of immunes had rolled in and taken charge; that much seemed obvious. Everything else amounted to so much speculation and only distracted him, but when he tried to put it out of mind his thoughts turned to that bizarre cave in the rainforest and the creature he'd spied within. Part of him wanted nothing more than to gather a posse and head back out there, a desire these immunes stood in the way of. But there was another part of him, a part he felt guilty about, that welcomed any task other than returning to the home of that nightmare. The thought crossed his mind, more than once, to forget all about the things he'd seen.

He'd walked all day. A long, circuitous route brought him around to the east side of camp, opposite of where he'd approached from before.

By the time he'd crawled through the foliage to study the scene, night had long fallen. His legs were rubber from the day of walking, his feet raw and aching.

He took a glance at his wristwatch. Three A.M. He'd slept for almost two hours. Eyes on the camp, Skyler reached down and grabbed his canteen. He swished the cool water through his teeth and then spit it out before taking a modest gulp. A growl from his stomach he ignored.

The invaders, as Skyler had come to call them, were organized and taking no chances. Their vehicles were parked in a semicircle around the north and west sides of the camp. One pointed outward, the next inward, in repeating fashion. Their bright headlights bathed the camp in pure white and complex shadows. Most were aimed dead center on the base of the Elevator, where the camp's improvised headquarters sat. A few, though, cast their light on the parking lot of aura towers.

Those trucks pointing outward cast wan illumination on the surrounding trees and low buildings, giving swarms of moths a stage for their evening dance.

Skyler's strategy to approach from the east proved wise. He'd walked well past the camp and followed the riverbank back, turning in at the tributary that roughly traced the camp's eastern border. The invaders were paying little attention to this side.

From his position on the sloped bank of the tributary, Skyler saw no colonists abroad. They were either confined to their tents and mobile homes, or they'd been crammed into the bellies of the five armored personnel carriers he counted.

Or killed. There was always *that* possibility.

A climber rested at the base of the Elevator, loaded with cargo. The construction crane they'd rigged to lift the thing still had truss lines attached to the frame of the spiderlike vehicle. Yesterday should have been the first real shipment of water and air to the space stations above. Having checked constantly for signs of the crawler rising above the city, Skyler knew nothing had gone up. Tania and the others would be rationing now, and the farms would be even more at risk than before. He wondered how much they knew of the situation here. Whoever the intruders were, Tania would try to talk to them if the comm functioned. A climber stuck at the base meant that nothing, and no one, could come down.

Skyler needed hard information, and the longer he waited, the closer dawn would be, stealing any chance of a quiet foray into the camp.

He allowed a half hour to study the invaders' movements. Sentries manned each vehicle, either atop a mounted gun turret if available, or just sitting on the roof with an assault rifle across their knees.

A few patrolled on foot, giving a cursory flashlight inspection of the waterway. Skyler took some heart at this. If he had it right, only a handful of the invaders had any formal training in such things. Despite their matching gear and professional attitude, they were not all experienced militants.

When the next patroller wandered out of earshot, Skyler made his move. Running low, he went to the nearest friendly tent and ducked behind it. He waited, ready to bolt toward the river if any alarm rose. Hearing nothing, he flicked the canvas side of the tent with his finger. He repeated this a dozen times before he heard a whisper.

"Who's there?"

"Skyler," he said, voice low.

"Thank God," the person said. "We thought you were dead. Where have you—"

"No time for chat," Skyler hissed. "How many are there, who are they, and what do they want?"

The person inside the tent swallowed audibly. "Thirty? Maybe forty? I don't know what they want. We were shoved into random tents and told we'd be shot if we came out. I've heard three gunshots since then."

Whatever their goal, the fact that they'd kill for it told Skyler everything he needed to hear about. "Where's Karl?"

"I don't know," the colonist whispered. "I saw him talking to their leader, before they shoved me in here."

Skyler glanced around himself. Another patrol would come by soon. "Which one is their leader? Can you describe him?"

"I . . . I'm not sure. Tall, your height I guess. Military hair, you know, close-cropped. Goatee and sunglasses. That's all I saw."

"You're sure he was their leader?"

A pause. "I just assumed . . ."

Skyler heard footsteps to the south. "Okay, stay put. If violence is the only solution here, you'll know when I've started it. Follow Karl's lead if you can; otherwise just fight. There's no place to run."

"Take me with you?"

"Sorry," Skyler said, and meant it. "When they find you're missing, they'll double their guard and make trouble for everyone else. Right now they think I'm hiding deep in the city, and the longer they believe that, the better."

"Okay, okay. You're right."

The footsteps sounded closer. "Quiet now," Skyler said. He feared that a return to his place on the riverbank would take too long. Instead he moved farther into the camp, making use of every shadow he could. He reached a parked truck, the flatbed he'd seen on Mercy Road the day before carrying bed frames, and rolled underneath it.

For a long time he lay still, inhaling the rich aroma of chipped wood. Mud and deep puddles had plagued the center of camp in the first days after arrival, so Skyler had led an expedition for decorative bark, of all things. Tania and the others had balked at first, claiming medical supplies and food were all that mattered.

Once Skyler and a half-dozen volunteers blanketed the Elevator base in the ground cover, the complaints stopped. No mud in the tents, no bootfuls of cold rainwater to suffer. Tania even thanked him for being bullheaded about the idea, on one of her brief visits.

That the material suppressed sounds and held no footprints proved an unintended benefit. Satisfied no one had seen him dive under the truck, Skyler allowed himself to relax, and surveyed the center of camp from his fresh point of view.

One of the black-clad newcomers guarded the cargo container that served as the camp's headquarters. Karl, Skyler knew, spent most of his time in there, carefully managing the logistics of the alien towers. Where they were, who had responsibility for them, and when they would return. He and Skyler spent many evenings huddled around the map of Belém taped to the wall within, plotting and strategizing.

The comm, their only link to Melville Station above, lay within as well.

Skyler crawled forward. He could see the sentry up to the knees. He or she stood beside the door, casually leaning against the wall of the container, one foot crossed over the other. As Skyler moved toward the front of the truck, he saw that the guard's arms were folded, an assault rifle nestled within like a cradled newborn.

He hoped to find the person dozing, but when Skyler finally saw the face—a young man—the guard's eyes were alert and actively studying his surroundings.

An approach from here would be suicidal, as no cover existed. That the guard hadn't seen him dive below the truck was something of a miracle.

A rustling sound came from behind. Skyler shot a glance back over his shoulder and saw a colonist emerging from a tent, thirty or forty meters away.

"Hello?" the man said, voice raised. "I need to relieve myself."

"Stay where you are," the guard standing at the headquarters door shouted back. His voice carried a heavy accent. Brazilian, Skyler guessed. "I'll get you an escort."

"I'm just going to go behind the tent here," the colonist said. He started to walk.

Skyler glanced forward and saw the guard standing alert. The man took a few steps forward, readying his gun.

"Remain still!" the guard yelled. Then he slipped two fingers into the corners of his mouth and whistled three times as he continued to march toward the noisy colonist. His path brought him right next to the truck Skyler lay beneath, and he stopped just centimeters away. "I mean it, asshole, stop."

The camp began to stir. Skyler heard voices and the zippers of tent flaps. Some invaders, across the camp and out of view, were shouting queries about the whistle.

"Stop, I'm serious," the guard urged. Then he muttered, "Shit," and started to run. Skyler glanced back again and caught a glimpse of the colonist racing off into the darkness, toward the river. The guard bolted toward him even as more of the invaders came from the other side of camp. Shouts went up and bleary colonists stumbled out of their tents.

On pure instinct, Skyler crawled from beneath the truck and sprinted to the improvised headquarters. In a former life, the structure had served as a shipping container. A doorway and window had been cut out of one side, and given the darkness within, Skyler assumed the place was empty.

As the commotion in the camp escalated, he ducked inside and closed the door.

"Who's there?" someone called.

Skyler swung his gun around and flicked on the light. The bright beam lit up the face of a black-clad stranger, lying on the floor atop a sleeping bag. Halfway to a sitting position, the man froze at the sight of Skyler's gun barrel just centimeters from his face. With the weapon so close, the beam from the mounted light only lit a circle around the man's mouth.

"Not a bloody peep," Skyler whispered. He moved the light to the man's eyes, and the off-duty guard squinted and blinked, turning his face partly away.

"Okay, relax," he said.

"I need answers. Who are you people?"

"Survivors," the man said, his voice faltering. An American, judging by the accent.

"Do better than that. Quickly now. How'd you come to be here? Who's your leader?"

Fear radiated from the poor man's face. "Please. They'll kill me."

"I'll kill you," Skyler hissed. "*They* don't need to know we ever met."

Eyes closed, the man swallowed hard and managed a terse nod. "I ran a factory in São Paulo. Everyone started dying, or . . . worse. I hid for a while, and when things quieted down I decided to make my way back to Colorado."

"Skip the life story, okay?"

The man went on. "Gabriel found me on the freeway, near Rio. I could barely walk I was so hungry."

"Gabriel?"

"Our leader. He brought all us survivors together, ever since the . . . He's building a new society from the ashes."

Skyler took a second to digest the information. The man's voice held a reverence that could mean nothing good. "Why did you attack our camp?"

The man opened one eye, trying to see Skyler and failing in the face of the flashlight. "What would you do, if you came across a scene like this?"

"I'd probably cheer at the sight of so many more survivors."

"You spacemen are not *true* survivors."

Skyler had opened his mouth to argue when the blade of a knife flashed inches from his face. He leapt backward as the man slashed again. Blinded by the bright flashlight, the invader misjudged the distance on both swings.

A gunshot here would have the whole lot of them bearing down on the room, so Skyler flipped his gun around and smacked the butt into the man's face. He heard the sound of bone breaking as the weapon hit.

The man roared and fell back, clutching at his ruined nose. Skyler darted forward and lunged with his weapon again, then a third time, until the American fell silent.

He had no doubt the entire camp heard the man's anguished shout. Skyler turned and fled, stopping just shy of the door. Linked pairs of handheld radios lay in a tray bolted to the wall. He grabbed a set and knelt, placing his gun on the floor so he could work with the light it provided.

A strap of Velcro held the two devices together. He ripped

the material apart and set one device aside. Fingers dancing, he turned on the radio in his hands and then wrapped the Velcro strap around twice, pulling it tight so that the transmit button remained down.

He turned and scanned the room. Prompted by a nearby shout outside, Skyler knew he had to leave. He slid the modified radio across the floor and it vanished beneath the table where the comm terminal sat. He could only hope it would remain unfound.

Skyler snatched the other radio and ran from the room. He ignored a cry of warning from somewhere behind him, taking a zigzag pattern around the truck he'd hidden under before. A deafening report from an assault rifle made him duck and change directions again, as bullets thudded into the side of the truck.

He didn't bother to turn and look. There were too many of them. Instead Skyler kept running, straight back the way he'd come, pumping his legs as hard as he could. He stuffed the radio into his pocket and flicked off the flashlight on his gun as he went.

When he passed the tent where he'd spoken to a colonist, the man was emerging from the flap, brandishing a folded umbrella.

"Not yet," Skyler said as he raced by. The colonist, an older man, ducked back inside as more gunshots rang out. Skyler crouched and altered his angle twice more before finally reaching the sloped bank. He leapt into the tributary at a narrow point, hoisting his weapon above his head, landing in knee-high water with a huge splash.

Out the other side, he turned and knelt. When the first invader's head appeared above the sloped bank, Skyler fired, killing the person instantly.

He spun and ran up the far bank, diving over the top and rolling in the tall grass beyond as more bullets traced paths through the vegetation around him.

In any other scenario he would have fired wildly in return, hoping to send the enemies diving for cover. But with the colony as a backdrop, the risk was too great. Instead he flipped the holo-sight on and took aim at the closest invader. Skyler squeezed the trigger and sent the person sprawling, clutching their leg.

The others took cover as their second comrade hit the ground.

Satisfied, Skyler began to crawl through the meter-high grass. He went east, or so he hoped, moving to a bent-over run as soon as he thought it safe to do so. Twice he tripped in the darkness. On the second fall his head smacked into a rock buried in the deep grass, cutting his forehead. He bit back a groan and ran on as blood began to trickle from the wound.

The immunes chased him through grass fields and rainforest for an hour before Skyler happened upon a flimsy boathouse.

Double images blurred before his eyes. He swayed on his feet and needed every ounce of concentration to keep his legs under him. Throwing caution to the wind, he kicked his way into the feeble structure and turned his flashlight on again, finding the single room empty. A concrete channel full of black water held a tiny, two-man fiberglass boat, tied down with a single nylon rope.

The water went out through the wide-open fourth wall, ten meters out through a mangrove cathedral to the swift Guamá. Whatever smugglers used this place in the past hid it well from above.

Blood still trickling from his forehead, Skyler lumbered forward and stepped into the boat, his foot splashing in stagnant water that had pooled in the hull. He ignored the foul smell and lay down on his back. After three tries to grab the yellow rope, which swam and blurred in front of him, he finally found it and undid the simple knot. Fighting the searing pain in his skull, he reached over the side of the boat and probed with his hand until he found concrete. Using just his fingertips, he pushed with all the strength he had left. After what felt like an eternity, he cracked his eyes open enough to see the roof of the hidden boathouse pass above him, giving way to tangled mangroves and dark sky beyond. The pain soon became unbearable and he let his eyes close.

Voices nearby. Shouting. The door of the feeble shack being kicked in again. Brittle wood shattering this time. Skyler lay still, aware his pursuers argued at the water's edge, their words a meaningless jumble. They had not fired at him, not with intent to hit him, since leaving the auras behind. The thought flickered in a corner of his mind, then danced away, intangible.

Adrift, skull throbbing, Skyler felt rather than saw the transition into the swift and churning waters of the wide river. As the light of dawn began to touch the sky above, he lapsed into unconsciousness.

11

DARWIN, AUSTRALIA

1.MAY.2283

Vaughn shifted in his sleep. He rolled away, his moist skin separating from hers in a sound that made her think of peeling a banana.

One sweaty arm still draped across Samantha's stomach. She lay on her back, on the floor of her cell, naked and glistening from their roll in the hay. Despite his mirthless personality, Vaughn performed remarkably well for his first time with her. Fit, young, and otherwise bored proved a good mix, if enthusiasm counted for anything. He wouldn't win any awards for originality, but she didn't care. He slept now; that's all that mattered.

She lay there in the humid air and musky smell until he did not stir when she lifted his wrist from her stomach. On the previous three tries, he'd resisted having his arm moved, despite his regular breathing and rapid eye movement. This time she lifted his arm and dropped it back to her stomach in a wet slap. Satisfied, Sam slid from under him, her skin breaking into goose bumps when his fingertips brushed across her waistline.

In any other circumstances, you'd make a decent sparring partner, Vaughn, my boy. He'd declined to tell her his first name when she'd finally asked after rolling off him. Something about how they shouldn't get to know each other too well. "We just fucked," Sam had replied.

He'd grunted, considered for a moment, and said, "Fine, it's Bruce."

Sam had never met an actual Australian man named Bruce, but she didn't press it.

The tiny window on her cell door cast a square of dim light onto the concrete floor. Sam pulled the guard's clothing into the beam and went through his gear. A nightstick, Taser, and red utility knife she set by the exit, on top of her discarded clothing.

In one pocket she found a set of old-fashioned metal keys, the card-swipe system having apparently failed a year earlier, something Vaughn griped about every time he entered. Six silver and bronze keys dangled from the ring. She clasped her fist around them, pulled them from the pocket, and set them carefully next to the other gear, her ears tuned to the sound of his breathing.

The door squeaked when she slipped out. Not enough to stir the guard, but plenty to send her pulse racing. She left her clothing behind. If Vaughn stirred she thought she could return to his side and raise no suspicion. Now out of the cell, she figured her naked state would give her a brief advantage to anyone coming across her.

Samantha padded down the hall and poked her head into the office the guards used. In the middle of the night, Vaughn appeared to be the only person on duty.

She set the nightstick on the desk there and checked all the drawers for proper weapons, a futile effort. One of the keys she'd taken might open a weapons locker somewhere in the building, but a search could take awhile.

A clipboard on the wall caught her eye. A stack of stained papers was tucked under the metal fastener, rows of names written in one column and numbers in another. Using the weak light coming in from a curtained window, she scanned the names. On page two, she found it: Adelaide, cell listed as "Royal 004." Samantha's own name noted cell "Main 212." The numbers were rooms, she guessed, but the words held no meaning for her.

"Royal 004," she whispered to herself over and over. Near the door an idea struck her, and she snatched up a half-empty bottle of some alcohol or another. Fermented cider, Darwin's poison, if the smell was any indicator.

Leaving the nightstick behind, she held the bottle loosely in one hand and clutched Vaughn's keys in the other, and stumbled out the door in what she hoped looked like a drunken swagger.

Her bare feet splashed in puddles on the cracked sidewalk outside. A half second later a spray of warm rain dappled her bare skin. She paused a moment and closed her eyes, enjoying the feeling of freedom, both physical and metaphorical.

"We have a dress code within the walls," someone said.

She whirled around, slipped, then righted herself. Liquid sloshed in the bottle, a splash of it clapping onto the ground. The clumsy move fed into her ploy. "Thass a new rule!" she barked.

The man stood between her and a yellow LED bulb mounted on the wall by the guard's office. How he'd gotten behind her, she had no idea. He wore an overcoat, and had slick hair. Shadows hid his face.

"True," he said. "However, a rule is a rule."

"Can't make an exception in my case, sweetheart?" she said, and tried to strike a flattering pose, deliberately off balance.

"You may be the worst actress I've ever seen, Samantha Rinn."

She dropped the façade and whipped the bottle around in her hand, holding it like a club. The alcohol poured down her leg in a noisy gurgle. "Who are you?" she asked. "How do you know me?"

As an answer, he sidestepped into the light.

"Grillo . . . ," she said.

He tilted his head to one side. "It's been awhile since you declined my job offer."

"The bennies were shit," she said through a tight smile. He'd tried to hire everyone on Skyler's crew, after Skyler declined to join his operation. He even tried to pay poor Jake to assassinate their leader, claiming an accident. Jake said no, of course, and told Sam about the offer only after a night of hard drinking at Woon's.

Her hand tightened around the keys, and she set her feet wider, ready to pounce or run. "What the hell are you doing here?"

"I came looking for you," he replied.

A pair of laughing Nightcliff regulars came around the corner. At the sight of Samantha they pulled up. One hooted at her nakedness; the other froze in wide-eyed recognition of a captive on the loose.

"Move along, gentlemen," Grillo said to them without so much as a glance in their direction.

"Sir, she's a prisoner," the stunned guard said. "Dangerous. Russell said no one was to touch her."

"I'm in charge now," Grillo said. "You may have heard. Miss Rinn is an old friend and is going to accompany me to my office."

"She is?"

"I am?" Samantha said. She draped an arm across her breasts and crossed her legs.

At some point Grillo had slipped a pistol from his coat pocket, and it now rested against his thigh. Samantha couldn't decide whom he meant to threaten with it.

"You," Grillo said to the guard who still gawked at her, "you're almost tall enough. Give the young lady your jacket and pants."

"Huh?" he managed.

"Please do not make me repeat myself," Grillo said. His even voice intoned deadly threat.

Ten minutes later she found herself seated at Grillo's desk, the stiff and smelly borrowed jacket itching her skin, too-tight black pants covering her legs.

She asked for scotch; he gave her water.

For a time they sat in uncomfortable silence, sipping their drinks. The office was cluttered with mismatched furniture and obnoxious decorations. Blackfield's things, she surmised. Skimmed from years of impromptu searches of returning scavenger ships. Sam even recognized a painting on the wall as one she'd grabbed in haste in a mansion in China. Abstract and tacky, it nevertheless reminded her of entwined limbs, like some crazed orgy. The same impression hit her now, and the painting seemed even more out of place here than in that party official's home. Nothing in the room matched Grillo's personality.

Lightning flashed outside, followed a few seconds later by

distant thunder, as wet season made its curtain call.

"So you're running things now?" she said.

He considered his words. "Russell needed order in the city, and I'm the man for the job."

"How come you were skulking about outside my cell in the middle of the night?"

"As I said," Grillo replied, "I was looking for you. You seemed . . . busy, so I thought I'd wait."

"Looking for me, why? The others either want to scrape a knuckle or get in my pants. Sometimes both."

"I need your help."

"Go fuck yourself. I know how you work, crime lord, and it's not my style."

He frowned, if only for an instant. "I never understood that moniker. Crime, by definition, does not exist in an anarchy."

"Slumlord, then."

Grillo swirled the water in his cup and watched the vortex that formed for a moment. "It's integral to my plan for Darwin that the scavenger crews return to full capacity, that they cooperate. My unfortunate rivalry with them over these last five years does not make me the best person to try to convince them of this fact."

"But me . . ."

"You they love."

Sam shook her head. "Forget it. Our independence is, was, the only reason we bother."

"Not the greater good?"

Samantha chuckled. "The only people who ever ask that can't afford to hire the crews. Look, forget it. I'd rather rot in this place than help you and Russell Dickfield."

Grillo leaned to one side and looked toward the door they'd entered through. He raised his voice and said, "Bring her in."

The doors opened a second later, and Samantha rose from her chair as two nurses wheeled a stretcher into the office.

"Kelly Adelaide," Grillo said.

Samantha rushed across the room and took her friend's hand. Kelly didn't grip back, and Samantha eased, afraid she would crush bone.

Fighting tears, Sam whirled on Grillo, who now stood near the center of the large office. "What did you bastards do to her?"

Grillo took a step back, holding his hands up before him. "Let me explain."

Without thinking, without a care in the world, Samantha balled her fists and stormed across the room. She threw the punch without a second thought, her calloused, meaty fist whooshing through the air.

Grillo dodged it. He sidestepped with uncanny agility, his calm expression never changing.

Momentum threw Samantha off balance and she stumbled forward. The failed attack only fueled her rage. Before she could stop herself, she swiped an arm across Grillo's desk, scattering papers and sending a comm terminal crashing to the floor.

"She's been sedated," Grillo said.

Sam gripped the wooden desk, squeezing with all her might to release her anger. Tears threatened to spill from her eyes and she fought to keep them within. "Bollocks," she managed. "Why?"

"Because the two of you together are a rather volatile combination," Grillo said.

"You think this will convince me? I'll tear your arms off and shove them up your bloody ass before I help you."

Wisely, Grillo moved to stand on the opposite side of the stretcher. By the time Samantha crossed to face him, her sympathy for Kelly quieted the rage within.

"Here's your choice, Samantha," Grillo said, voice low. "Get the crews running, and Kelly lives. Refuse, and her next injection will be drain cleaner. You'll remain in your cell until Russell finally gets tired of waiting for you to be a willing bedmate."

When the white-hot rage faded, Sam saw only Kelly's serene, vulnerable face. She knelt beside the bed and took her friend's hand again, a light grip this time. Kelly's eyes fluttered beneath the eyelids in reaction. "I won't help you if she's rotting in a cell alone."

"I understand," Grillo said. "But I can't have the two of you together, at least until I know where your allegiance is. Sorry, but I know what you're capable of."

"Think of something."

Grillo mulled it over for a moment. Then he turned to the two nurses. "Take her to my facility in Lyons, a guest room with a barred window. When she wakes, tell her that if she tries to leave Samantha will be shot." They nodded and wheeled the woman away.

For a time Samantha just stared at the empty space where her friend lay. Grillo kept back, respectful of her turmoil.

"Let me get this straight," she said when her grief and anger had faded. "I convince the scavenger crews to work for you, and you'll let Kelly live in your mansion?"

"Not exactly. Tacit agreement from the airport crews does me little good, and I sense you want more for Kelly than just 'house arrest' status."

Samantha turned to face him. She towered over the man but somehow felt his equal. The way he'd avoided her fist, the unnerving calm in the way he carried himself. This man demanded respect in a way Russell Blackfield could only dream of. "So," she said, "what then? Stop being vague."

His head tilted to one side as he spoke. "You'll ask the scavengers to work for *you,* not me. You keep them flying, you supply their missions based on my needs, and you take responsibility for the success or failure."

"What's the big push? Russell asking for more guns, or does he want fine art and gold chains now that he's the big boss?"

Grillo shook his head. "Soil," he said. "Fertilizer. Shovels, hoes, and spades. Weed killer. Seeds."

"I thought the 'traitors' took all the farms?"

A thin smile flashed on Grillo's face. "I work for Darwin, first and foremost. I intend to change the face of this city."

Sam blinked. "I'll be damned. You're full of surprises. It sounds like you actually give a shit."

"Not the words I'd use, but yes. And thank you."

Samantha crossed her arms. "So what about Kelly?"

"Work for me," Grillo said, "and you'll no longer be a prisoner. Kelly will remain under my care, house arrest, until I'm convinced you're a believer, a partner in the metamorphosis. At that point, when I no longer fear you might flee, I'll release Miss Adelaide to you."

"And Blackfield is on board with all this?"

That flash of a grin again. "I have broad authority here."

This time Samantha grinned. "He doesn't know, does he?"

Grillo met her gaze, and allowed his smile to stay this time. "Mr. Blackfield doesn't know a lot of things, Miss Rinn, and that's the last we'll talk about it."

12

BELÉM, BRAZIL

1.MAY.2283

Radiant amoeba-like shapes swam in a sea of molten orange, and any attempt he made to focus on one served only to obscure it further.

A long time passed before Skyler realized he was looking at the inside of his eyelids.

A feeble attempt to open them resulted in stabbing pain, so he gave up and focused on the sounds around him: birds overhead, water lapping softly against wood and stone. A distant wind chime tapped out random harmonic chords.

His lips were dry and cracked. Throat and mouth so dry he couldn't summon enough saliva to swallow.

The sun sat directly overhead, it seemed from the heat on his face. He hoisted one arm to block the painful light and felt the world sway. His head pounded, a steady drumbeat from the back of his skull.

After what felt like an hour, Skyler opened his eyes against the blackness of his arm. Moving one careful millimeter at a time, he lifted his wrist and let his eyes adjust to the blaze of daylight.

"Don't move," a voice said. A girl.

Skyler let his arm fall. He tried to say something but managed only a weak cough.

"Sit up."

"Don't move, or sit up?" Skyler croaked.

When no reply came, he grunted and propped himself on an elbow. A wet tearing sound signaled more pain when his hair, matted with dried blood, detached from the floor of the boat. The drum in his head turned to a marching band, and Skyler ceased moving to let the throbbing pain subside before finally pushing himself to a sitting position.

Blinding light forced him to squint. He turned away from it, only to find it in all directions. "Fuck. Enough with the flashlight, eh?"

No response. Gradually his eyes adjusted and Skyler saw white sand reflecting sunlight up from below. A beach, stretching twenty meters to a row of vacation cottages. Behind the homes he could see the vague forms of skyscrapers against the white sky. Downtown Belém, he hoped.

The girl stood between him and the cottages. She wore hiking boots and long, dark blue shorts. Tan, toned legs filled the space between. An oversized white T-shirt was stretched tight across her chest by the black straps of a backpack, accentuating small breasts.

"I know those legs," Skyler found himself saying.

She shifted in the sand, and he realized she held a pistol pointed at him.

"I know that gun, too," he added.

"Stand up," she said.

He groaned. "Would if I could."

"Are you drunk?"

In answer he turned so she could see the sticky blood coating the back of his head and neck. From her sharp intake of breath, he knew it looked as bad as it felt.

"What are you doing out here?" she asked.

"I could ask you the same," Skyler replied. "Though I'd rather know why you were dancing the other day. Lovely as the performance was, it's a damn dangerous place for a recital."

He saw her face clearly then. Light brown eyes and a little bulb of a nose. Her cheeks were dappled with dark brown freckles that matched the color of her hair, which she'd tucked behind each ear. If not for the suspicious scowl on her face, the worried brow, she'd be rather cute.

The girl held her ground, shifting her weight again, adjusting her grip on the weapon. "You're following us."

Skyler rubbed his temples. "Us. You're with this Gabriel character?"

The girl jumped forward, her gun filling Skyler's field of view. A stream of curses in a language Skyler didn't know flew from her lips. Spanish, he guessed, not Portuguese.

"Not with Gabriel then," Skyler said, looking down and away. "We've got something in common."

She flexed her fingers on the grip of the weapon and seemed to will herself to be calm. "If you're not with Gabriel then what are you doing here?"

Skyler met her gaze and held it. A fleeting moment of clarity came to him, and he realized she'd shot at him in that courtyard because she thought he was one of Gabriel's people, one of the invaders. He'd scared her much more than he'd realized. Skyler tried to swallow. "His people hold our camp, and I escaped in this boat. Hit my head in the process and . . . that's the last I remember."

She studied him for some time. "How far to your camp?"

"Depends on where I am."

"Are they following you still?"

Skyler pinched the bridge of his nose as a wave of nausea crashed over him. When it passed, he said, "Probably. They seem hell-bent on finding me."

The girl swore again, her eyes sweeping the horizon behind Skyler's right shoulder. Upstream, he guessed. "*Imbécil,*" she muttered.

"That I understood."

She renewed her aim, square on his chest, and narrowed her eyes. "Why are they chasing you?"

"Give me some water," Skyler said, "and I'll tell you."

* * *

She led him at gunpoint to a cottage a full kilometer farther down the beach.

"Davi?!" she called out as they approached the stand-alone structure, part of what once must have been a luxury resort.

A young man poked his head up from a hammock on the patio. When he saw Skyler, the kid rolled out of the rope bed and emerged a second later with a rifle in hand. He called out in Spanish and the girl replied in turn.

She circled around Skyler, her aim never straying from his torso, and held up a hand for him to stop when they were ten meters from the tiny vacation home.

"What's your name?" she asked.

"Skyler," he said. "He's Davi, I gather. Who are you?"

She studied him for a second before replying. "Ana."

When the young man joined them on the beach, Skyler saw their resemblance. Other than gender differences, the two looked exactly the same.

"Immune twins," he said. "I'll be damned."

"He's the one I saw in the courtyard," Ana said, ignoring Skyler but speaking English for his benefit.

"Are you with Gabriel?" Davi asked.

Skyler shook his head. "I'm with . . ." *How to explain?* "You've seen the thread going up into the sky?"

"The space elevator," Ana said.

Skyler nodded.

"Like the one in Australia."

He nodded again. "You've heard of it, good."

"We had an education," Davi said with pride. "Before . . ."

"I'm with the group that came down this one," Skyler said, gesturing toward the sky. The motion made him dizzy. "From space. From Australia before that."

Ana spoke rapidly to Davi in Spanish again. Soon the boy stood a few meters away from Skyler, a healthy dose of skepticism on his face.

The girl came to her brother's shoulder, standing just behind him. "They'll find his boat," she said under her breath, but loud enough. "And search the beach."

"I know, *manita*. Let's move to the other place."

* * *

The pungent aroma of grilled fish filled Skyler's nose and he found himself salivating.

Gingerly, he turned his head to one side. He lay on a bedroll a few meters from a small cookstove painted in glossy red, the kind Skyler imagined rich adventurers would buy before a guided trip up the Amazon. Fortunes spent to see an actual rainforest, to set foot in wilderness, before it was too late. Who knew back then that it would be the humans that vanished. The forests had the better end of the Builders' bargain.

On one burner, half a gutted fish lay in an oiled steel pan, sizzling. A pot of canned beans and rice steamed away on the second burner. Skyler licked his lips and found they had been coated with ointment.

A plate of food lay near his head, he realized, white picnic fork daring him to get up. He couldn't resist, and struggled to one elbow, trying to remember exactly where they were and how they'd come here. He remembered the beach, and walking in silence through the twisted city streets. He'd been too tired, and still a bit dazed, to pay much attention. Now he cursed himself for it.

He had a forkful of fish in his mouth before he noticed Ana and Davi, sitting opposite the stove. They both sat cross-legged on the hardwood floor, a plate in the right hand, fork in the left. Ana had tied her hair back, and if the two of them had worn matching clothes Skyler might have failed to tell them apart.

Dim light came from an LED lantern set so low it barely chased the darkness from the otherwise empty, windowless room. Skyler shoveled a forkful of beans into his mouth and wondered if they'd set the lantern that low for safety, or out of sympathy for his head injury.

"Delicious," he said after scraping half his plate clean. "I mean it. Best meal of my life, I think." Even as he said the words he wanted to take them back. Prumble, and that bowl of ramen, still held the top spot. The memory made his eyes water.

"It's time we talked," Davi said. "Are you well enough?"

Skyler nodded, then hefted the last of his food from his plate. He chewed as long as he thought polite, savoring every last second of the flavor. Ana crossed the room and set a bottle of water in front of him, and he'd gulped half of it down before she even returned to her place on the floor.

He probed his head and found it had been wrapped in gauze. It still hurt to touch the gash, but not so much that he saw the heavens. Belatedly he noticed his gun, leaning against the wall behind his two hosts. "You start, or shall I?" he asked.

Davi nodded to him.

"Me first, then," Skyler said. He sat, cross-legged as they were, and wrapped the blanket they'd given him around his shoulders. Part of him became aware of the foul stench his body and clothing emitted. Something to resolve tomorrow, he decided, and told his story.

He left out only the details of the shell ship he'd found, and the transforming subhuman he'd seen within. There might be a time for that, he thought, but right now it would only complicate matters. The twins hung on his every word when he explained what had happened in Darwin over the last five years. They'd heard nothing since the disease spread, save for a rumor or two that Darwin was safe, which they had assumed was just that . . . rumor. Ana asked far more questions than Davi, especially about the aura towers, and Skyler quickly assessed that she was the brains of this brother-sister team.

The idea that there could be survivors who still could catch the disease rattled their worldview in a way Skyler could only imagine. He guessed they must have been sixteen or seventeen when the disease struck, and within months must have found themselves alone, forced to survive while being attacked constantly by the subhumans that ran rampant in those first days. How these two kids managed to last he had no idea.

When he told them how he found Camp Exodus overrun by the militant immunes, they both leaned forward, eyes narrowed. He explained his attempt to enter the camp and recounted what little he'd learned from the immune he'd questioned. Davi nodded constantly, confirming the information whether he meant to or not.

"So who are these people?" Skyler asked. "What do they want, and how do you know them?"

Davi did most of the talking. While he spoke, Ana set a pot of water on the portable stove and removed a trio of instant coffee packets from her backpack.

They were twenty-two years old, the son and daughter of wealthy winemakers in Argentina. A world-renowned brand, Davi claimed, though Skyler had never heard of it. He said he was a "coffee man," which earned a smile from Ana just as she handed him a steaming cup.

Their life had been one of large family gatherings, private tutors, and vacations to all corners of the world. Then the disease arrived. They were seventeen at the time.

For a year they'd stayed on their family land, defending it from subhumans and living off the garden and livestock there. Eventually they had to make forays into the nearby town. Davi spoke with pride about teaching Ana how to shoot a gun, and the day she made her first kill. Skyler gathered that the girl had been something of a princess before the disease came. Having seen her graceful dance in the flowing white dress, he had no problem picturing that. He wondered if Davi knew she still clung to that part of herself.

A fire ultimately drove them from their land. How it started they had no idea, but Skyler had seen enough of the world to know that failing electronics and other equipment often sparked such infernos. Entire neighborhoods, even towns, would be reduced to ash with no one to fight the flames.

They moved north after that, deciding it better to seek out other survivors, with all the risks that entailed, than to live in solitude.

Not long after entering Brazil, they came across Gabriel and his group, just eight strong then. Davi spoke at length about Gabriel's charisma, his innate way of forging friendships and loyalty. Before the disease, he'd been an undercover police officer working the drug-ridden slums of Rio de Janeiro. He never spoke of himself as the leader of the group; everyone just knew he was and accepted it.

Davi and Ana had found a family again, and happiness.

A sense of purpose, too. They joined gladly.

Things changed, though. So slowly Davi and Ana didn't notice at first. It wasn't until the group met an immune who refused to join that Gabriel showed his true colors. The reluctant immune was held captive, and Gabriel spent hours every day talking to the man in hushed tones, usually alone but sometimes with his closest members present.

Eventually the man joined. Still in the group now, in fact, and one of Gabriel's closest members.

"Brainwashed," Skyler said.

The two nodded. Davi then explained what happened with the next immune who declined to take up with the group. She'd left in the night, Gabriel had explained, with his blessings. Anyone could leave provided they spoke with Gabriel first.

Davi saw the body by accident, later that morning while gathering firewood. Bound hands and feet, a dry trickle of blood running down the back of her neck. The poor young man spoke of it like any seasoned war veteran might.

"Why is he doing all this?" Skyler asked. "Banding all the immunes together, I mean."

Davi spread his hands. "To start over. He thinks those of us who survived were meant to build a new world."

"*He* thinks. But you disagree?"

Davi glanced at his sister. "Right or not, his methods are what we fled. He runs the group like a cult."

"A religious nut, then?"

"No," Ana said, before her brother could reply. "If Gabriel has a god it is himself."

"Don't get her wrong," Davi added. "Gabriel has a calling; it just comes from his own warped head. He gives those who resist plenty of time to see things his way, but if they make a move against him, or fight him, they vanish."

Skyler nodded, noting the intense hatred on both their faces. He sipped the rest of his coffee while Ana excused herself for a few minutes. Davi spent the time with his nose buried in the screen on a handheld electronic device. A book or video game, Skyler guessed.

The gadget reminded him of his paired radio. Skyler rummaged through his backpack and found the device. He turned it on, heard static, and turned it off again.

"What's that?" Davi asked as his sister returned. She stood behind him, an eyebrow raised.

"I hid the other one in the main building of our camp. We can listen in on them, if we get closer."

When Ana sat down again Skyler set his mug aside. "Tell me," he said, "if you two escaped from this cult, why stay so close to them?"

Davi's eyes became distant for a moment, and Ana just stared at her brother, waiting for him to decide what information they would share. Her constant deference to him made her dancing in the courtyard all the more curious. Sitting here, Skyler could not imagine her straying too far from her brother's side.

"There are more like us," Davi said after a time. "More who started to question, and more who never believed in the first place. Friends of ours, in other words. Gabriel holds them captive, eleven that we know of, and we intend to free them."

"But we have to find them first," Ana said.

Skyler found himself nodding. The pair may be young, but they spoke as if an extra decade had been dumped on their shoulders. *Just like Samantha,* he thought, who was barely a year older than these two. He'd forgotten all about her youth within a few weeks of meeting her. The death toll caused by the Builders and their vicious disease was so omnipresent that Skyler rarely thought about it, but this—stolen childhood. Kids who watched everyone they knew die or become wild, only to find themselves caught up in a murderous cult of personality.

With sudden clarity he understood why Ana danced. Why she'd set aside her gun and her clothing, her shoes, her very persona, and risked her life to spin and twirl in that square. Without moments of escape like that, her life was one of constant terror.

"Eleven, you say." Skyler focused on Davi. "Gabriel now holds a few hundred of my people at our camp, and he's effectively trapped a few thousand more up in space. They'll die without air and water from down here."

Davi's mouth twisted with anger. He rose to his knees and pointed off to his right, presumably toward the space elevator. "You mean your people are more important than ours?"

"Hear me out," Skyler said, motioning for the young man to sit back down. "We find and free your friends. With them on our side, we can retake my camp, and take down Gabriel in the process."

Davi's head shook before Skyler had even finished. "Your camp is your problem."

"Oh, Dav," Ana said.

"We'll rescue our friends and get away from here, with or without your help."

"You do that," Skyler growled, "and all you've done is traded eleven lives for two thousand. And for the rest of your life you'll know Gabriel is still out there, gathering others just like you. Can you live with that?"

"Davi," Ana whispered, a hand on her brother's shoulder.

He recoiled from her, muttered something in Spanish, and stormed from the room.

"What did he say?" Skyler asked.

The girl waited until her brother's footsteps faded down the hallway beyond. "He just needs to think. You are right, and he knows that, but he doesn't like it when his plans are changed."

She set to work cleaning their cups, using leftover water from the pot on the stove. When Skyler offered to help she waved him off. "Rest, please."

"I need to use the bathroom," he said.

Ana looked at him, then toward the door her brother had exited through.

"You still don't trust me," Skyler said. "It's okay. In your shoes, I'd be a skeptic, too."

Her mouth turned down in silent apology.

"Here," Skyler said, removing his boots. "I can't get far without these, and my gun and pack are here. Fair?"

She nodded and pointed toward the hallway. "Take a flashlight. Down to the end, and I suggest you breathe through your mouth."

Digesting the ominous warning, Skyler removed a small key-chain LED from a pocket in his vest and set off down the hall. Hardwood flooring creaked under his feet. He trailed one hand along the wall as a precaution against dizziness, feeling the ridges where bands of red and gold wallpaper met. Without working air-conditioning to chase away humidity, the glue that held the covering up had started to degrade, leaving edges peeled and folds where the heavy paper had gone slack.

Gold numbers on the doors implied the building was a hotel. An ancient low-budget one, if the communal toilet said anything. At the end of the hall, Skyler found the bathroom door open. He paused before entering when he noticed a stairwell directly across, leading up and down. Though he had no intention of fleeing, a quick jog up to the roof held a certain appeal. The sensation of not knowing exactly where he was grated on some corner of his mind, like an itch he couldn't scratch. The hotel they'd brought him to could be a hundred meters or a hundred kilometers from the space elevator, for all he knew.

Nature called, though. Skyler slipped into the cramped bathroom and nudged the door closed with his toe. A janitor's bucket served as toilet, the real item rendered useless by lack of running water. A faded wooden toilet seat lay propped against the wall, removed at some point for the screws that held it to the bowl. Moonlight from a small window on the back wall provided enough light, so he set his tiny flashlight on the porcelain counter and unzipped his pants. What felt like a minute passed as he relieved himself, and he had to prop his elbow against the wall to combat a mild wave of dizziness as the bucket filled. Finished, he hoisted the bucket out the tiny window and flipped it over. He shook it to make sure nothing remained inside.

Rapid footsteps came from outside the door. Davi, he thought, bounding up the stairs in a hurry. Skyler heard him turn the corner and race off down the hallway.

"Ana!" Davi shouted, muffled by the door and his distance down the hall.

Then Skyler heard others. Heavy footfalls now, in the stairwell. He stood frozen in place, holding the waste bucket out the window in the night air, unsure if he should move or keep silent.

The footsteps stopped right outside. Two or three people, and not subs, Skyler guessed by the fact that they had halted at the stairwell exit. He pulled the bucket back inside and set it carefully on the grimy tile floor.

Davi shouted something from the far end of the hall, but the words were too muffled for Skyler to understand. A pair of gunshots followed, though, providing all the translation he needed.

He knew Davi and Ana had chosen a room with only one exit. An amateur mistake he doubted they would make again, should they live. A quick search of the bathroom did not yield any obvious weapons. All Skyler had was his clothing, the key-chain flashlight, and the flimsy bucket, none of which would do much good.

Then Skyler eyed the wooden toilet seat; he hoped it wasn't just painted plastic.

Gunfire just outside the room made him jump. More shouting followed, whether in Portuguese or Spanish he couldn't be sure. It mattered little. Skyler used the commotion to grab the toilet seat. It had the satisfying heft of real wood.

Gripping the oval seat by its narrow side, Skyler crossed to the door and gripped the handle. He waited, his eyes beginning to water in the stale air of the old bathroom. A cough brewed in his chest, and he knew it would escape soon.

Davi shot at the intruders again, his bullet cracking into the wall at the end of the hallway, just outside Skyler's door. He heard the enemies talking among themselves. A tactical argument, from the tone. Skyler had been through enough of those to recognize it despite the foreign tongue.

When they returned fire, Skyler acted. He twisted the handle, yanked, and threw the door wide open. Even as their faces began to turn toward him, Skyler took the toilet seat and flung it like a saw blade.

The thin edge caught the closest man full in the face. Surprise and horror came through in the man's gurgling scream. He fell back into his friends, both of whom were equally caught off guard. The three of them tumbled backward in slapstick fashion, ending in a tangled mess of limbs on the dark landing below.

Skyler brushed away the idea of running to Ana and Davi. He leapt into the stairwell instead, landing squarely on the chest of the first man. Hands clasped together, Skyler brought his fists down like a hammer into the man's face.

The man went limp. His two comrades were close to disentangling themselves.

Skyler ripped the weapon out of the unconscious intruder's hands, swung it around, and put two bullets into each of the other men. One fell against the wall, a splatter of blood dotting the surface behind his head. The other fell to his knees and toppled forward, down the next flight of stairs.

Heart pounding, Skyler tossed the weapon aside and used his legs to push up the stairway backward. "Davi!"

The young man appeared behind him seconds later, gasping at the sight in the stairwell. Ana was right behind him.

"Tell me," Skyler growled, "that you have another way out of here."

"Those are Gabriel's men."

"No shit."

"We have to get out of here. Get away."

"Hence my question."

"No, Davi," Ana said. Her voice carried a sternness not there before. "Not away. Closer. Closer so that Skyler's radio will work."

Davi stared at his sister for a long time, his gut instinct to flee dwindling with each passing second. "Okay, okay. But if we don't hear anything by morning, we will have to grab one of them. Force them to tell us."

Skyler turned to him. "Let's go."

SHOES?

13

GATEWAY STATION

3.MAY.2283

Alex Warthen laid three gray slates on the table.

"What's this?" Russell asked. He angled his head to get a better look, and took a noisy sip of his vodka. Each panel showed a schematic of some sort.

Pointing at each screen in turn, Alex said, "maps of the space stations along the Elevator. Past, present, and future. Future being later today, if we all agree on the plan."

Ten Backward had been cleared for the meeting, not that the tavern had seen much activity lately. Everything, even alcohol, was on ration until things settled down.

Sofia Windon, the only other council member genuinely motivated to retain her former position, loomed at Alex's shoulder. The others had faded away when Russell disbanded the group. Good riddance, as far as he was concerned.

The woman, Sofia, hovered like a gnat, annoying and difficult to dismiss.

"Okay," Russell said. "Station maps. And?"

He couldn't ignore the stark difference between the maps from before and after the farms were stolen. The platforms made up the bulk of the Platz-built stations, and their absence after the traitors fled stood out like missing limbs.

A twang of pride coursed through Russell when he compared that to the future map. The vacant gaps between the lonely habitat stations were partly filled in again.

"The farms were originally clustered in groups of four," Sofia said, "at specific altitudes. The higher up, the more time the stations are in sunlight. As you can see, a few members of each cluster are being returned."

"Sunlight's good, right?" Russell looked at each of them. "Why not move them all to the top?"

Sofia shook her head. "The scientists had all this tuned to perfection. Some crops do better with more sunlight, yes, while some provide better yields on a more normal diet."

"We're talking percentage points, though," Alex Warthen said. "What I'd like to do is re-cluster them all down here, closer to Earth."

Russell slurped his drink again. "Why?"

"Logistics. As long as we're in a state of emergency like this, the closer the farms are the easier it will be to move—"

Russell held up a hand. "Look, do whatever the fuck you want, eh? What the hell do I know about crop yields? I got you the farms, my work is done. Debating details like this is exactly why I told the council to piss off in the first place."

"You said you wanted all major decisions submitted for your approval. We're just trying to explain—"

"Approved then. Jesus fucking Christ. Do the needful, as the blokes in Rancid Creek say."

A technician rapped his hand on the open door to the tavern. "Mr. Blackfield?"

"What now?" Russell barked.

"Tania Sharma is on the comm," he said. "Asking for you."

Russell took in the words like a sweet song. He met Alex's gaze. "Hear that? Asking for me. I deal with the runaways, you deal with the day-to-day."

"Provided we get your approval on everything first," Alex said.

"Not everything. The big stuff."

"Can you define 'big' for us, please?" Sofia asked.

Russell considered telling her to look at her own ass in the mirror, but thought better of it. "Use your best judgment," he said. "No, don't do that. Until we've learned to work together, assume everything is big. I'll tell you what is and isn't."

Alex and Sofia exchanged a glance, then Alex sighed. "So not everything, just the big stuff, which is everything."

"Now we're getting somewhere. What else do you have for me today? Just the big stuff, please." Russell winked at him, enjoying the confusion on his face.

"Nothing, really. Shore-leave requests, we can prioritize those."

"All declined," Russell said evenly. "That is big stuff. We've got a mountain of work to do, shore leave can wait. If anyone bitches about that, have one of my boys kneecap 'em, all right? All right. Let me know when the farms have been reattached."

The tech wanted Russell to take Tania's call in a cramped little communications room. "Can you set it up anywhere?"

When the man shrugged, Russell beckoned him to follow and strolled to Section H, the portion of the station Neil Platz used to use as a satellite office. He thought it might be nice to let Tania see him sitting at Neil's old desk, even if it wasn't his true office on Platz Station. Mentally he set that place as his next destination.

As he strolled through the vacant area, a large meeting room caught his attention instead. Red carpets surrounded a sunken area in the center lined with black leather couches and chairs. A wet bar lay open on the wall to his right, empty. Looted by the cleaning staff, probably.

None of this held Russell's attention. He walked instead to the far wall, which didn't exist. An illusion of course, but a damned good one. The transparent panel that spanned the entire back of the room must have cost a fortune. Russell's stomach fluttered at the sight of Earth below them. Darwin, and the rest of Australia, lay partly in shadow, the time being just after dusk.

"Put the comm on the table," he said without looking back.

While the technician worked, Russell took in the entire horizon of the planet. Tania was out there, somewhere, along with Zane Platz and who knew who else.

"All set," the tech said. "Let me know when you're done."

"Oh, of course. I'll make it my number-one fucking priority," Russell said. "How about you just come back in an hour."

"Yes, sir," the man said. He slipped out of the room with his shoulders hunched.

Alone, Russell let out a long breath. The blue crescent of the planet below begged to calm him, and he decided to let it. Show Tania a face of control, even one of relaxed ambivalence.

He put on his best smirk, testing it in the faint reflection on the glass. Satisfied, he turned and went to one of the leather chairs. He carefully arranged the comm's camera to catch him with the spinning blue globe behind him. Then he leaned back, folded one leg across the other, and took the call.

"Good evening, Miss Sharma."

She looked haggard. Dark bags under each eye ruined her otherwise flawless face. Her black hair had been pulled back in haste, judging by the uneven strands that framed her cheeks. "Blackfield," she said with a slight nod.

"I'm told our exchange is going smoothly; is this a social call then?"

The tics in her facial expressions proved a fascinating puzzle to decipher. Russell noted her lips purse slightly, her eyes narrow. He wondered if a recording of the call could be reviewed later, for a deeper study.

"We have an additional request," she stated. She waited for him to say something, to ask the obvious question. When he didn't she visibly gathered herself and went on. "An aircraft, one capable of atmosphere reentry."

"Those don't grow on trees."

"I'm willing to trade additional food—"

"How about another farm," he said.

She froze, blinked. Then the woman mumbled something and put the feed on hold. *Always putting me on hold when a decision needs to be made,* Russell thought. She must have her own halo of gnats buzzing about, a veritable flock of Sofia Windons, all anxious to be part of the leadership process. Hell, Tania was probably a gnat herself. He could see them now, huddled around the bright screen of a slate and making lists of pros and cons.

"Make sure all voices are heard, Tania," he said to the blinking screen, smiling. "No rush."

Russell sat back and clasped his hands behind his head. At this rate he'd have all the farms back without breaking a sweat, and the traitors would be at his mercy. He'd have food enough for Darwin, too, which would kill the steam driving Grillo's ambitious plan. Still, he could let the slumlord ramble on for a while. Even if 50 percent successful, he'd deliver a much more cooperative city before Russell relieved him of duty.

Tania's face reappeared on the screen. "We can't afford to part with another farm," she said. "Perhaps our shipments could increase—"

"No farm, no plane," Russell said, and ended the call. She'd call back. He tapped the station directory on the screen and selected the Nightcliff interconnect, then Grillo's, or rather his own, office.

Kip Osmak's face appeared. "Mr. Blackfield, hello," he said.

"Where's Grillo?"

"Uh," Kip muttered, his eyes dancing left and right.

"Doesn't matter," Russell said. "Tell him I need an aircraft, one that can drop from orbit. No pilot, no crew, and nothing military. Get it up here on the next climber."

The sickly man only just managed to nod before Russell killed the link. Then he dialed Alex Warthen. It took a moment for the security chief to answer.

"Yes?"

Russell leaned in to the camera. "Do you have another tracking device? Like the one you stuck on that briefcase, months ago?"

"I'm sure one of the technicians can cobble one together. Why?"

"With video?"

"That's harder to do. What's on your mind?"

Russell recapped Tania's request, and his idea. Place a remote camera in the aircraft's cockpit, and feed it back to Gateway. They could learn all manner of interesting things, he pointed out.

"It'll be complicated," Alex said. "The range on such things isn't great, so we'll have to patch it into the comm system. If we're not careful, they'll detect it."

"So be careful. It's worth the risk to get a fix on their location, perhaps even some pictures. Lay of the land." An icon appeared on the comm's screen. Tania, calling back, he guessed. "Put it together, and quickly."

He disconnected before Alex could respond, and tried hard to contain his glee when Tania's face reappeared.

14

BELÉM, BRAZIL

3.MAY.2283

He had the dream again.

The same one he'd had before the Japan mission, of falling from a great height toward a vast engine. A machine that spread from horizon to horizon, pistons firing, massive metal gears turning, all laced with a maze of circuits upon which electrons raced.

As in the previous vision, he sped toward the apparatus and braced himself for the impact with it. Last time he'd punched through the surface like it was tissue and continued to fall, but he flinched and braced himself nonetheless.

This time, though, an iris opened before him, revealing a warm, pulsating glow. He fell into it and hovered. The energy seemed to snake toward him, tendrils as thin and fine as the Elevator cord itself, lacing out from the greater field and worming their way into his ears, eyes, and nostrils.

A flood of memories came to mind all at once. Clear and yet eluding any attempt to focus on their specifics.

And then the light vanished. The memories disappeared with it, and he fell once again, punching through the machine in an explosion of parts.

He flipped over in the air to look up at the damage, and found that the machine was just the other side of the sky. *Now* he fell toward the ground, the endless jungle with its dark heart.

Skyler felt the evil lurking beneath the canopy again and resolved to face it this time. His pace slowed toward the end, and the leaves at the greatest height began to tickle his arms. He ignored them, brushed them aside. Someone stood in a clearing directly below. A person wearing a suit of black. Black like the Builders' material. Red light sizzled along the fine lines in the surface, gradually coalescing into what might be called eyes.

The branches grew thicker as he fell toward the being. They slapped at Skyler's face, and he frantically tried to shove them away to see below.

In the clearing, the being looked up, arms outstretched, and waited to catch him.

Skyler woke with a start and sat bolt upright.

Next to him, Ana knelt, her hand still held out from gently slapping his cheek.

"You were dreaming," she said.

Skyler nodded and rubbed his eyes. They'd camped within the mansion he'd found, the one he'd scavenged the motorcycle from. A third-floor master bedroom with a grand balcony that overlooked the southern district of the city. From that viewpoint they had line of sight on the encampment at the base of the Elevator, and Skyler knew the home was relatively safe, given that it had not been looted or soiled by subhumans.

"Is it my watch already?" he asked.

Ana shook her head. "There is talking on the radio. Come and listen."

She tiptoed back across the opulent room and out the balcony door without another word. Skyler could see Davi already standing out there, leaning against the railing, a pair of binoculars trained in the direction of the colony.

Crawling from his sleeping bag, Skyler stretched and threw his jacket over his shoulders. He glanced at his watch, 3 A.M., and took a healthy gulp from his canteen before joining the twins outside.

Ana sat cross-legged on the Spanish-tile surface of the wide balcony, holding the radio in both hands like some kind of holy relic. She dialed the volume up slightly when Skyler took a seat next to her.

The first voice he heard was Karl, and a flood of relief coursed through him.

". . . water supply. And these we placed to gain access to the hospital."

Skyler closed his eyes and pictured the control room, set up inside a modified cargo container. He imagined Karl standing before the map of the Belém on the wall, tracing a finger along the aura roads.

"And you cannot travel beyond these . . . auras?" A new voice, thickly accented.

"Gabriel," Ana said, distant and cold.

"Not without a protective suit."

Silence followed. Skyler heard a tinkling sound, like a spoon rattling against a teacup.

"So, the suit contains some of the aura? It can be bottled like wine?"

"No," Karl said. "As I said before—"

"Never mind what you told me before," Gabriel said, his tone light, conversational. "I want to hear it again."

"The aura puts the disease into a kind of stasis. If you bottle air within an aura, and pump it into a special suit, the disease will stay asleep. It's only when it comes in direct contact with the live disease that it will wake up again."

"Fascinating," the other man said. Another long silence.

"Please," Karl finally said. "*Please,* let us ship air and water up to orbit."

Gabriel chuckled. "We'll discuss that tomorrow. I'm tired."

"You've said tomorrow four times—"

The *smack* made Skyler jump. Ana did, too, and Davi turned from his vigil.

Another *smack*. Then the distinct sound of a person toppling to the floor.

"And I'll say tomorrow as long as I wish, *pendejo*. Take him back to his tent."

Sounds of rustling, grunts of men hefting a body. Skyler gritted his teeth when he heard the scraping of feet across the floor of the room. Then a door slammed shut.

Again came the sound of a spoon stirring tea. Then a new voice, a woman's, in Portuguese. Skyler looked to Ana and Davi, who both shrugged. They didn't understand the words, either.

Gabriel replied in turn, and the door opened and closed once again.

No one spoke for a minute. Then two. Skyler motioned for Ana to turn the volume up again, and soon they could hear the sound of someone sipping a hot beverage. Then chewing.

When the door opened again the new arrival spoke in Spanish. Gabriel replied and a quick exchange occurred.

"Gabriel asked for a status," Ana said, "and the other man, Carlos I think, said the scout team still hadn't reported in."

"Those must be the men we fought," Skyler mused.

Ana held up a hand to quiet him as more conversation spilled out of the radio's tiny speaker. "Carlos wants to lead a search party at dawn, but they're arguing about how they'll watch all the prisoners."

She listened to their words, her eyes dancing back and forth. Then she glanced at Davi and her eyebrows arched.

"What is it?" Skyler asked.

"Carlos said if they don't have enough people to watch all the newcomers, they could start the trials early, which would reduce the population."

"Trials?"

Ana shook her head. Then, "Hold on."

A long back-and-forth between the Gabriel and Carlos followed. There was laughter, as well as periods of serious tones.

Their conversation continued but grew quieter; then Skyler heard the door close and they could no longer be heard. "What were they saying?"

"Carlos noted excitement about the start of the trials. But Gabriel urged patience. He said when the trials start the *incerto* will panic, and they'll need everything ready. Then he said he wants someone to go out to the lodge first thing in the morning and bring the others back."

"What trials?"

Ana shrugged, her look apologetic. Whatever Gabriel was

planning, he expected it to cause panic among the colonists, and that meant nothing good.

"Tell him," Davi said to Ana.

Skyler glanced at him, then at the girl. Her eyes were downcast.

"Gabriel said it's critical that the 'rogue' be captured or killed before then. That he'd prefer you be taken alive so that he could try to talk to you, but because you had killed some of his own family—he refers to us as his family—he realized you may have been among the *incerto* too long, and will never claim your place within the new society."

"*Incerto*?"

"It's like . . . uncertain. Or, untested."

Skyler stood and went to the railing. He stared at the horizon, in the direction of the Elevator, trying to see any sign of the camp in the darkness. Davi offered him the binoculars but Skyler waved them off.

A second later he changed his mind, took the glasses, and studied the buildings closest to the encampment.

"What are you looking for?" Ana asked.

"High ground," Skyler said.

"Why?"

"We need to get moving," Skyler said, otherwise ignoring her. "We don't have much time."

"An attack now is suicide," Davi said. "The deal was that we would free our friends, then—"

"I know," Skyler said. "The lodge he mentioned, is that where your people are being held?"

"My heart says yes," Davi answered. "We can't know for sure until we look."

Skyler handed the binoculars back to him. "That's why we need to get moving. He said they were going to 'bring everyone back,' so we need to act before that. When the sun comes up they're going to send someone to this lodge, and we need to track them. Follow them there, and rescue your friends. We can't do that unless we see which road they take out of the camp."

"High ground," Davi repeated, understanding.

"Pack the gear," Skyler said to them. The twins set to work immediately.

Later, as he rolled his sleeping bag and tied it, he tried to pinpoint when he'd become the leader of this little group. Only the night before Ana barely trusted him to go to the bathroom unsupervised. Considering his track record as captain of a crew, Skyler resolved to look for a way out of the position as soon as their goals were accomplished. They were kids, after all, and people under him didn't have the greatest survival rate.

By the time the three of them began their trek toward the camp, the sky in the east had become a purple stain, growing brighter with every minute. Skyler set a hard pace and showed them how to move between cover positions so that one of the three was always still and vigilant.

Moving through the dark streets, he weighed the situation. No air or water had been delivered up the cord in a week, and supplies had already been strained before that. From what they'd overheard on the radio, he guessed Tania was still in the dark as to the situation in Camp Exodus. Who knew what was going through her mind right now?

Whatever happened, Skyler realized, when he finally attempted to retake the camp, if all else failed he must clear the base of the cord so that climbers could come down again. At least then Tania and the others who huddled in orbit would have an option. A choice, if they wanted it, that wasn't to turn tail and head back to Darwin.

If he only accomplished one thing, Skyler would give them that.

15

ABOVE THE ATLANTIC OCEAN

5.MAY.2283

In the dead of night an aircraft dipped into the atmosphere high above the Atlantic Ocean. Heat generated by friction with the air made the underbelly glow bright orange, and the fighters inside clutched their harnesses with white knuckles against the bone-shaking turbulence.

The aircraft, a long-range paramilitary troop carrier originally built for the Thai army, began to turn in a wide circle once the violence of reentry ended. It set itself on a course for Belém and began to drift lower as the coast of Brazil approached.

A small device, installed in a cavity behind one of the instrument panels in the cockpit's ceiling, transmitted telemetry information sapped from the ship's computer to a relay in orbit. The relay, bolted to the top of a small inspection robot, sent the information to a terminal in Alex Warthen's office on Gateway Station.

No one aboard knew about that, though. They'd searched, twice in fact, but not to the point of dismantling anything. Even Tania had poked around when the vehicle first arrived, looking under seats and inside every storage compartment. The urgency of the situation didn't allow for diligence beyond that.

The crew were all in back, slipping out of their jump-seats and pulling on their gear. Ten men and two women all armed to the teeth after a carte-blanche rummage through "Room 17," the armory Neil Platz had stocked inside his secret station.

Environment suits went on first. Much debate had gone into whether the bulky protective outfits were needed. The aircraft, programmed to land between the colony and the reservoir to the east, would set down in a clearing that fell within the "aura road" set up to link the two locations.

The soldiers balked at the idea of trying to fight with the suits on. But as they planned their mission, it became clear the precaution would be wise. They had no guarantee the aura road had even remained in place. Whatever had befallen the colony, it was possible the aura towers had been moved, scattered, or pulled back to camp. No one knew.

"Five minutes," someone said.

"Five minutes," a voice in the background said.

Russell leaned in over Alex's shoulder and studied the image. The camera had a perfect view right down the middle of the cockpit. The aircraft, another loaner from Grillo's dwindling fleet, had a side-by-side pilot and navigator seat layout. Flat monitors made up the bulk of the dash, showing virtual instrumentation along with maps and other indicators.

Both seats were empty. The colonists apparently didn't have anyone who could pilot the ship—an interesting detail—but they'd been able to program the autopilot system.

The view out the vehicle's window was too small and grainy to discern anything yet, but the location of the traitors was now known: Brazil.

Russell hadn't stopped smiling since that bit of information came in. Already he'd thought up and discarded dozens of attack plans, always thinking up something more spectacular than the last.

He watched as the craft slipped over the coastline and followed the edge of a river. It skimmed low over the ground. Russell saw treetops zoom by above the height of the plane.

"Interesting," Alex said.

"What?"

"Flying so low; it's a risk. Like they're worried someone might see them if they came in at a normal angle."

The aircraft banked again and followed a smaller river. This time there were hints of a cityscape to the west. Russell glanced at another window on Alex's terminal, which showed the physical location of the tracking device on a map. The plane followed a river that marked the northern edge of a city called Belém, heading east and then southeast.

"One minute," the voice in the background said.

At a bridge spanning the river, the aircraft slowed to a crawl and then turned to follow the road that extended out from the bridge back toward the city. The road, Russell saw on the map, snaked around to eventually meet the city's southern edge, where dockyards lined a wide river.

Then the plane slowed completely and hovered. The sound of the thrusters spinning down could be heard. Their view out the cockpit showed the black shapes of the metropolis's skyline against a clear, starry sky.

"They're going in dark," Alex said. "Taking pains to land in secret."

The plane turned in place to orient itself toward the south. Treetops replaced Belém's skyline. The rainforest spanned the horizon.

A second later the aircraft's engines stopped and the landing lights came on.

The aircraft had landed in a clearing alongside a dirt road. The road went up a small rise maybe thirty meters away and then dipped back down and out of sight. Dense rainforest lined both edges, the trees still rippling from the exhaust wash generated by the landing.

Russell ignored all of this. His eyes were locked on a black tower that sat beside the road, not far from the craft. The object looked to be about as tall as a two-story home, and its square base was perhaps two or three meters wide.

It looked wholly out of place in the surroundings. And,

despite being on the sloped road and uneven ground, it sat perfectly upright.

After a second Russell realized that another tower loomed in the distance, just over the rise. A black, angular monument against the night sky, completely out of place among the dense trees.

"The fuck are those?" he whispered.

Alex shook his head and continued to study the screen. He zoomed in slightly to remove most of the cockpit from their view.

Within seconds a squad of environment-suited soldiers flowed past the nose of the aircraft, rallying at the base of the nearby tower. They crouched there and waited until the entire group had exited the plane.

"Hmm . . . odd," Alex said.

"What?"

"They're wearing environment suits, but according to the map they're only about one klick away from the Elevator."

"Maybe it doesn't have an aura like ours."

The idea explained a lot about Tania's recent requests. Air and water, in exchange for so many of the Space-Ag platforms, made total sense if they had no way to scrub Belém's air of the disease. The supplies would only buy them time, though. Maybe they had some plan to activate the aura? He racked his brain, trying to figure out how any of that would require a commando squad to fly in the dark. Whatever it was, this mission was worth nine farm platforms, almost all of Tania Sharma's remaining leverage.

Russell watched with bemused interest as the combatants readied their gear. Gun-mounted flashlights were activated, the beams sweeping across the ground. Some part of him yearned to be there with them, gearing up for a fight. That corner of his mind didn't care whose side they were on, or what their purpose was. Combat just got his juices flowing, in a way no woman could. None he'd yet to meet, at least.

The camera's view became obscured as someone entered the cockpit. Alex quickly zoomed out to the full view again, and they watched as the person began to tap commands into a touchscreen near the pilot's seat.

"Power-down sequence," Alex noted. "The camera is tapped into the flight computer's power line. We'll lose our feed in a minute."

The person in the cockpit tensed suddenly and dropped to a crouch. The muffled sounds of machine-gun fire thumped through the speaker.

Outside, the gathered soldiers were shooting in all directions. Rapid muzzle-flashes lit up the surrounding trees like lightning.

A human dressed all in black was among the fighters, Russell saw. He quickly realized "human" might not be accurate. The being clawed and punched with terrifying speed. Bodies fell with each blurred swing of the thing's arm.

Some of the fighters broke and ran, one toward the aircraft and another toward the cover of the trees. But a second creature emerged from the foliage, galloping on all fours. It pounced on the back of the nearest fleeing enemy, and the pair collapsed into a rolling ball of flailing limbs.

The creatures moved like subhumans. Russell knew that, and yet their appearance was very different. They were clad from head to toe in some kind of skintight black outfit.

A bloodbath unfolded on the screen. Russell saw one of Tania's fighters stagger away from the carnage, his environment suit torn to shreds, both hands clutching at his neck, where blood flowed freely. One of the creatures spotted the man and raced over to him. It swung, raking a hand across the back of the man's head. The poor bastard collapsed in a sickening heap, dead before he hit the ground.

The man in the cockpit stepped backward, blocking much of the view. A third creature appeared in front of the plane, illuminated fully by the landing lights. The black material it wore seemed to have hardened panels, like armor plating.

As Russell watched, a flash of red light appeared to emanate from the creature's eyes, as if it had trained a laser on the cockpit window.

Then it jumped.

In a split second the being reappeared right outside the window, clinging to the fuselage. It tilted its head at the cowering man in the cockpit. Then it raised one hand and placed it on the glass. Light erupted from the creature's palm in a blinding flash. The tempered glass shattered into a thousand tiny pieces, but it held its shape.

A black-clad fist punched a hole straight through the thick barrier. The hand then swiped violently, knocking the shards away, and the creature was inside. It dove on the man and the two fell out of the camera's view.

The sound of the man in the cockpit being torn to pieces was so revolting that Russell reached out and turned the volume down. Alex sat perfectly still, making no effort to stop him.

Outside the aircraft, the battle was already over. Broken bodies lay everywhere, and the armored, outfitted subhumans were gone, vanished into the forest as quickly as they had appeared. Not twenty seconds had passed since the first shots were fired.

The instruments and screens in the cockpit started to go blank, and the landing lights turned off, plunging the grisly scene outside into darkness.

A second later the feed ended.

Russell swallowed. He realized he'd put a hand on Alex's shoulder and gripped the man's shirt in a white-knuckled fist. He let go and stepped back. "What the hell did we just see?"

Alex half-glanced over his shoulder. He opened his mouth to say something, and then snapped it shut and looked back at the blank monitor.

"I mean," Russell said, "what the actual fuck? And what were those towers?"

"I'm not sure I want to know," Alex replied, his voice laden with naked dread.

A long silence followed. When Russell finally got his breathing under control, he began to chuckle.

The chuckle turned into a rolling, uncontrollable laugh.

Alex turned to him. "What's so funny?"

"Tania," Russell replied. "She. Is. *Screwed*. Totally, utterly, royally screwed!"

The dire look on Alex's face only made him laugh harder.

16

DARWIN, AUSTRALIA

5.MAY.2283

Samantha took one last swig of her cider and flipped the cup over on the bar.

"Done," she said.

Woon bobbed his head at her, his constant smile almost hidden beneath the long white beard and mustache he wore, both extending down to his waist. He spoke very little English, and Sam knew only a few words of Mandarin. This left their conversations one-sided, with Samantha blathering on about whatever she felt like talking about, and Woon just nodding. His smile seemed painted on, and even if she launched into a lengthy, solemn diatribe about the fates the rest of her crew had suffered, his grin never faltered.

She pointed at the glass with two fingers, her thumb up to create a mock handgun. "My tab," she stated, and winked at him.

Woon, of course, nodded. His eyes, so narrow they looked closed, still managed to twinkle in the dim room.

Samantha climbed off her stool, yawned, and stretched. She dropped to the floor and rattled off ten push-ups in rapid succession, then flipped over onto her back and did the same number of sit-ups.

She bounced to her feet, waved to Woon, and headed for the wide entrance to the hangar-turned-kitchen. Both of the massive doors were open, rolled to either side of the front of the building. This indicated Woon was open for business, but the stools and tables were mostly empty.

A glance at the old digital clock on the wall told her the time in large, amber numbers: 3:14 A.M.

Two scavengers sat at a table off to the side. One had his head down on the table, one arm curled around to block his face. The other flipped through a worn paperback book, its cover weathered to the point of being unintelligible. Sam recognized the second man as Lee, the pilot of a short-range boat. They'd flirted here, once upon a time. She turned toward their table and took an empty seat. Lee's eyes flicked up to her, then back to his book.

Not even a hello, she thought.

"Lee," she said.

"G'day," he muttered, and flipped a page. A greeting used for random strangers passed on the street.

Sam jerked her head toward Lee's sleeping friend. "Looks like you need a new drinking partner. I could grab us a bottle."

He glanced sidelong at her then, and some silent deliberation passed through his mind. "Thanks, but I'm okay."

The lingering effects of Woon's cider jumbled her thoughts. Six months ago he would have invited her to stay and drink, and within an hour they'd probably be in the cargo bay of his plane, making the beast with two backs.

But not now. No hint at all of that camaraderie.

"C'mon," she said, leaning forward in hopes of earning more than a glance. "Shots, you and me. We can go to my roof. Dawn is still—"

"I fly at dawn," Lee said. He dog-eared a page in his book and set it down carefully on the table. "Your orders, remember?"

She did, vaguely. Grillo wanted more output from the crews, and two missions a day was the only solution Sam could find. She doled out Grillo's requests not based on profit or eagerness, but on things like range, readiness, cargo room, and capacitor charge time.

None of the crews liked it, but they didn't have much choice. No one had seen hide nor hair of Prumble in months, and anyway the days of picking and choosing missions were long gone. Grillo says jump, the crews jump.

"Maybe we should inspect your bird then," she said with what she hoped was a coy smile. "A thorough examination, just you and me—"

"Sam," Lee said with an annoyed sigh, "it wouldn't be good for others to see us cavorting. Sorry, just the way it is."

"Cavorting? Jesus. I'm not proposing fucking marriage, I just want a quick tumble. What's the big deal?"

"Not a good idea, Sam. Sorry." He picked up his book again and pointedly began to read.

She stood so fast her chair tumbled over backward. Lee winced but kept reading, and with that Sam turned and strode away, the warmth of alcohol in her head transforming instantly to a cold desire for more. She told herself they would come around. Grillo's plan required time before the rewards would be clear. Until then, she doubted any of the crews would smile and wave at her when she passed, much less jump between the sheets.

"Maybe I'll go visit Vaughn," she muttered to herself as she stalked down the center of the runway. She'd used him to escape, only to end up not escaping at all, not really. Grillo had agreed not to punish the guard for allowing her to get away, but she'd not seen Vaughn since then. Perhaps, she thought, he'd be up for some makeup sex.

Samantha stopped walking and hung her head. "Why," she said to herself, "am I so damn horny all the time now?"

The constant fantasies that ripped through her mind like runaway trains had become an annoyance. She walked on, pondering the reasons behind her distracting thirst all the way to the hangar, the same hangar she'd called home when Skyler ran the show.

Maybe, she thought, *it's because I've not seen any combat in two months.* Perhaps some part of her had grown addicted to the tension and violence beyond the aura and sought to fill the void in other ways. Or maybe it was because she was no longer living with four men. Skyler, Jake, Angus, and Takai were all gone now. The bond they'd shared had been something different. Primal, sure, but born of a shared reliance on one another to survive. None of them had ever shown her attention of a physical kind, and she'd never sought it from them.

She laughed aloud at another thought. *Maybe I'm just suffering from twitching ovaries.* She was twenty-three, too young for such concerns in a pre-disease world. And now, all bets were off. The idea of birthing a child into the hell that humanity now lived in seemed foolish at best.

Besides, Samantha had no desire for motherhood. Three times in the past five years she'd been asked, sometimes subtly and sometimes directly, if she thought an immune woman would give birth to children with the same attribute. She doubted it, but the question was pointless. She had no intention of being the guinea pig in that experiment. Though she knew of no other immune women, she did not want to be a lab rat.

The hangar depressed the hell out of her. With no aircraft dominating the vast floor, it felt like an empty cavern. Add to that the lack of her crew mates, and it served only to remind her of everything that had been lost.

As she did most nights, Samantha pulled the blanket and pillow from her bunk, tucked them under one arm, and made her way to the roof. She left her tent behind, this time, the sky being devoid of rainclouds now that wet season had made its usual swift departure.

The stars were bright and clear tonight, and a half-moon provided plenty of light by which to move. She laid out her blanket and pillow, stripped to her underwear, and fell asleep under the stars only after a quick and lackluster session of pleasuring herself. Up until a few weeks ago she'd engaged in that activity only a few times, those needs fulfilled by the regular brush with danger, the proximity to and the dealing of death. Lately, though, it seemed she could not find rest unless she coaxed her body into some release, however limited it might be.

* * *

She awoke shortly after dawn to the sound of her name being shouted.

When she opened her eyes, the morning sun lanced into her eyes like lightning bolts. Samantha winced, and rolled onto her side, pulling the blanket over her. The motion made her head hurt, despite a tame night at Woon's. "Fuck off!" she shouted back.

"Come down here. I have something to discuss!"

Grillo's voice. *Bloody hell.*

Frowning, Sam threw the blanket off and pulled her clothes back on. A stained white tank top, black cargo pants, and steel-toed boots with bright yellow stitching. She rubbed the back of her neck as she stalked across the roof, weaving her way between planters flush with ripe fruits and vegetables. Her stomach grumbled despite the hangover, and so she plucked a ripe plantain from a heavy branch, peeled it, and devoured the bland fruit in three bites. At the cistern she filled a bucket with cool rainwater and dunked her head in it, twisting left and right violently until she couldn't hold her breath anymore. Water flew in an arch when she yanked her head from the bucket, and she kept her eyes closed as the runoff flowed down the sides of her face, letting some of it flow into her mouth. This she swished from cheek to cheek while she wrung her blond hair out and knotted it into a quick braid.

"Good enough," she growled, and trudged down to the hangar's catwalk. From her room she grabbed her favorite black vest. It was laden with pockets and made of a stiff woven nylon. A patch on the left breast bore the Australian "Special Operations Command" logo. There'd been another patch below it when she found the garment, bearing some soldier's last name, but she'd torn that off.

Zipped up, the vest constricted around her torso and made her feel even taller than she already was. Something about the stiff, tight material served to give her confidence, and a certain swagger that made people listen.

At the front of the hangar she punched the red button that hung from a chain by the doors, causing the big barriers to roll back with a loud gnashing of gears and pulleys.

Grillo stood just outside, in front of a black armored truck. He wore a business suit, as usual, and gripped a ledger of some sort in his left hand. "Good morning," he said.

Two similar trucks were parked behind his. She noted that each had both driver and passenger seats occupied.

"What's with the caravan?"

"Safety in numbers," he replied.

Samantha grimaced. Grillo's relentless drive to subjugate the roofers around Nightcliff, and their gardens, was often discussed by the scavenger crews. A few seemed to fall every day. The leaders of those enclaves were once a steady source of business.

The slumlord gestured, his eyes darting to the interior of the hangar.

"Come in," Sam said. "Take a load off."

He nodded and stepped inside. She led him to the circle of couches and chairs that the crew used to sit in when planning missions. Grillo deliberated for a few seconds before selecting a wooden chair. Sam flopped onto the black leather couch opposite him and tucked her feet up beneath her legs. "You could have just sent a list."

"It's not that kind of mission," he said flatly.

Samantha waited.

"Do you recall," he said, "the explosion just south of the aura, in Old Downtown, a few months ago?"

"Sure. I heard the, um, 'traitors' tried to blow up Nightcliff. Good thing they missed, too, since I was locked up in there. Look, we've talked about this. I'll keep the crews in line and all that shit, but I draw the line at doing anything that might hurt my friends."

Grillo held a hand out, waving her off. "Our arrangement is well understood. Hear me out."

"Okay . . ."

The slight man leaned forward in his chair. "The site of the explosion is seeing some"—he searched for words—*"activity."*

"Huh? Subhumans?" She thought that unlikely. Old Downtown sat beyond the aura, yes, but it was only connected to land inside the aura, effectively making it an island. The small subhuman presence that existed there in the first weeks and months of the disease had long died out, leaving the place a ghost town.

He shook his head. "A cloud blankets the whole area. Darwin gets fog on occasion, but this is localized to just that area, and it's been there for two days now."

Samantha studied him. "So their bomb hit some subterranean infrastructure. Ruptured a pipe or a mini-thor's cooling system."

"Maybe so," he said.

"So what's the problem? It's walking distance from the aura. Send a team in environment suits to scout it out."

"We did," he said. "Yesterday."

His tone implied the result.

Grillo went on. "Five suited men hiked down there, but the moisture obscured their helmets. Zero visibility. They said they were going to turn back, but got lost. And then we lost all contact."

"Subs," Samantha said, "probably. They can track by sounds, so the fog wouldn't slow them down much."

Grillo spread his hands. "That's what we'd like you to find out. You don't need a suit, and you're the only—"

"The only immune. Hooray for me," she muttered.

"I'd just like you to poke around. Find out what happened, and that's it. I'll send a few good soldiers with you, yours to command. Men who fought in the Purge and know how to handle an environment suit."

She'd prefer to go alone, but Grillo had a certain tone he used when something was not debatable, and he'd invoked that now. Maybe he feared she would run off.

"Clear the place out," he added, "if you can, and then we'll get some engineers in there to make sure whatever is generating that steam is not a danger to the city."

She folded her arms and leaned back into the plush couch. "Our agreement was that I would get the crews flying again, which I've done. You never said anything about playing sub bait, or babysitting your goon squad."

His face remained a mask, but she caught his grip tightening on the leather-bound book in his left hand. "Do this," he said, "and I'll bring you to my compound afterward to visit your friend."

"And if I refuse?"

Grillo shook his head. "This is not an ultimatum, Samantha. I'm asking for your help because you're the best person for the task. Whatever is going on out there, it may pose a threat to us all."

Samantha shrugged. "Okay then. Sounds easy enough. When will your people be ready?"

"They're waiting outside."

The drive, despite being only eight klicks or so by road, took more than an hour.

Samantha sat in the back of the armored vehicle, rocking back and forth as it trundled over Darwin's battered streets.

The two thugs Grillo brought along remained silent after the briefest of introductions, as if they'd been ordered not to chat with her. The taller one, David, had a ragged beard worn in contradiction to his neatly cropped black hair. His teeth were yellow and crooked, and there were wrinkles at the corners of his hard eyes.

The other was a Middle Easterner of average build and height. He'd said his name, Faisal, with a strong accent, and had not even made eye contact with her. *Perhaps,* she thought, *he still believes women should cover themselves.*

Darwin's filthy streets blurred by. The morning sun would soon become intolerable for most, giving urgency to the foot traffic and makeshift street markets. Children chased after the caravan, laughing and waving until they could no longer keep up. Then they would bend down and pick up the nearest rock, hurling it at the trucks with total abandon, as punishment for not stopping.

Eventually the vehicles turned down Cavenagh Street and surged in speed. This close to Aura's Edge, the people out and about were the lowest of the low. The single-story buildings here were all crumbling, looted shells. Hardly any had gardens on the roof, Samantha noted. Too easy to raid, too hard to defend.

Groups of citizens huddled in whatever shade they could find, all dressed in dirty rags, their faces skeletal and arms stick-thin. They watched the trucks roll by with hollow stares, having lost hope years ago of anyone coming out here to help them. Samantha glanced at Grillo. He sat in the front passenger seat, his back to her, and she expected him to be ignoring the heartbreaking view. But he wasn't. Grillo was turned toward the window, his face scanning back and forth as he studied the sights. His lips were pressed into a thin line, and though she couldn't see his eyes behind a pair of small, round sunglasses, she suspected there was no disgust to be found there.

After a few blocks the trucks reached the barricade and fanned out to park side by side. Samantha squinted when Faisal opened the back door of their APC and hopped out. Sunlight flooded the compartment, reflected off a dusty concrete sidewalk they'd parked on.

"After you," David said, the only words he'd spoken the entire drive other than his name.

Outside, Samantha waited while the two mercenaries pulled on bright yellow environment suits that were produced from the back of one of the other trucks. The final truck held a selection of weapons and a comm terminal. A black woman in civilian garb sat at the screen, pulling a headset on. She smiled halfheartedly when their eyes met, then focused on the equipment in front of her.

Sam glanced over the weaponry arrayed along the floor of the truck, but there was nothing tempting. She made sure her own machine gun was loaded and ready. She'd yet to find a replacement for her beloved Israeli shotgun, lost when the *Melville* crashed. Someday, soon perhaps, she resolved to take a crew out into the Clear just to find another. For now, one of Skyler's extra rifles would have to do. She'd found it in a private, hidden stash shortly after returning to the hangar. The place had been ransacked by Nightcliff's finest, but in their haste they'd missed a few spots.

Skyler, despite his many faults, knew how to keep a weapon clean, and so she had no qualms about carrying one of his guns on a mission. In some weird way it felt like a small tribute to his memory.

"Up here, Samantha," Grillo said. He'd scaled the barricade and now stood atop it. The mound of trash and debris roughly marked Aura's Edge along the entire circle, except where it went out into the ocean. Beyond, a no-man's-land extended for a hundred meters. Here the aura's protection rippled, shifted, and weakened. Only fools ventured beyond the barricade without some form of protection against SUBS.

Sam bounded up the five-meter-high "wall," hopping from one broken chunk of concrete to another, avoiding a rusty bit of chain-link fence that protruded from one spot.

Up top, Grillo waited with a pair of binoculars already extended to her. She took them, but didn't raise them to her eyes just yet.

The street beyond the barricade was markedly different from the portion inside. Because so few dared to venture there, very little had been looted or picked over. Cars dotted the road. They weren't packed in like sardines here, because Darwin's Old Downtown was effectively an island, cut off by the aura. Farther west, Larrakeyah Army Base found itself in a similar state of isolation, but it had been one of the scavengers' first hunting grounds for useful items.

Sam's gaze settled on the area just beyond no-man's-land. A group of tall buildings marked the local government offices, half a kilometer away. She could only see the very top floors. Everything else lay blanketed under a thick cloud that hugged the ground despite an ocean breeze. The gray-white haze swirled and billowed gently.

Grillo tapped her shoulder and handed her a headset. She slipped it over her head and adjusted the boom mic to rest near her cheek.

"Sound check," a woman's voice said in her ear.

Sam glanced back at the truck below her, and said, "Testing one two."

"You're clear," the woman replied.

The two mercenaries, David and Faisal, were suited now and climbing the barricade. They both carried matching assault rifles, standard army issue stuff. David, she saw, had a couple of grenades on his utility belt. Oddly, both men had towels wrapped around their left forearm, as if they expected to get bitten by a police dog.

Next to Sam, Grillo cleared his throat. "I'm most interested in what is causing that cloud. If you can find yesterday's party, please ascertain their fate, and salvage what you can."

"And the headset is so I can call in reinforcements?"

"Do you want the truth?"

"No," she said. "Glad-hand me."

Grillo's eyebrow twitched slightly but he did not smile. Sarcasm seemed to be the only thing that rattled his calm veneer. "The headset is so you can report back what you are seeing," he said. "Up until the end, if need be."

No offense, mate, but I'm not risking my life just to give you a little intel. She kept this to herself and nodded. "Let's go, boys."

She hopped down the other side of the barricade and stepped onto the dirty road beyond. When her two companions didn't immediately join her, Sam glanced back to egg them on, expecting to see them eyeing the Clear with worry.

Instead, she saw them standing in a rough circle with Grillo, their hands clasped and heads bowed.

What the fuck is this? Prayer?

The posture only lasted a few seconds, and then in unison they broke their circle and the two men jumped down the mound of debris to join her.

17

DARWIN, AUSTRALIA

5.MAY.2283

Samantha took point, with Faisal and David following a few paces behind, off to her left and right, respectively. The air processors on their backs hummed each time they took a breath.

They walked in this formation through no-man's-land and into the Clear beyond. *Clear,* of course, being a misnomer. Samantha often chuckled when the term was used to describe the world outside Darwin. With no more humans polluting the shit out of everything, the theory went that the world would "clear up," hence the name. Some thought that might be why the Builders confined everyone to a single city. A punishment, or judgment, of sorts. A chance for the planet to recover.

And the world may have indeed cleared up in places, but so many factories, chemical plants, power stations, and other bits of infrastructure were abandoned in haste that many of them ran on their own for *years,* unchecked. Fuel stations caught fire and burned for so long that they would shroud an entire metropolis in dark smoke for months. Samantha had seen all of this in her forays. Yet even she used the name Clear. It's the name that stuck, and if it had a tinge of irony to it, so be it.

Fog started to envelop them. Samantha called a halt by raising her fist and then motioning for them to lower into a ready crouch. She felt a bit more confident when both men complied like such a silent command was old habit.

She instructed them to come to her position. "The thicker this gets, the closer we bunch, understood?" she asked when they were next to her.

Both men nodded. The masks of their environment suits were already dappled with condensation. Faisal raised his left arm, the one with a towel wrapped around it, and wiped away the moisture.

"If you get separated, stop and do a quick little whistle, nothing more. Subs are wired to attack humans, and our speaking voice is something they key on. Despite your helmets, a loud shout of surprise will still carry."

Whether they knew this or not, they both flashed her an a-okay with their hands. She'd made the comment more for Grillo's benefit, and for the woman operating the comm, so that she wouldn't have to provide a running commentary.

"Okay," Samantha said. "Follow me."

Less than ten meters into the cloud, Samantha could hardly see her hand in front of her face. The swirling fog was cool on her skin, and in no time her body glistened from the water as if she'd been caught in a morning drizzle. She glanced back. Faisal and David were nothing more than apparitions in the fog. David drew his towel-wrapped arm across his mask, leaving a swath of clear plastic through which to see.

She faced forward again and crept farther into the thick mist.

The crystalline spike appeared so suddenly that she almost ran into it.

A needle point of pale blue glass, just a few centimeters in front of her face. Samantha halted and raised her hand for the others to stop. "Found something," she said in a low voice.

"Bodies?" Grillo asked in her ear.

She ignored him and moved sideways to look at the strange tendril from the side. It was segmented, each length of it as long as her hand, connected by bulbous sections like bony knuckles. The material was not like anything she'd seen before. Slightly opaque, and coated with a fine dust, or moisture perhaps. She moved closer and saw both theories were wrong—the spike had thousands—no, millions—of tiny thorns jutting out of it, each thin as a hair and no longer than a grain of sand.

"What is it?" David asked.

Sam shook her head. "Beats me," she replied. She stepped around it only to be poked in her stomach by something sharp, felt even through her thick combat vest. She looked down to see another of the long, thin crystal branches protruding through the cloud.

Looking up, and around her, Samantha realized they were standing at the edge of some kind of massive lattice. A complex, chaotic system of branches made up of the queer, pale blue segments. The tips of the branches were sharp as needles.

Samantha slung her weapon and tugged at her pant leg, pulling a section of it tight and away from her thigh. Then she waddled a few steps over to a spike protruding at that height and watched in horror as it poked through the cloth like a knife through warm butter.

"Guys," she said, "back away. Very slowly."

Faisal turned first. "God help us," he muttered, and froze.

Facing him, Samantha saw that the lattice of branches had grown over and around them. Even as she watched, she could see new knuckle-like tips blooming on the thorny ends of branches, and new segments beginning to stretch.

"What's going on?" Grillo asked, urgency in his usually calm voice.

Faisal crouched low and ran, ducking under the jagged tentacles. She saw him drop to a belly crawl before he vanished completely in the soupy gray haze.

"David, go!" Samantha shouted.

But the man hesitated. The spikes were getting lower to the ground with each passing second.

"I'm out!" she heard Faisal yell from somewhere nearby.

The opportunity to flee passed just seconds later. Samantha thought they would be skewered on a thousand of the knifelike points, but the growth seemed to stop when it neared them, leaving them inside a bulbous cavity, surrounded on all sides.

"We're trapped," David said. Now a hint of fear shadowed his gruff voice. If any one of those spikes poked his environment suit, he'd be infected and the headaches would start. After that, if he didn't get back to the aura in time to snuff out the early part of the infection, he'd die. Or worse.

Sam unslung her rifle again, took the clip out, and ensured no round was in the chamber. Then she flipped it around to hold it like a club.

"Samantha, I need an update," Grillo hissed in her ear.

"There's some kind of . . . growth here. I think it's . . . alien."

David nodded at her with grim determination. He'd converted his own rifle into a club as well, and stood ready to start hacking.

"We're completely surrounded by it," Samantha said. "Going to try to smash our way out."

Glancing around, she realized that every direction looked the same. She couldn't remember the path Faisal had taken. "Which way?" she asked David.

He glanced around, then dropped to a knee to study the ground. "I think he went that way," the man said, pointing. There were so many blurred boot marks on the ground, Sam didn't think he could really tell.

"Faisal?!" she called out.

"Here," his voice came back. It seemed to come from everywhere, but she thought it stronger in one direction. Better than nothing, she decided, and turned to face that way.

She swung the butt of her rifle with all her strength.

The gun swept through the crystal branches with a whoosh. The bony arms rattled against the butt of the gun like deadwood. They swayed from the impact and bounced back, vibrating silently along their length. Not a single one broke or even showed signs of damage.

After a few seconds of rattling back and forth, the branches settled back into their original positions and continued to grow. Sam felt like a diver, trapped below some kind of coral reef grown with time-lapse quickness.

Soon she and David were completely enveloped in a pocket within the strange structure, needle-sharp tips pointing at them from every direction except the ground. David crawled to the center of the cavity and sat there, glancing frantically around himself, waiting for the thorn that would puncture his suit and doom him. But the growth stopped, as if it wanted them trapped inside.

"We're stuck in here," Samantha said for Grillo's benefit. "Some kind of plant, I don't know. It's surrounded us and the tips will cut David's suit if he moves."

"Try a grenade," Grillo said.

Samantha filed that advice. She'd not yet reached that level of desperation. Kneeling, she wiped her right hand across her shirt to dry it, then reached out and tapped the side of one branch with her index finger, as gently as she could. The semi-transparent stick, which snaked off into the cloud in a line roughly parallel to the ground, swayed slightly from the pressure. Sam examined her finger and saw a dab of moisture there. Water? Some kind of secretion? She couldn't be sure, but it tingled.

Leaning in close, she noticed fine wisps of mist coming from the microscopic thorns along the length of the branch. "I think this thing is creating the cloud," she said, to no one in particular.

"Grenade?" David asked.

"Hold on," Samantha said. "If it shatters and falls on us, you'll be fucked."

He grunted. "Good point."

Slinging her weapon again, Sam held out her hands to either side of the closest branch, twitched her fingers, then gripped it below a knuckle a half meter down its length.

Pinpricks of pain forced her to yank her hands away. "Son of a damn bitch" she barked, examining her palms. A hundred little dots of blood formed and welled. "Jesus H. fucking Christ that hurts." She unzipped her combat vest and gripped the white tank top beneath to put pressure on the wounds. Her hands began to feel cold and numb, as if she'd rubbed eucalyptus oil into them, and she gripped her shirt tighter, biting her tongue against the pain, until the sensation subsided.

Sam sat down next to David, aware of his measured breaths through the speaker on his suit.

"Sod this," he growled. "Grenade."

"No," Samantha said. She let go of her shirt, leaving two dark red handprints on it, and flexed her fingers over and over until the numb feeling vanished entirely.

Knowing it futile, she searched the pockets of her vest and pants for a pair of gloves, and found none. She rarely carried them unless on a mission somewhere cold.

In another pocket she found a chrome Zippo lighter, dented and scuffed. She'd picked it up in Japan, she thought, but couldn't recall for sure. *Worth a try,* she figured, and moved back to the edge of their pocket within the lattice.

She rolled the knobby igniter, swallowing a bit of pain from the still-raw needle pricks on her thumb. It failed to catch, and she had to thumb it four more times before the sparks finally lit. A meager yellow flame sprouted from the tip of the lighter and held.

Slowly she guided her hand underneath the same branch she'd tried to break. When the flame licked a portion of the crystalline stick, it turned beet red and shrank away. The red discoloration rippled along the length of the branch, fading into the cloud. Soon the thin arm of the alien structure absorbed the redness and returned to its original pale blue.

Sam jabbed the flame under it again, and once again the branch recoiled away, as if growing in reverse. She kept the flame under it, watching in fascination as the length receded and pulses of bright red coloration flowed along its length.

"It doesn't like fire," she said brightly. "We need to make a torch."

It took a few minutes to improvise one. David's assault rifle was modular and easily broken down. He removed the butt of it to serve as the handle of their torch. Sam pulled her vest off and set it on the ground, then hoisted her bloodied shirt over her head. David actually averted his eyes at her partial state of nudity, only refocusing on the torch when she pulled her vest back on. The thick nylon rubbed against her skin like sandpaper.

Then she took apart the Zippo while David kept a close vigil on the hundreds of needle-tipped branches around them. Sam dumped the lighter fluid onto the shirt, but only a few drops came out. "Shit," she muttered. "Grillo, anything flammable in your vehicles? Liquor, a butane stove, anything?"

"We're checking," he said.

Sam quickly reassembled the lighter, before all the fumes vanished. She rolled the wheel and this time it produced a flame on the first try. Brow furrowed in concentration, she held it to the makeshift torch and watched with grim satisfaction as the torn, bloodied cloth took flame.

"We found some road flares," Grillo said in her ear. "Would that work?"

"Worth a shot," she said. "Faisal! You still there?"

"I'm here." His voice sounded faint, and in a different place than before.

She told him to run back to the barricade and get the flares from Grillo. While he did that, Sam had David stand in the center of their cavity while she walked around him, waving the torch at the closest branches. They receded more violently from the bigger flame, making a sound like two shards of glass rubbing together when they moved. Gradually she managed to increase their space to something the size of a small car. A few new branches tried to snake their way in, so she kept at it until the bright red glow of a signal flare could be seen in the haze.

"I see your torch," Faisal said.

"Meet you halfway. Be careful, they grow back in behind you pretty quick."

A minute later the three were reunited. Faisal handed an extra flare to both her and David, and Sam saw he had one extra stuffed into his front pants pocket. She inspected hers and saw text on the side indicating it would last for one hour.

"All right, Grillo," Sam said. "Your mystery fog is coming from some kind of bizarro plant. Or . . . reef. A strange fucking alien tree. I don't know what the hell it is, but if you want my opinion, it's not ours. Are we done here?"

"Faisal described it to me," Grillo said. "I think it's worth exploring the crash site. The traitors dropped a farm platform here, and if there was something related to the Builders aboard, that would be very interesting to know. Especially if it has now been . . . unleashed."

She grimaced. "The flares only last an hour."

"Then you'd better get started," Grillo replied.

Sam bit back a snide response and looked at her two

companions. "You're both wearing environment suits in a forest of knives. You can bug out if you want; I'll handle this."

In unison they shook their heads, and Sam understood. They had orders.

"Follow me, then," she said for the second time.

With fire, traversing the nightmare forest became easy. Sam went first, swiping her makeshift torch in slow, wide arcs. The branches shrank away with their glassy crackling sound.

She glanced over her shoulder every few steps. The two soldiers waved their flares about as if they were trying to flag down an aircraft. Sparks dripped from the bright red fires, and thick smoke billowed off until it merged with the foggy soup around them.

Every ten steps or so Samantha dropped to a knee, listened for a moment, and then selected a few pieces of the rubble that littered the ground. She arranged these in an arrow pointing in the direction in which they walked.

After a few hundred meters of this, she began to see signs of the explosion that resulted when the farm platform came down. Blackened debris littered the ground, skittering away when kicked by their boots as they walked. The asphalt road, as worn as any in Darwin, had a web of cracks laced across it. In places entire chunks were gone, revealing the hardpan beneath.

The sky grew dark above them as they went. Sometimes the fog above Sam's head would dissipate enough to see more than a few meters up. The lattice of crystalline branches extended far above their heads here, half as tall as the office buildings she knew loomed around them, hidden by the cloud and the darkness.

Then, as suddenly as it had enveloped them, the branches ended, and the cloud thinned dramatically, turning from a static, oppressive soup to a patchy, swirling, silent maelstrom. Lit by her torch and the men's reddish flares, the wafts of fog looked like otherworldly ghosts.

Samantha called a halt and took a knee again.

She realized they'd come to the edge of a giant dome within the glassy lattice. Twenty meters high at least, and the same across, she thought, perfect in its shape. Distances were hard to ascertain as wafts of the thick fog still drifted through the area. These puffs rose from the center of the space, as if hot air pushed them from below. If she had a religious bone in her body, she might have said they looked like souls ascending.

"Heat," she muttered. The tension of their situation, and the long walk, had masked it, but she now felt the oppressive heat of the place.

David and Faisal knelt behind her, taking in the dome in silence from behind the curved plastic masks of their environment suits. Their breaths fogged the clear material in rapid puffs that vanished a heartbeat later as processors pulled moisture from the sealed outfits. Faisal drew his towel-wrapped arm across his mask to wipe away a fine pattern of droplets. The towel looked soaked.

She glanced at each of their chests, noted the green light of containment on each, and turned back to the view.

The ground beneath the dome sloped downward. A crater, she realized, and they were perched on the lip. She followed the broken ground to the center and sucked in her breath.

Faisal gasped. He saw it at the same time she did.

The boot and leg of a yellow environment suit, protruding through the morass of swirling fog. Whether the human contents were still within she couldn't see. More scraps of thick yellow material lay beyond the leg, forming a rough line toward the very center of the dome's floor.

"This mission," Samantha said, "just went off the 'what the fuck' chart."

"What are you seeing?" Grillo asked, his voice laced with static now.

Sam rattled off the important details quickly: bits of a suit, torn to pieces. Some weird dome around a crater, the swirling mists. "My tactical instincts are telling me to get the hell out of here," she concluded. "But I'm guessing you feel otherwise."

"I do."

She grunted, annoyance brewing within. Skyler would have argued with her. He would have left *room* for argument, and no matter what harebrained scheme he'd cooked up, if Sam said "scuttle," he'd almost always do just that. Grillo's manner somehow made her feel guilty when she disagreed, and his commitment to the mission bordered on dangerous.

She wondered what would happen if she told him to get fucked, and went back. Would he throw her back in jail? Threaten Kelly?

Would these two tagalongs even let her retreat? For the first time she saw them as escorts rather than helpers. Maybe they'd turn their guns on her, force her to proceed.

Best not to test it, she decided. The previous group Grillo had sent in was not combat trained, or so he'd implied. So far she hadn't seen anything here she couldn't handle.

"Fine," she replied to Grillo, and then looked at her two companions. "Let's keep moving."

She stepped slowly toward the center of the crater, giving a wide berth around the severed pant leg. A dinner-plate-sized pool of blood surrounded the open end of the garment fragment. She decided not to check if a leg remained inside; the answer seemed obvious.

Breathing became a chore. The air stifling, like a sauna run amok. Sam watched as the improvised torch in her hand burned out, and she set it aside. David would want to get his rifle back together, but the stock would need to cool first.

She decided to save her flare for now and crept farther ahead, aware of her two companions following behind. They still held their flares aloft, more to light the strange alien cathedral than for any other reason.

Near the center of the impact crater, the ground ended at a jagged edge of earth and concrete. It was a circular opening to some kind of pit, descending down into blackness so choked with fog that the fiery light from the two flares could not illuminate much beyond the lip.

A twisted bundle of the glassy branches, thick as a tree trunk, rose up from the middle of the hole, stretching high above them before disappearing into the cloud. The fog wafted off this column in thick tendrils, rising swiftly toward whatever was above.

Sam looked at Faisal and jerked her head toward the hole. He took the hint and tossed his flare in. The beacon fell into the cloud, like an upside-down view of a firework launched into smoky skies. The light became a faint glowing orb and came to rest ten or fifteen meters below. The shape of the reddish glow resembled a crescent moon, and Samantha realized the flare was partially obscured by some giant boulder or object resting on the floor of the depression.

That's what made the crater, she realized. *And sprouted these vines.*

"I don't think they dropped a farm platform here," she said for Grillo's benefit.

"Explain," he said.

"We found a pit, in the center of the crater. There's something at the bottom, big as one of your trucks, and round. Round*ish*."

A brief silence followed. David took advantage of the pause to put his rifle back together and wipe moisture from his helmet's curved plastic mask.

"Could be some piece of machinery that survived reentry. A reactor, even."

"Well, whatever it is, it's what these goddamn branches are sprouting from."

Faisal sucked in a breath. She glanced around, looking for what spooked him, but saw nothing. When she turned to him, he was staring at her with disgust. The expression vanished the instant their eyes met.

"Something wrong, Faisal?"

He looked down his nose at her and shook his head.

Grillo's voice brought her back to the moment. "Can you climb down and get a closer look?"

Sam knew that no answer other than "Sure" would fly. She sent Faisal back to the truck to get a rope. When he left earshot, she turned her headset off and looked at David. "Why's he so uptight all the sudden?"

David regarded her. "You should watch your tongue."

"What the fuck did I say?"

David narrowed his eyes. "I'm not as devout as them, so I can tell you. 'Goddamn' is like a punch in the gut. Show some respect. It doesn't cost you anything."

Samantha thought back to the little prayer circle she'd witnessed just before they climbed down the barricade. *Them? Grillo is a fucking Jacobite?*

She thought up and promptly swallowed a half-dozen snide, disrespectful replies, and waited. In the silence she pondered the revelation. Grillo certainly did have a minister's demeanor, but his reputation as a ruthless slumlord didn't mesh. She thought it possible he was just pandering to the sect to earn their support, and anyway it didn't really matter if he'd thrown in with the weirdos or not. Her situation had nothing to do with it.

Faisal returned ten uncomfortable minutes later with a bundle of nylon rope. The two men helped Samantha tie it around her waist, across her shoulders, and then through loops on her pants and vest.

In no time she found herself leaning backward over the vertical pit, holding the rope with two hands, her toes resting on the edge of the precipice. She leaned farther to put her full weight on the line, watching David and Faisal as they grunted with effort to hold her in place.

"Lower me down," she told them. "One step at a time, yeah?"

The heat became unbearable. Sam could do nothing on the descent except focus on her footing and breathing. The walls of the pit were a cross section of hard-packed earth, layers of foundational concrete reinforced with iron rebar, and the odd bit of pipe or wiring conduit. None of this showed the charred, blackened evidence of a major explosion like the crater above.

Near the bottom she cleared the fog, and the floor of the pit came clearly into view. Sam unslung her rifle and flipped on its barrel-mounted LED, bathing the place in crisp white light.

"Stop!" she called out immediately. The rope tugged her in a rough snap, her progress halting.

The floor of the pit shimmered and rippled. Black water, how deep she couldn't guess. *This is a sinkhole,* she thought. The object had impacted above, and in the violence of that, runoff water had begun to pool down here, eventually causing the ground above to collapse. The water moved in one direction, implying a drainage path that kept the hole from filling to the top.

"Sam? Report," Grillo said, almost unintelligible with the static. She ignored him.

In the center of the circular pit, partially submerged, lay an oblong shape that reminded her of pictures of the Builders' shell that capped the space elevator, only much smaller in scale. The surface of it was so black it seemed to drink in the light when her beam swept across it. Flickering light from the partially submerged flare cast the walls of the pit behind it in a dance of bright red and deep shadow. Backlit so, the object took on a demonic quality that brought goose bumps to her arms despite the stifling heat.

From the object's "tail" came the bundle of glassy, segmented branches. The tangle of alien limbs stretched up in a straight line into the fog above. Unlike the black alien object from which they came, the branches seemed to glow in the light from her gun, their pale blue coloring almost jewel-like without the fog surrounding them.

"You okay down there?" David called out.

"Yeah," she whispered. Then louder, "Yes. Lower me a meter or so. There's water."

After a series of short drops and barked commands, David and Faisal managed to lower her slowly into the balmy water, warm as a bath. Her feet touched broken, uneven ground when the depth had submerged her to mid-thigh. "I'm down," she called up.

Sam crept slowly around the perimeter of the pit, her gun trained on the alien mass that loomed just a few meters away. The heat, she realized, had a pulse to it, rising and falling a few degrees every second or two. The air smelled of tar and burned charcoal.

After three steps the "drain" through which the water escaped came into view: a wide concrete pipe, cracked in half by the collapse of the ground above it. The dark water rushed into it in sloshing gulps as the wake from her passage pushed waves into its wide maw.

Lapping against the pipe's opening, a body listed gently in the water. Clad in the trademark yellow of an environment suit, the limp form bobbed with each ripple.

Samantha saw parallel cuts in the legs and back of the suit, as if claws had raked it. The sight filled her with sudden fear. She pressed herself against the wall and swept the beam of her rifle's light across the entire space, looking for any sign of what had caused such damage.

But the place was quiet. Dead. She slowly exhaled and spoke

into her headset. "Found another of your lost crew," she said. "Something cut him to shreds, I don't know what. Can you hear me?"

A garbled response came, full of scratchy hisses and deep clicks.

"Piece of shit," she growled. Grillo could get the highlights later. She continued on her path around the object, stopping long enough to inspect the body. She rolled it over in the water and cringed at the face inside the suit. The mask had been shattered, as had the face. Bruises covered the nose, one cheek, and an eye.

Something must have given this poor bastard a haymaker of epic proportions, she thought. That, or he fell in. She flipped the corpse back over and turned to the alien shape in the center of the pit.

Three more steps into her route, Sam froze. The flickering red flare lay only a few meters away from her now, and its dancing light illuminated a gaping hole in the side of the object. She trained her own beam on the opening. Not a hole, she saw, but an actual entrance, square in shape.

Inside the shell was a cube-shaped cavity, roughly two meters on a side. The walls were laced with thin grooves, drawn in sharp, straight lines and perfect ninety-degree corners.

Thin arms jutted out from the corners of the cavity, converging near the center around a cube-shaped object, perhaps a half meter tall and wide. A channel three or four centimeters deep ran down one side. Sam knew somehow that the thin black arms were not connected to the object, but rather were holding it in place.

The cube had the same angular patterns of lines etched into its otherwise smooth black surface. But these lines were different. As Samantha watched, pale blue light rippled along their lengths, the same color as the thorny branches above. To Sam the cube's surface almost looked like a circuit board, or city streets viewed from high above.

"Sam?" David called down from above.

"Here," she called back. "I've found something."

Wading through the warm water, Samantha approached the cube, unable to take her eyes off the fine patterns of blue-white light that rippled beneath the lines etched into its surface.

She reached the opening on the side of the shell and climbed up onto it, warm water dripping from her legs and sloshing in her boots. The liquid should have pooled around her feet, but instead the Builders' material drank it in. For a moment she marveled at this before turning her attention back to the cube suspended in the center of the chamber.

Flexing her fingers, Samantha reached out for it. The blue laser light pulsing along its surface shifted, growing brighter where her hands were about to touch, and darker elsewhere, as if sensing her presence. She paused only for a second, gave a small shrug, and gripped the cube by two sides.

A pulse of light exploded from the cube, blinding her. The object hummed under her hands as if she'd gripped a live electrical wire, and she couldn't let go.

Above her came an avalanche of noise, like a thousand butcher's knives being sharpened at once, so loud it hurt to hear. Somewhere beneath that noise she thought she heard a scream, silenced abruptly. Something splashed in the water at the bottom of the pit. Something large. Sam turned but all she saw was the afterglow of blue light.

Her hands remained clasped to the cube, vibrating. She yanked, hard, and the cube came free. It weighed as much as a concrete block, and she stumbled, falling backward out of the shell and into the warm water.

The cube landed on her stomach and forced the air from her lungs. A mouthful of gritty water flooded into her mouth and nose and she tried to spit it out, but she had no air to do so.

Somehow she found her footing, rolled over, and stood up. The raking, calamitous sound of glass sliding against glass continued above her. Sam coughed and retched the water from her lungs. When she opened her eyes, she could see again.

The cube lay in the water at her feet, still pulsing with blue light. She turned and looked up. Above her, the bundle of glassy limbs that stretched from the top of the shell were writhing. They'd taken on the color of fire, and burned as bright. The glow faded the farther up the trunk she looked. Above the pit, she could see the latticework of branches flailing about violently. The segments no longer had a pale blue color. Now they were blood-red. She thought it must be like standing in a whirlwind of barbed wire up there. "David! Faisal!" she shouted. No response came.

The violent movement of the branches dispersed the fog, and Sam could see that the alien structure stretched at least fifty meters above her head.

She focused on the thick trunk of tangled branches that jutted from the tip of the shell. Gritting her teeth, Sam unslung her rifle, set it to fully automatic, and took aim.

Her bullets raked across the bundle, punching through the tendrils easily, and sparking as they ricocheted off the wall of the pit beyond. Each branch that she severed turned gray instantly. By the time she'd depleted her ammo, most of the trunk was gray, and the violent motion above had all but stopped. Two or three branches still swayed, so Sam reloaded and took care of those, too. Her ears rang from the sound of gunfire.

"Faisal?! David?!" she shouted again.

The rope they'd lowered her on still rested against the pit wall, a few meters away.

A shape in the water caught her eye. Another body in a yellow suit, the material sliced into tatters, tainted with fresh blood. She waded over to it and flipped the corpse over. David's eyes stared back at her, glassy and wide with terror.

"Fuck," she muttered, and pushed his body away.

Shaking, Sam climbed the rope, leaving the alien cube where it lay.

At the top of the pit she found Faisal's body, or what was left of it. He'd been farther from the lip of the sinkhole, and sliced to pieces when the thorny branches went haywire. Bits of his flesh hung from the gray limbs, along with pieces of his environment suit. Yellow and red ornaments on a dead alien tree.

"Grillo," she coughed into her headset. "Come in."

The device had shorted out, she decided, from her fall into the water. She ripped it off her head and threw it angrily into the pit.

From a pocket on her vest she produced the flare Faisal had given her. Sam closed her eyes and wished for luck as she cracked it open. Even after being submerged when she fell, it crackled to life and soon a red fire blazed on its tip, dripping sparks.

Gingerly, Sam held it out to the nearest branch, wondering if the now-dead segment would recoil as it had before. Instead of shrinking away, the material blackened and disintegrated.

After what felt like an hour, Sam finally emerged from the alien forest and trudged back to the barricade at Aura's Edge. The sight of Grillo standing there, waiting for her, was a strange comfort.

Sam sat in the back of the APC, wrapped in a blanket and nursing a bottle of water, when the cavalry arrived. Dozens of trucks filled with armed fighters encircled the area, securing it. Grillo's private army.

She stared beyond them, at Darwin's dirty skyline. Unable to focus, she had only a vague awareness of the activity around her. A dozen people gathered, clad in environment suits, armed with flares and torches. They walked out of her field of view toward the barricade.

They were talking about the space elevator. Something about a vibration along its length, and a surge of power, when she'd removed the cube from the crashed ship. They were laughing about it, like someone laughs after walking into a surprise birthday party, so her action must not have caused any damage. Still, it meant the object was connected, somehow, to the alien cord.

Numb and exhausted, Sam pulled her blanket tight and fought to stop shaking. Despite everything she'd seen, the only image that she seemed able to conjure was David's dead eyes, staring at her, accusing her. Like Jake's, in a way. She shuddered at the memory.

Sam hardly noticed when the group returned later. Four of them carried a cube-shaped bundle of blankets, and were moving with slow, deliberate steps. The people around them cleared the path, and soon the package disappeared into one of the newly arrived trucks.

The group began to remove their environment suits once the crate was secure. Dazed, Samantha hardly recognized their

Jacobite garb before the rear door of her APC was thrown shut, blocking her view.

Seconds later she heard the vehicle's caps begin to whine. She swayed in her seat as it lurched into movement. Sam leaned back, closed her eyes, and let the gentle rocking of the vehicle lull her to sleep.

18

MELVILLE STATION

5.MAY.2283

She was in the cargo bay, helping unload a shipment of apples, when the station rattled. An alarm went off somewhere, one she hadn't heard before.

"What the?" Tania said to no one in particular. The people working around her looked as worried as she felt.

"Collision?" someone asked.

Tania doubted it. The vibration seemed to come from the Elevator cord itself. "Excuse me," she said, and pushed off for the intercom on the wall. Her mind raced as she flew across the room. She imagined Blackfield's troopers swarming through the station like they had on Anchor.

At the wall she steadied herself with a handhold and tapped the activation switch. "Tania here. Someone talk to me. What's going on?"

Tim's voice came through a few seconds later. "Unknown. A vibration rippled up the cord. Black Level reported it first, then the farms a few seconds later. Now us."

"It started at the shell ship? An explosion or . . . ?"

"Some kind of electricity discharge, hence that overload

alarm. Our draws on the cord went into emergency disconnect mode when the surge hit us."

Tania frowned. The cord generated electricity due to friction with the atmosphere, something the stations tapped as a backup source. The climbers relied on the source exclusively to make their journeys. A change in that would be catastrophic.

"Everything's fine now," Tim said. "Greg says all systems are reading normal up there."

Memories of Darwin's Elevator malfunctions raced through Tania's mind. Nothing like this, but still, if something similar was happening again . . . "Put all stations on maximum alert. All personnel should be required to check in. If the aura failed . . ."

"Already done. Commanders will report within the hour."

"Thanks, Tim. Keep me posted." Her hand shook as she switched the intercom off.

Tania sat cross-legged on the floor of Room 17, her chin resting on steepled fingers.

The room, which had been stocked to the brim with weaponry by Neil Platz, was all but empty now. A few crates remained here and there, mostly gear no one knew what to do with. That simple fact seemed to encapsulate for her everything about the state of the so-called colony. Gear and resources depleted, and no one who knew what the hell they were doing.

She sighed, exhausted from the mental effort it took to stop thinking, even in brief spans, about the fate of the aircraft she'd sent down to the planet below. Crew and craft lost, and they hadn't even made it to the edge of Camp Exodus. By any measurement the entire endeavor had been a complete fiasco.

The bizarre fluctuation along the cord didn't exactly help her nerves, but all personnel were accounted for and there'd been no repeats of the event.

Failings aside, what bothered Tania more was that she had no idea what to do next. The strike team had been her last-ditch effort. She glanced around the nearly empty room. "You'd know what to do, wouldn't you?" she asked, her voice echoing from the walls. She wasn't quite sure if she'd meant the question for Neil Platz, or for Skyler.

The soft sound of a key-card swipe came to her from outside, and the door behind her opened.

"There you are." Tim, of course.

"Here I am." She felt immediate guilt for the unappreciative tone in her words. He'd been trying, hard, to lift her from the melancholy she'd fallen into since the failed rescue. It seemed wholly unfair to treat him badly for the effort.

"I brought chai," he said. "Can I sit with you?"

With a sigh she hoped she'd hid, Tania nodded and patted the floor next to her.

He handed her one of two mugs and mirrored her cross-legged position. "Spared no expense," he said, gauging her reaction.

The cup had a twist-on lid and when Tania opened it the warmth and smells contained within hugged her like an old friend. "This is the good stuff, isn't it?" she asked.

"Mm-hmm. You gave me two bags of it for an early simulation result, a few years ago."

"I remember," she said, lying.

"Been saving it," he added, then sipped. Tim winced from the heat and set his cup down. "Oh, blimey but that's hot. Might want to wait a minute."

Tania followed his lead. In truth she was content just to let the complex, spicy scent drift up and around her. It smelled like her mother's kitchen. "Thank you for the tea," she said earnestly. "And the company."

"No problem." He shrugged, settled himself. "So what are we doing in here? Concocting a new plan?"

"I wish," Tania said. "Unfortunately I don't think we have many options left. I mean, look at this place. We're overextended everywhere. No supplies are coming up. Who knows what the hell is going on in camp. . . ."

She let her voice trail off. Tim knew all this, and the last thing Tania wanted to do was rehash it all again.

Tim, mercifully, said nothing. He tried his tea again, hissed through clenched teeth, and set the cup back down. "You think you have problems—I can't even boil water right."

Tania elbowed him, laughed lightly at his mock show of

pain. "Anything new to report on that vibration that the cord exhibited?" she asked.

"It was some kind of power surge, we know that much. Beyond that, nothing new. No damage reported, at least."

"How's Zane?" she asked, desperate to change the subject.

"He retired early. Between us, I think all this stress is getting to him. He's always tired, and doesn't eat enough."

"Sounds like he's the one who needs chai," Tania said.

Tim grunted, and looked over at her. "If you're saying I should leave . . ."

Tania turned and met his gaze. Even in the dark room, she could see the sparkle of intelligence and energy in his eyes. "I'm trying to find any excuse not to think about our dire situation."

"A distraction," he concluded. "Good. Did you, er, have something in mind?"

Tania searched his eyes. "Yes," she said sternly. "Let's make Zane some dinner."

Tim readily agreed, and for the next hour they took over the mess kitchen. The meal had to be improvised, but Tania thought the result was a reasonable curry, something she knew Zane loved.

They called him down from his cabin and the three of them ate together, even shared a bottle of wine. To Tania's delight, for that evening at least, no one mentioned the plight they faced. For the first time in a while, they were just three friends sharing the simple, sacred pleasure of a meal well prepared.

19

BELÉM, BRAZIL

5.MAY.2283

Skyler and Davi lay side by side in the brush at the top of a small rise.

Ana worked in silence behind them, securing their excess gear. She'd become more and more withdrawn during the last stage of their trek. When Skyler asked, Davi had chalked it up to fatigue.

Skyler held a scavenged pair of binoculars to his eyes, scanning the shallow valley below while Davi used the scope on his hunting rifle. Skyler had found the weapon, too, and spent an hour each morning for the last few days teaching Davi how to use and clean it. The young man had none of Jake's natural skill, but he could hit a target if he focused.

The lodge appeared intact. Beyond it stood a barn, doors closed and latched, the muddy ground in front churned and laced by tire tracks.

A dirt road, obscured by knee-high weeds, served as the primary way in and out of the complex.

"Fresh tire tracks," Skyler said. He kept his voice low.

"I see them. This is the place."

Over days of cat-and-mouse with Gabriel's people through the streets of Belém, Skyler's radio picked up the needed hint to find the hidden immunes: a call to help free a truck stuck in mud. From that they knew the road being used by Gabriel's people to move back and forth between their base of operations and the colony at Belém's Elevator. Tracing their exact path proved easy enough, as the heavy military vehicles Gabriel's people used left plenty of evidence in their wake.

Skyler pulled the binoculars away from his face and took in the whole scene below him.

A shallow ravine lay below, carved by a thin stream that snaked down from lush foothills to the west. Morning fog obscured the eastern end of the valley, where the grassy field gave way to rainforest, and the stream met a stronger river.

Nestled in the center of the valley, in a wide clearing, was a lodge. A tourist hotel, Skyler judged, with maybe twenty rooms on two stories. A barn stood a short distance from the main building.

Two black personnel carriers were parked between the two structures. Neither had moved since dawn, nor had any signs of activity within the buildings been seen. The quiet made Skyler wonder if the location had already been abandoned, but the presence of the two vehicles threw doubt on that theory.

"Let's go," Davi said. "They're probably all sleeping."

Skyler caught movement through his binoculars. "Hold up."

Three men marched along the ridgeline on the opposite side of the valley. Skyler put them at half a kilometer away. Only their heads were visible above the weeds.

"See 'em?"

"I see 'em," Davi said. "Keep still."

They watched the men for a tense few minutes as the trio worked their way toward the lodge.

Davi sucked in his breath as they came into full view. "What the hell?"

Through the binoculars, Skyler saw something that raised goose bumps on his arms.

An old man with a thick gray beard led the group. The other two each carried long metal poles, with loops of rope at the end.

The ropes were lashed around the neck and torso of a woman, or what was once a woman. The subhuman was nude, filthy, and very much alive. She bled openly from a number of lacerations on her belly and legs.

"Jesus," Skyler said. "Davi."

"I see it."

"They captured a sub."

"I fucking see it," he hissed. The young man glanced back at Ana.

Skyler looked, too. Twenty meters away, her back to a tree trunk, the girl worked methodically to load the new weapon he'd given her. The compact assault rifle fired small .22-caliber rounds, easy to handle but lacking punch. That shortcoming was made up for by the grenade launcher slung under the barrel.

Skyler broached the question he so desperately wanted to keep inside. "Are you sure you want her to come with us? She could guard our bags."

"She comes," Davi said. "Trust me, she gets very upset if you try to shelter her."

"Okay then."

"But," Davi added, "if you could give her the least dangerous part in the plan . . ."

"I understand," Skyler said. He meant it, even though he knew it would be impossible to do. There were too many unknowns. But it couldn't hurt to give Davi a little reassurance.

He made a *took-took* sound through pursed lips. Ana glanced up and waved back. She finished loading the gun and jogged up the hillside to join them on the ridge, crawling the last few meters before lying next to Skyler. The corners of her lips were curled up in the hint of a smile. She was, Skyler realized, enjoying this. Her mirth drained when she saw the men below with their captive subhuman.

Davi fiddled with the scope on his sniper rifle and took a long, measured breath. "What's the plan—"

The subhuman prisoner, now twenty meters from the lodge, clutched at the bar that held her torso and began to howl, her nose held high in the air.

"She smells something," Skyler whispered. *Us?*

A response came from somewhere inside the lodge. Ten voices, maybe more, took up the same, wild, subhuman cry. Something rang different about it, though. Skyler had heard such cries all over the world, and they always sounded the same. These, from the building, sounded feeble. Weak.

Skyler swallowed hard and said, "I've got a really fucking bad feeling about this."

The two immunes who held the female captive in the valley below struggled to keep her under control. She began to buck violently, left and right and again. One of the men slipped. The leader, in front, turned and walked back to them. He was shouting something, impossible to make out against the wailing of those within the lodge.

"Here's the plan," Skyler said. "We'll surround the lodge—"

Ana leapt to her feet and rushed down the hill. She ran hard, holding her rifle across her chest. Not even a glance back.

Skyler started to shout after her, but reason won out. The immunes were too busy with their prisoner to notice the woman racing toward them. She would cross the distance in no time at her adrenaline-fueled pace.

If she had some kind of death wish, Skyler hadn't caught it before. Though in hindsight, her dancing alone in that courtyard had a suicidal aftertaste to it.

"Ana, Jesus!" Davi hissed through clenched teeth.

"Don't panic," Skyler said. "Take a shot before they spot her."

Ana was less than fifty meters from the men now. Davi took a deep breath. He sighted downrange, and on an exhale let off a round.

The big leader's head jerked wildly. He sank to his knees and toppled over.

The thunderous sound from the rifle brought a brief shocked silence from all around.

Davi wasted no time, unleashing two more bullets in rapid succession. Panic filled the valley. The second of the three men dove to the dirt, letting go of his metal pole in the process. The bullets meant for him did nothing more than generate two puffs of dust from the trail.

Skyler watched as Ana crouched down. She raised her rifle and began firing at the third enemy.

The man shoved the subhuman toward Ana, turned, and

hustled away for the safety of a small mound. The subhuman spun in circles, poles still attached to her, moving like a frenzied animal.

Another deafening clap from the hunting rifle dropped the subhuman in a whoosh of dirt and outstretched limbs. She twitched on the ground only for a second, and then nothing.

Skyler heard the sound of breaking glass, coming from the lodge. He saw a shotgun barrel poke out of a window on the side of the building facing the valley. It was far enough away from all of them to be of no concern, but it meant the three immunes were not alone here.

Battle instinct took over.

"I'll flank," Skyler blurted. He was up and moving, keeping low behind the edge of the ridge.

As he ran, he heard the battle continue. Another salvo from Ana's gun. Two shots from a gun he hadn't heard yet, from somewhere in the valley. Davi answered those with another booming shot.

Skyler angled for a thin copse of trees that bookended one side of the lodge. He kept his machine gun angled low, at the ready. As he rounded the edge of the wooden house, the sounds behind him faded, until he heard nothing but his own labored breath. He paused to gather himself, just for a few seconds, then crouched below the window height and moved along the back wall of the structure.

At the far edge, he took a quick look around the building before bouncing back. Two more of the immunes stood next to an open door. One held a pipe wrench. The other's hands were not visible, but from the way he stood, Skyler suspected he had a handgun.

Best not to take any chances.

Skyler jumped around the corner and lined up the holographic dot his gun provided on the second man's back. He squeezed off a controlled burst, adjusted, and followed it with another. The two men were dead.

Surprise no longer on his side, Skyler moved up to the door the men had come through. He peeked quickly inside, but found it too dark to make much out.

Then the howling started again, from within. The sound was gut-wrenching. More pitiful than frightening.

There were, he realized, other shouts mixed in. Human cries for help.

Skyler flattened himself against the wall by the door. Off to his left, he saw nothing along the trail except dirt. The occasional echo of a gunshot rolled down the valley floor to him.

Then Ana appeared, running toward him, her gun pointed down as he'd shown her.

He motioned for her to stop and luckily she saw him. The girl crouched next to a shrub beside the trail.

Skyler pointed at his gun, then at her, then at the barn. *Secure the barn,* he mouthed.

She looked from her weapon to the large wooden structure and nodded.

Satisfied, Skyler renewed his focus on the door to the lodge. He readied himself to rush in when Ana's movement caught his eye.

Or rather, her lack of movement. She wasn't moving toward the barn—she was taking aim on it.

Realization hit him just as she fired the grenade launcher.

Skyler covered his ears as the massive rolling door on the front of the barn exploded into a million shards of thin wood.

Then a second, much bigger explosion hit. Skyler was slammed into the wall of the lodge by the force of it. He dropped to a fetal position and threw his arms over his face as shrapnel peppered the entire area. Even from here he could feel a flash of intense heat.

Every window on the lodge shattered. Bits of flaming debris smacked into the walls and roof.

More blasts followed. Skyler peeked between his elbows and saw nothing but a cloud of smoke where the barn had stood a moment earlier. Gabriel's people must have been storing explosives inside, or fuel of some sort. Hopefully no one friendly was in there.

The worst of it over, Skyler leapt to his feet and ducked inside.

The main hall ran deep into the building, into darkness. On either side were empty door frames, every three meters. Anyone waiting inside would expect an intruder to enter the first room, so Skyler bolted right past the first two openings.

The tactic worked. Two gunshots, one from either side of him, both late. They shook the walls of the old building, nothing more. Skyler saw that the next door on his right was a bathroom. He ran into it, stopped abruptly, and pressed himself against the tiled wall.

He closed his eyes and counted to ten. When he opened them, his vision had adjusted to the darkness.

Skyler realized that the subhuman wailing came from below. A basement, then. Cries for help came from both below and above.

A creak from the floorboard in the hall focused him. Skyler half-spun out of the bathroom. He gave himself a split second to make sure Davi or Ana hadn't followed him in. They hadn't.

An older woman stood in the hallway, overweight, dressed only in a threadbare nightgown. She raised a shotgun, aiming from her waist—a clumsy motion. The weapon discharged into the wall a meter from Skyler.

He answered with two rounds. One took her in the gut, one in the chest. She gurgled as she slumped to the floor.

Eyes adjusted, Skyler now saw the interior of the main hall. He stalked toward the front of the house, stepping over the old hag's corpse.

He'd heard two shots when he first entered. Someone was still there, he knew; he did a somersault across the entryway.

A shot rang out, hissing through the air above him, where his head would have been. He came up firing, a *rat-tat* that shook the very walls. The bullets hit the chest of a teenage boy, adding two red holes to his dingy shirt. The kid fell backward with the impact, lifeless, landing on an overturned milk crate, smashing it with his weight.

A damn kid! Skyler had no time for remorse and shoved the look on the boy's face aside. The sound of footsteps drifted down from above. From the second floor.

"Skyler?"

He turned at Davi's low voice, coming from the doorway. "In here," he replied. "Two down, more upstairs. And subhumans in the basement."

"I'll take the basement," Davi said, readying a pistol.

"No," Skyler said, "I've got it."

"You sure?"

Skyler nodded. "Where's Ana?"

"Stunned from that explosion. I told her to guard the door in case we flushed anyone out."

"Good," Skyler said, genuinely. "Right. Shout an all-clear when you can, and exercise caution. We still don't know where your friends are."

Davi nodded and led the way down the main hall. They came to a narrow stairwell. To one side of it, an open door gave way to another set of steps leading down.

Skyler stopped only to take a brief look down the stairs. The steps looked aged: cracked wood nailed atop older rotten planks. He crept forward, leaving Davi to deal with the second floor.

The smell from below overpowered him—worse than the bathroom. A mixed scent of death and human waste. Skyler stopped halfway down and vomited. He could not hear his own retching above the agonizing cries from below. After a time, the nausea passed. Another four steps, taken slowly, and Skyler reached the basement.

When his feet hit the floor, the wailing stopped.

It felt markedly cooler in the subterranean room, enough to make him shiver. He placed an arm across his mouth and nose to quell the odor, and moved inside.

His shoes encountered a sticky, wet patch. Skyler thrust out a hand to brace himself, just preventing a slip and fall. He paused to gather himself, to let his heart rate slow.

The room spanned ten meters on each side, following the footprint of the building above. In the near darkness, Skyler could see poorly erected rooms—pens, or cages, he sensed—lining the other three walls. In the center of the space, an area three meters square was marked off by sections of chain-link fence.

Inside the center cage, a naked woman was crouched on hands and knees. Her head tilted slightly when Skyler's eyes met hers. The movement reminded him of a cat. She had the wild eyes and unkempt hair of a subhuman, but not the starved leanness. Her hands and feet were held in place by metal braces. A section of fence behind her had been cut away, allowing . . . access.

Skyler swallowed, a knot of realization forming in his gut even before the thought came fully to mind. The restrained subhuman woman was filthy save the part of her pressed against the gap in the cage. A steel bucket sat on the ground just outside, a soiled towel hung carelessly over the lip.

He shot a glance at the cells along the far wall. A female subhuman form loomed within each, save one that was empty, the door slightly ajar.

The knot within him tightened. Skyler turned to the opposite wall. More cells, more prisoners, though these were different. He saw six naked men and women, all devoid of that animalistic glare. Immunes. Two slept or were, perhaps, dead. The others stared at him with hope in their eyes.

Skyler didn't need to see any more. He'd heard enough about Gabriel and his followers to guess what was going on here: breeding.

The subhuman woman hissed at him. Within seconds, the shrieks and wails from the other cells began anew.

Time to end this.

He shot the subhuman woman in the cage at point-blank range, between the eyes. She made no effort to avoid it. Skyler had a vague sense that she wanted him to do it, the way she closed her eyes just before he fired.

With a methodical march along the far wall he found six more of the poor creatures. Skyler put a bullet in each, ending their misery. The anger in him morphed, became resolute, a white-hot coal. This was evil, pure and simple, and whatever else happened he would make sure Gabriel paid for it. The world had enough problems without this kind of shit.

Turning back toward where he'd entered, Skyler faced the immune prisoners.

"I'm here to help you," he said.

Combination locks secured each cage. Skyler made a cursory search of the room for bolt cutters or anything of the sort, but found nothing. "Get back," he said to the prisoners. The order registered for those awake and they hobbled toward the wall.

Four gunshots later the cages were open.

"Carry them," he said, pointing to the sleepers. "Get outside and wait for us. I'll try to find you some clothes."

One mumbled thanks. Skyler ignored them and went back up the stairs.

Davi waited for him at the ground-floor landing, carrying a young girl in his arms, three or four years old. She hugged him fiercely, face buried in his shoulder, her chest heaving with sobs. At the door to the lodge Skyler saw a few other immunes, shuffling out into the bright sun.

"Find anyone?" Davi asked.

"Six," Skyler said. "We're burning this place when we leave. No debate."

Davi held Skyler's gaze for an instant. "Okay."

The immunes shuffled up the stairs, carrying their brethren. Davi greeted the first one by name and a flicker of hope flashed on the man's face. They embraced as well as they could.

"Take them outside. I'll look for clothing and blankets," Skyler said.

When the others cleared the front door, Skyler bounded up the stairs to the second floor and searched it again. Davi might have had little formal training, but he'd killed two armed men in the central hallway. Skyler stepped over the bodies and entered the first bedroom he found. In the closet he found black uniforms like those worn by Gabriel's people in Belém. Skyler grabbed the garments and tossed them on the bed. He found one pair of hiking boots and some underwear, and threw that on the pile, too.

As he ransacked the place for useful supplies, the rage within him turned cold. It froze into a deep resolve. Whoever this Gabriel fellow was, he'd not just held these people against their will; he'd forced them to breed. And not just with each other, but also with subhumans. Try as he might, Skyler couldn't keep his imagination from painting what this place must have been like an hour before they arrived, and what kind of sickness lived within the people who ran it on Gabriel's behalf. He felt no remorse at killing those he'd encountered on the way in, and would feel none when he put a round through Gabriel's brain, either.

* * *

Outside he found Ana cradling the young girl Davi had rescued. She wept openly, as did the child.

The two unconscious prisoners were being tended to by the rest. In all, a dozen immunes had been freed.

Skyler set the blanket in the dirt and unfolded it to reveal the items he'd scrounged, then walked away to let the group dress with a modicum of privacy.

Davi brushed the hair from Ana's face. "Wait for us here, sis," he said, and followed Skyler over to examine the wreckage of the barn.

Smoking debris littered the ground for hundreds of meters around the structure. Whatever explosive they stored in here was either very potent or in a large quantity. Skyler saw bits and pieces of food packaging, and signs of less critical things like toiletries and charred books.

Nothing remained of the barn itself. Skyler could only hope no one had been inside. No one friendly, that is. He sighed. Clearly Gabriel's people had stored their reserve supplies here, and it might have been worth rummaging through. No point in worrying about it now.

"Your sister . . . ," Skyler said without looking at Davi.

". . . takes risks," Davi said, finishing. In tone and terseness, he said he didn't want to talk about her actions.

Skyler let it go. He'd force the topic before they returned to Belém, but more pressing issues were on his mind. "The purpose of this place, Davi. Not just a prison."

"I know," he said.

"Did you know about this before we arrived? Is this what you two escaped from?"

Davi shook his head. "I . . ." He searched for the words. "Gabriel talked often about how just finding immunes wasn't enough. We needed to create more. I thought he meant to force Ana . . ."

To breed. Breeding immunes. Skyler didn't know if the trait even worked that way, but the presence of the young girl seemed evidence enough. She couldn't be more than five, Skyler guessed, and that meant she'd been born after the disease ravaged the planet, beyond the aura.

Had there been others who didn't have the protection? Dashed against a wall or drowned for their inferiority? Skyler shivered.

Together, Skyler and Davi walked the perimeter of the compound, and then through the field of wreckage that had been the barn. Other than a few cans of food, and a box of pain-relief pills, they found nothing salvageable.

"The two vehicles are a gift," Skyler said. "We might be able to sneak up on the colony in them. There are a couple of uniforms, too."

Davi said nothing and avoided Skyler's gaze.

"Pack anything useful into the trucks. We'll move back to the clearing tonight and head to Belém at dawn," Skyler added. He watched the young man carefully and saw the distance in his eyes. "You do intend to come back with me, right? We had a deal."

"Yes," Davi said, his voice defensive. "At least give us some time to tend to our friends, after what they've been through. I can't think about tomorrow right now. Even without . . . all this . . . Ana and I have been on the move for months."

Skyler thought of Davi sitting in a hammock on the beach in Belém, but kept it to himself. "How long are you talking? A day? A week? My people are under Gabriel's thumb back there, and those in orbit—"

"Just . . ." Davi swallowed whatever he intended to say, and then lowered his voice. "Can we just wait until morning to decide? Let my friends rest, and not have to ponder a rush into danger so quickly after they've been freed?"

That's when their thirst for revenge will be strongest, though, Skyler thought. He kept it to himself, though. Davi feared the dangers ahead, too, he guessed. Maybe some time would help him remember the purpose of their plan.

Those who were able spent the rest of the day hoisting what supplies they could find onto the cargo racks on the tops of the two trucks. Ana sat atop one vehicle, organizing the meager goods and tying them down. Davi stood atop the other truck, rifle at the ready, scanning the surrounding countryside for any approaching subhumans.

When finished, Skyler told Ana and Davi to drive to the clearing where they'd camped the night before. "I'll hike out there after I've had a good look around," he said, and waved them off.

In the common room he found nothing except blood and furniture. The tables could be burned for firewood, but then so could the entire cursed building. He left everything where it lay and didn't bother to search the corpses.

He moved on to the kitchen. In one pantry he found a box of packaged noodles with bouillon packets, a discovery that made him think of Woon, and Prumble, and the old airport. Skyler hadn't thought about Darwin in a day at least, and the realization filled him with a mixture of guilt and sorrow. He may have had next to nothing left there, but he'd abandoned it all, and for what?

For Tania. For Tania, and the future.

She'd be desperate by now, he guessed. Air and water would be running short. He wondered if she knew anything about the situation on the ground. Maybe she'd taken the stations back to Darwin, for sheer purposes of survival. He couldn't blame her if she had.

In a drawer Skyler found a bag of hot sauce packets. Past their expiration date, but if he'd learned anything in the last five years it was that expiration dates were grossly underestimated. The ubiquitous Preservall could keep most foods safe for many years, something food manufacturers must have found bad for sales, so they shaved months or years off the printed date. The hot sauce went into his bag with the freeze-dried noodles.

Out the back door he found a small garden, blissfully free of mango. Skyler left the plants untouched, deciding he could send someone else back here to pick anything edible. Next to the planters he found gardening tools, and a hefty axe that had been recently sharpened. This he kept in hand as he circled the building.

He went upstairs again. A methodical search of each bedroom produced a few additional items: ammunition, two modern handguns, and a suitcase full of women's clothes. Skyler put the weapons and bullets inside with the clothing and tossed the whole thing out the window to the dirt below.

In the master bedroom he found a sleek black briefcase on the top shelf of the closet, pushed way to the back. The locks were in place and required both a combination and a thumbprint to open.

Or an axe.

Skyler set the thing in the middle of the hardwood floor. He brought the blade down with all his strength, aiming for the front edge just behind the locks. It took two such swings to sever the front of the case. Sweating, Skyler dumped the contents onto the bed.

A passport spilled out, along with a thick leather wallet, two stacks of crisp one-hundred-euro bills, and a bag of cocaine.

Skyler flipped open the passport and read the name. *Gabriel Zagallo.*

The passport had stamps from every drug-infested hellhole on pre-disease Earth, along with travel visas for China and India. Skyler studied the photograph. The worn passport was dated a decade earlier, so he couldn't be sure how much the man in the picture had changed since then. The man he saw had well-groomed black hair, combed neatly to one side. His head was tilted down, giving his eyes an animal quality that chilled Skyler.

This man had been a gangster, before.

The contents of the wallet contradicted that conclusion. A credit slate, its screen dead due to a lack of spooling, had chipped corners and grime on the screen, implying heavy use. A stack of receipts for small meals, and a few small bills in the local currency. A driver's license that confirmed the name on the passport. Most important, though, was the badge. The words across the top read POLÍCIA FEDERAL.

Gangster, or cop? Maybe both. Skyler wondered if the man had worked undercover. That might explain the bag of narcotics, and the money. Strange things to pack in the face of an apocalypse, but Skyler had seen plenty of odd choices in the belongings people tried to bring on their flight from the disease.

An undercover role also explained Gabriel's ability to draw others to him. He would have the acting skills needed to lure people in. The ability to make up lies on the spot.

Skyler slipped the passport and wallet into his bag, and left.

Exhausted and hungry, he hiked along the ridgeline above the lodge. Dusk fell, and with it came a wild symphony from the rainforest that ringed the valley. Birds sang a countless variety of songs that all blended into one constant chatter.

The group of immunes sat around a small campfire nestled within a copse of trees, a few hundred meters past the ridge. They ate noodles in a spicy chicken broth and raw vegetables plucked from the garden behind the house. Skyler sat near the edge of the ring, and stuck to the noodles, in hopes of settling his stomach.

Between swatting insects from his neck and slurping broth, he stole glances at the prisoners they'd freed.

Aside from the child, the others were all adults and in relatively good health. The oldest, a woman with tired eyes and a quiet manner, was perhaps fifty. Skyler doubted she could help in retaking the colony, nor the young girl, but the other ten looked every bit the hardened survivors that he would have expected, five years on since SUBS scoured Earth.

At the end of the meal a bottle of rum was passed around; it had been found behind the driver's seat in one of the armored trucks. By the second time the bottle reached Skyler, much of the somber mood had lifted. Davi laughed freely at a comment from one of the other men, while Ana played an improvised game with the young girl, using rocks and a stick.

Skyler wanted to talk of the next step in the plan, but Davi had been right. There was no harm in letting the freed immunes have a quiet evening before the storm that would follow.

The insects grew increasingly worse as the evening turned to night, and no one wanted to sleep outside. So they divided up into two equal groups and slept inside the armored trucks. Skyler took a driver's seat that, though cushioned, did not recline, and his legs were pressed painfully against the dash. Eventually he gave up and climbed to the roof of the truck.

For a while he kept watch, but when an hour passed with only the constant din of birdsong wafting down from the tree line, he nestled himself amid the frayed backpacks and ragged canvas bags the group had cobbled together. Skyler pulled his jacket up around his head and lay down with his rifle cradled across his chest.

* * *

The smell of toast and strawberries greeted him when he woke.

Dawn had long passed, and the sun hung above the eastern horizon in a crisp, clear blue sky.

Half the group huddled about a cook fire, warming toaster pastries on a slab of charred wood. The sweet, buttery smell made Skyler's stomach growl loud enough for others to hear and turn their heads.

A blue box lay near them, its edges charred. The lid had been torn open, and Skyler could see more of the breakfast pastries within, still wrapped in Preservall bags.

"Found it near the ridge," someone said, munching on one of the golden squares. "Must have been blown a hundred meters by that explosion."

Skyler set himself down beside one of the men and smiled. They offered him two of the pastries straight from the fire.

"One second," Skyler said. He unzipped his backpack and rummaged through it until he found what he wanted. Straightening his face, Skyler produced a handful of instant-coffee packets. A cheer went up around the circle, and Skyler traded with the man offering him the pastries. Two of the treats for a dozen silver-foil packets of powdered coffee.

Within ten minutes, the others came to join them, called by the irresistible smells. Ana and Davi arrived in unison. They were dressed, armed, and breathing hard. Patrol duty, Skyler recognized. He smiled at them. Ana smiled back, Davi did not.

Tomatoes from the garden were roasted on the same wood plank, and Skyler felt like a magician when he produced a fistful of white packets from his bag—salt and pepper. The red fruits were sour and not quite ripe, but with the seasoning they made a perfect counter to the sickly sweet pastries.

Now or never, Skyler decided.

"My name is Skyler," he announced. They all knew this by now; he'd made his introductions to each, and promptly forgotten most of their names. "I came here from Australia, and the Netherlands before that."

All eyes were on him.

"I've spent my years since the disease came traveling all over the globe. Half of it, anyway. Japan, Vietnam, Sri Lanka, India, Russia, Hawaii. Everywhere, really."

For ten minutes he recounted the events that had transpired on the other side of the planet. The Elevator they knew of, but the aura had only been rumor, discounted by everyone gathered. Skyler explained what led to his flight from Darwin to Belém, taking care to point out the sacrifices and heroics of all the others who'd come with them. He also told them of his old crew, and the sacrifice they'd made. "Immunes, like you," he told them. "A voluntary band, six strong at our peak. We had an aircraft and went around looking for, well, whatever those trapped in Darwin needed. There's a million people living there, by some counts, and just like you were trapped in that house, they are trapped in Darwin. Only they can't ever leave. Not really."

Skyler downed the last of his coffee and set the mug at his side. "Some made their way here when the new alien vessel arrived, and they found something remarkable." He told them of the aura towers, and how pockets of safety were now possible for those without the immunity. He explained the lofty goals that Tania, Zane, and the others had set for themselves.

"The future," he said in conclusion, "remains a mystery. If the Builders keep their schedule, according to the scientists they'll be back in twenty months or so. What they bring, or do, this time is anyone's guess. All we know is, we need to get this new colony established, defended, and prosperous before that time arrives."

Everyone stared at him. Total silence, save for a meager cough from the child.

"That's all in jeopardy now. Gabriel, and his . . . people . . . have overrun the camp. They're preventing supplies from being shipped up to orbit, and the people up there will be forced to return to Darwin soon if the siege is not broken."

He left out his larger concern, that of the strange black-clad subhuman he'd seen inside that cave. Routing Gabriel, he knew, would just be the start.

"I need your help," he said. He made sure to look at each of them, and let his gaze linger on Davi. "You know firsthand what this Gabriel character is capable of. I plan to put an end to his group, but I can't do it alone. Will you help me?"

One of the women cleared her throat. Skyler nodded at her.

"I've been held here, or places like this, for over a year," she said, her voice even and thickly accented. "Raped almost weekly." She paused to let those words settle, as if now was the first time she'd admitted it even to herself. "Made pregnant twice, both ending in miscarriage. Held in solitude with no one to talk to except those who came to attack me: Gabriel, and many of his circle."

Skyler felt his hands ball into fists, his jagged fingernails digging into the flesh of his palms. This woman would help—

"I cannot assist you," she said, and Skyler's heart clenched. "I'm sorry, but I can't. I just want to go, to flee and find somewhere quiet to live."

Others were nodding, but some were not.

"What you've been through," Skyler said, "was horrible beyond comprehension. I cannot even begin to imagine the terrible things that have befallen you. But if you walk away now, Gabriel will just continue to do the same to others. He had a dozen of you here, but there are hundreds in Belém and a thousand more in orbit. This is the best chance to stop him before he hurts anyone else."

"I'll come," Ana said. "I'll fight that bastard."

"Me, too," said one of the men in the circle, a short, gaunt man with pale skin and distant blue eyes. He looked at the woman who'd spoken first. "I understand how you feel. I'll fight for you, so that you can have peace."

In the end, four others agreed to join Skyler and Ana. Davi was the last to speak.

He stared for a long time at his twin sister. For her part she alternated glances at Skyler and the ground in front of her, withering under her brother's gaze. Skyler wondered if they'd agreed to leave now that they'd freed their friends, despite the deal they'd made.

Finally Davi shrugged. "Okay," he said. "Let's do it."

Ana closed her eyes, and the hint of a proud smile formed on her lips.

"What's the plan?" Davi asked.

"No plan yet," Skyler admitted. That drew some concerned stares. "I've done enough missions in my day to know that plans are worthless if made too early. We go back to Belém, we scout, and once we have information we choose a tactic and act, immediately."

Whether that assuaged their fears or not, he couldn't say. But within an hour the goodbyes had been said. The two groups, those coming and those not, divided between the two armored trucks and went their separate ways.

Despite initial protest from Davi, Skyler first drove back to the lodge. While his volunteers watched from the humming vehicle, he built a small fire in the dirt just outside the door. When the flames took, he poked a long stick in until the end of it burned, then walked to the house.

Skyler stepped into the building one last time and threw the flaming log onto an old couch pressed against the wall.

By the time they drove from the valley, the entire building was engulfed in flames. A plume of ugly black smoke rose high above the rainforest, marring an otherwise perfect sky.

20

MELVILLE STATION

6.MAY.2283

Tania could not sleep. The semblance of peace that her shared meal with Tim and Zane conjured had already vanished like the bittersweet departure of a good sunset.

The sound of waves, lapping gently on a beach, failed to help, and she'd stopped the sound effect almost as soon as she'd started it.

Eight laps around the central ring hadn't helped, either. She'd run hard, treated the people she passed like an obstacle course, ignoring their concerned stares. If they were concerned for her sanity, or the air she churned through exerting herself, she didn't know, and didn't want to know. The only certainty was the question that waited on their lips: *What's your plan? What are we going to do?*

Greg and Marcus called, at Tim's urging no doubt, and offered to host her on Black Level for a few days. They ran the now-fledgling research station, flush with scientific equipment but lacking in computational power to handle analysis as Green Level was left behind above Darwin. They'd turned to old-fashioned methods—pen and paper, long nights in front of a whiteboard—and seemed wholly reinvigorated by the change in pace. To escape there tempted her more than she cared to admit, even to herself. It still constituted escape, a flight from her responsibilities.

Next Tim offered to find her sleeping tablets from the station's supply rooms. When she declined, he offered to bring her a bottle of wine, an upgrade from chai, apparently. Drowning her failures seemed like a feeble move, though, and so she'd declined that, too.

Sleep lay beyond a barrier of horrors. Every time she closed her eyes, Tania saw an imagined version of the carnage that had befallen her so-called rescue team. She'd sat in bleak silence with Zane, Tim, and a few others, listening in total shock as the team was systematically butchered.

There'd been too much noise on the comm to know for sure what happened. Screams and gunfire and shouts of alarm. A horde of subhumans must have swarmed them the moment they stepped out of the aircraft. An aircraft that had cost her an entire farm platform, and now sat abandoned on Water Road northeast of camp.

A soft knock at her door broke the monotony.

"Go away," she groaned. She knew who it was and found herself in even less of a mood to entertain him.

"It's me: Tim."

Tania sighed, stood, and crossed to the door. She opened it a crack, as if she weren't presentable. Maybe she could pretend to have slept; if anything it would make them worry less about her.

"You look terrible," he muttered. "Um, I didn't mean . . . still can't sleep, eh?"

"Nice to see you, too." His concerned expression remained. He seemed to be staring through her. She had not noticed before, but he showed all the symptoms of sleep deprivation, too. Bloodshot eyes set behind dark rings. "What is it, Tim? Has something happened?"

"Would you come with me?" he asked. "I want to show you something."

"I really should . . ." Her voice trailed off. His tone suggested the visit had nothing to do with their present predicament, but at this point she'd take any distraction over the war for sleep. "Sure, why not?"

He led her in silence to a section of the station called the quad—a large common room that ran the length of four of the station's rings. The wide, open space had deep blue carpet contrasted by walls the color of desert sand, its floor dotted with groups of couches facing in on one another, tables for taking meals, an improvised bar, and two low-quality sensory chambers. Two crewmen sat on as many couches, both quietly reading from well-worn paper books. They barely looked up when Tania and Tim entered. A group of six crowded the small bar, sharing a box of white wine. They motioned for the newcomers to join them, but Tim begged off and continued to the back of the room.

Tucked into one corner was some sporting equipment, all folded up and stowed. Tim rolled out one wheeled piece. It looked like a folding conference table. He fiddled with some latches on it and gave it a shove near the center. The object transformed into a hard green table with perfect white lines and a net dividing the playing surface that dominated the space.

Tim grabbed two paddles and a ball from a small brown bag someone had tacked to the wall, and took the side of the table that faced in on the room, leaving Tania only a view of the walls and Tim himself. He threw one paddle to her.

Tania snatched it out of the air. "I haven't played in—"

"Good," he said in a comically shrill voice. "For I shall destroy you."

She hefted her paddle and took a wide stance at her end of the table, bouncing from foot to foot in what she hoped was a taunting fashion. "Bring it on, tough guy."

"One rule," Tim said. "No talking about air, or water, or the colony."

Tania grinned. "You read me like a book, Tim."

He responded by striking an exaggerated server's pose that looked halfway to something out of an old kung fu movie. He gripped his red paddle upside down in his left hand and glared at her. When Tania chuckled he served, bouncing the white ball past her.

The game was on.

By the third point Tania abandoned a sense of guilt for enjoying herself in such a dire situation. The repetition of the game, at once exhilarating and monotonous, cleared her mind of all other thought.

By the tenth point, she'd worked up a sheen of sweat and found herself wholly engrossed in the friendly battle. It was Tim who halted the game, as he nodded past her shoulder.

Tania turned to see Zane approaching. He looked haggard, as if he'd aged ten years since their meal the previous evening.

His lips formed a thin, grim frown. "I've been looking everywhere for you. Come to the terminal room. Karl is on the line."

"Karl?" Tania blurted, setting her paddle down.

Zane held up a hand. "It's not good news, from the way he sounds. The way he looks."

She nurtured a flicker of hope anyway. The game forgotten, they jogged together to the junction hallway and then toward the room two levels away where the ground-linked comm had been set up. Zane struggled to keep her pace, stopping at one point to steady himself against a wall, his breaths coming in gasps. She slowed for his benefit. "What did he say?"

"Just that he needed to speak with you, *alone*. He wouldn't say anything else."

"Should we wait outside?" Tim asked.

Tania glanced over her shoulder at him. "Why?"

Tim spread his hands. "Karl said 'alone.'"

"So stay quiet and off camera," Tania said, too terse. "I want you both there."

Zane cleared his throat. "Er, he reiterated the 'alone' request a number of times, Tania. I suggest we honor it."

"Fine," Tania said. "But I'll record the conversation so you can review it afterward."

The two men exchanged a glance and kept to her pace.

At the door Tim and Zane stopped and took places on either side, like guards. Tania gave each of them a reassuring pat on the arm and warmed slightly at the smile this earned from Tim. Then she entered the comm room. She sat in the center chair at the desk and held a finger above the hold icon on the screen.

After three long breaths to calm herself, she swept her hair back behind her ears with her left hand.

"Relax," she whispered. Then she tapped the button.

Karl's face did not greet her. Someone else stared back, someone she didn't know. A man, his skin deeply tanned and smooth. Thick black hair parted to one side and closely shaved around the ears, as if he'd just visited a salon. His eyes caught her attention more than anything; brown flecked with yellow, and bright with cunning and vigor.

The man wore a smile so vulpine and false it made her squirm.

"You must be Tania," he said, his voice thickly accented.

"Where's Karl?" she asked. Inwardly she cursed the weakness and confusion in her voice. Tania willed herself to be strong.

"Sent him back to his tent," the man said. "I'm Gabriel."

"Are you in charge there?"

Gabriel's smile broadened, revealing two rows of perfect white teeth. "I suppose so, yeah. Time we talked, I think."

Tania steadied herself. "I'm listening."

"Karl tells me you've got a lot of people up there. People who are in need of supplies?"

Gabriel had an easy manner about him. His voice and body language all said "Trust me" in a way that made her skin crawl. She hadn't felt that since last speaking with Russell Blackfield, though for different reasons. Russell's eyes undressed, but Gabriel's disarmed. She held his gaze and nodded.

"Let me tell you," Gabriel said, "how this is going to play out. I'm what you people call an immune, as are the rest of my family. Though we just think of ourselves as human beings."

Tania couldn't mask her surprise. "Your whole family is immune?"

It seemed impossible, and in answer his smile broadened. "They're not blood, just people I've met over the last five years. Survivors who have joined me, who follow me."

"I see."

"You call us immune, Tania, but our perspective is different. We call you *incerto,* untested. I understand that no one but Karl has taken a breath of air down here, air that hasn't been . . . what's the word you use? Scrubbed? Scrubbed by these alien towers."

He practically spat the word *alien*.

Tania's mind raced. *What have they done with Skyler? Do they not know of his immunity?* Maybe no one had given up that detail. "What are you asking, Gabriel? You *are* asking me something, correct?"

Gabriel spread his hands before the camera. Long fingers bearing gold rings, a flashy watch on his wrist. "Not asking, Tania. I'm telling you how this'll play. Two things are going to happen. First, you and all your friends up there are going to come down here, in groups, and take our test."

"Test?" she asked. "You mean to force us outside the aura."

"Karl did that, and he seems okay other than a bad headache. But there's another option if people fear to breathe the air."

"Oh?"

Gabriel clasped his hands together. "We have kits, found them in a government laboratory outside Rio. They can test for the immunity from a simple blood sample."

Nonsense, Tania thought, but she held her tongue. Anchor Station scientists as well as doctors on the ground sought just such a solution for years after the disease spread, hoping to discover a way to inoculate people, but no such test was ever devised. The engineered disease was simply too alien.

"For those who don't want to step outside the 'aura,' the blood test is their alternative. We'll take them in groups to a ranch near here, with one of your remarkable towers in tow for their safety, test them, and return them."

"Return them?" Tania asked. "What happens if someone is found to be immune?" *Skyler.*

"The 'immunes' will join my family and help find others like us until we're all together as one people."

"You realize there's a million so-called *incerto* in Darwin? Do you plan to go there next?"

Gabriel's eyes glimmered at the prospect. "Someday, maybe. It is our goal to bring everyone immune to the disease together. Earth is ours now, and we must work together to begin again."

He sounded as if he believed it. Tania wondered if what he really craved was the role of hero in such a scenario. Attention, glory, and all the other perks.

Tania said, "What happens when the tests are done?" *What happens to those of us who don't fit into your plan?*

"When everyone has been tested," he said, "you can continue as you have been. However, you will confine yourself to the city of Belém. If we find any of your alien towers beyond the city's edge, we will shoot on sight and keep the towers for ourselves."

"And anyone found to be immune goes with you, whether they wish to or not?"

"Yes. Exactly right."

Tania knew that the odds of immunity were fantastically low. She'd be surprised if anyone was found to have the trait. Anyone except Skyler, of course.

Assuming Gabriel could enforce a blockade on the entire city of Belém, which she highly doubted, the city represented years of supplies and plenty of land to expand to. It would be a long, long time before the fledgling colony would have to test the threat.

But time was not a luxury humanity had. If her calculations were correct, and the Builders stuck to the predicted timeline, they would be back in less than two years. What they sent this time was anyone's guess. "Let's be ready," Neil would have said.

We don't have time for this kind of infighting, Tania thought. Why did no one else seem to realize that?

Perhaps they could test Gabriel's threat much sooner. Get it over with, and then move on.

Unless, she realized, he had a *lot* of immunes with him. She tried to picture this man, wandering the South American continent for five years, fighting off subhumans and wooing every immune he came across. How many could there have been? Darwin had fewer than a dozen. Of course, the city was full of people who had never set foot beyond the aura. It stood to reason there might be a few dozen more hidden within the population, unaware of their special trait. If Gabriel really did have a way to test . . .

The situation might never get that far, she realized. Gabriel offered a chance to bring people to the ground. She had no idea how big his group was, but it seemed unlikely there were enough immunes on his side to stop a full-blown uprising by her colonists. The prospect of violence chilled her, but not as much as it once had. Submission was worse.

"You said there were two things," she said, while her mind worked through all the ramifications.

"Yes," he said, lingering on the s. "I know of one immune among you already. Skyler, I believe he's called."

A knot twisted in Tania's stomach.

"He's been harassing my people, even murdered a few in cold blood, people who sought only to make contact with him. He must be delivered into my custody and face his crimes. Once he's paid his dues, he will join us."

The way he spoke reminded Tania of the stereotypical tough-cop characters in old films. Perhaps this man had been an actor himself, before the fall. "Skyler's not in the camp?"

She regretted her response as soon she'd voiced the words. From the look on Gabriel's face, she'd just confirmed something he'd only suspected.

"No," Gabriel said. "But I'm told you have a strong relationship with him. You will convince him to come back, unarmed. Promise him all is forgiven if he just returns."

"Except that all is not forgiven, right?"

"He doesn't need to know that."

"Skyler will know I'm lying," she said, unsure if the words themselves were true.

"He'd better not, for your sake. From now on, for every one of my people he so much as wounds, I will take ten of yours and tie them up outside the aura until they go mad or the afflicted come for them. Starting with Karl."

"I don't have a way to contact Skyler," Tania said. "How am I supposed to convince him to come in?"

Gabriel shrugged. "I don't care if you stand at the edge of your aura and shout his name all day and night: Just make him listen."

Tania glanced down at the table in front of her and hugged herself below it. "I need some time to think about this," she said.

"No, no," Gabriel replied. "Sorry. I said before, these are not requests. I've set some of your people down here to work clearing the cable so that you can begin shuttling people down here. Start immediately, and you'd better be among the first arrivals. I want this Skyler fellow in my custody before he can do any more damage to our important work."

"I understand. It's just . . . There's logistics to—"

"See you in fifteen hours, Tania."

The screen went blank.

Tania slumped back in her chair and exhaled. An intense pain began to form behind her eyes, and she rubbed the bridge of her nose between thumb and forefinger. "Guys," she called out, "come in here."

"This guy sounds mental," Tim said. "Completely mental."

Zane shook his head. "Be that as it may, we're stuck between him or a return to Darwin. Abandon our people on the ground, or bring everyone down there to face this test."

"The test," Tania said, "and to hand over Skyler. Don't forget that."

"A world of immunes," Tim muttered, not listening to either of them. "Nice vision, I guess, if you ignore the million or so other people living in the aura's shadow."

"Tim," Tania said.

"I mean it," he said. "What a bloody prick! He means to turn Belém into a concentration camp and control the rest of the planet with a superior breed of human. Sound familiar to anyone?"

The comment brought silence to the small room, save for the whir of a fan somewhere behind the wall panels.

"Do we all agree," Tania asked after a moment, "that returning to Darwin is not an option?"

"It's an option," Zane said. "Just not the preferable one."

He and Tania both looked at Tim.

"This Gabriel fellow sounds worse than Blackfield," the young man said.

"So you'd rather go back?" Tania asked.

"I don't know," he admitted. "They both need to be stopped."

"Suppose we just give him what he wants?" Zane said, his voice not much more than a whisper.

Tania glared at him. "Skyler, you mean. Say his name, Zane."

Zane spread his hands. "One man, for the safety of the colony."

"None of us would even be here if not for him."

"Granted. Don't get me wrong, I like the man. He's resourceful, smart. A fighter, and clever as anyone. This Gabriel means to mete out some kind of justice and then have Skyler join his group. If anyone could escape, Skyler could."

"I can't just . . . hand him over. I won't. What if that justice is something like losing a limb?" she asked. Zane's mouth clapped shut and he looked away, contemplating her question. She couldn't believe that he would advocate in favor of going along with Gabriel's demands. Yet the very fact that he was somehow sobered her. She'd come to trust Zane's matter-of-fact opinion on things, his ability to divorce emotion from facts. As a scientist she'd prided herself on being able to do just that, too, all her life.

"Tania," Zane said, an echo of his brother's tone in his voice. "For all we know, Skyler is in the wrong here. Maybe it was a mistake, or an overreaction. We may never know. But what if he really did kill some of these immunes without cause?"

She started to protest but Zane held up his hand. "Just . . . listen. Regardless of how things ultimately end up, Gabriel stated plainly that he will punish innocent colonists if Skyler continues to assault these immunes, correct?"

Tania nodded.

"Then realistically we have no choice," Zane said. "We have to at least go down there and try to defuse this situation. Talk to Skyler, if we can. Come to some kind of agreement. Perhaps if we give Gabriel surplus food or supplies he will let us handle Skyler's punishment. Confine him to orbit, for example, until things return to normal."

"You don't actually believe that."

"I don't know what to believe," Zane said quietly. "All I know is, if we just turn around and go back to Darwin, we've given up this chap Skyler and everyone else down there. But if we go, and talk, and cooperate if it makes sense, we may find a solution that benefits everyone. Including, dare I say it, a solution that includes these immunes working *with* us. Certainly a large group of them would be extraordinarily useful in the coming months."

Tim, Tania realized, had been shaking his head the entire time Zane spoke. She looked at him, beckoned for him to speak.

"This guy is mental," he said again, as if that negated everything Zane had said. It well might, Tania thought.

Zane sighed. "That *guy* has been scrounging out a living for the last five years in this hellish world with no knowledge of the aura in Darwin, no idea that a city full of people still survived. Put yourself in his shoes for a moment. At first he probably thought he was the last man alive. Everyone he knew died or went primal, insane, and psychotic all at once. Five years, surviving, and ultimately finding others like him. Of course they would band together, thinking they're special. They *are* special, for God's sake. I can't begrudge the man the loss of a few marbles. Not after all that."

No one spoke, and Zane went on.

"And then to look up in the sky one day, and see a string of dark shapes moving down from space. He probably thought we were aliens. Still might, quite frankly. The idea of other survivors, large numbers of us, shattered his worldview. It needs time to register. If we talk to him, he'll come around. I'm sure of it."

Put that way, Tania found it hard to argue. But Zane's eagerness to give up Skyler made her see the younger Platz brother in a new light. Neil would never have done that, she thought.

No? Are you sure about that? Neil, at his core, was a businessman. Granted, he protected those he loved, but Skyler? Skyler was a smuggler he'd hired. An asset. Perhaps Neil would have found the terms Gabriel offered acceptable. After all, with the aura towers, Skyler's immunity was not so valuable—

Stop! Tania screamed inside. She shut her eyes tight and fought to banish such thoughts. No price could be affixed to Skyler, or any person.

Yet Zane was at least half-right; she couldn't deny that. Without information, without a chance to talk to Gabriel and evaluate his ability to follow through on what he intended to do, she was helpless. She had to go, had to cooperate. Buy time.

"Tim," she said as she stood. "Get a climber prepped."

21

BELÉM, BRAZIL

6.MAY.2283

Skyler turned off the handheld radio and stared at it.

He wanted to crush it, or dash it against the wall. Both. But all he could do was stare in disbelief. "I understand," she'd said. "It's just . . . There's logistics—"

Logistics? She understands?

Her situation must be dire if she'd agree to such demands. Of course she hadn't expressly agreed, but Skyler saw little point in picking apart the semantics. What she had *not* done was tell Gabriel to rot in hell, that she'd be damned before she subjected her people to his "test," or give him one of her . . .

What? What am I?

A tool, Skyler realized. In Darwin, he could walk beyond the aura and few could follow. But now, in Belém, he was a colonist who happened not to need an aura tower in tow when he bumbled around.

"Knock that off," he hissed to himself.

Tania's only knowledge of Gabriel came from the silver-tongued words he gave her. She had no idea what lay behind the mask. The prison he'd set up for his unwilling immunes, the forced breeding.

And that nonsense about a test for immunity. If it existed, which he wholly doubted, it went up in the fire, or vanished when the barn exploded. Either way, no such test existed, and so Gabriel's promise of a civil option was, in reality, utter bollocks.

But at least he offered to let them live on in Belém after his group moved on with their prize immunes in tow. Skyler had needed all his self-control not to laugh at that part.

None of this matters, he decided. Tania had agreed to hand him over, or else she'd lied. She really believed Gabriel's offer to play nice with those who didn't pass his test, or she suspected treachery but saw no alternative other than a retreat. The only truth in all of it was that Gabriel needed to be stopped, now.

Skyler stuffed the radio in his pocket, stood, and stretched. His ankles and knees cracked with the effort.

He slung his rifle and climbed down the maintenance ladder that provided roof access to the top of the building. A department store, once. Looted and vandalized almost beyond recognition, but the roof was all that mattered. Two kilometers southeast, the colony was just visible between trees and half-collapsed houses.

Out of habit, Skyler paused when his feet met asphalt. He studied the deserted street for a few seconds, but saw nothing, of course. The subhumans, he knew, were all gathered in the rainforest to the east, around that small Builder ship. He'd said nothing of its existence to anyone yet, despite the burning desire to share the discovery. Such revelations would only confuse the immediate goal.

Across the road Skyler jogged down a steep concrete embankment to a man-made river. With the wet season having passed—which in Belém meant it rained only half as often—the basin was mostly hard-packed mud, with a trickle that ran down the center, looking more like chocolate milk than water.

The others were camped beneath a bridge, their tents just silhouettes in the shadows below the overpass.

Ana and two others were awake. Once closer, Skyler recognized them as Elias and Pablo. The three were huddled together over cups of Skyler's instant coffee, heated on a small cap-powered stove as a cook fire might draw attention.

Elias was a soft man. Greasy strands of gray-brown hair were drawn across his nearly bald scalp. He'd probably once been as large as Prumble. Skyler guessed the man had lost half his weight or more in the years since SUBS swept across the world, from the slack skin on his upper arms. Months in captivity under Gabriel had taken a toll as well. He talked with nervous anxiety, and Skyler wondered how useful the man would be in a fight.

Pablo, on the other hand, stood tall and lean, corded with muscle. A curly mess of black hair spilled from the top of his head to his shoulders, over skin so tan and rugged it looked like he'd never spent a day indoors in his life, which was true enough. He'd been a farmer in Colombia and continued in that role for years after the disease took his family and everyone else he knew. His land was isolated, and so he had little trouble from subhumans. Then Gabriel's caravan had come through. Pablo had thanked them for the offer to join up, and asked them to move on. They had, until two men entered his meager home the next night, hog-tied him, and stuffed him into a truck.

Pablo spoke little and seemed perpetually in a dark mood. Skyler had seen him smile only once, a grin that revealed brown, crooked teeth.

"Fifteen hours," Skyler said as he approached.

Ana raised an eyebrow at him. "Until?"

"Until we raise hell," Skyler said. "I don't think they know about the ranch, about all of you. We need to use that to our advantage while we can."

Davi emerged from his tent at the sound of voices. A moment later, the final two members of the motley group appeared as well. Skyler nodded at both of them.

One was Wilson, a Canadian student who had found himself stranded in Brazil at the peak of the disease. He was gawky and socially inept, spoke too loud, and smiled at everything. Skyler had accepted his offer to come along despite a lengthy diatribe about his lack of skill with a weapon. All he could offer, he said, was a hatred of Gabriel and his inner circle. "What were you studying in Brazil? Medicine? Engineering?" Skyler had asked. Wilson had frowned. "Indigenous tribes of the upper Amazon. Useless, I know."

Last was Vanessa, a woman in her early thirties. She might have been a model or actress from her startlingly voluptuous body, but she had an imperfect face—a wide mouth that filled with teeth on the rare occasions that she smiled. In reality she'd been a lawyer, and the daughter of a Brazilian senator. She'd been practicing law when SUBS arrived. Her husband died early on, as did one of her children. The other child had survived the infection to become a subhuman, and she'd been forced to kill the girl, a story she'd told in a quiet voice long drained of any emotion. Skyler suspected she'd suffered more than the others while a captive of Gabriel's. She'd been beautiful once, and though battered and broken from her ordeal she still held an undeniable appeal. Skyler felt like a monster for even harboring such a thought. He could not imagine the horror she'd been through, and she never spoke of it. Her eyes told the story well enough.

"Fifteen hours?" she asked, tying her hair into a bun as Tania often had. Unlike the scientist, Vanessa's beauty seemed to melt away with the change, as if her chocolate hair somehow hid the worry lines, the bruises, the cracked lips and wide mouth. *Give her a Dutch accent,* Skyler thought, *and a bit of gray in that hair, and she could be my twin sister.*

"Yes," he said to all of them. They gathered about, some standing, some sitting. Skyler gestured toward the Elevator camp. "At that time, some of those stranded in orbit, the leadership I suspect, will be coming down the cord to meet with Gabriel. He means to test each of them for the immunity."

"How do you know this?" Davi asked.

Skyler tapped the handheld. "Overheard them."

Ana raised a hand and Skyler nodded to her. "What's this test? And what happens after?"

He sat on an overturned plastic box they'd salvaged as a chair. "Gabriel means to march each of them beyond the aura, see who is affected, and who isn't."

A bleak silence settled on the group. Wilson spoke up. "Won't most of them get infected that way?"

Skyler nodded. "Not as bad as it sounds, though. The initial infection brings on a devastating headache, but if they can get back inside the aura quick enough, the virus goes into stasis, and the headache along with it. They'll still carry that initial infection, yes, but as long as they remain in the aura, they'll be fine."

Davi's brow wrinkled. "That doesn't sound so bad."

"Maybe not," Skyler said. "We're assuming Gabriel and his people will let them back inside fast enough. They might suspect a true immune is faking the headache. It wouldn't be that hard. And some are so overcome by the pain that they collapse, unable to return to safety. Will someone be allowed to help them?"

"Knowing Gabriel," Pablo muttered, "no."

This earned frowns from the group.

"I thought not," Skyler said. "He offered an interesting alternative. Gabriel claims there's a medical test for the immunity, and that the kits to perform it are at 'a nearby ranch.' I assume he means where you all were staying."

"I never saw anything like that," Wilson said. The others nodded.

"So I guessed," Skyler said. "Gabriel probably intends to hold them there, as he held you. I don't think he knows what happened, that you're free. That's good news."

"Why wait?" Ana asked. "Why not attack now, before the people come down?"

Skyler made a point to wait a few seconds before answering. The eagerness in Ana's voice, and her brash actions during the assault on the ranch house, spelled trouble, he thought. If even a brief pause took some of the push out of her, he'd count it as progress.

"When the Orbitals arrive," Skyler said, feeling a twinge of bitter nostalgia at the slang term. "When their climber reaches the ground, Gabriel's people will have their hands full. Lots of colonists to watch, and that moment of heightened alert when the climber doors open. All eyes will be on it. We'll use this to our advantage."

"You have a plan, then, Skyler?" Davi asked.

He nodded, and told them.

Wilson and Vanessa had the least experience in handling firearms. The group balked when Skyler announced he would pair the two, but when he explained their role in the attack the murmuring stopped. This was not the time, Skyler argued, for weapons training, and he felt it best that the group's strengths be used to full effect.

For his part, Wilson didn't seem to mind at all. He had a pacifist's demeanor, and from the way he stole glances at Vanessa, Skyler guessed the kid was already romanticizing the mission to come.

Vanessa just shrugged. "Twenty years of jujitsu," she said with a laugh. "A lot of good that's done me."

He gave the two of them their marching orders and turned to the rest of the group.

Davi, Elias, and Pablo would team together, he explained.

"What about Ana?" Davi asked.

"She's with me," Skyler said. He fixed Davi with a hard stare that he hoped conveyed the reason. Davi would be too distracted with protecting his reckless sister, and Skyler wanted none of that. Young as he was, Davi had proved himself in combat, and all of that skill would be needed.

Whether the young man understood or not, Skyler couldn't tell. Davi looked to Ana, studied her, then turned back to Skyler and gave a grudging nod.

"You three," Skyler said, "will come in from the west. Ana and I, from the east. We move when Wilson and Vanessa's distraction is in full swing."

"And when do we start?" Wilson asked.

Skyler glanced upward. "When you see the first vehicle from space about to reach the bottom. Say, twenty meters from the ground. We'll give Gabriel and his people as many problems to juggle as possible, and use their confusion to our advantage."

The finer points of the plan were laid out, debated, refined. Elias commented twice that it would be better if everyone stayed together, but the rest of the group liked Skyler's plan. Come from every side, split up and confuse the enemy, get the colonists to join the fight from within.

An hour later, Skyler and Ana set out. Their trek was the longest, and Skyler had a few things he wanted to scavenge along the way. No goodbyes were said when they left, just some quiet well-wishes. Ana gave her brother a peck on each cheek, and tousled his hair when his frown didn't vanish.

"Be safe," Davi said to her, but his eyes were on Skyler.

"The greatest treasure in all of Belém," Skyler said with a mock bow.

Ana peered inside the building with a skeptical frown.

"I'll show you," he added, and wiggled through the security gate he'd torn open a month earlier with a crowbar. A gate that had, for years, saved the store and its contents from looters.

The dusty beam of his flashlight swept across a large banner hung on the back wall. AVENTURA NA AMAZÔNIA, it read. And below, SUPRIMENTOS DE SOBREVIVÊNCIA.

Row upon row, rack after rack, of high-end quality camping and survival gear lay before them.

Ana whistled, her eyes wide. *Exactly how I felt,* Skyler thought. He'd found the building ten days after initial landfall. Windows boarded, doors chained. Pristine, if a bit musty.

The girl crept inside and strolled slowly down the nearest aisle, past rolled sleeping bags, air mattresses still in boxes, tents of every size and color, and bundled blankets. She ran her hand along an entire wall of hiking boots, and picked up a bundle of climbing rope, price tag still attached. Skyler left her to wander, grabbed a fresh duffel bag from one shelf, and set about finding the items his plan required.

When Ana returned to him she sported a new vest, a pair of sunglasses, and a water bottle with filtration built into the cap. A confused smirk grew on her lips as she watched Skyler strip two mannequins of their fashionable survival gear.

"You want us looking good when we attack?" she asked.

In answer he disassembled the mannequins and stuffed their torsos and heads inside his bag. Her smirk turned to a knowing smile when she saw the rest of the duffel's contents.

"Let's go," Skyler said. "Plenty of time to ransack this place later."

"Just a second," Ana replied. She went to a rack near the cash registers and selected two more items: a pair of thin, tight leather gloves and a wide-brimmed olive-green hat.

"My hands get sweaty," she explained. "When I hold a gun, I mean. And now that the rains have gone, the sun makes me squint."

She put the hat on and stuffed the black gloves into the new vest she'd pilfered, a journalist's vest in desert tan. When she realized Skyler was watching her, she flashed him a thumbs-up and winked. In that moment she looked markedly younger than her twenty-two years, so much so that Skyler toyed with the idea of leaving her here, safe and out of harm's way. Hadn't she earned the right to that foolish abandon only young people can get away with? Those years had been robbed from her, after all. The battle to come was too much to ask of someone who'd lost what she had. Her parents, her world. Her youth. And even if they succeeded it would only be to face the thing that loomed in the rainforest. The cave. The black-clad subhuman with glowing red eyes.

But when her smile vanished, Skyler saw only Ana the survivor. She became a woman of startling maturity, a woman who'd been through unimaginable terrors over the last five years. That a fire of youthful recklessness still burned in there filled Skyler with a sudden sadness that he couldn't explain. The world he knew had no room for innocence anymore. Maybe that's why he'd never had similar thoughts concerning Samantha. All the innocence had long since been bled out of her. Somehow Ana still clung to it with a white-knuckled grip.

For the next few hours he led her on a winding path through Belém's ruined streets. Rain, the mortal enemy of asphalt, had turned the avenues and alleys into a moonscape of potholes and cracks. Littered on top were derelict vehicles of every size and shape. Trucks, cars, and buses. Many flipped on their side, or impaled into the side of a building. Some had skeletons inside, and more littered the road.

Skyler shook his head. Much of the carnage that occurred in those first days of the disease was due to panic and mass hysteria. A few infections in a city like this, even just the rumor of such, would have spurred the entire population into a desperate race to flee, riot, or hide. He'd mused, in nightly debates with Skadz during their own surreal journey to Darwin, that the disease's reputation had been just as deadly as the brain-crushing infection it carried. Skadz, the first immune Skyler met after discovering his own invulnerability to the disease, had a knack for stating things plainly. "We humans are a skittish bunch, that's a fact," the *Melville*'s original captain had said.

Soon they reached the city's border, where urban press met the imposing green wall of the rainforest, like two armies frozen in the initial clash of their front lines. Buildings and shanty homes gave way to a wall of emerald trees that fronted the dark, endless forest.

He paused there and glanced up at the zenith of the sky. Ana, at his shoulder, did the same.

A few meager clouds dotted the vast blue expanse, but above the view was clear. He thought he could see the Elevator cord, or hints of it. The hair-thin cable was hard to detect when no traffic marked its path, and his eyes often played tricks on him when he sought it. Being so close to the equator, Belém's cord didn't slope nearly as much as Darwin's did, but that didn't make the task much easier. Straight up still wasn't quite the right place to look. He scanned the sky for a moment just to be sure. There were no climbers yet visible. Tania, if she was indeed coming, was still hours away.

"Plenty of time," he said. "Let's keep moving."

Skyler followed a deliberately wide route toward their destination, always with a wary eye on the cloud that clung to the forest canopy a few kilometers south. The white haze loomed well off to their right, visible through the occasional break in foliage. If Ana saw the strange fog, she didn't mention it.

That place should be our focus, he thought. If Gabriel had brought a thousand trained killers down on the base camp, it wouldn't fill Skyler with the same dread as the subhuman he'd seen inside the cave. But he knew the colony must be liberated first if they were to have any hope of finding out the nature of that creature, and the ship from which it came.

The sun shimmered low on the horizon when their path brought them to the shore of the Guamá. With wet season gone, and the worst of the rains with it, the river's angry brown churn had given way to a more tranquil surface that reflected some of the sky above.

He glanced up again. At the sky's zenith, a small dark object seemed to hang in the sky, like the opposite of a star. "There they are," he whispered.

Ana put her hand on his back. "How long do we have?"

"Two hours. Maybe three."

They took a ten-minute break from their hike. Ana produced two granola bars from her backpack and handed Skyler one. They ate in silence, both watching the climber above. After he finished the tasteless snack, Skyler swallowed a few gulps of cool water from his canteen, and Ana copied him.

He turned off the dirt road when he found a game trail through the dense foliage near the shore. Thick vines and roots lined the ground like veins, and branches spanned the narrow trail every few meters. Their pace slowed to a crawl, but Skyler wasn't worried.

An hour later he spotted the smuggler's boathouse. He led Ana inside and instructed her to be silent for a moment. For five long minutes he sat perfectly still, crouched in the doorway of the tiny shed, listening. Birds, whispering branches, and the gentle lapping of the river against the shore were all he heard.

"Let's get to work," he said, and closed the door.

22

BELÉM, BRAZIL

6.MAY.2283

An hour later, the inflatable raft slipped out from the boathouse and into the river's current.

The two occupants sat side by side, facing the northern shore. One hunched over a hunting rifle, the other at the sniper's shoulder, a pair of binoculars pressed to a hooded face.

Skyler and Ana watched the boat drift away. In the waning sun, the mannequins looked a bit silly to his eye. He could only hope that the craft would drift out from the shore far enough that the ruse would work. If it bought them ten seconds of confusion, he'd consider the effort worthwhile.

"It's moving fast," Ana noted, an urgency in her voice.

And she was right. The current picked up pace a few meters from the shore, and in no time the boat began to bounce along nearly twice as fast as the leaf Skyler had used as a test run. If the craft beat them to base camp, and the diversion worked, it would be wholly wasted.

Skyler ran. He swept aside vines and ducked under branches, tripped twice on roots. Ana, right on his heels, helped him up the first time, and toppled onto him the second. She giggled as they untangled themselves.

Soon the game trail turned north, and Skyler had no choice but to push into the dense foliage that stood between them and base camp. He shot alternating glances at the tiny raft, which drifted along thirty meters ahead of them, and the climber car that ambled down the Elevator cord straight ahead. The vehicle was only a few hundred meters from the ground now and seemed to be racing the sun to the horizon. The sky blazed crimson, putting the climber in stark silhouette.

Skyler turned to Ana and raised a finger to his lips. A few steps later they came upon the stream that bordered the colony on its eastern edge. Skyler did not stop to look at the camp, tempting though it was to study the enemy's positions. He turned sideways and jogged down the embankment, one hand trailing the sloped mud wall for balance. Ana stopped at the top, her eyes wide as she took in the tent city on the other side of the stream, but her senses returned soon enough and she bounded down the slope. Skyler waited at the bottom for her to break her momentum, lest she splash into the meter-deep rivulet and give their approach away.

At the bottom of the ditch, Skyler unslung his rifle and made sure it was loaded, half his attention on Ana as she did the same. In the dwindling light, her expression showed no fear. He even saw a hint of a smirk on the corners of her mouth. When she flashed him the a-okay, her eyes sparkled.

He wanted to grab her by the shoulders and impress on her the danger they were about to walk into. He wanted to tell her this all wasn't some game. And he wanted to kiss her, he realized, a desire he quickly banished to the farthest corner of his mind.

Skyler shambled up the other side of the sloped ditch on his hands and knees, using his fists to keep dirt and debris from clumping on his palms and fingers. He crawled the last meter until his head just poked above the slope and the camp came into view.

The colonists all sat on the ground on the southern edge of camp, near the river. Skyler counted three armed guards circling them, weapons held at the ready. One of Gabriel's APC's was parked near the prisoners, its bright headlights trained on them.

Most of the captives sat facing away from the blinding beams, which left their faces in shadow. Even from here, two hundred meters away, Skyler could tell they sat on their hands. He wondered if they were bound, but he thought it unlikely.

Behind the glow of the vehicle's lights, he thought he could see the outline of one more guard, sitting atop the vehicle.

And beyond that, he saw the barricaded pen that housed the aura towers. The alien devices were crowded together. Too many of them, Skyler thought. Gabriel and his people must have gathered as many as they could, taken down Mercy Road and Water Road in an effort to give their prisoners nowhere to run.

At the center of the camp stood perhaps ten of the immunes, black-clad and armed. They arrayed themselves in a loose circle, centered on the base of the Elevator—the black alien disk that resembled a gear laid on its side. Portions of the intruders' circle were obscured by the large tents and modified cargo containers that ringed the Elevator's connection point.

Around the northern edge of the colony, the bulk of Gabriel's vehicles were still parked in a wide half circle, only now they faced outward. Their headlights were off, and in the half-light of the setting sun Skyler couldn't tell how many guards patrolled there. At least as many as in the circle around the Elevator, perhaps more. A handful of aura towers were interspersed between them, giving the border an odd similarity to a castle wall.

"Do you see Gabriel?" he whispered to Ana.

"Not yet," came her reply. "Wait, there, near the—"

A shout went up. Skyler almost leapt out of his skin at the sudden noise.

The yell came from the southern edge of camp, near where the prisoners sat. He glanced there and motion in the river caught his eye. A raft.

The raft! He'd almost forgotten. The inflatable boat ambled along, fifty meters offshore. In the near darkness the ruse couldn't look more perfect. Two shadows, and just the hint of a rifle poking out from one. A BB gun, in truth. Skyler smiled.

The guards near the prisoners shouted and pointed, and those near the center of camp yelled back. A few broke from the circle to run in that direction.

"Get ready," Skyler said.

"Oh, no," Ana whispered.

He was about to ask her what she meant when the rocket launched.

It came from the vehicle that stood sentry over the prisoners. Or, rather, from the guard who sat atop. A deep *WHUMP* preceded the launch, a sound Skyler knew well from the Purge. Then blinding light from the projectile's tail put the entire camp in daylight for a scant second. A single second was all the time it took for the weapon to knife through the air, hissing as it flew, leaving a straight line of smoke in its wake.

The raft erupted in a fireball that roiled up into the sky, reflected in the water below. Bits of raft and debris rained down into the river and onto shore.

Then the shooting started.

Gunfire rattled from the southwest, toward the docks. Davi, Pablo, and Elias, too far away to see, had started their attack early.

Skyler glanced northwest. "C'mon, Wilson. Where are you?"

He saw nothing there, heard nothing. As with any battle plan, Skyler recognized the moment when it all went out the window. "Time to improvise," he muttered, and came to a crouch. "Cover me."

In answer Ana settled onto the slope, her rifle at the ready. Inside its grenade launcher were the last three rounds they had, and her role would require the use of each.

Skyler ran at a crouch to the nearest tent, aware that the camp now flirted with chaos, exactly as he'd hoped. Gabriel's people were in disarray. Some held their circle near the camp's center, some ran for the river, others for the docks where gunfire still raged.

When he reached the tent, Skyler went to a knee and glanced back, ready for Ana to unleash her first grenade.

She wasn't there. He scanned the embankment in both directions and saw no sign of her.

"Shit, shit," he muttered. Where the hell was she? He felt trapped, caught between the urge to go back and find her, and the desire to press on. He knew she wouldn't have spooked and retreated. More likely, she'd run headlong into the northern portion of the camp, the recklessness Davi had warned about on full display. Maybe it had been a mistake to ask her to sit on the periphery and attack from afar.

A horrific sound whipped Skyler's attention around. The smash of metal and breaking glass, followed by a wrenching grind so loud it made his teeth hurt.

For a split second he thought the climber had fallen to the ground, and his heart skipped a beat at the idea of Tania inside, falling to her death. But when he glanced up he saw the vehicle above, still dawdling downward, now just thirty meters from the ground.

It would make landfall in less than a minute.

One of Ana's grenades, then. Perhaps she'd stayed put, after all, and he'd just lost track of her. According to the plan she was to put her explosive rounds into three of the trucks that guarded the northern edge of camp, forcing Gabriel and his people to devote precious resources to defending that angle.

Somewhere west of him he heard screams of pain, and more shooting.

A guard ran past, just meters away, heading toward the river. He saw Skyler and tripped in surprise, fumbling a handgun into the dirt as he went down. Instinct took over and Skyler fired, twice, into the man's torso. His position would be known now, so he ran.

From tent to cargo container to tent, Skyler weaved an erratic path that brought him closer to the center of camp. Fighting raged on the opposite side of camp, where Davi and the other two men were tasked with spearheading the attack.

People were shouting all around now.

Skyler ducked inside an empty tent and knelt to catch his breath. He would assume for now that Ana had simply moved to get a better angle for her part of the plan. That meant only Wilson and Vanessa were unaccounted for. Their task, to crash the captured enemy APC into a building a few hundred meters from camp, in hopes of drawing Gabriel's people out to investigate, should have started the overall attack. Perhaps the inflatable raft's arrival had preempted that, and so one ruse had caused the other to go ignored.

He could only hope they were okay. The two were supposed to crash the vehicle, then retreat to a safe distance, avoiding combat unless absolutely necessary.

Another explosion rocked the ground beneath him, sent him to one hand. Ana. *Good work, girl.*

Outside the tent the air smelled of smoke. A chorus of angry voices could be heard from the south side of the camp where the prisoners were being held. He hoped they'd joined the fight, but he had no way to know just now.

The climber car loomed just ten meters from the ground now, and Skyler surged forward. If Gabriel and his closest lieutenants held the base, at best Tania would become a hostage, at worst a casualty. He couldn't let either happen.

The vehicle slipped behind a cargo container and out of view. Skyler pumped his legs, throwing caution aside.

A third explosion tilted the ground beneath him.

He staggered, found his footing, and raced on. A woman in black combat gear appeared in front of him, her face hard and sly. He didn't hesitate, firing at her in a wild yet effective burst. The woman dove aside, a bullet ripping through her leg. Her own salvo missed, a line of dirt eruptions in the ground between them.

Skyler fired again, intent to put her out of the fight for good. He saw the other attacker too late.

The butt of a rifle caught Skyler in the stomach. Air rushed from his lungs and he could do nothing but curl into a ball as the sounds of battle raged around him.

As he fought for breath he felt himself being dragged through the dirt. His mind screamed to fight, to escape from whoever pulled him through the muck, but his body refused to do anything but breathe. Everything else seemed to fall away.

Suddenly he saw Tania in front of him. She knelt on the alien surface at the Elevator's base, the open hatch of the climber behind her. Tears lined her cheeks.

Skyler tried to reach for her, but his arms wouldn't cooperate. They were being held, gripped so tight he could feel his hands going numb. His legs lay in the dirt, but something or someone held his torso from the ground. The position bent his back in a growing agony. He glanced left and felt a lance of pain from his skull. Blood trickled into his eye, stung, and he blinked hard with little effect. He shut the eye and looked right instead. There he saw the boot and pant leg of one of Gabriel's immunes, a carbon combat knife sheathed in leather strapped to the thigh. The man held Skyler by the armpit, his grip like a vise, and Skyler realized another most be holding his left arm. It occurred to him then that some time had passed. Ten seconds or a minute? An hour? He had no idea how long the crack to his skull had knocked him out, but there was still the sound of gunfire in the distance.

Someone knelt in front of Skyler, boots crunching the dirt beneath. He turned and saw Gabriel's face, eye level with his. The man tilted his head, studying his captive. "Can you talk?" the immune asked.

Skyler spat in his face. He heard Tania gasp in shock.

The leader of the band of immunes made no effort to wipe the spittle away. He just frowned. "I'm not sure how I've wronged you, friend, but your actions are uncalled for. Call off your fighters, please, and we'll sort this mess out."

One eye closed tight, Skyler did his best to meet the man's intense stare. "Sergeant Zagallo," he said. He laughed at the confused expression on Gabriel's face, a chuckle that came out more as a gravelly cough. "Go fuck yourself, monster."

Realization dawned on Gabriel's face. His frown deepened, and he rose to his feet. As Skyler watched, Gabriel stepped to one side, bringing Tania into view. There were others behind her, cramped inside the climber.

Gabriel raised a handgun and pointed it at Tania's temple. She whimpered, her eyes closed now. "Call them off, or this one dies first."

"No need," someone said from outside the circle. Another group of guards arrived. One prodded Pablo forward, and the tall man stumbled into view. His hands were bound in front of him, and Skyler could see a trickle of blood running down his arm. *Elias? Davi?*

"Is it over?" Gabriel asked.

The guard in charge of Pablo nodded. "More from the ranch were with him. They're all dead."

Ana. Skyler felt a rage boil within him. He squirmed, only to incur tighter grips on both his arms. He tried to kick, and found his legs had been bound.

"Good, that's . . . good," Gabriel said, lowering his gun. He looked at someone behind Skyler. "You can silence him," he said.

Skyler closed his eyes and waited for the bullet that would end his life. Instead he heard the telltale sound of duct tape being unrolled and torn. The strip came over his head and was pulled across his mouth, then smacked hard for good measure.

Tania finally spoke. "What are you going to do with him?"

"That's a decision for tomorrow," Gabriel replied. "Right now we've got a little test to perform and I think we'll start with you."

Tania began to protest when another of the immunes grabbed her by the upper arm. She winced and tried to pull away, to no effect.

"Take her beyond this 'aura,'" Gabriel said. "Diego, bind the ones inside this sardine can and bring them next. After that, the ones down by the river, ten at a time."

Skyler tried in vain to free his arms again. When he looked up, Gabriel was kneeling in front of him once more.

"With any luck," he said, "we'll be done by morning. And then I'll decide what to do with you."

A sound caught the man's attention. The other guards came alert, too.

The whine of an electric motor, running at full power. Heavy wheels crunching over dirt and rubble.

Skyler heard a distant shout, from the northwest, the direction in which they'd begun to march Tania.

The man holding Tania by the arm cried in alarm, and then came a horrific sound. A deafening smash, metal grinding against metal, glass shattering. It came from the edge of camp, Skyler judged, and though he could only see darkness there, he knew with a certainty what made the noise.

Wilson and Vanessa. Late to the party, they must have ditched the plan of crashing their vehicle a few hundred meters down the road. Such a diversion would achieve little now, so they must have aimed the vehicle straight at the camp. Risky as hell, Skyler thought, and something he would have done himself.

Everyone in the circle, even Gabriel, hunched down

instinctively at the gut-wrenching sound of the crash. Skyler guessed the runaway truck had collided with one of Gabriel's own vehicles, and so the diversion had ended before it even really began.

But then he heard another *WHUMP* from the south, and the center of camp lit up as a rocket flare hissed just over their heads. Shadows swept across everything in opposition to the blinding light that whooshed across the camp.

The two guards who held Skyler ducked on instinct. He felt their grips loosen in tandem, and he should have run, but he couldn't help himself in following the rocket as it sped to its target.

Everything seemed to slow to a crawl.

Skyler watched in numb horror as the plume from the rocket lit the scene. The projectile flew wide, too high and too far left of the crashed APC.

Its path took it straight into the side of an aura tower.

"No!" someone screamed.

Skyler winced as the rocket exploded against the alien monument. Fire and smoke roiled across and around the device, and the entire mass moved backward a meter from the impact.

A half second of shocked silence fell across the camp. Skyler's guards momentarily forgot their task to hold him. He gripped the tape across his mouth and was about to tear it away when a horrifying sound began.

A deep, mechanical moan, so low it came more as a vibration felt in the gut than in the ear. He'd never heard a sound so ominous, so sinister, before.

It only grew worse. Louder. Deeper, impossibly deep.

He had no doubt it came from the tower that still smoked from the rocket's explosion. If the projectile had done any damage at all, Skyler couldn't see it, as darkness once again enveloped that side of camp.

When the other towers began to echo the anguished noise, Skyler felt a terror so deep he wanted to run. Some did, and panic began to take hold. He saw Tania, just meters away from him, her hands clasped over her ears. Gabriel stood next to her, mirroring her stance, though in one hand he still held a pistol.

And still the sound grew. Louder, deeper.

The ground began to shake. Dirt and dust loosened from the walls of the cargo containers.

Someone near Skyler fell to their knees and vomited. Two others tried frantically to flee, their hands against their ears, only to collide with each other.

Still the sound grew.

And then the camp began to glow. Red, green, and yellow, from different directions. Purple, brightest of all, from the south. Skyler looked at the towers arrayed along the northern perimeter of the camp and saw their black surfaces laced with glowing lines.

"What's happening?!" someone shouted. *Gabriel*, Skyler thought. The voice could barely be heard, and no one answered.

Skyler risked his sense of hearing to yank the tape from his mouth, wincing as it tore stubble from his young beard and skin from his chapped lips. The vibration from the noise shook his knees, and he stumbled to one side, into a guard. The man hardly noticed, and Skyler saw a handgun holstered at the man's hip.

He wrapped his fingers around the grip, pushed down and forward to release the gun from the holster, and pulled it free. The guard finally realized what was happening and gripped Skyler's wrist.

Only then did Skyler notice the fog.

The cloud enveloped the camp with astonishing speed. Within seconds Skyler could see almost nothing. The man he grappled with, and nothing else.

People were shouting, screaming. He couldn't hear anything except the tortured, steady moan the aura towers gave off.

The sound began to change. The deep groan remained, but a new voice emerged, higher and yet somehow more terrifying. A second later, a third voice joined. Then a fourth.

Skyler used his free hand to chop the guard across the throat, and when his shooting hand came free he pressed the pistol against the man's temple and fired. The bark from the weapon sounded dull and distant in the press of the towers' noise.

His legs still bound, Skyler dropped to the ground. The motion made him dizzy, his head pounded. They'd wrapped duct tape around his ankles and knees. Without a knife, the quickest way to freedom was to simply unwind the gray binding. He set the pistol in the dirt at his side and worked at the tape with his fingertips. The fog draped his world so completely now that he could not see his own hands working at his bound knees.

"Skyler!" he heard someone shout. *Tania? Ana?*

He dare not reply, not until his legs were free. His fingertips shook with fear and adrenaline. They groped along the slick tape and found no edge to pry. He wanted to scream in frustration.

Skyler remembered something. He rolled in the dirt to his right until he collided with the slain guard. He slid his hands along the man's limp leg until they brushed the combat knife. Skyler drew it free and sawed through the tape that bound his legs.

He bounced to his feet, coiled in a low crouch. The fog left him with only a meter of visibility, if that. Every direction looked the same.

The pistol. He dropped to his knees again and patted the ground. Someone ran past him and stepped on his fingers. Skyler yelped and pulled his hand back, shaking away the pain. He felt like a fool.

A shape emerged from the fog in front of him. A person.

Gabriel. Their eyes met and Skyler lashed out with the knife, but Gabriel moved quicker. The man lunged forward and tackled Skyler to the ground.

He was fast, relentless. Skyler scarcely hit the dirt when the first punch landed on his jaw. It rattled his skull, and the second blow was worse. A fist caught him above his eye, splitting skin.

Skyler felt the world slipping away as the third blow landed. He tried to raise an arm to block his face, but Gabriel smacked it aside. He straddled Skyler now, his fists up before his face as if they were in a boxing match. Three more punches landed in rapid succession, and Skyler's entire head felt like one massive bruise.

He heard something odd, a new sound above all the others, like a bulldozer rushing headlong through a pile of debris. The noise grew and grew, and beneath it he could hear shouts of alarm, screams of pain.

Gabriel stopped his assault and glanced around. Then a person loomed up behind him. Tania, and she held something in her hand. A length of pipe or a—

She swung viciously and the metal smacked into Gabriel's

neck just below the ear. He grunted through clenched teeth, his eyes unfocused. The impact wrenched the bar from Tania's hands, and she took a step back, suddenly frightened as Gabriel turned to see her. He thrust an arm out to try to grab her, his fingertips brushing the fabric of her pant leg.

Run! Skyler thought, and miraculously she did.

The opening might be Skyler's last, and he took it. The knife was still in his hand, and he flipped it around and plunged it into Gabriel's side, just above the waist. The man wore a thick police-style vest, though, and the blade's tip failed to push through.

"Motherfucker," Gabriel said as his attention swung back.

Skyler stabbed again. This time he aimed for the leg, and felt grim satisfaction as the blade buried itself up to the hilt in Gabriel's thigh. He felt it slide through muscle and then the sickening scrape as it slid off bone.

Gabriel grunted, winced, and then Skyler twisted the knife.

"EIIAAHHHHHH!" the man bellowed, so loud everyone in the camp might have heard it, if not for the cacophony of grinding metal and destruction that grew ever louder.

Head swimming, Skyler had just enough focus to lurch his knee upward. The move toppled Gabriel into the dirt, and the man barked in pain, the knife wrenching again as he rolled on top of it.

Skyler staggered to two feet. He knew he could not fight anymore. He could barely compel his limbs to move.

A pillar of brilliant purple glow emerged from the fog. An aura tower, alive with lines of light traced along its surface. A tent, poles and ropes and all, draped across the obelisk's base, along with various other debris.

Skyler held a hand out to push back on the tower, a technique he'd mastered in the last few months.

The tower kept coming. It bathed him and everything around him in a surreal, purple glow. It pushed him back and he stumbled over Gabriel, who had been attempting to crawl away. Skyler fell backward and just managed to break his fall with an elbow. A stinging sensation raced up and down his arm.

The tower did not pause. It continued to drift forward, and pushed Gabriel aside like a toy. The man cried out again, a noise that brought sudden focus to Skyler's mind. Despite the chaos around him, Skyler crawled around the gliding aura tower and over to Gabriel. He ripped the knife out of the man's thigh and gripped it with both hands.

Gabriel sensed the blow about to fall and raised one arm. "Not like this," he muttered.

"Yes," Skyler said, plunging the blade into the man's neck. "Exactly, like this."

The dying man pawed at the hilt of the knife weakly for a brief second, then slumped to the dirt, lifeless.

From Skyler's left came the sound of wrenching metal, and he saw the hint of another tower there, or rather the shimmer of emerald-green light on its surface. The alien object moved in unison with the one Skyler had just crawled away from. It collided with one of the cargo containers near the camp's center, and shoved the massive metal box aside as if it had been made of cardboard.

More of the alien objects came drifting into view.

All Skyler could do was to curl into a fetal ball and wait for the towers to pass him by. The fog began to thin a little then, and he saw many towers alive with emerald light disappear into the distance. Confused, Skyler came to his knees and glanced around. He saw another large group of towers, this one shimmering with yellow lines. They moved off at a slightly different angle to the first set.

As the fog receded, so did the sounds of battle, leaving behind a haunting mixture of screams, shouts for help, and sporadic coughing. Some of that would be from people suddenly outside the protective auras, the towers once protecting them now gone.

He knelt for a minute in the center of camp, near the Elevator, unsure what to do. Debris littered the ground. Bodies lay everywhere, some limp, some moving. A woman wandered in a daze. He smelled smoke, and blood, and churned earth. A voice in his head screamed at him to get up, to take action, but his legs wouldn't move. His hands shook uncontrollably. He looked down at them and watched, as if they belonged to someone else. Then he curled his fingers in, made fists tight enough that his fingernails drew blood, and willed calm. He closed his eyes, tried to focus on his breathing and ignore all the injuries he'd suffered.

When he cracked his eyelids again, he saw things with a bit more clarity. *Ana,* he thought. A pang of guilt hit him for thinking of her first. *Tania,* he corrected himself. She'd saved him. She'd come after Gabriel with a pipe and given him his chance. "Tania!"

"Here!" A weak voice, somewhere to his right. A cough followed the words, and for a split second he wondered if the Elevator's aura had failed as well.

He stumbled in the direction of her voice, calling her name one more time. The fog had all but vanished, and he finally saw her, hunkered down just inside the climber car. The climber itself, an eight-pronged scaffold built to lift cargo to orbit, had come down with only one car attached, the one Tania rode. The other arms of the vehicle were empty, and three were now badly bent.

The personnel car itself was tilted to one side and bore a long scrape across its surface.

Skyler came to the door. Tania reached out for him and he took her hand.

"The towers," he said sharply. "Tell me how you feel. Headache? Strange thoughts?"

"My God," she whispered, "your face."

"That handsome, eh?" he sputtered more than said. She was okay. Despite the towers' abrupt departure, the aura provided by the Elevator still held.

Tania laughed in relief, a pained sound. Tears were on her cheeks.

"Are you okay? Can you walk?" he asked her. More people were behind her, crowded within the dark space. "We should survey the camp."

Tania grimaced and shook her head. "Twisted my ankle, I think, when he tried to grab me. What's happening, Skyler? Did we lose them all?"

"I don't know yet. Most, I think. Some colonists were surely left outside the aura. Stay here. I'll come back."

"Don't go—"

"I have to," he said, too stern. Tania nodded, a grave look on her face.

He gave her shoulder a gentle squeeze and walked away to survey the camp.

23

BELÉM, BRAZIL

6.MAY.2283

Skyler cupped his hands over his mouth and roared, "Everyone to the Elevator! Now!"

He made his way south, where most of the towers had been, and where part of the colony extended past the aura provided by the Elevator. The survivors he passed, though dazed or injured, seemed free of the disease. At least, then, the Elevator still provided protection.

Ahead someone screamed. Others cried out in alarm. Skyler began to sprint, ignoring every ache and injury on his body.

When he rounded a half-fallen tent the tower yard came into view. Skyler froze in his tracks. "Oh hell," he whispered.

Well over one hundred towers had been there before, the rest employed along Water Road and Mercy Road.

Now he counted only twelve. They stood in a tight bunch, like some kind of tribute to Stonehenge. "Spread the towers out!" he shouted.

A number of colonists were in the area, but none of them heeded his order. They were all focused on something off to Skyler's left. He glanced that way and saw a colonist near the river. A man he thought, though it was too dark to tell for sure. The person staggered in erratic directions, hands clasped over his ears, moaning from abject torment.

Skyler had seen this many times before, most recently with Karl on that first trip down to Belém. He went to raise his rifle, only to realize he'd neglected to pick it up. And the knife—he'd left the knife buried in Gabriel's neck.

As the man near the river screamed in sheer agony, Skyler turned and searched the partially collapsed tent nearby. He found no weapon but did find a thick, polished walking stick made of hard wood. Good enough, he decided, and grabbed it.

Skyler strode toward the infected man with calm resolve. He knew it was too late for the poor bastard. Already the man acted more like a creature than a person. He still wailed from the pain between his ears, but he crouched now, and in his few fleeting moments of near-human clarity his eyes remained wild.

"Everyone get to the Elevator," Skyler said as he passed a few colonists standing slack-jawed nearby. "Or look away, at least. You don't want to see this."

Skyler walked right up to the subhuman, wound up, and swung. The walking stick hit the creature full in the face in a sickening, meaty thud. The sound of the impact was wet and marked with the crunch of bone and broken teeth. Skyler knew better than to pull punches when it came to subs, so he'd swung as hard as his aching limbs would allow. Hard enough, it turned out, to lift the man from his feet and send him sprawling into the water of the river, limp as a rag doll.

The current tugged at the body, gradually pulling it in until the corpse floated away from shore.

Somewhere behind Skyler one of the colonists broke into sobs. Someone who'd known the man, Skyler guessed. He threw the walking stick on the ground at his feet and stared numbly at the rippling water. Nothing could be done about it now.

The colonists behind him took the hint, finally, and backed off to a safe distance from the Elevator base, no longer trusting the few remaining towers. Skyler wandered back toward the center of camp, listening and looking for more subhumans. He found none, and for that he felt an immense relief.

An hour passed and he still hadn't pieced together exactly what had happened. Every person he spoke with, those who weren't tending to the wounded or in some state of shock, told only bits of the story, often conflicting with what others said.

Of his immunes, Vanessa found him first. Skyler's knees buckled at the sight of her, partly from simple relief and partly because it gave him hope that Gabriel's henchman had lied and more were alive. Vanessa had one forearm wrapped in gauze. Her account of the battle, seen from afar, filled in the most blanks.

The plan called for their diversion to happen first, in hopes it would draw away some of the enemy when the attack started, but they found their path through the city fraught with blockages and arrived late. When she and Wilson heard the raft explode, they rushed their attempt to crash the APC a few hundred meters outside camp. It missed the intended building and continued on down a Belém street for five blocks before smashing into a one-room home. The two of them spent the next ten minutes just reversing the damn thing, and by then Camp Exodus was in chaos.

Wilson had argued they should just hide and wait out the fighting. But Vanessa shamed him into action, and together they set the vehicle on a collision course with the camp itself, jumped out, and watched it go. "Stupid and reckless, I realize now," she said, her head down.

Skyler assured her the action might have saved the whole enterprise.

When the vehicle crashed into one of Gabriel's idle trucks, Wilson and Vanessa were already racing toward the camp, intent on joining the fight as best they could. Then the enemy's rocket had knifed across camp, missed the diversionary APC, and slammed into an alien tower.

The pair had watched the rest from a distance, baffled and awestruck. They heard the deep groan from the towers and saw the blanket of fog that enveloped the camp in less than ten seconds. Vanessa swore the fog seemed to come out of the air itself, but Skyler knew the towers had somehow created it. A defense mechanism, maybe, after one was "attacked."

"Where's Wilson now?" Skyler asked her.

Her lip quivered. "He's gone, Skyler. One of those towers hit him and just kept going. He went underneath. I've never . . . It was . . ." She covered her mouth and nose with both hands, her voice muffled when she spoke. "He deserved better."

Unsure what else to do, Skyler embraced her and let her sob against his chest. "Maybe you should lie down," he said, feeling helpless. Wilson he'd known for only a few days. A nice enough fellow, and an immune for all that meant. Skyler had seen the way the Canadian looked at Vanessa, but he'd also seen how she'd pointedly ignored the attention. "Don't blame yourself," he said, assuming she was doing just that.

Her sobs dwindled until she suddenly pulled away and wiped her face with one sleeve. "This isn't like me," she said. "I need to do something useful. I'm going to help with the wounded." Without another word she walked away.

Skyler had turned, intending to join her, when he spotted Ana a few dozen meters away. The girl stumbled toward them, her shoulders slumped and feet dragging. Smears of dried blood marred her face and neck.

Ana's gaze was on the ground in front of her, but every few steps she would glance up, as if gauging Skyler's temper. He waited, frozen in place by the sight of her exhausted, wounded form.

She stopped a few meters from him and started to say something. Her knees buckled, and Skyler closed the distance between them in two steps, catching her before she fell. Her arms wrapped around him and she began to sob.

"It's okay now," he whispered. "They're gone."

Between sharply drawn breaths she said, "I lost sight of you in the shadows, and moved. But I still couldn't see you, and then the raft blew up and I just panicked. I ran. . . ."

"Doesn't matter," Skyler told her. "You did good."

"I ran," she repeated. "I fled."

He held her tight, and when the sobs began to fade he checked her for wounds.

"The blood is someone else's," she said.

A short distance away Skyler spotted a cot tipped onto its side. He led Ana to it, righted the portable bed, and eased her down to a seat. When he offered her his canteen, she took a mouthful, swished, and then spat the liquid onto the ground beside her. Then she poured some water on her hand and began to wipe the blood from her face. Her effort only smeared the gore.

Skyler knelt before her, took out a fresh white handkerchief from a pocket on his pant leg, and eased her hand down. Ana closed her eyes and sat motionless as he cleaned blood, sweat, and tears from her cheeks and brow.

"My face," she said, "feels like yours looks."

It hurt to laugh, but he laughed anyway. "Now we're twins, eh?"

He heard footsteps behind him.

"Skyler, when you have a moment?" Karl's voice. The man sounded so haggard Skyler almost didn't recognize it.

Ana opened her eyes and gave Skyler a nod. "I'm just going to sit here a while," she whispered. "Then I'll find Davi and the others."

He brushed a stray strand of auburn hair from her face, offered the best smile he could, and went to Karl.

The man had two black eyes, and the rest of his face hid under a mess of bruises, cuts, and scrapes. "You look like hell," Skyler said as they embraced like soldiers.

"I always do. And anyway, speak for yourself," the man replied. He sounded as if his mouth were full of marbles. "Tania wants you at the climber, so we can start to sort out this mess."

"Later," Skyler said. "There's injured, dead. People missing."

Karl took the rejection in stride. "All but twelve towers are gone," he said. "Looks like even those deployed as roads moved out."

"Already with the bloody towers? Secure the colony, treat the wounded. Fuck the towers, we'll find them later."

The battered man held up his hands in surrender. "Calm down. Everyone's pitching in. We need to think about what happens at dawn."

"What happens at dawn?"

"The camp just got a lot smaller, Skyler, and our plans for water and medical access are shot. We need a new strategy."

Skyler had plenty of opinions but decided to wait until Tania was with them. He swept his arm toward the climber and followed Karl to the center of Camp Exodus in silence.

With the air now clear, the full extent of the devastation became apparent. The exodus of aura towers had moved through the camp with total abandon, leaving trails of broken tents, overturned supplies, and broken bodies. They had pushed vehicles and heavy steel cargo containers aside like they were toys.

Skyler asked Karl to halt near a cargo container flipped on its side. The gruff man waited as Skyler shimmied his way onto the roof, or what had become the roof.

From the top, he could see beyond the crowded camp.

Four paths stretched out from the aura's edge. Paths of devastation. The towers seemed to have moved off in tight formations, and in the distance Skyler could still see two of the groups working their way through Belém. One, lit in emerald green, moved north by northwest. The other ran northeast. The towers in that group shimmered with a milky purple light.

Both demolished every structure they came in contact with, instead of just stalling as a tower pushed by human hands would do. Belém consisted largely of shanty hovels built from plywood and laminate, and these fell before the towers as if they'd been made from playing cards and toothpicks.

The emerald group looked to be on a path that would take it through downtown, and Skyler wondered if the skyscrapers there would provide enough resistance to halt the alien objects' progress.

He turned toward the east. The remaining two groups were hidden by the rainforest. He saw their trails—swaths where no trees now stood. Yet even with such destruction in their wake, the forest had consumed them from view. The only hint was the glow they emitted, which lit the trees from beneath.

One moved east, colored with a yellow so brilliant it looked like sunlight.

The last went northeast. The scar it left through the forest left little doubt in his mind where it had gone. Even from here, he could see the cloud that perpetually clung to an area of the forest past the reservoir. The cloud now glowed red.

"Karl," Skyler said.

The man looked up at him. "Yeah?"

"Bring Tania and the others here instead. There's something they need to see."

* * *

By the time Tania reached the container upon which Skyler stood, a ladder had been found and placed against the giant metal box. She took the steps slowly while Karl held the base of it.

When she reached the top, Skyler offered her a hand and helped her off the ladder.

He was filthy, bruised, and smelled of dirt and sweat.

"Thanks," she said, brushing dust from her hands.

Karl joined them a moment later. Tania had urged him to seek out one of the few doctors in camp, but he'd just shaken his head. He looked like he had one foot in the grave already, his face bruised so. "I can't decide which of you looks worse," Tania said.

"Skyler," Karl said.

"Karl," Skyler said at the same time. "Where's Zane? Tim?"

"I left them in orbit," she replied. "In case this was all some trap."

Skyler regarded her for a moment. "That was smart."

She doubted anything she'd done recently could be called smart. Brushing aside the compliment, she looked out across the camp. Colonists already worked to re-stake the tents, and toward the river she saw a group of twenty or so people all huddled together, their arms stretched in unison as they pushed a cargo container onto its side. The sight of teamwork gave her a sudden pang of hope, until she saw the body that lay beneath the metal structure. Man or woman she couldn't tell; the body had been crushed and pressed halfway into the mud. Tania covered her mouth with one hand and forced herself not to turn away.

At least, not until Skyler nudged her. He pointed north, and for the first time she set her attention beyond the camp's perimeter.

Trails of devastation marked the paths the aura towers followed. As she watched, one group moved through the slums of Belém, half-hidden by night and the dust thrown into the air as buildings collapsed in its wake. The towers there rippled with murky purple light.

"They started moving the instant that RPG hit one," Skyler said.

"Four groups," Karl noted. "Why four? And why didn't they all go?"

"And where will they stop?" Tania added. "At least they'll be easy to track."

Skyler gestured east. "Those two groups crossed water already, so that answers one question. It would seem they don't sink."

"Oh hell," Karl said. "That means—"

"When they hit the Pará, or even the ocean, they may just keep going."

The words left both men silent. Tania looked at each path in turn, trying to form a hypothesis as to where the towers might be traveling, and why. Four groups, each at least forty towers in number, gone without any concern or care for what lay in their path. Was the movement some kind of programmed self-preservation? The fog and noise some kind of defense mechanism? One gets attacked and the rest instantly scatter to the four winds, in groups, on different paths?

She wondered if they would stop somewhere, or just keep going, eventually circumnavigating the globe and returning right back here. That didn't make much sense to her, but when it came to the Builders nothing seemed to make sense.

"Well," Karl said for everyone's benefit. "Who wants to talk first?"

Tania decided to take the opening. "I will. For what it's worth, four days ago we sent an aircraft down to try to secure the camp. Or at least help us figure out why we'd lost contact."

"What aircraft?"

She told them of the plane, and the fighters aboard it. "They never made it here," she whispered. For the moment she thought it best to leave out the price she'd paid for it, and for the air and water she'd acquired from Russell Blackfield.

"Gabriel's people must have spotted them, and set up an ambush," Karl said.

"Maybe," Skyler said. "Maybe not. Tania, where did they land?"

"On Water Road, about a kilometer from camp."

Skyler glanced in that direction, his eyes two narrow slits, his bloodied face grim and full of disapproval.

"We had no other options," Tania said, "and no information. After that failure, our only choice was to listen to Gabriel's demands."

If Skyler heard her he didn't show it. His focus remained on the northeast.

"And those demands were . . . ?" Karl asked. "I think I know, but I'd like to hear your version."

Tania started to speak but caught herself. How much to say? "Gabriel wanted to test each of us for immunity from the disease. He held some delusion that he was supposed to gather all immunes together to form some new society."

Karl nodded slowly. "He must've asked me a hundred times where Skyler was. I said nothing, because I knew nothing, not really. Didn't stop them from giving me a bruise or three. As if this constant goddamn subhuman headache wasn't bad enough. Remind me not to go without pills like that again."

"I'm sorry for that," Skyler told him. "And, for what it's worth, I'm grateful that you didn't cooperate."

"I might have," Karl admitted, "if I had known anything. Where the hell were you, anyway?"

Skyler told them of two immunes, twins in fact, whom he'd met in Belém. Escapees from Gabriel's flock. "They told me of more like them, ones who didn't want to be part of Gabriel's new world order. The dissenters were being held at a ranch house, in a valley west of here. So I made them a deal. I'd help free their friends, if they in turn helped me oust Gabriel from the camp."

"Your timing was impeccable," Karl said. He smiled then, and winced for the effort. With one finger he gently probed a cut on his lip.

"Not really," Skyler said.

"No?"

Skyler ignored him. He looked at the metal surface upon which he stood. "Tania, about this test. Were you coming down to take it? To get the others to, as well?"

She held his gaze as long as she could, then turned to Karl and found no strength there, either. "After the aircraft and crew vanished, I didn't know what else to do. Coming here seemed a better choice than abandoning everyone and returning to Darwin."

"Grim choices," Karl said. "I don't envy you."

"Did Gabriel want anything else?" Skyler asked.

Her stomach clenched, and Tania felt her cheeks grow warm.

"He wanted you," she admitted. "He wanted me to convince you to come in, to surrender."

"What did you say?"

"I told him no," she said, lying. *I didn't say yes, either, but I may as well have.* Lying to Skyler pained her more than negotiating with Blackfield, or caving to Gabriel. What choice was there, though? It was over, and thankfully the moment never came where she would have had to ask Skyler to lay down his gun. *Would I have?*

Skyler stared at her for a long moment, so long that Karl began to shuffle awkwardly. Tania suffered the gaze like a spotlight she dare not turn away from. "I'm just glad you're safe," she managed to say.

At that he finally turned away, and with it went the weight of her shame. Not all, but enough.

Skyler returned his focus northeast, and Tania followed his gaze. The reddish glow of the towers in the rainforest appeared to have slowed or even stopped.

"I think I know where one of the tower groups is headed," Skyler said a moment later. He pointed northeast, toward the reservoir. "I found something out there, in the forest. Something you both need to see. And it may explain what happened to that aircraft, too."

"What?" Karl asked. "What is it?"

"I don't know, exactly," Skyler replied. "Whatever it is, the Builders sent it."

Tania and Karl exchanged a glance.

"There's a shell ship out there where that red glow is," he said. "A small one. Crash-landed, or, maybe not a crash exactly." He visibly struggled to find the words to describe it, then sighed. "Sorry, I'm asleep on my feet. I'll explain better in the morning."

Karl nodded sympathetically.

Tania wanted to ask a thousand questions, but Skyler's mention of sleep suddenly made her own exhaustion come forward. "We could all do with some rest. Let's talk more at dawn," she said.

Once down from the overturned cargo container, Karl mumbled something about finding a medic to look at his face, then he wandered off.

When he'd vanished amid the bustle of the liberated camp, Skyler turned to Tania. "Follow me. I need to show you something."

A vague uneasiness festered within her as he led her toward the base of the Elevator. His path took them beyond it to another cargo container, the one that served as the camp's headquarters and comm station.

At the door, Skyler turned and handed her something. A small gadget made of metal and plastic. A handheld two-way radio, she realized. She stared at it, confused, and then Skyler reached out and switched it on.

"Stay here," he said, then went inside. A few seconds later she heard him speak through the tinny speaker. "I heard your conversation with Gabriel," he said, his voice gruff and metallic. "I make no judgment on your decisions, Tania, but you lied to me just now. You never told him 'no.' You said there were logistics. *Logistics.*"

Tears welled in her eyes and she made no effort to stop them. She just stood there, in the center of the wounded camp, surrounded by death and pain and despair, and stared at the radio in her shaking hands. The world around her receded to a blur, leaving nothing but the tiny speaker through which Skyler's voice lashed out at her.

Skyler went on. "I understand the dilemma you were in, Tania. One man for the safety of a thousand. Not a bad deal under the circumstances. But you lied to me. You'd let me believe that you stood up to that monster, when in fact you did no such thing."

I wanted to. I tried. The aircraft. I tried and I failed. "I never asked for this position. To make such decisions," she whispered, unsure if he could hear her.

"Go make rounds of the camp." Through the speaker he sounded so cold, and half a world away. "I'm not of a mind to talk about this more right now."

"I'm sorry," she whispered, frozen in place.

Skyler remained inside the dingy room and paced its length until his heart stopped hammering in his chest. *I should have just let it go,* he thought. For some reason, he couldn't do that.

Tania had been in a fog the last few months. Since Neil died, really. Skyler couldn't claim to know her well, but he knew enough to realize she'd fallen into some kind of pit within herself. Even if a rift now formed between them, at least he might have shocked her back into her true self. At least, he hoped that would be the result.

When he exited through the door, she still stood there, the radio held in two cupped hands, her eyes fixed on it. If she noticed him, she made no move to speak or even look up.

"See you here at dawn," Skyler mumbled, as he walked away.

He went to the south side of camp, first, where the colonists had been sitting on their hands when the battle started. Almost all the towers had been parked here, and had careened away to the north and east with reckless abandon. As such, the human toll turned out to be worst here. By now most of the dead and wounded had been moved, or at least covered. Sixteen dead, twenty-three injured, Skyler overheard. One older man was still being treated nearby. A crushed leg, and Skyler guessed from the look of it that it would need to be amputated. Mercifully, someone had brought a medical kit taken from the hospital and injected the poor fellow with a powerful painkiller.

Others were busy picking up the tents and other supplies knocked aside by the runaway towers. A few acknowledged Skyler when he passed. Some even thanked him for coming to their rescue. Just as many, though, looked at him with accusing eyes, and he couldn't blame them. They didn't know what he did, didn't know what Gabriel was capable of. As far as they knew, Tania had come down to negotiate some peace, and he'd ruined that effort.

A few had even seen him dispatch the newly infected subhuman. In hindsight he might have chosen a less brutal method, but there was nothing to be done about it now.

At the tower yard Skyler paused only a moment. The few towers that remained were silent, dead hulks. They almost looked lonely. A few of the colonists lingered about, working to reposition some of the huge monoliths. They guided the bulky forms with a newfound reverence, he saw.

Skyler hiked through the old university grounds west of

camp, then toward the dockyards.

He found the rest of his immunes in a small field between three buildings, huddled below a tree.

A few were crying, he realized. Ana knelt below the tree, a limp body in her arms.

Davi.

She looked up at Skyler, her cheeks wet with tears already shed. He wanted to look away, to fall to the ground and cover his head in guilt and shame. Anything but meet her gaze. He expected to find accusation there. *My brother is dead, thanks to you.*

Skyler forced himself to return her look. In her raw, red eyes he saw no accusation. Instead she seemed to convey one simple thought:

I have nothing now except you.

24

BELÉM, BRAZIL

6.MAY.2283

Tania slipped into the makeshift comm room shortly before midnight. The events of the day had drained her to the point of collapse, but there was one more thing she had to do before she could find sleep.

She closed the door behind her and flipped on the LED lantern that hung from an exposed bolt on the wall. For a long time she simply stood just inside the door, numbly studying the cramped and cluttered room. None of the tables or chairs matched. Maps and scraps of paper littered every horizontal surface, save for the few places where the communications equipment had been assembled.

She tried to picture Karl sitting in here, chatting with her when one of Gabriel's people had stormed in and clubbed him. The poor man had been through so much since the day Neil Platz had sent him to Anchor Station disguised as a common janitor. She couldn't recall a single time that Karl had questioned an order, or flinched in the face of danger.

Then she imagined Skyler, more recently, sneaking into this room while enemies lurked just outside. He'd had the presence of mind to hide a handheld radio, transmit button taped permanently down, so that he could spy on the intruders. She pictured herself in the same scenario and knew she'd never have thought to do something like that. She would have powered up the comm and tried in desperation to raise Melville Station before they came in and caught her.

She would have blown it, if she'd even made it that far.

A feeling ate away at her, the undeniable sensation that she did not belong in the role she'd somehow wound up in. That Neil Platz, for all his amazing instinct, had misjudged her ability as a leader.

She'd first entertained the thought the very moment she and Skyler had sealed Black Level and disconnected it from Anchor. For months she'd been able to talk herself out of such doubt. Surely being surrounded by so many talented, smart people would shore up any faults she possessed?

No, she thought bitterly. *No, I'm just a scientist lucky enough to be the daughter of Neil's old business partner.* She knew that if she'd not grown up as part of the Platz inner circle she'd be just another researcher trying to find that next materials or manufacturing breakthrough that would increase the company's profit margin.

Tania walked slowly though the narrow room until she reached the chair in front of the comm. With a deep breath she lowered herself into the seat and flipped the unit on.

Several minutes later, Tim's awkward, affable face greeted her. The relief in his eyes came through with such clarity that she looked away slightly. He mistook this for disappointment. "I'll get Zane?"

"No," she said. "Not yet."

He studied her, and the frown on his face grew deeper with each second that passed. "Karl called up earlier and told us what happened. How's your ankle?"

"My . . . who cares about my ankle, Tim? People are dead. The towers are gone, the camp is in ruins." The words tumbled out as if spoken by someone else. A heat rose behind her eyes and nose, the precursor to tears, and she couldn't stop it.

Zane Platz appeared at Tim's shoulder. His hair stood at odd angles in places, and he wore a plaid flannel shirt. "Thank God you're okay," he said.

A tear rolled down her cheek and Tania swiped at it angrily with the back of her hand. "Yes, that's it, praise the Almighty that Tania Sharma still lives. Everything's sure to be okay now."

The two men exchanged a glance.

"What is it, Tania?" Zane asked. "What's wrong?"

"Isn't it obvious?" She closed her eyes and tried to get her breathing under control. "I can't do this. It's in their eyes. I see it everywhere I go down here."

"They blame you for what happened," Zane said.

"No," Tania replied with a sudden sharp laugh. "No, that is what they should do! But there's no blame in their faces, Zane. They look at me with . . . hope. With the expectation that I'll know the path forward. They look at me and their eyes say 'we're with you, Tania, to the bitter goddamn end.'"

Everyone except Skyler.

"You're their leader, Tania," Tim said. "Our leader."

"Nonsense," she said. "We govern by consensus; that was the agreement. I'm just one woman."

Tim held his hands up. "That's not what I meant—"

"Isn't it? Isn't it?" Tania said with a force she hadn't intended. She inhaled a long breath, pressed her palms against the cluttered desk in front of her, and let the air out through her nose. "You meant that I'm the face of things, right? You said it before. That I'm the spiritual leader of this . . . whatever *this* is? Well, I'm telling you *that is not me*."

Neither of them spoke.

"I can't do this anymore," Tania heard herself saying. "I walk among these people and I want them to look at me as if I am responsible for the deaths of their friends. I don't want to see resolve or bloody admiration, as if this was somehow all worth it for my sake. Yet that is what I see, and I can't bear that. I can't. Do you understand, guys? I'm done. I quit. I just want to go back to my telescope. I want to walk through the farms again with Neil, stay up until all hours drinking wine with Natalie. I want . . ."

I want Skyler to look at me again the way he did when we first met.

No one spoke for a long time, and in that ocean of silence

Tania felt the weakness in her turning into something she could live with, like an ice cube melting into the water around it, soon to be indistinguishable from the rest.

"Well," Zane Platz said in a hard, level voice that echoed his famous brother, "what a bunch of crap."

Tania glanced up at the screen. She expected to see disappointment on Zane's face. More than that she craved it, because it would mean he'd accepted her resignation. Instead she saw a near-perfect portrait of Neil Platz—the face he took on when calling someone's bluff in a card game.

She glanced to Tim for support, but the young man was staring at Zane with the sort of mortified stare she should have. The longer he studied the older man, though, the more Zane's reaction and posture seemed to flow into him, until they both looked at her in some unspoken united front.

"Think of it however you like," Tania said, "but that's how I feel. I resign. I—"

Before she could finish her sentence, Zane erupted in a fierce coughing fit. He held up an unsteady finger as the racking sounds erupted out of him in rapid succession. The man leaned away and covered his mouth. Tim stared on helplessly before turning to Tania with a shrug.

"Zane?" she asked. "You okay?"

The question seemed to force him to get his breathing under control. "The air up here," he said dismissively. "Been through the recyclers one too many times, I think." He glanced down at a cup of water that Tim produced from offscreen. "Thanks," he said to the young man, and sipped.

"We can finish this later," Tania said.

"I'm fine, and no, we should finish this now." He drank half the water and set the cup aside, then ran one hand down his tired face. "Tania," he said, "did Neil or your father ever tell you about when Platz's operations in India were scuttled?"

She squinted, confused. "I remember bits and pieces. That happened before I was born."

"Your father, Sandeep, championed that initiative when it started. He believed with absolute conviction that the old superpower still had potential. Neil had his doubts, but he agreed

Sandy should run with it. It was the first time your father had spearheaded a business operation."

It felt strange to hear someone refer to her father as Sandy. Only a few of his close friends had used the nickname. "Okay . . ."

"The company took a massive write-off, massive even by Platz standards, when our partner companies collapsed. The venture failed spectacularly. Billions of dollars vanished overnight. Thousands of people lost their jobs."

"So it runs in the family, is what you're saying?"

"Not in the way you're thinking. Sandy wanted to quit then, just like you do now. He couldn't imagine why anyone, much less Neil, would want him around after such a debacle. Your dad had never dabbled much in the business side of things before that, and he vowed never to do so again. I was there when he returned, hat in hand and eyes downcast. Neil walked straight up to him and clapped him on the shoulder. He said, 'Think of it like any other experiment. The result is just data, and even if it's not the data you wanted, you can still learn from it.'"

Tania saw the sense in the words, and could even hear Neil say them. "I still don't see what this has to do with me."

Zane leaned in and lowered his voice enough to force her to concentrate on what he said. "Your father woke up the next morning and left without a word on a hopper back to India. He went in like a demon with a completely different plan. Bought up the choicest patents, surplus equipment, real estate, and talent left behind by our failed partners. Things that would have either faded away or fallen into competitors' hands had Platz Industries pulled out completely. Then he bundled all that wreckage together in a package our competitors salivated over, and offered it as a partnership to the most eager one. Six months later your father acquired that former competitor, completing a turnaround even Neil hadn't thought possible.

"It was brilliant, and it was all because your father had that scientist's knack for treating anything, good or bad, as data that can be learned from. A trait I'm fairly certain you possess, too. He just needed a little prompting from Neil, and today I'm giving you the same advice. This whole venture, everything we're doing, is a grand experiment. Allow yourself to do what you do best, to step back and impartially analyze. You do that, and whatever actions you take will have the conviction behind it that people can't help but follow."

Tania slumped back in her chair and let the words settle into place. "Why me?" she asked them. "Can't you two do that?"

Zane shook his head. "If Tim and I have one thing in common it's that given a task we will get something done. Coming up with the tasks? That's something we have never been good at. I hope you don't mind me speaking for both of us, son," he said to Tim.

"It's the truth," Tim replied. "Why do you think I was a technician on Anchor, instead of in the science lab?"

Tania felt a smile tug at the corners of her mouth at that. They'd worked aboard Anchor together in proximity for years, yet she'd known him only well enough to greet him on the rare occasion they passed each other in a hallway. It wasn't until he came forward in that moment of desperate need, and offered to pilot Black Level away from the rest of the station, and Darwin, that she really knew him. She'd given him a task and he'd risen to the occasion.

"And why," Zane said, interrupting her memory, "do you think I was left to handle things like the Platz Charities? Neil and I both knew I'd make a mess of anything else."

"That's not true," Tania protested by reflex. Zane's quickly raised hand silenced her.

"It is true. No need to sugarcoat it." He shifted farther in his seat and tilted his head quizzically. "Come on, now, Tania. We need you. Don't make me look to the kid here for my orders. Tim will have us resolving disputes with table tennis."

"I stand by that suggestion," Tim said.

Tania laughed, and only partly succeeded in suppressing it. She knew then that she couldn't walk away from these two.

Zane went on. "This little triumvirate doesn't work if it's just Tim and me. We need you. You're part of this. You're what makes it work."

"Okay, okay. If you two keep going on like this I'll be in tears. I'll . . . try. That's the best I can offer right now." And she would try, for their sake more than her own. But deep down she knew that Skyler had carved the hole in her confidence, and that wound would fester unless she did something about it.

"Get some sleep, guys," she said. "There's something I need to do."

Tania rapped on the rear door of the APC and took a few steps back.

The camp around her had finally settled into a strangely peaceful silence. The gentle sound of the river filtered up from the south like a calming fountain. Sprinkled just above that came the flirtatious chatter of nocturnal birds, the occasional mew of a feral cat in the slums just north, and the muffled talk of the few colonists still awake. Nearby, a group of them still toiled to right a collapsed tent, and it occurred to her she should help them since Skyler seemed unlikely to rouse.

The sound of the APC door unlatching dispelled that idea.

She'd neglected to bring a flashlight or lantern, and realized suddenly she was standing in near total darkness outside the door. The door swung open just enough for Skyler to poke his head out. "Who's there?"

"It's Tania," she said.

"Oh."

He climbed out with a tired sigh and latched the door behind him with deliberate care. Without a word he led her by the elbow a few paces away, to where a campfire had burned earlier. A few embers still glowed in the fire circle.

"I'm tired, Tania," he said when he let go of her elbow. "And I'm not sure there's much else to say."

"There is," she said. "Just one thing, and then you can go back to sleep."

She felt, more than saw, the serious look he gave her. Despite herself she inhaled deeply, hoping to find some strength in his scent. But all she found was the smells of smoke and churned earth, of ash and rainfall. The action made her feel pathetic.

"Go ahead then," he said.

Tania looked up at his face, just a shadow against the faint glow of starlight that filtered through the cloudy night sky behind. Somehow not being able to see his features, to stare into those narrow brown eyes that always seemed to be scouring the horizon for any looming danger, helped focus her resolve.

"I'm sorry for lying to you," she said. "It seemed innocent enough at the time. Easier than explaining the truth."

"And what is the truth, exactly?"

She looked up into the shadow that hid his face. "That I agreed to Gabriel's demands. That I would have turned you over if it meant saving everyone else. At least, that's what I let the others convince me to do. And that's the real truth. I've been letting others do my thinking for me, Skyler, because I'm terrified of making a mistake. The future of all these people, hanging on my every decision, is crushing me. I don't feel like myself, I feel like an actor on a stage. Or a . . . or a . . ."

". . . a politician," Skyler said flatly.

"Yes, exactly. And I hate it. It's not the person I want to be."

He stood still for a long moment, staring down at her. "I'm not sure what you want me to say. Are you here for forgiveness? I forgive you."

"No," she said. "I didn't ask for that."

"Then what?"

"I guess I'm here to tell you that your little trap to catch me in a lie was childish and disrespectful. You knew the truth and *you* made me say otherwise."

"I didn't make you say anything."

"You created the opportunity for me to shed something I wasn't proud of, something I hated myself for. Of course I'd take that. It would shock me, frankly, if you wouldn't, too, had the roles been reversed."

He seemed on the verge of saying something, but instead he sighed and looked away toward the rainforest.

"What I did was wrong," Tania said, "but I resent how you handled it. As far as I'm concerned, we're even. Maybe not back to where we once were, but I hope at least we understand each other enough that we can get back there someday, because I need you, Skyler. We all do."

If he'd intended to respond or not, she didn't know. Before he could reply she turned and walked away, toward the colonists working to repair the fallen tent. She stepped in and helped to stabilize one corner, the person next to her grunting thanks.

A minute later she turned to see if Skyler still stood there, by the remains of the campfire, but he was gone.

25

BELÉM, BRAZIL

7.MAY.2283

Dawn proved too ambitious a goal.

When Skyler woke, the sun had already cleared the horizon, and the APC he slept in had become stifling.

He shoved the rear door open and drew in a long breath of fresh air. Parked as it was, the back of the vehicle faced the rainforest. The cloud of thick fog that hung over the crashed Builders' ship was now visible to the naked eye, and he knew that everyone in camp would have seen it.

The path gouged by the red-lit aura towers traced a perfect line toward the hazy blanket.

Ana slept soundly on the bench opposite his. Skyler had suggested she share the vehicle with Vanessa, as much in the hope that the two women could console each other as in propriety. But the young woman had insisted Skyler stay. In fact, she'd scarcely left his side since he'd found her kneeling in the dirt, her brother's lifeless body clutched in her arms. *Have I adopted her, or she adopted me?* He studied her sleeping face for a time and decided there was truth in both.

"Now we're twins," he whispered. He'd said the same last

night as an offhand joke.

Yawning, Skyler tugged on his boots and left the vehicle, taking care to leave the door cracked so the small cabin would not become an oven as the sun climbed the sky. Outside only a few colonists were up and about. Two stoked a cook fire, and the smell of coffee drew Skyler to them.

Steaming mug in hand, Skyler made small talk with the pair as long as was polite, and moved on. He stopped at his own tent, a blue and black camping tent that he'd slept in only a handful of times. From inside he snatched two white towels scavenged from a nearby hotel's linen room, and fresh clothes, then headed for the river.

Stripped to his underwear, Skyler swam out into the cool water. He kicked underneath the surface, down and down until the water turned from cool to cold, and stayed there until his lungs began to complain. The water did wonders for the pain he still felt from his fight with Gabriel. Exhaling bubbles, he returned to the surface, inhaled deeply, and settled onto his back. He drifted on the current toward the docks west of the camp, then kicked hard and wheeled his arms against the water's strength. By the time he'd come parallel with his original entry point, the muscles in his arms and legs burned from the effort. Skyler rolled onto his back, drifted again, and repeated the process.

By the fourth repetition his thighs and shoulders screamed. It was a lot of exertion for the morning after a battle, and he felt sure he'd get odd stares from the colonists. Partly because he'd gone outside the aura to swim, and partly for exercising when there was so much work to be done. He'd take the risk: He needed to clear his head and wash the sweat, dirt, and blood from his body. After one more trip down to the colder depths, Skyler finally paddled back to shore. He placed one towel in the mud and stood on it while he dried off. As he pulled a clean gray shirt over his head, he began to form plans. Yet no matter what approach he thought up, he found himself unable to concoct a strategy for exploring the crashed alien ship. There were too many unknowns, the biggest being that black-clad subhuman. The image of the creature and its strange laser-light eyes brought goose bumps to his arms and the back of his neck.

He pulled on a brand-new pair of gray pants, which happened to match his shirt. The pants were made of a tough blended fiber, and the knees and lower legs were coated with a protective black material with a rubbery texture. Another find at the high-end supply depot for would-be Amazon explorers. There'd been no shortage of adventure travelers in the last hundred years, when the age of the computer petered out. The giant tech conglomerates and their sponsored universities ran out of clever tricks to increase the speed of processors. With no big leaps in performance, people grew bored, then outright rebellious at the previous generations who'd hid inside their precious Internet for so long, shunning real contact.

Kids eschewed the global Internet for invite-only HocNets. *All the data, none of the riffraff.* Skyler remembered the slogan. As for the adults, they rediscovered the physical world. Skyler recalled pictures on the wall of his childhood home in Utrecht. Photographs of his parents and their friends on camelback in the Arabian Desert, or mountain climbing in Unified Korea. So many others they blurred together.

Over the shirt he donned his combat vest. A pair of fresh white socks felt almost decadent against his cracked, battered feet, and it almost seemed like an insult when he yanked his worn black combat books over the clean, bright cotton.

Skyler ran the towel over his hair, dabbing gently in the places where bruises and cuts were still raw. He ran a hand over his ragged cheeks and neck, and scratched at the stubble there. "Why not," he muttered, and trudged back to his tent.

Ten minutes later he emerged freshly shaved. He'd strapped his machete to his left thigh again and donned a bushman's hat. Aside from the purple bruises that lingered on his cheek and forehead, he felt like a new man.

"Morning," Karl said, walking up from the camp center. "You sure clean up nice."

Skyler clasped hands with the older man. "You still look like shit."

"And I've the smell to go with it," the man replied. "Glad I found you. No one else here seems up for a little gallows humor." He glanced toward the river. "One of these days you'll have to teach me to swim."

Skyler cocked an eyebrow. "It's a deal. Seen Tania?"

"Yeah. She, um . . . She's rather down this morning."

The comment came as no surprise. Her camp had been badly damaged, lives had been lost. *And I had to go and call out her lie. What the hell was I thinking?* The woman had enough problems, surely. He'd been angry, though, and so tired.

Karl cleared his throat. "They're planning a funeral right now. For the dead."

"Funerals are often for the dead, I hear."

Karl rubbed his eyes with his middle fingers, something Samantha used to do. The thought of her quieted Skyler, and for an uncomfortable moment the two men stood there, saying nothing, watching the camp. Skyler decided not to ask the question on his lips. The answer seemed obvious: There was little desire, from anyone but him, to rush headlong into another battle today.

"I've posted guards, and patrols," Karl noted. "Two people already wandered out beyond the Elevator's aura, so we're re-marking the boundary. Gabriel may be gone, but a few of his people are still unaccounted for."

"Any captured alive?"

Karl grimaced. "Sorry, no. The poor bastards who were guarding our people were beaten to the point of being unrecognizable."

"Speak for yourself," Skyler said, looking the man's face up and down.

"At least I'm breathing," said Karl. "The headache is under control again, too." He tapped a pant pocket and Skyler heard the rattle of a pill bottle.

Dawn turned into noon. Then early evening, and no one had mentioned a sortie into the rainforest.

Every time Skyler saw the scars left behind by the wayward groups of aura towers, he felt the burning urge to go after them. But when his attention drifted to immediate matters, the desire vanished.

The next morning came and went without mention of the

crashed Builder ship that sat just a few kilometers east. Tania led a funeral procession, aura tower in tow, and carted down to the docks the bodies of the six colonists who'd died. Rafts had been prepared. Crude squares of logs lashed together by scavenged rope. One by one, the bodies were pushed out on rafts set afire, and those who wished to watch stood solemnly on the dock as the flames grew and the rafts drifted down the Guamá.

Ana disappeared later that afternoon. Her twin's body had not been among those released onto the river. She'd insisted on burying him, and when the business with the colonists was done, she took Pablo and Vanessa with her to find some quiet place to dig a grave.

At camp, a dozen tents needed to be replaced. Skyler offered to tackle that scavenging job on the morrow, when he could hopefully enlist the help of the other immunes, except Elias, who nursed a broken wrist. For the rest of that day, the entire camp pitched in to load two climbers with compressed air canisters and as much water as they could boil and purify with the crude means available. A cheer went up when the second climber began to amble its way up the cord. Despite the insects that swarmed camp every night, most of the colonists ate dinner together outside that evening, around a big campfire, watching the two climbers until they disappeared into the starry sky above.

Another morning came, and Skyler found himself pestering Karl and Tania with a halfhearted plea to venture into the forest. There was too much to do in camp, and the prospect of a battle with subhumans tempered even the scientist's desire to explore the crashed alien vessel. He'd yet to tell them about the strange subhuman he'd seen; he was unsure now if he'd really seen it or if it had just been some kind of hallucination. So Skyler spent the better part of the day with the other immunes.

He'd intended to chat with them about the future, now that Gabriel's hold on the camp had been broken. Skyler planned to ask them to stay with the camp. With so few towers left, the colony's ability to gather supplies would be greatly limited, and a group of immunes helping out would be extremely valuable.

But he didn't need to ask. Ana broached the topic almost by

accident. She'd had a bright idea, a surprise she said, and led them deep into the city. Only one subhuman accosted them during the walk, and Vanessa put it down with a single shot from a pistol she'd acquired. The woman performed the action with total efficiency, and no emotion. Skyler knew then he could trust her at his side in a fight. Pablo, on the other hand, said so little, Skyler had yet to form an opinion about him.

Ana was another matter entirely. She would run off with no notice. In dark, cramped alleys where Skyler urged total caution, Ana would sometimes laugh aloud, or point at something strange and blurt her excitement. For his part, Skyler couldn't decide whether to chalk her behavior up to immaturity, or to her experiences since the disease came. The loss of her brother seemed to unground her already reckless personality. *Someone needs to take her under their wing,* Skyler thought. He had no illusions as to who that "someone" was.

She redeemed herself when they reached her "surprise." Ana bowed and swept her arm when the fenced yard came into view, as he had done when he'd shown her the adventure supply store.

She'd led them to a parking lot. The back lot, Skyler realized, of a recreational vehicle dealership. Row after row of the long vehicles were crammed together in the huge square area. The fence that surrounded it was five meters high and had rings of razor wire across the top. Vines crept halfway up the barricade, and the thick ones had wrenched holes in the chain link big enough to walk through.

Skyler's excitement abated somewhat when they entered. The vehicles were all in wretched condition. Five years was a long time for such machines to sit out in the rain, wind, and dust. Vines and weeds choked the wheel wells and routed up through the electronics bays. If any of them ran, Skyler would be amazed.

But Ana didn't stop. She led the rest of them straight across the expanse to a giant garage with ten massive metal doors. All were closed save one, and that last had been rolled up only recently, Skyler judged. Ana had been here before, he realized.

Inside the enclosed bays were nine motor homes. Skyler expected a service garage, but once inside he realized they were in a showroom. These were the high-end models, and other than a coat of dust, they were immaculate. He laughed aloud, and Ana brightened.

It took some time to find the nearest building with power, and even longer to cobble together a cable long enough to reach the garage. By nightfall they started charging the first of the RVs: a sleek, silver box of a vehicle, fifteen meters long and opulent inside. Kitchen, bathroom. *A goddamn shower,* Skyler thought. *No,* nine *goddamn showers.*

The next morning they each drove one of the vehicles back to Camp Exodus. The smiles Skyler saw as they caravanned into camp were enough to make him forget about the task still to be performed in the rainforest. For a time, at least.

By the end of that day, all nine of the recreational vehicles were safely in camp, their water tanks filled and ultracaps charged. Before midnight, every colonist had taken a hot shower, and moods were decidedly improved.

Skyler had no doubt that arguments would ensue over who would live in the vehicles. He'd take no part in that. If the colonists were good at one thing, it was debating the optimal use of communal resources.

A full week passed before the topic of the Builder ship finally came up. Skyler was in front of his tent, strapping on his gear for the day, when Karl approached.

"I think it's time we finished our talk," the man said, his meaning plain. "Tania does, too."

Skyler looked him up and down. His bruises had faded. A few scabs remained. "Finally," Skyler replied. He grabbed a few more items from his tent: pocket utility knife, a watch with a built-in compass, and two pairs of compact binoculars. All went into pockets on his vest or pants, except one of the binoculars, which he handed to Karl. "Let's go talk to Tania."

The man nodded and led the way.

Tania leaned against the wall of the steel room, next to the tourist map of Belém. She had her head down against her chest, her arms folded across her stomach, and one leg tucked up behind her.

For a second Skyler thought she slept there, on her feet, but when the door closed behind Karl, Tania said. "They're here, Zane."

Skyler looked to the sat-comm unit on the table. On the screen were the faces of Zane and Tim, and Skyler felt as if he'd not seen them in months. It had been weeks, in truth. Both the older man and the younger looked tired.

"Good morning, gentlemen," Zane said. "Tania has filled us in."

Tim leaned in toward the camera. "Thanks for the supply delivery, by the way. It'll buy a bit of time, at least."

"More will be on the way soon," Tania said. She hadn't budged from her place against the wall, and hadn't looked up at Skyler, either.

Christ, I should have kept my damned mouth shut. Skyler had an urge to cross the room and take her hands in his, tell her not to blame herself. But deep down he wasn't sure he'd mean it. What good was a lie to comfort a liar?

With the thought came a deep and twisted stab of guilt, as if he'd wronged her instead of the other way around.

"Tania says you found something in the rainforest?" Zane prompted.

"I did," Skyler replied, grateful for the shift in focus. He crossed to the map, aware of Tania as she moved a few steps away, presumably to give him space. At least, the others would think that. "Here," he said, drawing a circle on the laminated chart with a dry-erase pen. "If I had to guess, I'd say it's one of the pieces Tania saw approaching with the shell ship above us."

"There were five, right?" Tim asked.

"Five that I could see," Tania said.

Skyler tapped the circle he'd drawn. "It carved a long, shallow tunnel when it landed, and sits half-submerged at the far end. There were, well, a number of subhumans surrounding the area. Humming some kind of chant."

"Singing," Karl muttered. "A chorus."

"Half-submerged?" Tania asked. Her gaze fell on the map now, her sulking mood forgotten with the news of a discovery. "So you entered the tunnel?"

Skyler nodded. "What I saw in there has given me nightmares since," he told them all. The silence that followed was absolute. "The side of the vehicle has a hole in it, or some kind of door.

Point being, it's open. The whole place is shrouded in some kind of haze, but I managed to get close enough to see inside."

"What was in there?" Karl asked, his voice a gruff whisper.

"A subhuman. Kneeling in front of some kind of . . . altar, I guess. Hexagonal in shape, and lit from within in red."

"Red?" Tim asked. "The tower groups that left last night were lit as well, we're told. Was the color the same?"

"The same as one group," Skyler said. "Each group had a different coloration, but the red group went to this place, from what we can see."

"Four groups," Tania said, almost to herself. "I saw five ships, but only four groups of towers departed. Maybe they're not connected?"

"Or maybe one ship didn't make it to the surface," Tim said, his excitement palpable.

Zane put a hand on the youngster's shoulder to quiet him. "What do you mean, the subhuman was kneeling?"

"On its knees," Skyler answered. He held up a hand before anyone balked at his sarcasm. "On its knees, with its hands outstretched. Grasping that hexagon thing with both hands."

"Weird," Karl said.

"There's more. The subhuman was being coated with some kind of . . ." He inwardly recalled the scene, as he searched for the right words. "Some kind of armor, or second skin. I can't explain. All I can tell you is, the subhuman was already half-covered when I found it, and when it turned to me . . ." He shivered.

Tania asked the question. "What did you see?"

Skyler looked at each of them in turn. "That red laser light, coming from within. Where eyes should have been." Even describing it made him shudder. The creature had only looked at him, and yet it filled him with more dread than any subhuman encounter he'd had before.

"Do you think it was—"

Skyler held up a hand. "I'm not going to speculate; it'd be a waste of our time. My advice? We go out there, in force, and make a judgment based on what we find. Maybe get those towers back so the camp can keep progressing."

No one spoke.

"It's been almost a week since I saw the damn thing," Skyler added. "The only rampant speculation I'll make is that there may be more of them, these transformed subs, and now aura towers have moved into the area as well. What that means is anyone's guess. My gut tells me the longer we wait the harder it will be to do anything about it."

"No," Tim said. "Not necessarily. If we wait a month maybe the towers will run out of power, or these beings will die off, or leave. There's no way you can know—"

"Right," Skyler said. "That's the reaction I expected. Let me know when you've all finished debating." He turned for the door.

"Wait," Tania said.

When he stopped, she moved to the map and studied the spot he'd marked, as if it allowed her to see the place. "Skyler's right. Karl, open the gun locker, and put out a call for volunteers. As many as want to go and that we have environment suits for. We'll bring one tower. I don't want to risk more than that."

Karl's eyes darted between her, Skyler, and the screen. "You sure?"

Tania nodded once, her mouth a hard, thin line. Skyler guessed she was anything but close to sure, but he wasn't going to argue. He couldn't help but wonder, though, if her unilateral action was really a peace offering to him. Either way, it signaled a change in her, a flash of decisive leadership, and he'd take it.

"Okay then," Karl said.

Elias approached Skyler as he cleaned his sidearm. Skyler greeted the man with a friendly wave, and in answer the immune only managed a slight smile.

"You're leaving, aren't you?" Skyler asked, setting the weapon aside.

"It's that obvious?"

The man offered his left hand to shake, the right being in a spray-on cast, and Skyler clasped it. "Thanks for your help," he said. "I'm sorry about Davi and Wilson."

Elias kicked the dirt around his feet. "You rescued us; it's you who deserves thanks." He spoke so softly Skyler had to lean in to hear the words. "All this fighting, it's not in me. . . ."

"I understand," Skyler said. He gripped the man's shoulder. "Where will you go?"

Elias ran a hand across his scalp, smoothing strands of hair across the bald space. "Home," he replied. "It may seem stupid, but I wish to bury my family, to live somewhere I had happy memories."

"Not stupid," Skyler said. "I wish you well. You're welcome back here any time."

He lingered. "I wondered if I might take one of Gabriel's trucks. It's a long way."

Skyler winced, internally. Only four of the vehicles remained in functional shape. And though the colony now had nine motor homes, and an entire city to pick through for more, Gabriel's leftovers were armored, fast, and known to be reliable.

Elias sensed the hesitation. "A motorcycle would be better on these roads, but beggars can't be choosers."

At that Skyler grinned. "Actually, a bike I can help you with. Fully charged, even." Skyler provided him with a description of where he'd left it.

The quiet man thanked him again and wandered off. Skyler finished strapping on his gear and walked across camp toward the tower yard.

He took a route that brought him near the black vehicles Gabriel's people had left behind. Without a word, the other immunes fell in with him, as if they had some silent agreement. Ana, Vanessa, and Pablo were all decked out in scavenged combat gear, and Skyler couldn't help but feel a rush of pride.

Not a word passed between them. Skyler walked on, with the three immunes on either side of him. Everyone they passed stopped their work to wave, or simply stare. *We must look like quite the badasses,* Skyler thought. He fought to keep a smile off his lips. People had died here, less than a week ago. Many of the colonists had lost friends, or even loved ones. And then there was Ana. . . .

She walked in lockstep with Skyler, at his right. Her face and posture exuded grim determination, as if the prospect of more combat could keep her brother's death from her mind. Maybe it could. Skyler feared the loss might only continue to increase her reckless behavior. For the immediate future, he thought the best place for her was right next to him.

Twenty people had gathered by the tower yard, looking every bit the ragtag posse they were. About half of them wore environment suits, but Tania he saw had opted for plain clothes. It surprised him that she'd eschew the extra protection of the suit, and he wondered if it was just a show of solidarity for the rest of those going without. More surprising was the handgun she wore in a shoulder holster. He resisted the urge to ask her where she'd gotten it, or when she'd learned to fire it.

The mood of the crowd changed, flickers of hope or concern, perhaps both, as he strode up with his three armed-and-outfitted immune friends in tow.

A large water pail sat in the dirt near the group. Skyler flipped it over with one foot, then stood on top of it.

"You've all heard by now, I'm sure," he said. "We've seen scant few subhumans since arriving, and now we may know why. I found something in the forest, past the reservoir. A crashed Builder ship, we think. And it seems to have drawn the creatures to it. It's tempting to just let them be, but with a good portion of our missing towers now there, we need to go find out what we're dealing with. If possible, we'll bring those towers back."

Grim faces stared at him. Grim, tired, and yet amazingly determined.

"The camp's success depends on it," Tania added.

Skyler went on. "Form two groups. Those with suits in one, the rest with the tower. These people with me are immunes, former captives of Gabriel. Some of you may have met them over the last few days. They'll be with me, scouting ahead, roving between groups as needed."

Some in the group offered waves and nods to the newcomers.

"Bring a little food, but don't go overboard. We'll have to come back by evening since the suits are air-limited."

He gave them all a long, deliberate look. "Remember, subhumans or not, the rainforest has plenty of dangers. Snakes, jaguars, and so on. Keep alert, and keep quiet when possible. We'll leave in five minutes."

A few of the volunteers darted off toward their tents,

presumably to fetch more supplies. The rest shuffled into two groups, one designating members to handle the movement of the aura tower.

Exactly five minutes later, Skyler turned and began their march. The rest of Camp Exodus came out to watch, forming lines along either side of their path. Some offered words of encouragement, but most were silent. They simply stared, their expressions a blend of gravity and hope.

26

BELÉM, BRAZIL

7.MAY.2283

At the edge of the unnatural cloud, Vanessa nudged Skyler and pointed off to their right.

Half-obscured by the dense haze, amid a ghostly forest canopy, an aura tower loomed. He saw the traces of red light first, washing across the grooves on its surface as if a flame burned within the huge black object.

The tower had come to rest right at the point where the cloud became unnaturally thick.

Skyler called a halt.

He glanced left, but if another of the red towers sat in that direction, he could not see it through the haze or the dense forest.

By now the strange droning hum of subhumans had become a constant background noise. The creatures, however, remained obscured within the mist. Skyler reminded himself that most of the members of their party had never seen one of the creatures up close, much less fought one. The visibility within the cloud would only make things worse.

He called the leaders of the two ad hoc "squads" into a tight circle, urging the rest of the colonists to spread out a bit and stay alert. Tania joined, too, as did Ana.

Skyler leaned and spoke in a hushed voice. "If everyone goes in, and we're attacked, we'll end up shooting each other as much as the subs. Worse, people will lose their sense of direction."

Everyone nodded.

"I think," he went on, "we should form a wedge here. We immunes will go in and try to draw them back out. No one shoots until we're behind the line. Understood?"

"What do we do with our tower?" one of the group leaders asked.

Skyler peered over their heads and did a quick survey of the ground around them. The wayward red-lit towers had carved a path through the rainforest, uprooting small rubber trees and monstrous kapoks alike. Some were just scattered splinters now, as if exploded from within. *At least our path home is obvious to everyone.* But as the towers neared the crashed ship they'd spread out and formed what appeared to be a circle around it, leaving patches of thick forest between their divergent paths.

He pointed where two large trees stood to either side of the forged path the group now stood on. Both trees were tucked within the embrace of strangler figs and together looked like two pillars guarding the entrance to the area. "Keep the tower between those trees," he said. That would put it sixty meters or so away, he guessed, leaving plenty of room for the colonists to work within the aura it provided, without having the tower too close to the action. The last thing he wanted was to spark another defensive system, as the poorly aimed rocket had done the previous night. "Those not in environment suits will form a second firing line between here and there, in case the rest of us need to retreat. If we're overwhelmed, anyone who can should rally at the tower."

That last brought a pang of fear to the face of the suited squad leader, an expression the man quickly tried to hide. The other seemed content with the plan. For Tania's part she still wore a mask of determination and cold confidence, a face she'd maintained throughout the entire march. If Skyler hadn't seen how she handled herself in Hawaii, he might have questioned her comfort level. Once again he eyed the gun strapped under her arm. This time he arched an eyebrow at her. She simply returned the expression, questioning the fact that he would question her.

He let it go. "Have your people fan out, take what cover they can, and when everyone's in position we will go in."

Both squad leaders nodded. Tania did as well.

"Right, then," Skyler said. "Ana, Vanessa, Pablo . . . with me."

A breeze picked up and stirred the silent army of trees around them into a swishing morass. The haze that blanketed the crash site shifted with the change in wind, pushed into the colonists' positions. With a wave from Skyler, the two groups moved back a few more meters and hunkered down again.

Skyler crept ahead into the cloud and crouched, gripping his gun lightly with both hands. Ana fell in beside him without a word, and a few meters to his right, Vanessa and Pablo paired up as well.

In no time the thick haze enveloped them. A glance back provided no evidence at all that the colonists waited just ten meters away. Soon Vanessa and Pablo became ghostly shapes at his right, and Skyler made a point to move closer lest they get separated.

At the point where the humming sound only came from the left and right, rather than ahead, Skyler called a halt with a subtle *tick-tick* sound. He pulled Ana gently by the sleeve until they were next to the other pair, and whispered to all of them.

"They're on either side of us now. I suggest we halt here, and go that way." He motioned in a line perpendicular to the direction they'd been going. "First sub we run into, we put it down and then retreat back to the others, and see how many follow."

Pablo's brow furrowed. "Suppose we find none, or go a long way. Everything looks the same in here."

"If we keep the compass needle—"

A low, guttural sound killed the words in his mouth. It came from his left, behind Ana.

The girl reacted with incredible speed. She whipped around and brought her rifle up in one motion, a split second before a bony, filthy subhuman emerged from the swirling mist. It dove toward Ana, outstretched hands so dirty that for one terrible heartbeat Skyler thought they were coated in that black armor.

Ana fired two rounds. One missed. The second went through the throat of the creature, which clutched at its neck even as it crashed into the young girl.

Ana sidestepped, shouldering the sub off her and turning all at once. The being fell to the ground and lay there writhing.

Skyler had only just begun to raise his weapon when Pablo shouted. Another subhuman appeared in the cloud, from the opposite direction. Pablo squeezed a fully automatic burst, his gun chattering as bullets peppered the creature and the ground around it. At the same instant, Ana put a second round into the brain of the one that lay at their feet.

Vanessa began to shoot, though at what, Skyler couldn't see. He felt trapped between two fights. Another shadow emerged from the mist, again by Ana. Then a second appeared just behind it, loping on all fours. The young woman fired in rapid succession, trying to divide her attack between the two. It served only to make her miss both.

Skyler found his wits then. He whipped his gun up to his shoulder and felt it slap against his collarbone as brief plumes of fire erupted from the barrel. His salvo took down the first creature while Ana managed to wing the second just before it reached her. The sub collapsed as one leg went useless beneath it. Skyler put a round in its back before it hit the ground.

Pablo's gun barked in successive attacks. Vanessa hissed curses in Portuguese as she did the same.

"To the line!" Skyler shouted. "Back to the line, now!"

He gripped Ana by the shoulder and pulled her, but the girl twisted and wrenched free. She dropped to a knee and raised her weapon again, ready for the next assault.

Not this time, Skyler thought. He gripped her combat vest by the collar and yanked, hard. The girl scampered back to keep from falling over, a grunt of surprise escaping her lips.

Another subhuman appeared, just a vague shape in the cloud. Skyler fired one-handed and the shape retreated. Unsure if he'd hit it or not, Skyler flipped his gun from semi to full automatic. As he marched backward, pulling Ana with one hand, he pulled the trigger of his gun and held it down. He swept the barrel across the cloud, in the direction the subs had come from, at chest level.

Pablo picked up on the tactic and did the same on his side. Vanessa moved backward in a crouch, firing sporadically at phantom shapes when they emerged.

With a click, Skyler's gun ran empty. Eighty rounds in less than five seconds. Pablo's followed a heartbeat later. By then Ana had relented and moved backward on her own, firing as Vanessa did.

"Run," Skyler urged, when he heard Vanessa's clip deplete.

He turned toward the direction in which they'd come, and sprinted. Part of him became aware that the surreal humming sound had stopped. What replaced it gave him an odd sense of reassurance. Subhuman grunts and growls. Shrieks and snarls, from behind. *That* was normal. That he could fight.

Vanessa sped past him, a natural sprinter, Skyler noted. Pablo struggled to keep up, a few paces behind his left shoulder. Ana . . .

Skyler glanced over his right shoulder. Ana's vague shape receded behind him, and he slowed. Her gun still clattered off rounds in bursts of two. "Ana, dammit! To the line!"

She began to move backward in modest steps. Skyler couldn't see the creatures she fired upon, but her gun moved in quick arcs, stopped, fired, then moved again. He had taken a step toward her, intent to force her to retreat, when her clip finally emptied.

She turned and ran then, and Skyler thought he saw the hint of a smile on her lips. *She's addicted to danger,* he thought.

Shapes formed behind her. Skyler drew his handgun from his hip, aimed, and fired. *Pat, pat, pat, pat.* The Sonton pistol rattled off bullets with mechanical ease. Ana reached him and together they sprinted for the waiting wedge of colonists. Skyler could hear snarls behind him. Snorts and even the whimpers of wounded and fallen subs.

"We're coming!" he shouted ahead, though he couldn't see the others yet. "Get ready!"

He burst through the edge of the cloud three steps later, Ana right beside him. Twenty guns pointed straight at them. Forty terrified eyes. Skyler ran straight for the middle, where Pablo and Vanessa had taken cover. He dove past them, into the dirt.

All hell broke loose.

Twenty guns of every shape and caliber thundered to life as

the filthy creatures sped out of the cloud and into the trap.

The noise was deafening. Skyler rolled in the dirt, came to a knee. His pistol went back into its holster, and he yanked a fresh clip for his rifle from the bandolier built into his vest.

The roar of weapons firing in concert blotted out all other sound. The barrage was so intense and effective, it bordered on ridiculous. Even still, Skyler jumped back to the line and added his own weapon to the mix. To his right he caught a glimpse of Tania, standing behind two crouched men, her pistol raised in outstretched hands as if she'd learned how to shoot from a sensory thriller, which was probably near the truth. She fired with careful, deliberate aim. He wondered if she'd hit anything, how she'd react if she did, but then he realized that wasn't the point. She was doing her part and earning respect, he realized, nothing more.

Subhumans streamed from the cloud, only to fall a step later. Some collapsed dead, shot in multiple places. Others simply tripped over their own slain comrades and flailed on the ground as they tried to get up. Bullet holes erupted across their bodies until they lay still.

More came. They seemed to never end, and Skyler started to hear colonists on the line reloading. "Conserve ammo!" he barked, doubting anyone could hear him. He could barely hear himself.

And then, as quickly as it had begun, the flow of enemies trickled and stopped. The forest went silent, save for the few colonists who had the wits to reload in the lull. The carnage before their wedge was absolute. Skyler guessed at least forty in the dirt and leaves before them. Someone off to the left hacked, then vomited, a horrible sound to hear coming from within an environment suit. The colonist backed away from the line and sought help from the backup squad to get his helmet off. Another person on the front line, somewhere right of Skyler, let out a laugh born of adrenaline and fear.

"We did it!" someone shouted.

Others began to cheer, to congratulate one another.

"Shut up," Skyler hissed. "Keep quiet!"

They weren't listening, though. People began to high-five, to hug.

Idiots!

The black-clad subhuman slipped out of the cloud like a ghost. It made no sound at all, and moved with a cold ruthlessness that chilled Skyler to the bone.

The armored creature was among the colonists before they even realized it. It swiped at the nearest person with a flat hand, the speed of the attack a blur. Skyler saw the poor man's suit and neck tear open, as if sliced by a knife. The man fell dead, the creature already on its next victim.

Someone screamed. Skyler heard a gunshot and he cried out for restraint. The black-clad sub was in their midst, and shooting at it would only put their own people at risk. His call went unheeded, though. People panicked, firing wildly. All the while the dark enemy slashed and punched. In the space of a second, three more colonists fell.

A bullet finally found the enemy. Skyler saw a spark fly from the being's chest as the round ricocheted off. No penetration then, but the subhuman did recoil, almost fell. It seemed surprised, and Skyler saw its "eyes" flare with red light. In that moment of respite, the colonists closest to the creature, the ones still alive, leapt or crawled away in terror. They retreated toward the tower, and he felt a pang of relief to see Tania moving with them.

Other colonists sensed the opening and began to barrage the creature. Skyler joined in, and the monster bucked and shrank under the fire. Then it turned and raced back into the cloud.

It's vulnerable, Skyler found himself thinking.

Another scream arose from the crowd of colonists, a shriek of terror that stopped as abruptly as it started. The noise came from the left, and Skyler spun in that direction in time to see one of the colonists topple over and a black shape recede into the cloud.

"More than one!" Pablo shouted. He fired blind into the cloud where the subhuman had vanished. Others did the same.

Two, at least, Skyler thought. *And they're using the cloud for cover now.* "They'll pick us to pieces!" he yelled over the sporadic crackle of gunfire. "Retreat to the tower, away from the cloud!"

Everyone, even Ana, fell back at the command. Many turned and ran, but some walked backward, their weapons still trained on the edge of the unnatural cloud, Skyler among them.

Five people remained at their original positions, motionless lumps in the dirt.

A new wedge formed, and Skyler fell into line next to Tania. Her face was pale despite her dark complexion. Her eyes were wide and unblinking. She held the pistol in two shaking hands.

For a long minute no one spoke. All guns were trained on the shrouded forest, and the bodies that lay in the shifting border of the cloud. Parakeets and macaws began to settle back into the dense canopy above, chattering as if nothing had happened.

The cloud shifted and pulsed. It pulled in and then pushed back out, with no rhythm that Skyler could discern. At one point, the thick haze sucked inward a significant distance, enough to reveal the shadowy forms of two more red-lit aura towers off to either side of the first one they'd spotted.

Skyler heard murmurs of fear from the group, and focused back on the scene of the battle. In the retreated haze, two humanoid forms stood. Dark shadows within the cloud, like blurred photographs. Skyler's finger tensed on the trigger of his gun by pure instinct, but before he could shoot—before anyone could—the cloud pulsed outward again, and the beings were gone.

"They're staying close to that murk," Vanessa said.

Skyler raised his own voice. "Everyone reload, prepare to concentrate fire." He had started to double-check his own weapon, when Tania spoke up.

"No," she said. "Belay that."

He turned his head slowly until their eyes met. "What?"

Tania's wide-eyed gaze remained on the cloud where the two creatures had stood. "It isn't wise to continue this."

"We're hurting them," he said. "We should press the attack."

Tania's lips tightened. She shook her head. "We leave, Skyler," she said sharply. "We're outmatched by these creatures, physically and tactically. We need to rethink this. A better plan."

With a shift in the breeze the cloud receded again. The two dark shapes at the cloud's edge remained there, unmoving, watching. *Waiting*, Skyler thought. He had to remind himself that inside they were subhumans. Unless the Builders' altar had rewired their brains somehow, the creatures would still move and act in primal, predictable fashion. Not that he'd ever seen subhumans just stand around like this, biding their time. But if these two were constrained to the area of the cloud . . .

"Everyone stand down," he said. A silence fell over the colonists. Then Skyler raised his gun.

"What are you doing?" Tania asked.

In answer, Skyler lined up his holo-sight on the chest of one enemy and fired a single round.

The creature stumbled backward a step, one arm flailing about for balance. The other sub dropped to a crouch, moved left a step, then right. When the one Skyler had shot recovered, both of the augmented subhumans moved back farther into the cloud until their forms vanished.

If that had been a grenade, Skyler thought, eyeing Ana's weapon. *We can beat them.*

"They're stuck in the circle," someone said. "Just like us in the aura."

"Leave them alone, then," Tania said. "Skyler, this is too risky. I won't have it."

Skyler walked to her and leaned in close. He lowered his voice. "We can't ignore this place forever, not if you want to explore that ship. Not if you want those towers back."

She remained steadfast. "For almost three months we've ignored it. A little more time to develop a plan and revise our arsenal can't hurt. The colony can survive without the towers."

"Can I speak with you?" Skyler asked her.

He led her by the arm a short distance, until they stood by the aura tower parked at the rally point. Once the colonists were out of earshot, Skyler stopped and turned Tania to face him.

"The violence here," he said, "it's unspeakable, I know. But Tania, if we wait it will only be worse. We should press the attack, now, before more of these advanced subhumans are created."

She shook her head.

Skyler went on, undeterred. "You saw it recoil from that bullet. They're not invincible. Plus they're trapped. Ana has grenades, we can dart in, dart out—"

"No," Tania said. "*No.* This site is off-limits for now. We need a better approach. To continue now would only result in more losses on our side. The dead from your battle with Gabriel are still being mourned."

"*My* battle with Gabriel?"

Her eyes flared. "You initiated the combat. We were coming down to negotiate."

"Right. By sacrificing me. Never mind that your sneak-attack aircraft had already failed."

"So your life is worth more than those who died that night?"

He barked a laugh. "You tell me! You're the one dealing in human fucking resources."

Tania slapped him across the cheek. Not hard, but enough that it stung. Her hand immediately shot to cover her own mouth, as if she'd surprised even herself by the action. "I'm sorry," she said in a meek voice from behind her cupped hand.

"Hell," Skyler said as he rubbed at his jaw. "I probably deserved it."

The scientist steadied herself. A vein in her neck pulsed with anger, frustration. "We've been through this already, Skyler, and I apologized. I don't know what else to do."

"Just forget it," he said. "It's in the past."

Tania's lips parted, as if she wanted to say something more, but she relented.

A frosty silence followed, and Skyler decided he'd lost this battle. "Retreat it is, then. Do me a favor, though? Monitor this place. When we do come back, and we will, I'd like to know the situation before we arrive."

Tania turned back toward the cloud with a grudging nod to Skyler. "If you want to find the equipment to signal back to camp, set it up, and maintain it, I'll make sure we have people keeping an eye on it."

Skyler sensed she wouldn't give any more ground than that, but he pressed his luck anyway. "I'd recommend clearing the trees around here, too."

"Why? The creatures don't seem to be moving beyond the circle of towers."

"Maybe they just haven't figured out how to move the red towers yet."

Tania's gaze whipped back toward the cloud. She hadn't considered that.

"Anyway," Skyler went on, "I'm less worried about the ones inside, and more worried about new subhumans entering this place. If the ship in there is slowly converting them into these augmented versions . . . ."

". . . and there's a steady supply," Tania whispered, "we may never break through to explore that ship."

"Exactly," Skyler said. "One way or another, Tania, it's going to be a battle. You're just delaying the inevitable."

Tania stared at him, looking every bit the woman he'd fled Hawaii with. A mix of terror and determination, like two warring armies behind her eyes. "I just . . . I can't, Skyler. Not so soon. We've lost so many already."

He stared back at her for a long moment, hoping she might swing in her opinion. The idea of taking on the creatures within that haze didn't appeal to him much, in truth, but he knew the odds might never be better. When Tania's expression remained steadfast, he gave her shoulder a squeeze. "Fine," he said. "We retreat. Do me one last favor, though."

She squinted at him, waiting.

"Get Karl to show you how to handle that gun."

27

BELÉM, BRAZIL

8.MAY.2283

The missing aircraft was found the next day.

A team of scientists came across it while making the trek along Water Road out to the reservoir, and within an hour Skyler arrived to survey the scene.

Bodies littered the ground, each hidden under a blanket of flies. Clouds of the plump black insects took flight when he swung his rifle at them, only to return before he'd completed the swing.

Rivers of ants flowed in from the rainforest floor, their targets being the undersides of the corpses where the flies could not reach.

The revolting smell forced Skyler to tie a bandana around his face, and even that did little to quell the nausea he felt. Belém, like all cities on Earth save Darwin, was littered with the skeletons of early SUBS victims, so many that the sight of them hardly registered anymore. Rotten flesh was a different matter.

He decided the bodies could wait. They weren't going anywhere; at least the bones weren't. The aircraft that rested nearby was much more interesting. As he walked toward it, he felt his right hand twitch at the thought of holding a flight stick again.

Any hope of getting the vehicle airborne vanished as he came closer. A massive hole had been punched into the canopy. "Bird strike?" he wondered aloud. The cause didn't make any difference—no one alive had the knowledge or equipment to repair such a thing. No one he knew of, anyway.

The rear of the craft lay open, and his boots crunched on an unnoticed line of ants as he ascended into the belly of the vehicle. Skyler knew then that more horror awaited inside. He soldiered on, intent to know what had happened here, and found his answers within the cockpit.

No bird had punctured the window. He found the pilot lying on the floor between the two seats. Ants flowed into his open mouth, which gaped far wider than any human could achieve. Something had pulled the poor man's jaw open so savagely that the bottom portion had come unhinged.

Skyler gagged, and stumbled from the morbid scene. Outside he emptied his stomach into the dirt and staggered away.

"Only those black-clad subs could have done this," he told Tania and Karl via radio.

"So they aren't confined to that cloud," Karl noted.

Skyler took a swig of cool water from his canteen, swished, and spat it out. "They certainly appeared to be yesterday."

"Perhaps," Tania said, "the red towers are what confines them, not the cloud. This attack happened a week ago, before the towers lit up and encircled the cloud."

"Good point," Skyler said. "Still, all the more reason to make sure that cloud is monitored twenty-four/seven."

"Agreed," Karl said.

Skyler said goodbye and clicked off. He ventured back into the aircraft once, decided nothing within was valuable enough to keep him there, and left. He paused only long enough to close the rear door. Outside, he instructed the scientists who'd found the site to burn the bodies that littered the ground, then return the next day and recover any weapons left behind by the flames. "The guns won't be reliable," Skyler told them, "so toss the lot in the river. I'd rather nobody picked one up and tried to use it only to have it fail when actually needed."

* * *

In the days and weeks that followed, life in Camp Exodus returned to a semblance of normal, and mourning turned into stoic resolve. The luxury of movable auras had basically vanished, and with supply shipments to orbit still irregular at best, the area within the Elevator's aura became very crowded. Skyler found himself called upon daily to fetch things from the city, and his request list grew faster than he could fill it.

Of the two hundred original aura towers, only thirteen remained in camp after one lone surviving tower was found on what had been Mercy Road. That "road," along with Water Road, had to be abandoned.

With so few towers left, Tania and the others were hypersensitive to any request for use. Unless absolutely necessary, the towers were held in reserve. So it fell on Skyler, and his group of newfound immunes, to scavenge.

A mystery lingered, one that Skyler found himself often thinking about despite the willful denial exhibited by the rest of the camp. Where had the other three groups of towers gone? Only one such group was accounted for—"red circle" as it had come to be called. These were parked in an area around the Builders' crashed ship near the reservoir, a place now labeled off-limits.

The other three groups remained unfound and unsought, much to Skyler's chagrin. Every morning, or at least those he spent in camp, he would wake to the sight of their paths. Carved straight through trees and buildings, the scars left behind by the tower groups felt like an invitation to seek them out, and he wondered constantly where they'd gone.

It didn't take a lot of imagination to conclude they now ringed other crashed Builder ships. But only four groups had vacated Belém. Tania saw five small ships through her telescope, spread out from the main vessel when the second Elevator arrived. So where was the fifth? And why didn't it need a group of towers around it?

Perhaps that one would be the easiest to explore, he mused.

As of yet, the colony had no capacity to link into old mapping satellites and download the imagery they continued to compile. Anchor Station used to have that capability, but it came from a combination of Black Level and Green Level, a marriage that no longer existed.

With each passing day Skyler felt the desire grow to follow them. He figured they'd find the same terrifying creatures at each, but perhaps one would be easier to assault than the others. Fighting creatures that moved that fast in a dense cloud was one thing, but add the rainforest to the mix and the prospect of beating them seemed impossible.

Often, in the dark of night, with only the songs of nocturnal curassow and the occasional cry from a night heron to keep him company, Skyler found himself studying a child's school slate. He'd found the devices by the dozen in a Catholic school not far from the Elevator, and a few still held a charge. One program on the device taught geography and included a highly detailed map of Earth, replete with satellite photos from as recently as 2260. He'd traced three lines across it, radiating out from Belém and color-coded to the still-missing tower groups: purple, emerald, and a yellow he called "sunlight." The red towers near Belém he'd marked as well.

Certainly the exercise provided no clue as to where the towers had stopped. He even went so far as to draw the lines all the way back around the planet, reconnecting with Belém as they came around the other side. One night he calculated how long it would take them to circumnavigate the globe, assuming their speed remained constant. He doubted they'd return that way, but it passed the time.

The child's learning tool also proved useful for scouting Belém. He could zoom in on details as fine as five meters across, and even alter the angle to get some sense of perspective.

Each time the sun rose, Skyler dreaded the hours that would follow. Two things happened each morning in camp. First, Karl would inform him of the new additions to his growing scavenger wish list, a list the man now curated at Skyler's request. Karl had become his Prumble, in that sense, and life became a bit more bearable when Skyler could tell people to talk to Karl if their request didn't make it onto the day's priority list.

Second, Skyler would seek out the other immunes and casually invite them to join him in his foray into the city. It had been a rude awakening, the first morning after they tried to reach the Builders' ship, when Skyler gave the immunes orders. He'd forgotten what they'd all been through, and forgotten that no formal agreement existed as to how long they would stay, or if they would even help. They were free for the first time in years, and so to avoid the appearance of bossing them around, Skyler had to dance around the subject and take care to avoid giving orders.

So he would ask, nice and casual, over breakfast. "Going over to that plumber's supply today, for more PVC pipe and pumps. Anyone up for a hike?" A different question each time. More often than not, Pablo and Vanessa would agree to come. He suspected they were sticking around only because they hadn't come up with a better idea yet.

As for Ana, well, Skyler suspected he could not get rid of her if he wanted to. She went everywhere with him, and if he hadn't insisted that she move into Vanessa's APC, he sensed she would want to continue sleeping on the bench across from his. Skyler didn't need the gossip that would cause.

For the most part, though, he didn't mind her at his side. The young woman was bright, alert, and could hold her own in any conversation. Good company, on the whole. The erratic reckless actions seemed to come and go with no rhyme or reason, but with each day that passed since Davi died she seemed to get herself a bit more under control. Once in a while she would descend into a state of deep depression, lasting hours or even days. Skyler quickly learned a delicate balancing act for such times: Leave her alone, and make sure she doesn't wander off.

One evening he found himself sitting alone with her at the edge of the river, each with a fishing pole in hand. She'd been quiet the entire day, since Skyler had chastised her for shooting at a snake that had surprised her in the slums. Not ten minutes before she did that, they'd spotted evidence of recent subhuman presence in the area, and he'd ordered absolute silence as they trekked through the crumbling neighborhood. The echoes of her gunshot rolled through the streets like thunder, and though no subhumans came, he'd let frustration and anger get the better of him in admonishing her.

"Ana," he said, his voice breaking the trancelike state brought on by watching a lure bob on the rippling water.

She glanced up at him, a slight defiance still in her eyes.

"I'm sorry I spoke harshly earlier. I shouldn't have said what I said."

"You called me stupid."

Skyler feigned confusion. "I don't remember the specific words—"

"Specifically," Ana said, "you said it was a stupid fucking move, and that I needed to get my 'shit' under control."

He winced. "Like I said, I'm sorry. I just . . . I'd appreciate it if you tried to follow my orders when we're out there. That wasn't the first time, and it puts us all in danger. Part of being in a squad is keeping everyone in mind when you act, not just yourself."

Her eyes flared and she came right to the precipice of flying into a rage, but then, remarkably, she backed down. She visibly deflated, and after a few seconds of staring at the dazzling twilight sun that glinted off the river, she began to nod. "Davi used to say the same. Well, not exactly the same; he knew how to speak to a lady even when angry."

"I'm really sorry."

"It's okay. You're right, and for you I will try. I'll try to get my shit under control." She grinned as she recited the line.

Skyler found himself smiling, too.

Unlike Darwin, which dried up like a prune when wet season passed, Belém still received a healthy dose of showers. Not nearly as much as when the colonists arrived, but enough to keep the world around the camp green and lush. Gardens began to flourish within the limited space inside the aura, though they required constant tending. Luckily there was no shortage of bored colonists to pull weeds, trim overzealous vines, or maintain the insect nets.

Rats became a problem. A big problem, once they started to get into the supply tents. Skyler and Ana brought back as many traps as they could find, but they were either ineffectual or in too short supply.

One day, when the sun blazed overhead, Skyler and Ana hiked out down to the harbor in hopes of finding watercraft that could be moored on the river within the aura. Another boon to the livable space within the protective sphere, just like the motor homes. So they hoped, anyway. As they ambled toward the boatyard, Ana noted a line of houses that had become overrun with cats. The felines lounged all over the decaying structures, their tails flapping back and forth as if they hadn't a care in the world.

"I bet there's no rats in there," Ana joked.

"Not likely to be, no," Skyler agreed. The idea hit them both at the same time.

They returned to camp and borrowed one of the flatbed trucks. After a quick stop at a veterinary clinic for cages, Skyler and Ana spent an afternoon befriending as many of the feral creatures as they could. Many had lost their trust of humans, but some seemed to be survivors from before the disease and remembered that people meant a life of constant pampering. These entered the cages without too much struggle, though by sunset Skyler found his arms were laced with scratches. Ana fared better, having worn long sleeves.

"Might be a good idea to give each other rabies and tetanus shots," Skyler noted, frowning at the red lines on his forearms.

Ana grinned and winked at him. "Oh, *el diablo*! Your bunk or mine?"

He chuckled but said nothing. Her flirtations started innocently enough, but she grew bolder with it every day. Sooner or later he would need to sit her down and clarify their friendship, but for the time being he was loath to do anything that might trigger another bout of depression in the young woman. She'd been through a hell of a lot, and at an age when hormones raged within her. She'd spent most of her years of puberty as a member of Gabriel's clan, with all that entailed, or alone with only her brother for company. He couldn't begrudge her a little outlet for her emotions, not now.

Besides, it reminded him a little of Samantha.

* * *

The cats were a huge hit, as much for the entertainment they provided as their rodent-catching skills. For the first time since the towers left camp Skyler found colonists smiling, saying "hello" or "g'day" when he walked by.

Two months passed with no further sighting of the black-clad subhumans, save for the occasional report of shadows lurking near the edge of the cloud.

Jury-rigged security cameras placed around the roughly circular haze picked up subhumans entering the area on two occasions. After that, no one questioned the need for constant monitoring of the site.

Skyler assisted in a complex project requiring four days and a dozen people. They took two aura towers out to the site of a skyscraper abandoned while under construction. There, the group set upon a tower crane that had yet to be lifted to the topmost floors. The machine was separated from a loading winch, and two smaller cranes were used to hoist the massive object onto a flatbed truck. This took an entire day. The other three days were spent navigating the twenty-meter-long steel lattice arm back to camp.

After another week of trial and error, the camp soon had a working cargo loader. One of the scientists even figured out how to program the controls so that it could repeat the same function with little supervision. Push a button and the huge arm would move whatever had been attached to it up and over to a waiting climber. Press it again and the motion was reversed.

The system still required a team to spin the climber car forty-five degrees so that the next slot could be loaded or unloaded, but no one complained. The process of lifting cargo to orbit had been significantly streamlined.

Idle hands also made short work of the construction of a wall around camp. At three meters tall, the barricade had nothing on Nightcliff's massive metal face, but it would keep subhumans and larger wildlife out.

On one rare afternoon when not a single cloud marred the sky, Ana came to Skyler. She'd been gone all day with Vanessa and

Pablo, and he hadn't bothered to find out where they had been. "Follow me," she said simply.

Intrigued and a little concerned, he agreed. Vanessa and Pablo waited at the edge of camp and fell in with them. None of the other colonists asked where the group was going, as they often left without a word save from Karl.

As Skyler walked with the other three immunes, he realized they all shouldered backpacks, whereas he had only the usual equipment he carried on himself. They took him west, leaving Mercy Road on a route that would bring them to the modern buildings and harbors that lined the waterfront along the Pará.

"Where are we going?" Skyler asked.

"Shush," Ana replied.

He caught a playful undertone in her voice and decided to let the mystery continue. His eyes, though, kept returning to the backpacks they wore. *They've provisioned a boat,* he thought. *They're going to say goodbye and sail off. Maybe they'll ask me to come along, out of earshot of the other colonists.*

It startled him to realize that he didn't know what answer he would give if asked.

Well before the harbor, though, the three immunes turned from the road and entered the marble lobby of a luxury hotel. Other than a few skeletons near the welcome desk, the place showed no signs of wear or use. Skyler realized that tiny LED spotlights recessed into the ceiling were on, creating pools of warm yellow light at regular intervals along the space.

Skyler followed Ana into a well-lit elevator, and when she tapped the button for the penthouse, the doors slid closed.

"I'm not sure this is safe," Skyler noted, as he imagined the cables that pulled the metal box up the shaft. "Five years of neglect . . ."

Pablo chuckled.

The indicator on the wall counted through all fifty-six floors before reaching "PH." A chime sounded and the doors slid open once again. A small lobby greeted them, and beyond that a pair of fine wood doors. Someone had hacked them open with an axe, which leaned against the wall nearby.

"After you," Ana said, and bowed. "Tonight, we set the real world aside."

Skyler found himself inside a spacious apartment, trimmed and furnished in luxurious fashion. The modern décor was a study in hardwood and shades of gray: bleached slat floors, black carpets, and walls done in two-tone vertical gray stripes. Black leather couches and chairs were backed by brushed-metal supports. The kitchen had every convenience imaginable, all stainless steel surrounded by black marble and whitewashed hardwood cabinets.

All of this paled compared to the curved glass wall that ran the entire length of the space. The sky outside blazed orange and red around a sun half-set behind the mountains to the west.

As Skyler took in the view, Ana set to work in the dining area, placing cutlery and candles upon the thick wood table. Vanessa took to the kitchen, hoisting her backpack onto the counter and removing the contents within. Two bottles of wine, plus something wrapped in brown butcher paper and tied with string, as if she'd just popped out to the corner store.

Pablo ventured out on the balcony and dropped his pack near a professional grill built into the wall beside an empty lap pool.

"What's going on?" Skyler asked Ana.

"It's my birthday," she said, and offered him a half smile as she lit a candle.

"Isn't this a bit excessive—oh." He swallowed the rest of his comment, realizing his mistake. Ana's birthday meant it was Davi's birthday, too. "Shit. Sorry."

A loud *pop* saved him from further embarrassment. In the kitchen, Vanessa giggled as champagne erupted from a green bottle and splashed onto the floor. It might have been, Skyler thought, the first time he'd heard the former lawyer laugh.

Dinner consisted of chops Pablo had cut from a boar he'd felled that morning. He'd grilled the meat to perfection and it dripped with hot grease as Skyler shoveled the first bite into his mouth. For a side Pablo had roasted vegetables inside packets of aluminum foil with a dash of cooking oil, salt, and pepper.

The trio had brought enough wine for each of them to claim two bottles, and a wet bar within the apartment offered up a dozen different options for harder libations.

For a time no one spoke, at least not verbally. The chatter of cutlery on porcelain, the murmured coos of pleasure brought by rich, flavorful food, said everything that needed saying. The meal eclipsed everything Skyler had eaten in months. *No,* he thought, *years,* as he savored a sip of the merlot. Better even than the bowl of ramen that Prumble had served him after his journey through no-man's-land.

And then Vanessa poured the wine. She said a toast in Portuguese, then wished happy birthday to Ana on behalf of the whole world.

Ana blushed and took a healthy gulp of wine.

With food and alcohol consumed the birthday party started in earnest. Skyler and Pablo handled the task of clearing the table by flinging dirty dishes from the fifty-seventh-floor balcony. Ana fiddled with the entertainment panel until she had the entire place flooded with music that blended electronica, fizz-def, and traditional Latin instruments. Soon she and Vanessa kicked off their shoes and the two danced on top of a polished teak coffee table, Ana with a bottle of champagne in hand, as the deep rhythms boomed.

Skyler thought back to the first time he'd ever seen her, twirling in graceful arcs, a long white dress flowing around her toned body. Her movements had been fluid, even delicate. Now, dressed in khaki shorts and a stained tank top, her hiking boots kicked off, she showed a different side. Skyler thought of the university girls who filled dark clubs in Utrecht on the weekends. More than a few had warmed his bed back then, during the peak of his transition to manhood, before he'd joined the Luchtmacht. The Darwin Elevator had arrived a few years before, but the explosion of hope the device created in the world's youth still raged. A fine time to be an eighteen-year-old, he mused.

Ana's eyes were closed, lost in the thumping, aggressive tune that blared from recessed speakers in the walls. For her to come of age in a post-disease world somehow filled him with more anger at the Builders than all the billions who had died or succumbed, and all the survivors who remained trapped within the auras. They'd stolen a proper, carefree childhood from this young woman, and so many others. Ana just had the fortune, or misfortune, perhaps, to live on as an immune. How could he begrudge her the desire to act with reckless abandon now and then?

She had earned the right, and much more.

Well after midnight, the four immunes lay haphazardly on cushions they'd amassed on the wide balcony. Stars filled the sky above, and the silken voice of Ella Fitzgerald wafted over them from the penthouse suite, just loud enough to fill the occasional lapse in conversation.

Each immune shared their story, in more detail than previously given. Pablo, with a little wine, showed signs of a sly sense of humor under his strong and silent façade. Even Vanessa, who spoke last, opened up somewhat. The mental scars she bore from her imprisonment in Gabriel's lodge ran deep, though, and she avoided the topic entirely.

Skyler's experience in Darwin fascinated the others, and so he spent the most time talking. He told them of the events that led to Tania's discovery of the new Builder ship, and how they wound up coming to Belém. He also told them of the scavenger crew he'd run, and the fate that had met both them and their beloved aircraft, the *Melville*.

Wine began to dwindle as dawn approached, and the gaps in conversation widened. Soon the others slept soundly under the stars, but Skyler found it difficult to snooze there. He'd always preferred a dark, quiet room. More than once he found himself jerking awake, caught halfway between a dream and reality. At some point Ana decided to use Skyler's stomach as a pillow, and he had to cup her head in both hands to get out from beneath.

He left the three of them there and crept inside. A long draw from his canteen chased the aftertaste of alcohol and roast pig away. More time would be required before it could do the same for the headache he felt coming on. He relieved himself out the window of one of the bedrooms, then grabbed a blanket and pulled it over his shoulders.

Yawning, Skyler settled on the big leather couch in the main room of the suite, and slept.

* * *

He woke to bright sunlight, reflected into the west-facing room off the white marble pillars that lined the edge of the balcony outside, and promptly snapped his eyes shut again. *It must be past noon already,* he thought, and wondered if their absence from the colony had become a concern. He'd neglected to bring a handheld.

The smell of coffee kept him from a return to sleep. When he sat up, he realized a mug rested on the table near him, steam rising from its lip. He rubbed his eyes and took in the room. Ana, Vanessa, and Pablo all sat on the floor around the low table, each with a mug of their own in hand.

"Morning," Skyler said, and sipped. He would have used more sugar, but he didn't complain.

"We need to speak with you," Pablo said.

Uh-oh. "Should I switch back to wine first?"

"Stick with the coffee," Ana said, her voice light.

He didn't know exactly how to take that remark. After a quick study of the dark brown liquid in the cup, he tilted it back and downed the remainder. "Right, then. What's on your mind, birthday girl?"

"The three of us have been talking," she said, "since dawn. Talking about our future, and yours."

"Is there more coffee?" Skyler asked, glancing toward the kitchen.

"We talked about what you told us," she went on, ignoring his lame attempt at evasion. "About your crew, I mean."

"Oh," he managed to say. The three of them looked very serious now. All the previous night's revelry banished with the break of day. *My old crew. Yeah, I really fucked that up, what about it?* "Is there more wine?"

"We thought it might be best to make this little band we've formed official," Vanessa said, imparting an authority in her voice like only a lawyer could. "We want to be your new crew."

Skyler stared at the three immunes in stunned silence.

Pablo spread his hands. "We already are, really. It's just never been . . . eh, stated."

"You all are free now," Skyler said. "You don't have to do this. Stay if you like. Relax. Hell, you deserve that. Or go, as Elias did. I don't need—"

Ana moved to sit beside him, and rested a hand on his shoulder. "Skyler, each of us decided to stay for our own reasons, since that night. Since Elias left, though, things have been different. It's like none of us want to become too close, in case someone else leaves."

"Or dies," Pablo noted. The offhand comment stalled Ana's speech.

"Yes. Or that," she agreed, her eyes as distant as her voice. After a second she shook her head slightly and focused on Skyler again. "You shouldn't have to wonder if we'll be around tomorrow. You shouldn't feel guilty asking us to help on your scavenging trips. We want this little family, this crew, to be official. So the camp will know they can rely on us. So you can rely on us."

Skyler stood and walked to the kitchen. He emptied another packet of powdered coffee into his mug and poured hot water on top. *A new crew*. The thought repeated over and over in his head.

The faces of his former crew flashed in front of him. Jake, Angus, Takai . . . all dead. Then there was Samantha. Skyler felt guilty about a lot of things he'd done since the disease drove him to Darwin, but none more so than the day he left Samantha behind on Gateway. For all he knew, she was dead, too. He wondered if he'd ever find out.

Why anyone would want to follow him he couldn't fathom, and yet it seemed to be a curse he couldn't shake. But deep down he knew one thing for certain: He didn't want any of his new friends to leave. He wanted them at his side. Needed them. No matter how much he might try, he would always be the oddball among the colonists. The idea of spending the rest of his life as some loner, some freak of nature, filled him with dread.

Skyler stirred the coffee with an ornate silver spoon. "If you guys fall in with me, call me your leader, wouldn't that make me some kind of replacement Gabriel?"

"No. For starters," Vanessa said, "you're not a complete asshole."

"Or a murderer," Ana added.

"Or a rapist."

Pablo said the last, and to Skyler's surprise Vanessa didn't recoil from the word.

Skyler fought a smile and focused on his drink. "That may be true, but I don't want to be some dictator here. If we're going to be a crew it'll be a crew of equals. I may call the shots on one mission; maybe it's one of you on the next. Everyone gets a say in where we go and what we do."

"Fine with me," Ana said.

"Yes," Pablo said.

Vanessa nodded.

Only after he'd said the words did he realize he'd just proposed that their crew run the same way Tania ran the colony. Consensus, discussion, mutual respect. He wondered if he'd been too hard on her. Karl and the others, too.

A few seconds of silence followed, and then Skyler raised his mug and held it over the table between them. "A crew, then."

Each raised their own cup, and the four clanked together.

"Wait," Skyler said. The others froze and watched him retreat to the kitchen again. He found four clean champagne flutes in a cabinet, and an unopened bottle. "Where I come from, it's bad luck to toast with anything other than alcohol."

They each smiled and plucked an offered glass. "To the crew," Ana said, raising her flute. The toast was echoed in unison, and everyone drank. Skyler never cared much for champagne, but here, now, the bright and sweet liquid seemed the perfect choice to seal their pact.

"So," Vanessa said when her glass was empty, "what will we do first?"

Despite all of Skyler's talk about being equals, they all looked to him. He finished his drink and set the glass down. "First? I think we'll become teachers."

28

DARWIN, AUSTRALIA

30.AUG.2283

Grit and sand filled the air of Nightcliff's landing yard, churned by the thundering engines of the *Advantage*.

Even from within the windowless cabin, Samantha could hear the fine powder blast the aircraft's fuselage. Some portion would get sucked back into the turbofans themselves, which meant hours of cleaning and tests later.

The *Advantage* had been originally specced for short-range delivery work. Packages and parcels mostly. As such the interior had no conveniences for passengers. Just a pair of hot seats that butted against the cockpit wall. The rest of the cargo compartment was all bare steel walls, ugly rivets, and rows of ring hooks on the floor and ceiling to attach plastic nets.

The netting draped over four large stacks of pillow-shaped bags, each filled with topsoil from a field in nearby Queensland. On the trip out, the same space was occupied by fresh environment suit packs. More aura-scrubbed air and water for the workers who filled the dirt bags.

She'd made the trip dozens of times in the last few months. All the scavengers had. The crews ran like clockwork and worked like slaves, all under her stern direction. And she under Grillo's.

The craft lurched and Samantha heard a dull thud. "Secure on pad three." The pilot's voice came through her borrowed flight helmet. She didn't bother to acknowledge. Instead she stood and tossed the helmet into the foldout seat she'd occupied. Tired legs carried her past the cargo to the rear-loading ramp. At the flip of a switch, the aircraft's rear hatch opened like a whale's mouth.

Bright sunlight began to fill the cabin, in a sharp line that climbed her boots, then her legs, then her torso. Sam raised her arm instinctively as the glaring rays reached her face.

Once her eyes adjusted, she realized a welcoming party waited outside. The sight gave her a brief flashback to the inspection Russell Blackfield had made of the *Melville,* so many months ago. Only it was Grillo who now waited at the bottom of the ramp, and his posse of bodyguards were plain-clothed.

She'd seen little of Nightcliff's leader since the alien cube had been recovered from Old Downtown. He'd left her at the airport gate that night, almost as an afterthought, before he and his Jacobite friends had caravanned off with their strange prize.

What had become of the object, Sam had no idea. Grillo had not mentioned it once, and she'd been reluctant to ask. *Whatever the hell it is, I don't want anything to do with it.* Nightmares of that mission still woke her some nights, and Sam wanted nothing more than to forget she'd ever seen the thing.

Since that day, all of her scavenging requests came via messages delivered by courier. His promise to allow her a visit with Kelly had not been mentioned, and with each day her desire to keep working for the man dwindled.

"Dirt," Sam said by way of greeting. "Six tons. As requested."

"Nutrient-rich topsoil," Grillo said to correct her. "Excellent work, Miss Rinn. As always."

Sam shrugged, leaned against the aircraft's wall, and studied the men with him. They made no move to come aboard and start the unloading process. "Dump it here as if my plane had a bowel movement, or . . . ?"

"A crew is on the way to handle transport," Grillo said. "I came to see you, actually."

"Well, here I am."

A patient smile formed on the slumlord's thin lips. "Would you come with us, please?"

"Am I in some kind of trouble?"

"No, no," Grillo said. "The opposite, in fact. Kelly's here. I thought you might want to see her."

Sam bounded down the ramp, the clangs from her boots echoing off the interior of the cargo bay. "Here? Why?"

Grillo dismissed her concern with a wave. "To get her some fresh air, I suppose."

"What kind of hole have you kept her in?" Sam asked. Four heavy steps down the ramp and she stood in front of Grillo, towering over him. His bodyguards moved forward, hands reaching for concealed weapons.

"Relax, everyone," Grillo said. His voice had an uncanny ability to calm, and he used it to full effect. "Kelly waits for you on the roof above my office. I'll give the two of you some time to chat, and then we can discuss the future."

The future. Sam let her fists unclench, and she thought back to the terms Grillo had set when she started working for him. He wanted to be convinced of her allegiance. Only then would he release Kelly.

He gestured toward the control building that straddled the Elevator cord. Sam glanced back and barked an order to her pilot, James, to return to the airport after the workers emptied the cargo bay. The old man waved from the interior door. A former commercial pilot, he had no nose for combat but handled any aircraft they sat him in as if it were an extension of himself. When sober, at least.

Grillo set a languid pace across the dusty yard. In dry season Nightcliff became a miserable place, hot and bone dry. The sweet salty smell that came in from the ocean during the wet months turned into an odor Sam liked to call "rotten seaweed." Gusts came in from the water in irregular intervals and filled the air with that stench. Less than a minute out of the *Advantage* Sam found herself breathing through her mouth.

"Three months," Samantha said. "I've been wondering when you'd make good on your promise. I figured you'd forgotten about it after we found that—"

"I must remind you not to talk of prior missions," Grillo said in a rush. "Forgive my delay. I've been busy."

He had at that. Though Sam had not been allowed to leave the airport, she had heard plenty of talk at Woon's. Garden buildings fell to Grillo on an almost daily basis. Every week one of the skyscrapers that still had power seemed to suddenly find reason to form an alliance with the man. Those that didn't were increasingly isolated, and talk of running street battles was a constant topic at the tavern.

Gardens flourished on the rooftops of those buildings that did join his fold, and they were defended with zeal by Jacobites according to the gossip. Indeed the sect seemed to be experiencing an explosion of converts. Some spoke of groups of the religious freaks patrolling streets around the fortress and out into the Maze. Temple Sulam, the Jacobites' original house of worship in Darwin, attracted huge crowds on Sundays now. Ten thousand worshippers on a recent morning, by some accounts.

Sam stole a glance at Grillo and wondered how deep his ties to the cult ran.

The inside of Nightcliff's control tower offered little respite from the repugnant furnace of the yard. A bit cooler, perhaps, and the smell changed from ocean decay to the stale, sweaty scent of a locker room. *Air-con on the fritz,* Sam guessed. She knew of at least a dozen places within a two-hour flight from Darwin to fetch spare parts for the equipment, but she kept that to herself.

Grillo took the stairs with the same maddeningly slow pace. Sam mustered every last ounce of self-control not to elbow him aside and rush to the roof to see her friend.

The flights of worn concrete steps ran together in a blur. Sam had made this trek once before, when Grillo summoned her the night of her escape attempt, but it hadn't seemed so far. Her thighs burned from the effort by the time two of Grillo's bodyguards stayed behind on a landing, an indication that they were close.

The slumlord opened the next door and Sam was hit by a wall of humid air. He went through and led her down a narrow corridor that vaguely reminded her of Gateway Station, and for a second she saw herself back there, Kelly in front of her as they scurried from one junction to another evading Alex Warthen's guards. Unpainted concrete walls were almost hidden beneath pipes that rusted at their joints. The heat made breathing a chore.

A door at the far end entered into another stairwell, and here Grillo went *down. Odd route,* Samantha thought. Grillo must be trying to prevent her from seeing something. That, or he didn't want her to be seen. Either option made gears turn in her mind.

He descended only one flight before he pushed through another door. This one led into a foyer Samantha had previously seen. It fronted the office Grillo used, formerly occupied by Russell Blackfield.

"Still warming Blackfield's chair?" she asked before her brain could tell her mouth to shut.

Instead of a spoken response, Grillo forged ahead through double doors.

Sam barely recognized the office within. None of Russell's sloppy furnishings or tasteless decorations remained. Cramped and haphazard before, the space had seemed modest, if not small.

Now, though, the room bordered on palatial. A simple wooden desk sat at the middle of the far wall, with two identical chairs on either side of it. A matching wood file cabinet was parked underneath. To Samantha's right, two large windows framed the corner of the room, with a wide view of Darwin's crowd of skyscrapers.

The view of the crumbling city from here impressed her, despite the fact that she'd seen Darwin from aircraft a thousand times. Samantha could see east to the horizon, over the garden-studded rooftops of the chaotic Maze. South loomed a wall of skyscrapers, the lower floors hidden under a crust of bolted-on rooms where living space had been extended to the maximum. The upper floors were a patchwork quilt of glass panes and improvised coverings in the numerous places where the glass had long ago been broken. Drapes, blankets, and plastic tarps of every color and pattern filled the holes. Some open windowsills had cups, bottles, and buckets along the bottom to catch what rain they could. In wet season every window would, but during these months the chances were few and far between.

With an effort she focused on the immediate room again.

Natural light streamed in and fell upon four red love seats that formed a square. Two men sat there, each with a cup of tea in hand. They both stared at her but made no move to get up and greet her. Neither said a word.

"I'll be with you in a moment, friends," Grillo said to them. He went to his desk and sat behind it. Above him on the wall an enormous painting had been hung. Two meters tall and a meter wide, the image depicted a ladder stretching up into a cloudy sky. The rails and rungs of the ladder, on closer inspection, were composed of people. They stood on one another's shoulders, clasped arms, teamed together to hoist others higher, all in order to keep the ladder's shape solid. The strain on their tiny painted faces was evident, even from where she stood. A superimposed image of Christ on the cross covered all this, with the ladder of course forming the vertical portion.

The presence of the artwork dashed all remaining doubt Sam had as to Grillo's level of involvement with the sect. He was in deep. Pigs in a blanket.

"Where's Kelly?" she asked.

Grillo pointed toward a door off to her left. "You have an hour."

An hour. We could flee. Scale the wall down to the yard and run.

As she stepped through the door, Sam pushed that line of thinking away. Grillo had promised to release Kelly to her if he decided she could be trusted. Months of hard work had her close to that goal, and once achieved they could flee on an aircraft at their whim. Find somewhere far away to live, or—Samantha reminded herself Kelly was not immune. Maybe they could join the runaways, then, wherever they were. Hide somewhere in Darwin as a last resort.

That last would be difficult, she knew. Grillo's grip on the city spread like a flu, and unless Darwin's thousands of neighborhood kingdoms got their collective shit together, no one would be able to challenge him. She'd never been a big-picture kind of girl, and she still couldn't decide if Darwin under Grillo would be a bad thing. There'd be food, order, and law. But she guessed there wouldn't be much in the way of fun.

Beyond the door, Samantha found another narrow flight of stairs that led to a heavy steel door. A faded plaque indicated "roof access." Sunlight poured in as she pushed it open, and gravel crunched under her boots.

Sam raised a hand to shield her eyes from the brightness as she scanned the rooftop. Kelly was nowhere to be seen. Instead, a Jacobite nun stood near the edge of the roof, in a hooded robe of white flowing cotton. If not for the frayed hemline at the woman's feet, the garment could have been brand-new. The Jacobites' red ladder-and-cross sigil had been painted on the back of the robe. Someone once told Sam the symbol was painted with the acolyte's own blood as some sort of initiation rite. But she'd seen enough blood splash on her own clothing to know the color was wrong. Too bright, too *red*.

"Hello?" Sam called out. "I was told I could find Kelly Adelaide here."

The priestess half-turned, and Samantha recognized her friend instantly. "Hello, Sam."

Unable to hold it back, Sam erupted into laughter. "What the fuck are you wearing *that* for?"

Her laugh died when Kelly's expression remained impassive. She looked thin, and her mannish hairstyle was gone. Gray-brown hair came down to her neck, combed straight and simple and framed by the white hood.

"No, seriously," Sam said, composing herself. "What the fuck are you wearing that robe for?"

"I took the vows," Kelly said simply. She held out a hand and added, "Come and speak with me."

Samantha crossed the roof one slow, tentative step at a time. When she stood next to her friend, the woman seemed like a complete stranger. All the fire, all the spunk was gone. Instead she seemed almost demure. Pious, Sam decided, and she wanted to spit.

"It's good to see you," Kelly said as if reading a script. Her eyes flicked up and met Sam's for an instant, and then she cast her gaze downward. "You look well."

"And you look . . . Shit, I hardly recognize you," Samantha said. "What have they done to you?"

Kelly's lips pursed. "Nothing. I've simply discovered my true self, and found salvation."

The words sounded sincere on the surface. But Samantha knew Kelly. She'd heard her bluff past workers and even guards on Gateway Station.

A gust of hot wind swept over the roof. The white robe billowed around Kelly's body, revealing her shape beneath, a thin frame. Too thin, Sam thought.

As the wind gusted around them Kelly whispered something. It sounded like "Listen to the ghost. . . ."

The wind died out, and her strange words trailed off with it. Kelly's mask of piety returned.

For a time they stood in silence, Kelly soaking in the view of the city and Sam staring at her, looking for some hint as to what she meant. *Listen to the ghost? I'm standing right here. How could I not be listening?* Possibilities flooded her mind. Scenarios that would lead Kelly to don such vestments, which must be a deception. Perhaps it was part of some elaborate escape plan. Perhaps Kelly didn't know that Grillo would soon let her leave to stay at the airport.

"Have they treated you well?" Sam asked carefully.

"I have my own room," Kelly said, as if that settled the matter. Then she saw the dissatisfaction at her answer on Sam's face and went on. "It's not a cell, don't worry. Your work has spared me from that. No, this was a hospital room once, but now it's more like a hotel. I can see the city from my window. The stadium is *magnificent* to behold at night. But nothing compares to Jacob's Ladder, when the climbers are on it. I can see that, too, if I lean against the window."

Sam's mind raced. There were enough clues in that statement to guess where they held her. A hospital complex near Grillo's headquarters in Lyons, just north of the football stadium. Samantha wanted to shout at her friend in frustration. *Why tell me this? So I can break you out? You know Grillo plans to release you into my care, so what the hell are you up to?*

"Still," Sam tried, "nothing beats fresh air, yeah?"

"I get all the refreshment I need from reading the Testament," Kelly said.

In any other situation, Sam would have doubled over in laughter at such a statement from her friend. Here, though, it served only to unnerve her further. Kelly sounded like she meant it.

Kelly stole a sudden glance back toward the door, then leaned in toward Samantha and lowered her voice. "I think they're hiding something there, at the stadium. What it is I'm not sure, but it's important. A 'cube,' someone called it. I have to find out—"

"I know what it is," Sam said. "I found it for them. It came from—"

Kelly stepped back, her face hard and judgmental. She pressed a finger to her left ear. "The bird sings," she said.

Samantha didn't understand. "What?"

Kelly paid her no attention. "She spoke of it. She's not ready."

Before Sam could say anything she heard the sound of the metal door creaking open. She turned to see Grillo at the doorway. He stepped out, and Kelly went to him, taking a place just behind his left shoulder.

"Sam . . . Sam . . . ," Grillo said. "I thought we'd come further than this. You disappoint me."

She thought of protesting or playing dumb, but there seemed no point. She'd been sucker-punched by her last friend in the world, and all these months of work for this jackass were scattered to the hot wind. Sam felt a strong temptation to turn and step off the edge of the roof. She thought this must have been how Skyler felt when he crashed the *Melville*. Everything gone, taken. Skyler had fought on, though.

"You've failed this little test, Miss Rinn. I can't really blame you, though. You value your friends above all else. To a fault, unfortunately."

"Nail me to a cross then, asshole."

Grillo sucked in his lower lip, the composure on his face faltering for the briefest instant. "Anger is understandable. Your words, forgivable. But blaspheme again, Samantha, and I will show you pain far beyond what the redeemer experienced."

Any urge she may have felt to test his promise fell away when she saw the calm in his eyes, the absolute confidence. All of a sudden she wanted to be very far away.

"This transgression need not mean an end to our arrangement, Samantha. Just a delay, I'm afraid. I need to know you can be trusted, that you're truly one of us. Kelly has seen the path—"

"It's not Kelly anymore," the thin woman said.

Grillo turned to her, one eyebrow raised.

"I'm ready to take my sister name. I'm ready to leave my former self behind."

Samantha could only stare at her, the shadow of the woman she thought she'd known.

"Have you chosen a name?" Grillo asked.

"I have," Kelly replied calmly. "It was my mother's name."

Gabby, Sam thought. Kelly had told her many stories of her mum, Gab Gab, and how she'd been the very embodiment of the name. Always talking, always at ease in social settings. Kelly had envied that quality in her childhood, and strove to channel it as an adult.

"Josephine," Kelly said. "My mother would smile if she could see me now."

"She can, Sister Josephine," Grillo said. "I'm sure she's as proud as I am."

The name tripped Samantha, like the wrong punch line to a familiar joke. She realized her mouth was agape and snapped it shut, grateful that Grillo was looking at Kelly—Josephine—and not her. *Josephine.* The name rang a bell. Kelly had mentioned it before. No, Sam thought, she'd used it before.

On Gateway they'd needed access to a new set of security codes, and set about stealing them from a room that stored archival data for the entire station. Sam had assumed they would wait for the room to be empty, but Kelly told her to wait and listen. She'd proceeded then to bluff her way in, claiming to be Josephine and saying she'd forgotten her key card. Her acting had been masterful, Sam recalled, and the technician on duty had waved her in as if they were old friends.

Josephine. A persona Kelly had donned to steal something important. *Listen to the ghost.* Kelly is working an extremely long con, Sam realized, and this moment, right now, was the tipping point. Her friend wanted to remain in captivity in Lyons, or else whatever plot she'd cooked up would be ruined.

And whatever she was up to, it was important enough to throw Sam under a bus.

With sudden clarity she realized Grillo had been playing

them both on the same angle. Convince him of their sincerity, and he'd reward them. Sam had been going along to win Kelly's freedom, fully intending to escape with her friend at the earliest opportunity. Kelly's reward seemed to be stature in the Jacobite church. To what end, Sam had no idea.

"So what happens now?" Sam asked, buying time.

Grillo turned back to her as if he'd forgotten she was there. "I'm afraid we're back to square one. You'll return to your duties and try to earn my trust again. That, or rot in a cell, I suppose."

"Maybe I could take the robes, too," Sam said. "Say my Hail Marys or whatever you guys do."

"I'm afraid not," Grillo said. "I'd hoped sending Sister Jo to live with you—Sister Jo, I do like the sound of that! I'd hoped she could bring you to our flock, but I think more time is required. Return to your duties, Sam, and meanwhile I will think on what has happened here."

"What if I refuse?" she asked.

Grillo sighed. "Then you'll leave this roof the quick way."

Outside, the sun baked the city. Dry air raked across the dirty yard of Nightcliff, whipping up bits of trash along with the constant spray of fine sand. Sam could taste the grit of it in her mouth, and would have spat if she could muster the saliva.

The two guards who had escorted her from the building informed her that a car would be along to take her home. Courtesy of Grillo, they did not neglect to mention. Whether it was an offer or an order, she didn't care. Sam told them she'd rather walk, and she slipped through the patrol door adjacent to the fortress gates before the pair of goons could stop her.

In wet season Ryland Square was a sea of mud. Now, under the crush of sunlight and hot wind, the surface had become a cracked, brittle wasteland that crunched under her boots. Pigeons scattered as she crossed the center of the wide space, but would land again behind her the moment she passed. They squawked and fought over the corpse of a mouse, half-buried in the cake of mud.

It would take hours to walk back to the hangar, but she needed the time and space to think, and that wouldn't happen unless she avoided the scavenger crews. Lately they seemed incapable of even taking a piss unless she ordered it.

Ryland Square butted against Nightcliff's southern gate, and skyscrapers framed it on the three other sides. The square, a vast expanse of baked hardpan and broken concrete, was eerily quiet. Food riots, an almost daily occurrence during Russell Blackfield's stand against the Orbitals, were now a fading memory. Whether that was due to ample supply, or suppressed citizens, Sam didn't know. The cynic in her assumed the latter, but she'd brought enough soil and gardening equipment to Darwin in the last few months to wonder.

Power remained stable on the Elevator's cord, a fact that Blackfield tried to take credit for, and the city's endless supply of street urchins would believe anything as long as their bellies were full.

Grillo understood that tactic as well.

A third explanation for the empty square became obvious as she approached the edge of it. Jacobites milled about the gaps between buildings. She saw only a few at first, but as she walked closer the shadows came alive. There were a dozen of them at least, at just this one entry point. They spanned every age, race, and size, and all were armed with simple hand weapons. One carried an AK-47 on his back. The leader of the little troop, Sam guessed.

She realized then that she'd walked into Darwin unarmed. No wonder Grillo's bodyguards were so surprised at her refusal of the ride home. The Jacobite thugs nodded at her as she approached, though. They must have watched her since the moment she left Nightcliff's gate, and no one walked out of there alone and unarmed unless they were damn important. Sam hoped so, anyway.

She ignored them as she passed, save for the one with the rifle. To him she gave a simple, stern nod, which he returned. A gesture of respect, she thought, though his eyes held a measure of contempt. Most likely because she did not wear their robes.

Beyond Nightcliff's shadow, the city began to show signs of life. Filthy couriers dressed in rags shuffled about barefoot, carrying sacks of unknown contents over their backs. Few people of means braved street level themselves. Much of their business was done with adjacent buildings, and wherever possible zip lines and crude rope bridges spanned the gaps of alleys, high above the ground. For matters that required venturing farther from home, it was far better to send some skinny ground dweller to deliver goods or pick up supplies.

Grillo's mark was evident out here, too. Jacobite thugs patrolled the streets in packs of four or five, and Sam noted how the ragged citizens gave them wide berths. She wondered if the slumlord's sudden piety had more to do with the army he now seemed to command than it did any fervent belief as to the nature of the alien cable that stretched up into space.

Whatever. They're still freaks.

The image of Kelly, wearing those robes as she stood above Darwin, brought the sour taste of bile to Sam's throat. That moment would haunt her, no doubt. Tomorrow couldn't come soon enough, and hopefully she could leave the past where it belonged.

"Keep telling yourself that," she said.

She reached the airport unmolested. A couple of teens slipped out of an alley in front of her at one point, but it took only the gesture of cracking her knuckles to send them racing away. No mugger wanted a victim who would fight back, especially with all the Jacobites patrolling the area.

The guards at the airport gate were all Nightcliff supplied, and they waved her through without any fuss. Sam noted the total absence of swagmen around the gate. In times past, there would always be a crowd of hopeful petitioners loitering there, hoping to bend the ear of a scavenger to fetch something for them. Skyler used to stop and listen to them, in the early days. Eventually even he had to snub them, though. There was no room for charity work in this world. Not anymore.

A raucous sound came from Woon's tavern. Laughter and loud voices, common in the late evenings, was rather unusual for two in the afternoon.

Sam saw the backs of twenty people crowded near the door, facing within. Even more patrons were packed inside, all facing the bar. Another roar of laughter went up, and drinks were thrown back.

"What the hell?" she whispered.

She elbowed her way inside, and those behind her quieted. Others picked up the change in mood, turned, and went silent as well. By the time Sam reached the back of the room, all of the merriment had died out.

Their attentions had been focused on a man who sat at the bar, and for a split second her heart leapt. *Skyler?*

The man's hair dispelled that. Dark, sloppy dreadlocks. Sam knew that hair, and couldn't keep the grin from her face as she shouldered past the last row of onlookers.

"Skadz," she said. "You goddamn son of a bitch!"

"Sammy!" her old captain beamed, a broad smile flashing across his dark-skinned face. " 'Bout time you got here. I was running out of jokes to feed these blokes."

She drew him into a soldier's embrace. "They've heard 'em all, I'm sure."

"Didn't stop them from laughing."

She released him from the hug and held him at arm's length. Skadz, co-founder with Skyler of the original immune crew. The two had traveled together from Amsterdam to Darwin, and found her in no-man's-land fighting off a pack of subs. She'd killed four by the time they arrived to help, and probably could have handled the rest. Nevertheless, they'd been kind to her, and the three had their immunity in common. With nowhere else to go she'd stuck with them.

Jamaican born, Skadz was adopted by a Dutch family early on. As he told it, his adoptive parents then moved to England to follow the father's job, before coming back just before SUBS broke out. All this combined into one of the most unique people Sam had ever met. Skadz had the easygoing demeanor of an islander, the enlightened worldview of the Dutch, and the snooty accent of a Londoner.

"You look like you've seen a bloody ghost," he said.

"I'm looking at one," she shot back. *It has been a day of ghosts already.*

"Drink?" he asked.

Sam looked around. "Let's take a bottle to the hangar," she said.

He nodded, then added a grin that faltered slightly. He'd been away for more than a year, and must have noted the Nightcliff guards at the gate, and at his old hangar. No *Melville* inside, and no Skyler to greet him, either.

"You've got a million questions, I'll bet," Sam said. She grabbed a random bottle off the counter and offered a peace sign to Woon, who just nodded. Everyone loved Skadz, and Woon perhaps most of all. Outside the old crew, and Prumble, Woon had been the most surprised when the Jamaican had walked away from everything without a single goodbye.

"At least that many," her old captain agreed. He knew enough to hold them back, though.

She led him toward the hangar in silence. By now word of his presence at the airport had traveled to everyone, even those who didn't know him from before. A half-dozen people shook his hand or simply said "welcome back" as they weaved through the ragtag armada of scavenger ships that sat on the crumbling tarmac.

Sam stole glances at her old friend as they walked. He looked five kilos lighter than when he'd left, and a thin black beard grew on his chin and neck. His hair looked like a dirty bird's nest, but that was nothing new. There'd been a time when Skadz fussed over maintaining his throwback hairstyle. Clearly that hadn't been a priority while living outside the city.

A pair of Nightcliff guards stood to either side of the hangar door. They eyed the newcomer with open suspicion but said nothing. Sam rolled the heavy doors closed behind them and waited until the booming *clang* reverberated through the building before she turned to face her friend.

Whatever she'd been about to say, the words died on her lips. Skadz stood facing the empty hangar, shaking his head. "I thought maybe you guys were out on a mission, and the blokes at Woon's were just fucking with me."

"It's no joke," Sam said. "The *Mel* is gone. Crashed."

"Skyler go down with it?"

"Many think so, but no. He survived. A lot of shit's happened since then, though. If he's alive now, I have no idea. It's a long story."

Skadz digested that for a moment, and grunted. "So where is he? Where's Jake? And where's Prumble? I stopped at the garage on my walk in and it looked like the place had been bombed."

Samantha bit back her answer. There were more important things to discuss. "What are you doing here, Skadz? What do you want?"

"Huh?" he asked, and glanced over his shoulder at her. "This is my hangar."

"Like hell it is."

He burst into laughter then, and pointed at her. "The look on your bloody face! C'mon, Sammy, relax. I came in for a bit of trade with the big man, and thought I'd say hello. Let's open that bottle, yeah? I'll stay the night, and we can trade our stories."

"Stories," Sam repeated.

"Yeah. Though I'll be damned if mine is even a tenth as interesting as yours. Holy shit, Sam, what the hell happened here?"

She ignored the question. "You walk away without warning, for a year, and the reason you come back is to do business with Prumble? Where the hell have you been?"

"Here and there," he said with a shrug. "Spent some time down in Derby, but mostly I just wandered. Walkabout, the locals call it, yeah? It's as boring as it sounds."

"If it was so boring why'd you go? Why'd you stay away so long?"

"Boring is exactly what I wanted, Sammy. What can I say? I cracked. I hated being the candy man for an entire city."

She stepped up close to him, using her height out of habit, and looked down into his bloodshot eyes. "That's it? You couldn't handle the responsibility?"

He said nothing. Instead he gave her an exaggerated shrug.

"What a crock of shit," Sam said.

Skadz swallowed hard. "Fine, you need to know? Someone died."

"Lots of people die. Everyone, in fact."

"Someone died because I didn't scavenge what they needed."

"Who?"

"Remember Mary? The sheila I was seeing down in Hidden Valley?"

Sam nodded. "Shit. She died?"

Skadz shook his head. "Her daughter. Seven years old, cute as hell. She had this condition, called . . . doesn't matter. I promised to find the meds she needed." He hung his head. "No, fuck that. It's not that I couldn't find the damn pills, it's that I bloody forgot, all right? The lists back then were huge. Our missions totally mental. One request out of hundreds slipped my mind and Mary's little girl died."

"That . . ." Sam paused, searching for words. "It's tragic, but not the worst thing—"

"You want to know the worst part? Okay. Mary told me to apologize to the girl, before they cremated her. Told me to say something that might make her understand. And I tried, Sam, I fucking tried, but I . . . I couldn't remember her name, Sammy. The little girl. Her name was just, gone. Mary spotted it in my face and flew into a rage, threw my scatterbrained ass out, and told me never to come back. I still can't remember that little girl's name, Sam."

Sam backed off a step. "Jesus H. Why didn't you just tell us?"

"I already had to deal with seeing her accusing fucking stare every time I closed my eyes, Sammy. Didn't need to see the same every time I talked to you. You or anyone else."

"It wouldn't have been like that."

"Wouldn't it? I can see it now, in your freaky blue eyes."

"Don't. I'm just surprised to see my old friend, that's all. I'm not going to judge you, Skadz. That's in the past, and . . . Fuck, man, billions of people died. You're pretty damn low on the list of bad guys."

He glared at her. A flash of that temper she knew too well. Then Skadz sucked in a long breath through flared nostrils, and the hardness in his face melted.

"If it's any consolation," Sam said, "Skyler almost ran us into the ground after you left. But then . . ."

"Then?"

Sam motioned for him to sit. "Neil Platz hired us, and truly did run us into the ground."

29

DARWIN, AUSTRALIA

29.SEP.2283

Russell Blackfield wound up, sucked in a sharp breath, and heaved with both hands.

The Jacobite painting flew from the roof of Nightcliff's tower like a Frisbee, spinning in a flat trajectory for a moment before it banked and veered to the right. A second later the flight turned to more of a plummet, down into the depths of hell. *That's fitting,* he mused as he wiped his hands together.

He watched the canvas tumble and flutter until it disappeared just over the wall of the fortress.

"He scores!" Russell shouted as he thrust his fists into the air. A faint echo of his cheer rebounded off the skyscrapers that huddled next to the fortress like beggars at a trash fire. Somewhere a dog barked viciously, and he even saw a few candles lit in the tower windows at his booming cheer. Two in the morning might not have been the best time for his rampage, in hindsight.

He had to imagine the horrible excuse for artwork, now that it had left his field of view. The cult's sacred image, lying in a heap near Ryland Square, waiting to be ripped apart by Darwin's pickers when the sun rose.

It was almost enough to quench his rage. Almost.

Russell stood there, at the edge of the roof, and inhaled. The air tasted worse than it smelled. Stagnant ocean with a hint of piss, a classic Darwin vintage amplified by time spent above. Atmosphere on the space stations was sterile with a faint hint of metal and silicon. Once in a while he'd catch a whiff of flatulence not his own, but otherwise it was like breathing nothing.

He'd completely forgotten the giant armpit Darwin turned into when the rains went away. It would be even worse when the sun rose.

The skyline before him had changed since he'd last seen it. Seen in the dead of night it took him a moment to figure it out, but once he knew, he couldn't help but be impressed. *Gardens,* he thought. He could see the foliage, the greenhouse tents, silhouetted against a starry sky. *Fucking gardens everywhere.* Had the slumlord succeeded so completely? The thought bewildered him. Even more confusing was how they could water and fertilize so much growth. It implied a level of organization he would have sworn was impossible.

"No wonder they haven't been complaining about food," he said to himself. "And after I went to all that trouble to get some of the bloody farms back, too."

He shrugged. So Grillo had accomplished his task. *Good, now I can thank him and send him back to his maze.* Breathing through his mouth, Russell stomped back to the door and trudged down the stairs to his office.

My bloody office. It felt like an alien world. Grillo not only had decided his mandate included remaking the office, but the posh bastard also seemed to have a penchant for interior decorating. The space was clean, warm, inviting, and devoid of any personality.

The painting had been the only thing with any meaning. Russell grinned again at the thought of it crumpled and broken in the dusty alley below the wall.

A quick search of the room failed to turn up any alcohol, so Russell went to the double doors, opened them enough to see the anxious guards fidgeting there, and barked a request for vodka. The two men looked at each other as if he'd spoken to them in Swahili.

"Whatever you can find, then," Russell said. "I need a drink."
Neither man moved.

"Now!"

He shouted so loud that both men flinched. One finally broke away and shuffled off down a side hall. Russell sneered at the one who remained, then slammed the doors closed.

A few minutes later a soft knock at the door preceded the entrance of a bleary-eyed administrator.

"Kip Osmak," Russell said. He'd plopped himself into the sleek office chair Grillo had placed behind the simple desk. "What a pleasant surprise."

The greasy, feeble man stepped into the room and set a half-empty bottle of whiskey on the desk. He put a single shot glass next to it.

Russell plucked the cup and flipped it in the air, catching it deftly. He examined it, and though it looked clean he made a show of wiping it with his undershirt. "It's been awhile, Kip. How the hell are you?"

The man fidgeted. He turned back and forth between Russell and the exit, his stringy gray hair swaying about his face with the movement.

"Somewhere to be?" Russell asked.

"I'm fine. Good. No, nowhere especially."

"Sit," Russell said. "Drink." He poured a shot and pushed the glass toward the man.

"I'll pass, if you don't mind," Kip said.

"I do mind."

"Uh," Kip muttered. He wrung his hands together, relented, and picked up the glass.

Russell hoisted the bottle in a silent toast and tilted it back. The liquid burned in his throat before giving way to pleasant warmth. Kip only sipped his drink, Russell saw.

"What's the matter with you?" Russell asked.

"It's two in the morning. We weren't expecting you."

"Clearly."

Before Russell could interrogate the pathetic man for information, the doors swung open again. Grillo entered. Even at the odd hour, he wore a tailored suit and had not a hair out of place. Still, it had taken him an hour to get here since Russell stepped off the climber.

"You may leave, Mr. Osmak," Grillo said in a calm voice. "And thank you for the prompt alert of our guest's arrival." The two guards remained at the threshold of the room, and when Kip hurried past they stepped out and closed the doors behind them.

Russell leaned back in the modern, uncomfortable office chair and plopped his feet on the desk.

Grillo, to his credit, simply took the guest chair opposite, and clasped his hands in front of him. "Welcome back, Russell," he said.

"I thought we might chat."

"Of course. Please."

"Do you want to say a little prayer first, or anything like that?"

A flicker of anger shone in the man's eyes, then vanished. If he'd noticed the missing painting, he hid it well. "I'll be fine."

"Drink?"

"No. Thank you. Why are you here, Russell?"

Blackfield spread his hands wide. "This is my office. Am I unwelcome?"

"I mean on the ground," Grillo said thinly. "Of course you are always welcome, but I thought we had everything running to your satisfaction."

"Very much so," Russell said. "In fact, I was so impressed by your status reports that I found them hard to believe." He pressed the tip of his index finger onto the desk and held it there.

Grillo said nothing. His face betrayed nothing.

Russell Blackfield slid his finger across the desk and then checked it for dust. He found none, then smelled it just to be an ass. "Thought I'd come see for myself. First things first, you really ought to fire your decorator. This place is as bland as a piece of toast."

"I could have it restored to—"

"Don't bother," Russell said. "It suits you."

Grillo smoothed his pant legs. "Well, regarding my progress here. If you found my report unbelievable, perhaps another tour would dispel your concerns."

"Nah, I saw the gardens from the roof. Nice trick, that. How'd you do it? How'd you get all those fuckers to work together?"

"Don't you recall my demonstration? I offer them a carrot and a stick, and they get to choose one." The man's eyes narrowed. "Carrots are quite popular in a starving city."

Russell nodded. He understood that, though he preferred to offer two sticks. "Same goes for this Jacobite act? You give them a little hail-Jacob-on-high blah-blah nonsense, and they line up to suck your willy?"

Grillo's bottom lip pursed inward, his temples bulged. *There,* Russell thought, *I got under your skin for once. How's it feel?*

"My beliefs are my business," Grillo said. "And regardless, the Jacobites have brought peace to the streets. Something as alien to this city as the Elevator itself."

"Don't you mean ladder?"

Grillo leveled a gaze on Russell that could have withered a fresh rose. "My personal life is not your concern. You gave me six months," he said. "It's been five, and I have given you no reason to doubt my success."

"Darwin on a serving plate, yeah. But what happens at six months?"

At that Grillo shrugged. "That's for you to decide."

"Really?"

"It's your city. Do as you like."

Russell knew bullshit when he heard it, even from a true master of the art.

The glorified slumlord went on. "I hope you will see the benefits and perhaps extend our arrangement another six months. Your focus should be on the future of our civilization, after all, not which street gang holds which street."

"True enough," Russell agreed. He liked the sound of that and let it settle on his shoulders like a warm blanket. "Which brings me to the real reason for my visit."

"Oh?"

Russell took a swig from the bottle and set it down with a deliberate thump. "We've found our runaways, and the rest of the farms."

"That is excellent news."

"Thanks to both our efforts, the farms are no longer a card

they can play, though I haven't called them on that bluff yet."

"Why?"

Russell grinned. "If we still need food, we'll keep sending people for it."

"You intend to continue this trade?"

The grin on Russell's face widened. "One more time, is all. Ten squads, armed to the teeth."

Grillo nodded slowly. "So many men? That's a risk, isn't it? Your stations will be understaffed."

"That's where you come in." He felt a pang of pride at the way Grillo sat forward now. "I'd like you to send up a security detail to fill in. Temporary, right? Good fighters, loyal."

"That shouldn't be a problem."

Russell thought of that strange black tower, and the nightmare creature that cut through Tania's fighters like a machete. A shudder ran through him, and he hoped Grillo didn't notice. He would have a sudden change in plans when Grillo's men arrived in orbit. He'd send them to the meat grinder. Let them take the risk, and at the same time deplete Grillo's strength here. Then his own people could sweep in and clean up. *Perfect.*

"Perfect. Have them on a climber before the week is out," Russell said. "I'll need some time to train them for zero-g combat."

"A week is impossible. Every available fighter is deployed. A month would be better."

Russell shrugged. Tania wasn't going anywhere. A silence followed. He sipped from the bottle.

"Is there anything else?" Grillo asked.

"One more thing. I want to bring the immune, Samantha, with us when we go after the traitors. She was part of their little rebellion, and it might be that I can use her as bait. But when I went to the brig to fetch her, I found she wasn't there. The guard said she hasn't been there in months, nor the other. Kelly, I think her name was."

Grillo nodded, slowly. "I have other uses for them. It would be difficult to end that arrangement right now."

"No mention of that in your reports."

"There are numerous things I don't bore you with. I figured you wouldn't care about a couple of prisoners rotting in cells."

An old rage welled inside Russell Blackfield. A lot of things irritated him, but perhaps nothing more so than people who thought they knew his mind. He looked at the bottle of crap whiskey in his hand and thought of how satisfying it would be to smash the thing across Grillo's smooth-combed hair. "You found uses for them, eh? Playthings for your men?" He conjured an image of the tall blond immune, a head taller than he. *How I want to climb that mountain.*

Grillo had been looking at the floor, as if in prayer. He glanced up without moving his head, and for a second Russell saw wrath in those eyes. "Your brig proved insufficient to hold them, you should know. I thought it prudent to have them moved, but then I thought that still might not work. I realized I could accomplish two goals, then. So Kelly now resides at my own facility, under constant watch."

"And the immune?"

"Samantha is in charge of the scavenger crews at the airport."

"At the . . . wait, *in charge*?"

"In charge, and doing a fantastic job. Holding Kelly's safety over her has proved a remarkable motivator."

"I still think it's a bad idea. She's nothing special. Nice rack, hell of a right hook, and that's about it."

"She's immune. There are some who think that marks her as one of God's chosen."

Russell barked a laugh. "Or, you know, it's just some random genetic whatever. No need to get all biblical on the topic."

Grillo refused to rise to the bait. "The fact is, the scavenger crews were sitting on their hands after that business in Africa. Not anymore."

Heat rose on Russell's cheeks. His hand tightened on the neck of the glass bottle and it took a conscious effort to keep from swinging it. "Going to rub my nose in that again, eh?"

Grillo waved his hands. "That's not what I meant at all. I'm simply saying the crews were idle after that. Afraid and unsure of their status in your airspace. Samantha has them running like a Swiss watch now. It's really quite impressive."

"I'm sure." Russell found no path he could take to argue the point. He knew all too well the benefits of having a functional scavenger corps, and the immunes were the cream of that crop. It galled him, however, that Grillo had thought of it. More than that, he'd pulled it off. Scavenger crews running, the city calm and producing nearly all the food it needed . . . deep down he knew he'd never have been able to accomplish the same thing.

I did, though. I put this bloody rat in charge. Russell had no qualms about taking credit for that. Great leaders delegate.

The question was how hard it would be to undo.

30

BELÉM, BRAZIL

18.OCT.2283

Tania stepped down the rollaway staircase, each footfall producing a soft metallic click on the textured metal steps.

At the bottom, her feet met freshly poured concrete, and she smiled.

Compared to her last visit to the colony, almost two months earlier, the base camp was almost unrecognizable.

"Impressive," Zane said behind her. He came down the steps slowly, his attention shifting from his feet to the scene around him and back. Tim appeared in the climber's airlock next. The young man squinted in the sudden brightness, and then smiled as he took in the camp.

Large swaths of the ground within the Elevator's aura had been surfaced with concrete, and this had gone a long way toward reducing the mud, dust, and misery within the camp. The concrete had been poured in long rectangular strips, and the spaces between were surrounded by low brick walls. Black soil filled those walled-in areas, and in places she could see signs of vegetables beginning to poke through.

All of the tents were gone. In their place, a mishmash of

motor homes, modified cargo containers, and small prefab houses served as living space. These were placed in orderly rows along the concrete strips, with the spaces between them serving as narrow alleys. One wide avenue had been left, from the main entrance of the camp to the base of the Elevator, and then on to the shore of the river beyond.

She glanced west. Much of the work being done now focused on the nearby university buildings. These lay just outside the Elevator's aura, but a clever plan had been hatched to make a courtyard, open on the side that faced the Elevator, into the new impound yard for the aura towers. Two benefits came from this approach: The towers were naturally protected on three sides by university buildings, and in turn the towers provided a protective aura around the structures. This enabled their use for storage and, where feasible, more living space. But the buildings were in bad shape after five years of neglect, and so nearly half the colony now labored to restore them to a passable quality.

It had taken Tania some time to approve the plan. What if the few remaining aura towers suddenly "woke up" and plowed through the buildings like they were made from paper? Anyone inside would surely be killed in the resulting collapse. But as time went on, and no more aura towers showed signs of autonomous movement, she found it harder and harder to argue. At the ninety-day mark, she changed her vote to "yes" for the plan, and work started the next morning.

Tania turned east. That side of camp now looked like a garbage dump compared to the rest. No concrete had been poured there yet, and any equipment that needed repair or dismantling had been carted to that side temporarily. She saw three colonists climbing over a rusted piece of machinery she didn't recognize. They used wrenches and hammers to yank portions off the bulky object. Spare parts, probably.

Karl strode up. They shook hands and she saw he labored to breathe, as if he'd just run a kilometer.

"Welcome down," he said between gasps of air. He shook Zane's hand next, then Tim's.

"This is miraculous progress," Zane said.

Karl nodded, still short on breath.

"Are you okay? Is it the headaches?" Tania asked.

He grinned at her, took a few seconds to get under control, and then spoke. "Running late is all. Thanks for coming."

"Of course. I'm amazed at the progress, Karl. It's like a little city."

The pride on his face warmed her. "Well," he said, "no time to stand around. Come with me?"

"What's this surprise?" she asked as they walked northwest toward the wide gap in the camp's barricade. "The firearms training you promised, I hope?"

"Later, Tania. Right now, I have more progress to share." He led her through the camp entrance.

Four armed colonists, two on either side of the opening, waved at them as they passed. "Keep near the tower," one said, answering Tania's unspoken question as to the border of the aura. The wall marked it, roughly, but had been built five meters inside the actual radius to allow for some buffer. But one aura tower waited just outside, and Karl gave it a gentle nudge in the direction he wanted to go.

Once they rounded the corner and were outside the barricade, Tania saw the surprise he'd invited them down for.

Four aura towers were placed in a line formation along the Belém street north of the camp. At the base of each were four colonists, all decked out in survival gear.

Skyler and his three immune friends stood in front of the line, and Karl led the group to them.

"Is this what I think it is?" Tania asked. She flashed Skyler a smile and he returned it, but his expression had lost the warmth she used to find when their eyes met. She wondered if, or how, she could ever win it back.

"Tania, Zane, Tim, may I present your scavenger corps," Skyler said, gesturing.

The idea had not appealed to Tania when first proposed, and not just because such a setup would required the full-time assignment of four aura towers. She simply didn't relish the idea of putting anyone into harm's way, not after what had happened in the rainforest. Granted, with so few towers left the need to scavenge for supplies had become a critical necessity. To her, though, Skyler and his new crew seemed capable of handling the load. It wasn't until Karl had pointed out to her the marked difference in productivity between Skyler's outings and those arranged ad hoc by random colonists that she'd relented. "They just don't think like he does," he'd said to her. "We need full-time, dedicated crews."

"I'm impressed," Tania said to them, loud enough for all to hear.

Skyler came to stand next to her, and turned so he faced the crews as well. "Each group has a dedicated tower, as you know, and each is assigned a certain portion of the city."

The immune called Ana stepped forward and presented Tania with a map. She took it and smiled at the young woman, but she was looking at Skyler. *I know that look,* Tania thought. She felt her pulse quicken and a hollowness in her gut that she recognized as jealousy. The sensation surprised her as much as the affection she saw between Skyler and the newcomer. Tania forced herself to look at the paper in her hands, but she couldn't focus on any of it. What had she expected? Skyler to wait around for her? As if he had no more choice in the matter than the moon did in orbiting Earth?

Tim stepped in next to her, just behind her shoulder. "Let's have a look," he said, a bit too loud.

He gripped the edge of the map just below where her fingers pinched the page. Only then did Tania realize her hands were shaking. Not much, but enough that he might have noticed. Whether Tim had meant to rescue her from the moment or not, she felt grateful for the defusion.

On the map the city was divided into quarters of roughly equal size. Those in the more densely constructed parts of the city were a bit smaller, while the vast slums had larger blocks.

"Each section has a name," Skyler said, "and the crew assigned to that area shares the name." He leaned close and ran a finger across each section, calling the name as he went. "Tombstones, Dockyards, Ugly Church, and Eden Estates."

With each name, one of the crews arrayed before her gave a little call, like any military outfit might. At first she cringed at the silly names, but she knew they matched what the colonists already called those areas. The dark skyscrapers of downtown looked like tombstones. The dockyards spanned almost the entire waterfront. The others she could guess, save the last. "Eden Estates sounds nice at least."

"Oh, believe me, it's the worst of the lot. Sarcasm was in order, and I don't say that lightly."

"Okay," she said, a little disappointed.

"Now," Skyler said, "watch. Colton! If you please?"

A young man with the crew farthest to Tania's left nodded and began to walk away from his tower. He walked some distance, toward the invisible edge of the tower's protective aura, when suddenly he stopped and held up his arm. A wristwatch-like device was strapped there, and it beeped loudly. Even from here, almost two hundred meters away, Tania could hear it clearly.

"We found the devices in a pet store," Ana explained brightly. "Supposed to tell you when your dog has left the yard."

"Each tower has a beacon, and the crew assigned to that tower all wear matched receivers. Stray too far, we've set it for one hundred seventy-five meters, and the alert goes off."

"That's fantastic," Tania said. The fear she'd confessed to Karl, of such crews becoming careless, or losing track of the tower assigned to them during a fight with subhumans, faded. "Could we do something like this for all the colonists?"

"Maybe," Karl said before Skyler could answer. "The problem is that the receiver can only be paired to one transmitter. Works great for these crews, but that's because they're only worried about their own tower."

"We could at least provide them for those who stay near camp, tied to the Elevator cord itself," Skyler added. "But we need to find more, first. The store that provided these is now depleted."

"I see," Tania said. "Please do that; it would give the colonists some peace of mind."

Skyler looked at Karl. "Bump it up the list," he said.

"Will do."

Tania handed the map back to Ana and returned her attention to the crews themselves. "What else?" she said.

"Each crew has been trained," Skyler said. "Everything I could think of in terms of scavenging, plus some basic tracking and survival techniques thanks to Pablo, Vanessa, and Ana here."

Tania nodded thanks to the three immunes. She noted how

they all stood together. The fifth crew, she thought.

"In addition we've drilled them extensively in self-defense, tactics, and weapon use. They all have assigned arms they carry and are responsible for maintenance of. I've left it up to each crew to designate their leader."

"Leaders!" Karl shouted. "Come over here, please."

One member from each crew jogged up. The one called Colton was last to arrive, returning from his demonstration of the beacon.

"You all are to report to the comm room each morning that you're in camp, at eight, for your priority lists," Karl said to them. Then he turned to Tania. "I'll be the keeper of the master list, and everyone's been instructed to refer to me any colonist asking for something. I'll also keep an inventory list of what the crews bring in."

"That's a lot to do," Tania noted. "You should pick an assistant from the camp."

"I may even pick two," Karl agreed.

"Well," Tania said, "I'm very impressed, and I want to thank all of you for volunteering for this role. I know it will have its dangers, but your work will be vital to the success of the colony."

The leaders all smiled and muttered acknowledgments. Tania hoped the statement had enough sincerity. She heard the words as if they came from someone else—a politician or an actor, not her. In her heart of hearts, Tania would still rather be up on Black Level, alone in a quiet lab, poring over telescope data.

Absently she smacked an insect that had landed on the back of her neck.

The show ended, Karl dismissed the crews to begin working on the lists they'd been provided that morning. "No time to waste," he said, waving them off.

Tania watched with some fascination as each leader returned to their crew. Each group huddled over laminated or digital maps, and within minutes the first team began to guide their aura tower down the dusty street.

"That young man," Skyler said, "Colton, who demonstrated the warning beacon."

"Yes?" Tania asked.

"He's bright. Motivated. Someone to elevate when the time is right. Pardon the pun."

"Good to know."

Karl cleared his throat. "Same goes for that one next to him," he said, pointing. A dark-haired youngster in Colton's crew strode out in front of the tower, scouting ahead. Even from this distance Tania could see the innate communication between them. Body language and simple commands that kept each constantly aware of the other. "Nachu," Karl said. "A machinist from Platz Station. He and Colton both were, actually. Best friends. Each is clever as hell in his own right, but as a team they're a marvel to watch."

"Noted," Tania said. "As the colony grows we will need good leaders."

"Don't go stealing my people so soon," Skyler protested.

"Not soon, but in time. Before the Builders return . . . if they do . . . we'll want to have a task force that can be mobilized quickly, whatever happens."

"Agreed," Skyler and Karl said in unison.

A sober silence followed. She despised being reminded that the Builders might not be done. If their schedule held as calculated, the colony had a year and some few months before another "event" would occur. But what might happen was anyone's guess, and Tania detested speculation without data.

Yet the words of Neil Platz still haunted her. He'd been wrong about the third event, expecting a Builder invasion fleet to come and claim the planet, but that didn't mean his fear wouldn't yet be realized. Who knew how many Builder ships were lined up to reach the planet? There could be a hundred more events, until the point that they'd be arriving daily. *Hourly*.

Tania shivered at the prospect despite the heat. She struggled enough to imagine, or avoid imagining, what might come next. To dwell on it would only lead to what Greg and Marcus called "analysis paralysis."

"I do have one question," she said.

Both men turned away from the departing scavenger crew.

"Skyler, there's four zones on the map, but unless I'm mistaken we have five scavenger crews, don't we? What about you and your . . . ?" She nodded toward camp, where the three immunes had gone.

"My crew," Skyler said. His voice conveyed pride and sadness in equal quantity. "We'll help the other crews as needed, scout the border regions beyond the marked areas, and also explore the larger buildings where the towers can't provide full protective coverage."

"I see."

"There's more," he said. He shuffled on his feet. "I want to find another aircraft. We'll soon discover needs that Belém can't fulfill. And eventually . . ."

"Yes?"

Skyler looked north toward the horizon. "The other tower groups that left that night. We should find out where they went, I think, before . . . well, *before*."

"Before the Builders come back," she said, finishing for him.

Skyler nodded, grim-faced. "The group here, out in the rainforest, went to surround a crash site. The others probably did the same, and we'll find the same dangers, but you never know."

"And don't forget," Karl put in, "only four tower groups left. Tania, you spotted five of the smaller ships arriving, right?"

"Five that I saw, yes."

"So one is unaccounted for. We should consider seeking it, as well. Maybe there's one undefended by towers, one we can study easily."

"I hadn't thought of it that way," Tania admitted. In her mind she ran through scenarios, techniques that could be used to find all the ships.

"I want to follow one of the three remaining tracks, see where it goes," Skyler said. "Maybe we'll find they landed in some pattern, and the mystery fifth ship's location will become clear."

"Perhaps," Tania said. She'd had the same thought, but with no access to satellite imagery she had no way to confirm it. Skyler and Karl seemed to be waiting for her approval of the plan. "I'm loath to risk you, Skyler. You and your crew."

"Everything we're doing out here is a risk. And honestly I'd feel more comfortable in a plane than walking these streets."

Tania searched his eyes, trying to decide if he was deliberately looking to get away from the camp, or really wanted to seek the missing towers. Some of both, she concluded. "The colony comes first," she said. She noted his disappointment instantly, and held up a hand. "I just want to make sure the new crews are handling their roles before you go anywhere."

There were problems right from the start, and Skyler began to wonder if he'd ever be able to relinquish his role as the herder of cats.

Despite all the training, the new scavenger crews missed what should have been obvious opportunities with frustrating regularity. Not only that, but they took their marked regions on the map too seriously, and would bypass ripe sites just because they were on the wrong side of a street.

Logistics were a constant struggle. Karl and his chosen assistant, a former secretary to Neil Platz named Alfonz, struggled to come up with a decent method of cataloging all the sites within the city, their salvageable contents, and also what had already been returned to the camp. When the colonists' shifting priorities and daily emergencies were added to the mix, it became almost impossible to give the scavenger crews clear orders.

Skyler spent more time venturing out with the lowest-performing crews than he did with his own immunes. A woman named Rebecca ran the Tombstones crew efficiently enough, and the crew called Eden, for Eden Estates, took to their short-straw task of farming the eastern slums with surprising zeal and energy, thanks to their two inventive leaders, Colton and Nachu. But the other crews had varying degrees of success.

Worst of all, subhuman sightings began to rise sharply, as if the subs had been released from their vigil at the crashed Builder ship. Soon the crews were faced with almost daily encounters with the beings. The instinct they displayed to surround the crashed ship, and moan their strange chant, had apparently left them. Skyler feared that the armored versions would begin to show up, but as of yet no one had seen them, and the monitors placed at the circle showed no sign of them beyond shadows within the haze.

Those in camp could hear the distant, sporadic gunfire roll through the city, and often found crews returning empty-handed, or worse, with injuries that required tending.

On one rainy November morning, a battle erupted from the area called Ugly Church that lasted for almost an hour. So long, in fact, that Skyler gathered his own team and set out across the city to try to help.

Ugly Church was so named for the massive Catholic cathedral that dominated the cityscape there. The structure itself was, ironically, quite beautiful, despite the vines that now crept over and through its lower levels, or the rats that watched from every shadow. The "ugly" part of the name was due to the skeletons. Thousands littered the grounds, and no colonist had yet dared to venture inside.

Roughly five years ago, when the disease swept through here like a sudden thunderstorm, the pious had flocked to their house of worship, filled the place, and crowded around it in some kind of—ultimately useless—mass prayer.

Skyler and his team spotted the Ugly Church crew's aura tower near a low wall that partially ringed a traffic circle. The church itself was a few blocks away, but even here there were skeletal remains strewn about the ground. Time and rainfall had, at least, done away with the stench.

They arrived too late.

After a brief skirmish to finish off the remaining subhumans in the area, Skyler found himself amid a massacre. All four members of the Ugly Church crew lay dead. Two had apparently shot each other in an unfortunate bit of crossfire, though Skyler figured that may have been a mercy given what they were up against.

Skyler and Pablo cleaned up the scene as best they could while Ana and Vanessa stood guard. The fallen crew were buried in a shallow grave, after the useful equipment had been removed from their persons. Skyler worked methodically, having long ago abandoned any qualms about such things. Pablo, on the other hand, paused frequently to still his shaking hands.

Every other crew was called back to camp after that. The setback ate away at Skyler's optimism. Since Gabriel and his cronies were defeated, and the strange alien ship with its black-clad defenders had been willfully ignored, the camp had operated with surprising efficiency. But the relative lack of subhumans in the surrounding region had lulled the colonists. Many had still never seen a subhuman since setting foot off the climber car that brought them down. Now that the dam had broken, it almost didn't matter that the Builders had provided movable pockets of aura. Everyone cowered within the camp, patrolling the crude wall, crying alarms at every shadow that moved in the surrounding slums.

After much discussion a revised system was put in place. A new crew would be trained to replace the one they'd lost, but in the meantime the three remaining would be reshuffled to give each at least one skilled combat veteran. For a time they would forget scavenging, though, until the sudden population burst of subhumans could be dealt with.

Skyler had lived through one purge. *The* Purge, as it was called in Darwin. He'd fought in it, side by side with Jake, among others. Weeks of roaming the flat, scrubby lands around Darwin, killing every one of the creatures they came across. And in those days they were legion.

A similar effort was mounted in Belém. The scavenger crews, along with a handful of volunteers who could handle weapons, began to run sweeps back and forth in an expanding circle centered on the Elevator base. Skyler rode in the back of a pickup truck driven by Vanessa. Ana and Pablo were with him, and the three of them armed themselves with good high-power rifles. They drove back and forth along the line all day, helping if needed, scouting if not.

On the first day, no subhumans were encountered, but the circle had only expanded out two hundred meters from the wall. By the end of that week, they'd pushed out a full kilometer, and more than forty subs had been shot without a single injury to the colonists.

To go farther would strain resources to the limit. After a brief debate with all the various leaders, Skyler pointed out that unless they could somehow actually hold that ground, which was impossible given their numbers and the limited aura towers, the best course of action was to simply unleash the "ring of extermination" once a week, in order to keep the buffer zone around the camp as clear as possible. Any scavenging missions beyond that one-klick area would require special permission and would be handled by two teams working together.

By the height of wet season, the camp was running like a machine again.

Climbers worked their way up or down the Elevator cord daily, sometimes even in multiples. Subhuman encounters around camp dropped to manageable levels as the weekly purges became a camp routine. Indeed, the colonists became accustomed to the creatures, and most were now adept at fighting them. The sight of rifles slung over shoulders, or pistols holstered at the waist, became the norm.

Every month, with only some variance, Melville Station would receive another forty "volunteers" from Darwin. The people who could be vouched for by friends or relatives in camp always integrated quickly enough. Everyone else, those chosen via suspect criteria by Russell Blackfield, were kept on the station under guard for a few days, and then sent to places where they could be watched around the clock. To everyone's amazement, and intense suspicion, none showed signs of being spies. A few reported that Russell no longer bothered to pick the migrants, that he'd delegated the task to one of the old Orbital Council members. One migrant, Skyler heard, told of a newfound sense of purpose in Darwin. Gardens apparently flourished, and along with the farm platforms Russell had schemed out of Tania, the food situation was almost under control. Neither Tania nor Zane was overly troubled by this news, as neither felt the colony could handle too many more migrants. Soon the ecosystems surrounding each Elevator would no longer have need of one another, and this worried Skyler.

Skyler woke one December morning to the familiar sound of rain rattling against the roof of the APC, which had become his home. He checked the adjacent vehicle and found Ana's bunk was empty, which was not uncommon since she'd finished mourning her brother. Depression behind her, the girl woke early with an abundance of energy and often slipped out to wander the camp before Skyler stirred. She had a voracious appetite to learn, and he rarely found her in the same place twice when he called the crew together. Sometimes she would be helping load or unload a climber. He'd found her helping in the gardens, pouring concrete, dismantling electronics for parts, and fishing. Always she would be under the tutelage of one camp expert or another, and she made fast friends with just about everyone she spent time with.

None of this troubled Skyler in the least. A multitude of friends within the colony meant she wouldn't always be following him around like a puppy. Not that he didn't enjoy her company. She was bright and funny and, sometimes, impossible. Where Tania always seemed to enter into conversations as an equal, Ana either played the eager student or the headstrong, passionate firebrand. There was little in the way of middle ground for her, and it made her constant company an exhausting affair.

So her absence most mornings didn't bother Skyler at all, and indeed he learned to love the early hours as he used to. Coffee and a serving of oatmeal with fresh fruit or avocado. He'd sit around a small heater and sip his drink, discussing everything and nothing with whoever happened to join him. Pablo usually, though he talked little. Vanessa could hold her own on just about any topic, but tended to sleep late.

Karl would drop by to share a cup once in a while. They saw each other most mornings anyway, for the list reviews, and anyway the older man's motor home was all the way on the other side of camp. Word had it he'd taken a lover, a woman of similar age who had been some midlevel analyst on Platz Station, and Karl's rare appearances for morning coffee seemed to corroborate the rumor.

And so Skyler was surprised that morning when he found Karl seated at the cook fire, next to a pot of boiling water and a pair of mugs.

"This is a rare honor," Skyler said as he pulled on a sweater. All of the vehicles left behind by Gabriel were parked with their back doors facing one another, forming a ring. A fire pit had been set up in the center of this, surrounded by a mismatched collection of plastic chairs and tables. Rain drummed on a giant blue and white patio umbrella that covered the small communal space, tied to the roof racks of the surrounding vehicles.

"I miss seeing your pretty face in the morning light," he shot back. With two hands he carefully extended a full mug to Skyler. A few drops sloshed over the side and sizzled as they hit the portable stove.

After a careful sip, Skyler rubbed his eyes and settled into a low beach chair. The constant prattle of raindrops on the umbrella drowned out the sounds of the colony around them. "What dire problem has you making me coffee at six in the morning, Karl?"

"The comm's out again," he said flatly.

"Give it a good smack on the side."

"Tried that. But it seems some water dripped through a hole in the roof of the container and fried the antenna dish."

"Is there a spare?" Skyler asked. "Wait, don't answer. You wouldn't be here if there was."

Karl took a noisy slurp at his own drink. "I was thinking, maybe you and the others could bring back a larger dish, more powerful. We've got plenty of surplus juice coming in from the campus thor, and it would give us a lot more bandwidth to Melville. Hell, we could even reach the farms or New Anchor without the relays."

"Have one in mind, or are we supposed to track one down?"

In answer Karl slipped a slate from his inner jacket pocket and handed it across. The thin black tablet's screen came to life as soon as Skyler's thumb brushed its surface.

"Those boys from Eden have started an effort to do a photo survey of the city, so we can 'scout' from the comfort of the comm room."

"Smart," Skyler said. An image appeared on the screen of Belém's skyline, taken from the eastern slums somewhere north of the Elevator base. Karl had dropped a marker on one office building's rooftop. It appeared to be the largest building in Belém, with a logo of PGF marking its side. Skyler zoomed in. As he did, he realized the genius of a photo survey. The image was fantastically high resolution and even had illusory depth to it. Skyler tracked in until he looked at a single window on the building's top floor, and still he could make out small details. This one image of the city alone could be studied and marked up for potential scavenging all without leaving the safety of home. "Very smart."

He panned the image until he found Karl's marker again. The notation pointed to a white dish-and-antenna assembly on the roof.

"It's about a meter tall," Karl said. "Compact but heavy. I suspect you'll need bolt cutters or even a torch."

"Rain has hammered that thing for five years," Skyler noted. He usually eschewed electronics that he didn't find indoors. "It might not even work."

"Hydrophobic coating. I've seen that model before. Expensive as hell, but it'll last ten wet seasons without batting an eye."

Skyler zoomed in even farther, almost as impressed with the sharpness of the image as he was with the clean, white surfaces of the comm tower. Karl had it right; there wasn't a sign of discoloration or rust anywhere on it.

The rest was details. By noon that day, Skyler and his crew were clanging up the steps of Belém's largest building.

31

DARWIN, AUSTRALIA

10.NOV.2283

"Is he in?" Sam asked the stranger sitting outside Grillo's Nightcliff office.

"No," the woman said. She had frayed red hair and a narrow face laced with worry lines. Her gaze drifted to the parcel Samantha carried. "That for him?"

Sam looked down at the package tucked under her left arm. The plastic bag that covered the book had a visible coat of sandy dust on it, just like her clothing, skin, and hair.

"You can leave it with me," the woman said.

"No," Sam replied. "He asked me to bring it to him specifically. He was very clear on that."

"Well, you'll have to wait till Monday. He's gone to Lyons, and tomorrow is the Holy Day."

A shiver ran along Sam's back at the mention of Grillo's original base of operations, out on Darwin's eastern edge just beyond the Maze. As far as she knew, Kelly lived there now, supposedly as a Jacobite nun called Sister Josephine.

"Thanks," Sam said. She turned and walked out, the idea forming in her mind with each step down the long stairwell that would let her out of Nightcliff's tower.

Outside a stiff breeze whipped light rain about. She tucked the parcel back under her combat vest and continued to walk. Halfway across the yard she caught a glimpse of the door that led to the cell block where she'd been held. She flirted with the idea of dropping in to see Vaughn, to apologize for using him. To make amends. And perhaps . . .

No. Another time. She had a small opportunity here to find out where Kelly was, to perhaps catch some additional small clue from her friend as to just what the hell she was doing.

Sam walked on. She slipped through the side door next to Nightcliff's main gate with a polite wave to the guards, ignoring their suggestion that she wait for someone to escort her back. It was a halfhearted request, anyway, given the metamorphosis Darwin's streets had experienced.

She followed the fortress wall, leaving Ryland Square to the east. The skyscrapers quickly gave way to smaller structures ranging from five to fifty stories high, pressed together as if they'd been through a trash compactor. Tight alleys wormed between the loosely defined blocks, plunging into darkness.

Sam picked one at random and ducked into the Maze. The light rain that had been swirling about her like a swarm of tiny translucent insects stopped almost instantly, replaced by eerie droplets that tumbled down from the endless balconies and awnings above. Day turned to twilight and then night in the span of five steps, as completely as if she'd stepped indoors. She glanced straight up, past the clotheslines and exposed pipes, past the buckets that captured water or served as toilets, past the occasional face in the darkness, watching her out of vigilance or, perhaps, boredom. Above it all she could just make out a crooked gray line that was the sky. Even if the sun had been out she doubted she could have used it to tell her direction. She'd have to rely on asking, but this didn't concern her. She still wore her combat gear from the mission, and such garb made people wary even in a city as jaded as Darwin. Plus, her reputation among the Jacobites preceded her more and more these days. Grillo, it seemed, had put the word out that she was to be treated as a friend. A sneer-worthy heathen friend, yes, but still a friend.

She'd been through the Maze on foot only a few times before, but always with Skyler to lead the way. Things were different back then, dangerous in a different way. Swarms of people flowed through the twisting alleys like blood through arteries. Vendors and beggars alike shouted pleas for attention. Scrawny children dressed in rags would trail along behind them, gawking at their weapons, their combat gear, the sight of boots that didn't have holes worn through.

None of that remained. The alleys were practically empty of people. She passed one old woman who lugged a burlap sack that reeked of mold. A few turns later she came across two children, six or seven years old, splashing back and forth through a puddle. Their laughter seemed completely alien in this place. When they saw Samantha, though, the kids ran off. One whistled, a long blast followed by a short. Not ten steps later Sam heard and then saw a street patrol approaching; five young men in thrown-together Jacobite robes. They were armed with faith, but since that would go only so far they also carried clubs of various shapes and sizes. One carried a lantern that gave off bright yellow light from an LED.

The tallest, armed with a baseball bat, jerked his head upward once. The simple motion asked, "Who the fuck are you and what are you doing here?"

Sam was opening her mouth to explain when the light from the lantern illuminated her enough that recognition dawned on the leader's face. His posture changed in an instant. "She's okay," the lanky youth said. "Ang mentioned her, one of Grillo's." His companions followed his lead and visibly relaxed.

"Which way to Lyons?" Sam asked, still grappling with the idea that Grillo had passed word down this far about her. Whatever he'd said, it didn't appear to include detaining her if she was found wandering alone. She tapped the package under her arm in hopes it would imply she had a specific errand. The one with the lantern pointed in the direction they'd approached from. "Thanks," she said.

"It's a long way," the leader said. "We'll take you."

"That's all right," Samantha said. "Stick to your duty." She went for a tone that suggested she had some authority to tell them what to do, and it worked. The leader gave her a nod and continued down the winding street with only a single glance back.

Sam picked up her pace then. If word of her impromptu visit arrived ahead of her, she might not get the chance to learn anything useful. The narrow streets and crooked alleys began to blur together, and twice she found herself at a dead end, forced to double back and find another route. An old man with a bicycle-powered rickshaw gave her a lift past Rancid Creek in exchange for two of the candy bars she kept tucked in a pocket of her vest. Food bribes always worked best, she'd found. The threat of violence came in a close second.

He dropped her off just after sunset at the Maze's eastern edge, a few blocks west of the stadium, waving his chocolate payment in victorious fashion as he pedaled away. He clearly thought he'd taken advantage of her, but after catching a whiff of Rancid Creek Sam felt the payment was well justified.

She skirted the stadium and the streets immediately surrounding where Jacobite street patrols swarmed like flies. Once in Lyons she relaxed. The streets were all but empty, the population sparse enough that she could leave the main roads anytime she saw someone coming from the other direction.

Grillo's base of operations was a large campus of buildings that had once been Darwin's hub for the medical profession, the crown jewel being an ultramodern hospital. How he'd managed to gain control over the area in the early days of SUBS Sam had no idea, but seeing him methodically dragging Darwin into line over the last several months made the conquest of a little office park like this seem entirely plausible.

The guards at the campus gate were seasoned, older. Three flashlights and a dot of red laser light all converged on her before she'd come within twenty meters of the entrance.

"Who goes?" one of them barked.

She held up a hand in a fruitless attempt to shield her eyes. "Sam Rinn. I run the old airport for Grillo."

"And what are you doing all the way out here? He's not expecting anyone."

She held out the package under her arm, raising it up. "Package for him. He asked me to deliver it personally." Not strictly true.

Grillo had sent her on the personal errand two days ago. He'd said he wanted the book in his hands right away once she'd found it, and she figured this was a reasonable interpretation.

One of the four guards came forward and put out his hand. When Sam didn't move he beckoned with his fingers.

"He said for me to deliver it to him personally."

"I just want to make sure it's not a bomb or something."

Sam held it out so he could study the cover. He leaned in, read the handwritten words there, and glanced back up. "No shit?"

Sam shrugged. "The real deal."

The sod actually licked his lips, and read the words again.

THE TESTAMENT OF THE LADDER
Being the word of God
Transcribed verbatim in faith and obedience
by Sister Annabelle Katherine Haley
Perth, Australia, 2268

The guard fingered a cross-and-ladder trinket that hung around his neck on a gaudy gold chain. "Blimey. Right, then. In you go."

Sam tucked the book back under her arm and followed him to the gate. He twirled one finger in the air, a signal to open the gate, and then waved her through.

"Thanks," Sam said.

"Uh, the gun stays here." He nodded toward her rifle.

Sam slipped it off her shoulder and handed it to him, then turned and walked down the drive into the heart of the campus. She could hear the guards talking among themselves. From the sound of it, one of them spoke into a handheld. A response came back a few seconds later, too muffled for Sam to make out exactly. She walked faster.

"Oy!" the guard shouted.

Sam half-turned without breaking stride.

"Wait at the house. Surgery Center is off-limits."

She waved. "Surgery Center. Got it."

* * *

Once she was inside the compound, the presence of guards dropped to almost nothing. Sam walked past two brick buildings that once probably served some administrative purpose. Two nuns walked past her with their eyes downcast. She studied each of them, but neither was Kelly.

The road forked. To her right, at the end of a long drive, was a residential enclave of five or six impressive mansions, all tucked within a manicured forest of palm trees. Two of the homes were lit. Which one Grillo occupied she didn't know or care. The fork of the road that went left led around a slow curve that passed in front of the hospital complex. Sam went that way, walking as fast as her legs would carry her, determined to reach the entrance before anyone could question her.

A tingle danced across her shoulder blades. The thrill of malfeasance mixed with the fear of being caught, the combination as welcome to her as cold water on a hot, dry day. She felt the craving deep within her begin to come alive at the prospect of being sated. The mission to fetch the book, which carried all the potential for danger, had been a dull letdown. She'd walked into the revered woman's home, found the book in a desk drawer, nabbed it, and walked out. No subs, no action. Boring. Any jackass in an environment suit could have done it, but Grillo insisted she go. He wanted the best, and he wanted no mistakes.

Sam just wanted to shoot something.

There were no guards at the entrance to the hospital. The thought that this might be a bad sign flitted through her mind like a fly batted away. No guards meant she had options.

The lobby was dark and sparsely furnished. Some fading sunlight just managed to illuminate the first few meters of the space through floor-to-ceiling glass panels that fronted the building. The panels were caked with dust and grime, giving the light that made it through a greasy red hue. Sam guessed there had once been rows of seats here, to provide someplace to sit for the families of patients. None remained, though, giving the room an empty-dance-hall feel.

She tucked the supposed holy book into a large pocket inside her combat vest, then tugged a flashlight from a pocket on her pants and flipped it on. It was a tiny thing, Special Forces issue, with eight small LEDs driven to blinding intensity by a Zigg ultracap the size of a penny. The beam made a white cone of illuminated dust that spread from her to an even disk on the far wall. A hallway, wide enough to fit two buses side by side, left the back of the room and receded into darkness. To her left, a long reception counter ran the width of the room, save for a small gap to allow staff through. There were two doors on the wall behind the desk, both closed. Between these was a directory, too coated in dust to be read. Sam walked to it, her boots grinding noisily on the dirty tile floor.

Somewhere above her came a deep thud, then the distinct sound of people walking and muffled voices. One voice, above the others, caught her attention. Stifled screams, the shrieks of intense pain. The footfalls changed their cadence. On stairs now, and getting louder.

Sam acted on pure instinct. She leapt up onto the counter and swung her legs over to the other side in one smooth motion, landing behind the barrier in a coiled stance. She clicked the flashlight off and stuffed it back in its pocket with her right hand, simultaneously drawing a hidden knife with her left hand from a sheath tucked inside her boot. Gripping the hilt in both hands to stifle the sound, she thumbed the switch and felt a brief flicker of satisfaction as the blade sprang out and clicked into position. Only then did it occur to her how ridiculous it was to hide and draw a weapon inside her own employer's facility.

Somewhere down that long dark hallway a door was flung open. The sound of it echoed through the lobby, followed instantly by those gagged, anguished cries. Sam guessed by the number of footfalls that there were eight to ten people in the party. Beneath those sounds she could hear the scrape of feet being dragged across the floor.

That dragging sound transformed into a flurry of noises that Sam pictured as wild flailing. A few different people cursed and a lot of commotion followed, including what sounded like a barrage of punches and kicks. The struggle ended as quickly as it had started.

"You disappoint me," a voice said. Grillo, she recognized immediately. "Lift him up."

More sounds of struggle, though the spirit had gone out of it.

Grillo spoke again, his voice quiet, almost tender. "Tsk, tsk. This is behavior most unbecoming for a man of your stature."

Against her better judgment, Samantha turned and slowly raised her head enough to peer over the top of the counter.

In the center of the lobby, a squad of guards was crowded around two men. One was Grillo, and he knelt in front of the captive. The man being held was unrecognizable in the weak light. The guards had him by his arms, so that his torso was lifted from the floor enough that he was eye level with the kneeling Grillo. His legs were splayed out on the floor behind him, lifeless. One foot lay at an unnatural angle, turned opposite the way of the knee.

"Will you not even consider my—" Grillo's words were cut off when the captive man spit in his face.

A guard slugged the man with one meaty fist, and was coiled to strike again when Grillo stopped him with a simple upheld hand.

The punch had been a solid blow. Sam knew that sound well enough, but the captive hardly reacted. He just slumped and hung his head low. Blood trickled from his mouth.

Grillo took a handkerchief from his breast pocket and wiped the spit from his face. In the process he paused and plucked something from his hair.

"A tooth?" Grillo asked. "That's a nice touch. If you don't want them we could remove the rest for you. Gratis, of course."

A few of the guards chuckled. The captive groaned. A sick, wet sound that made Samantha's stomach churn.

"I really don't understand your resistance," Grillo said then, his tone light and conversational. "But your tolerance for pain is impressive, I must say. Enviable, even. So what we'd like to do now, if you have no objections, is retire to my home. I have your family waiting there."

This produced a feeble cry.

"Oh yes, that's right, I forgot to tell you that I invited them for a visit. A meal, a prayer, perhaps a happy reunion with Papa. Would you like that? To see your family again with the one eye you have remaining?"

The broken man, to Sam's amazement, tried again to lash out

at Grillo. His arms were held fast by the guards, however.

Grillo leaned in close to the man, looked his face up and down. Sam recognized the point of decision before perhaps anyone else, and felt herself go cold. She held her breath as the knife emerged from Grillo's pocket.

"Perhaps your ability to see is what clouds your mind," Grillo said flatly. He took a handful of the man's sweaty hair and jerked his head back so that they were staring at each other.

Sam lowered herself behind the counter and tried not to hear the sound of the blade puncturing flesh, or the guttural, inhuman cry of pain that followed. She heard liquid splash on the tile floor. Someone gagged. Sam wanted to, and fought to keep herself under control. She set her own knife on the floor and clasped both hands over her mouth, focused on keeping her breathing even and silent.

She heard the knife plunge again, then a third time, neither of which produced a reaction from the prisoner that she heard.

A vile silence descended over the lobby then. Sam closed her eyes and took a long breath through her nose.

"Well," Grillo said. "Disappointing after all that work, gentlemen, but I've had another thought. A revelation, you might say."

One of the guards chuckled.

"Toss him into the ocean," Grillo said, his tone still light. "The knife, too. It's soiled now."

Sam heard the guards heave the body from the floor.

"Come up to the house after," Grillo said. "Supper is on, and I do truly want his family to enjoy a fine meal when I break the news that beloved Papa has . . . well, I suppose we can say he's ascended up the ladder for some important work above. That's not too far from the truth, when you think about it."

A few more stifled laughs. Then the party was on the move again. She heard the double doors at the lobby entrance open and close, and she was alone again.

Sam waited a full five minutes, partly to give Grillo and his entourage plenty of time to distance themselves from the hospital, and partly to allow the crippling tightness within her to unclench.

Sam had seen horrible things in her time as a scavenger. She'd done horrible things, never thinking twice. But that had been in battle, faced with subhuman foes that fought with relentless insanity fueled by the disease. She'd never seen or done anything like this. Even the fingers she'd once severed to fulfill a mission had been from a corpse, the corpse of what amounted to an animal.

Had she missed every hint of this side of him? She'd certainly ignored, willfully perhaps, every story and rumor of his ruthlessness in running the Maze. He'd tried to bribe her and the rest of the crew away from Skyler, years ago, too. Offered to pay Jake to let a little accident occur. Piety apparently only ran so deep, if it was even truly there at all.

If Grillo's growing stance as some kind of spiritual leader was just a façade, what would happen to Darwin when it broke? Hell, what would happen to her? She was a critical part of this machine.

The sound of Grillo's knife sliding into the captive's . . . Sam shuddered. She felt sick, her skin clammy. *I've got to get out of here.*

All thought of trying to contact Kelly left her mind. Sam sheathed her knife and slipped back over the counter. She crept across the lobby floor, avoiding the smeared trail of blood that now marred the surface, and went through the doors. Nobody was about, and Sam took off at a run for the main gate, sucking in deep, rapid breaths of fresh air as she went. She slowed when the gate and its guards came into view, and forced herself to walk calmly toward them.

The guard who'd let her in raised an eyebrow when he saw her approach. "Well? What did he think?"

"About what?" Sam growled.

"The book, of course. He must be overjoyed to finally have it."

She'd forgotten all about the damn thing. Sam fished it out of her inner pocket and held it out in front of her. She'd never seen Grillo so excited, or anxious, about a mission into the Clear. Sister Haley's legendary notebook, the original handwritten version she'd been famously forced to leave behind in her own flight to Darwin, left to burn as her house crumbled in a vandal's flames. Even those who didn't follow the religion knew the story.

Grillo had apparently learned a bit more, somehow. The house hadn't burned. The book might still be sitting there. *"Sam, you have to recover it."*

So he could bask in the glorious words, or so he could trap Sister Haley in her little fabrication? Seeing Grillo through this new lens, Sam could see the angle. One way or another, he would use this to continue his rise within the cult. And she'd stupidly shown it to this guard, who'd probably told everyone he'd seen since about it. Her chance to ditch the thing had long passed. She handed it to him. "He wasn't available. You give it to him, with my, um, regards."

The man stared at the tome with such reverence that Sam wanted to slap him. "I don't think I have to tell you," Sam said, "to leave that bag sealed, to not lay even the tip of your fingernail on that thing. I'm trusting you here."

"I'll keep it safe," he assured her.

"Good. Run it up to the house, and tell him I dropped it off."

He nodded, and Sam walked away, toward home, toward sanity.

32

BELÉM, BRAZIL

5.DEC.2283

No functional power source served the building. There would be no shortcut via an elevator this time. The windowless stairwell was shrouded in pure blackness. Every step echoed along the huge vertical shaft. After thirty flights of stairs with a collapsible dolly cart in tow, Skyler's thighs burned.

On three occasions Vanessa called a halt to the climb. Faint, phantom noises came from within the darkened floors of the office building. Rats, more than likely. Subhumans rarely sheltered themselves so far above street level. Dark stairs and strange sounds reminded Skyler of a dozen previous missions, most prominently the foray to Japan that changed his life forever, though he didn't know it at the time.

At the end of each flight of steps they passed a door on the wall, labeled with the floor number and whatever business once occupied the space beyond. Most indicated various multinational banks, or local Brazilian financial institutions. At the fiftieth floor the sign brought a laugh to Skyler's lips, one he quickly stifled. PLATZ GLOBAL FINANCE, it said. Each floor after that repeated the same name. The PGF logo on the outside of the building now made sense.

Finally, after what seemed like hours, Skyler rounded a flight of the switchback stairs to see Vanessa waiting at one last door. The placard was in Portuguese, but it required no translation. They'd reached the roof access door.

A pictogram sign warned of high winds beyond, and as if to hammer home the point the door rattled slightly in its frame. With each gust, rain spattered against the other side of the barricade. Vanessa waited for Ana to join them, nodded to the group, and pushed open the door.

Outside the wind was stiff but not unmanageable, and anyway a thick guardrail ringed the entire roof. Rain sprayed around them in seemingly random directions, stirred by invisible vortices that roiled up the sides of all tall buildings.

Skyler's boots crunched into thick gravel, soaked from the downpour but free of any standing pools. Drains hidden beneath the covering of white pebbles were functional, then, which implied the rooftop was likely stable. He scanned the roof, squinting as a spray of rainwater lashed his face. The surface he stood on ran around the outer edge, like a walkway almost, with that thick metal rail around the perimeter. Inset closer to the center of the roof was a raised square area, one meter high and twenty on a side, with a slightly angled roof of corrugated metal painted in bright white and slick with rain. There were ventilation ducts and electrical boxes along the low sidewall of the square, indicating that the space likely housed air-conditioning and elevator maintenance access.

The antenna assembly loomed diagonally across from the stairwell doorway's position. Skyler studied the city as he walked around the edge of the roof, and quickly came to realize the fantastic vantage point this tower provided. Unlike the luxury hotel where they'd celebrated Ana's birthday, which was boxed in on three sides and provided only a western view, this skyscraper had almost clear views in all directions. On a clear day, if Colton and the rest of his team brought their camera here, they could image a good part of the city without moving much at all.

Skyler saw the flaw in the plan immediately. Although the aura towers allowed the other scavenger teams to move about freely, no one yet knew how high their auras went. The assumption was, at least as high as the tower itself, but no one had yet seen the need to test it. So any such mission by the Eden crew would require environment suits. Not a deal breaker by any stretch, but perhaps a better plan would be for Skyler's crew to borrow the camera for a day. He made a mental note to talk to Karl about testing the vertical height of the aura provided by the towers.

He and Pablo set to work on the comm antenna while Vanessa stood guard at the door. Ana, bored, began to wander the rest of the roof, studying the city below. As Skyler readied his gear, he watched her out of the corner of his eye until she returned to the stairwell door, said something to Vanessa, and reentered the stairwell.

Skyler was midway through cutting through the third of eight bolts when Ana emerged again. She shouted something. He cut power to the plasma torch and flipped protective goggles up from his eyes. Pablo already had his rifle in hand and was crouched defensively.

Ana was smiling, however. The largest smile Skyler had ever seen on her face. She raced over and grabbed his arm. "Forget that for a second—you have to see something!"

"See what? We're halfway done."

"Trust me," she said in a tone that left no room for argument. Her eyes had that reckless look in them that gave Skyler cause for worry.

Intrigued, he set the torch down and removed the heavy protective gloves that went with it. Ana bounced back to the stairwell door, forced to wait, once she reached it, for Skyler and Pablo to catch up.

"Come *on,*" she urged.

Next to her, Vanessa shrugged to indicate her lack of knowledge and followed Ana into the darkness.

Skyler bounded down the steps only to find the door on the landing open. Ana stood there, her grin too wide to dismiss as simple mischief. She waved him inside, behind Vanessa.

"First door on the left," Ana said.

Vanessa went through first, her flashlight on at full brightness now, and Skyler could hear a sharp gasp escape her lips. He turned the corner and added his own light to the room beyond.

Not just a mere room, he realized instantly, but an aircraft hangar.

The raised square on the rooftop above them was not a housing for machinery; it was a door. A massive, retractable door big enough to allow a VTOL aircraft in and out. The space reminded him of the cargo hangar on Gateway Station.

Like a child in a museum, Skyler stared in pure delight at the sleek vehicle that dominated the floor of the room. Even in the wan illumination their flashlights offered, he could tell the plane was brand-new. Or had been, before the fall. If it had been flown ten times he'd have been shocked to hear it.

The sharp nose cone tapered back from a needlepoint to form a narrow fuselage. Unlike the *Melville,* which had four engines dangling at the ends of as many wings, this bird had its vertical thrusters tucked up against the main body, below a pair of folded-back wings that would extend during normal flight. Two huge thrusters were mounted atop the craft, near the back by the rear fin.

"Oh," Pablo said from behind, "nice."

"Nice doesn't begin to describe it," Vanessa said. "It's gorgeous." She strolled along the length of the hangar, her flashlight dancing across the white body of the plane.

Skyler cleared his throat. "Workman Aeronautics Silver Flute," he said to no one in particular. "A Mark 5, I think. Executive class."

"Is it a good plane?" Ana asked from the doorway.

He turned to her and motioned with one hand for her to join him. When she did, he put an arm around her and squeezed. "Phenomenal. Very fast, and all latest flight systems and gadgets."

Ana beamed, and though Skyler studied the plane intently, he could tell out of the corner of his eye that the girl was looking at him, not the aircraft.

"Mind you it's not military spec. It'll have a luxury passenger cabin, I suspect," Skyler noted. "Minimal cargo space for luggage and whatnot. And no suborbital capability."

"So it won't work for us?" Ana asked.

Skyler squeezed her shoulder again to reassure her. "We can

strip out most of the cabin, maybe even knock through to the cargo floor to expand the space. The lack of thermal plating means we can't drop from space, but that's really just a range-extending feature. Besides, the only planes built with that feature were for use in Darwin. It wouldn't have been a big selling point here." Absently he wondered what the craft's maximum range was, his thoughts already on the three missing groups of towers.

"How will we get it out?" Vanessa asked, completing her circuit of the room. "I don't see a manual override for the doors, and there's no power."

"Portable cap?" Pablo offered.

"That would get the doors open," Skyler agreed, "but the bird is likely dry, too, and we'll need a lot more juice to spool it."

"So we run a line," Ana said. "Find the nearest building with a reactor and run a cable up here."

Skyler cringed. Sixty floors with a spool of high-gauge cable. The effort would take days of backbreaking work. Still, this was the first aircraft they'd found in operable shape. In the early, chaotic days of SUBS, if there was one thing the rumor of a safe Darwin caused, it was that anyone with access to an aircraft took flight for the city. Thousands of planes crashed either in the chaos of takeoff, or when their caps ran dry on the long flight. Still more reached Darwin only to find crowded skies and a protective local population that swarmed many of the vehicles on landing. Most of those who did make it became scavengers, the airport being the only place they could find refuge.

"Skyler?"

He glanced at her and saw a hope in her eyes he'd not noticed before. He knew then she relished the idea of getting away from Belém. Whatever travel she'd experienced as a child was long gone, and the journey she and her brother had undertaken was nothing short of a nightmare. The city of Belém was home for her now, and home was something to flee for a girl of twenty-two years.

"Yes. Hell yes, let's do it," Skyler said. "The least we can do is see if it will power up."

* * *

Two technicians, formerly stationed on Anchor, were enlisted to help with the project. A good thing, too, since they devised a solution much simpler than Skyler's: Restore power to the building.

Still, the job was complicated and difficult. They had to decouple a nearby shopping mall from its thor, snake heavy cable through Belém's mottled streets, and find out where to make the necessary couplings in the electrical room three floors below the tower's lobby. All of this had to be done with one loaned aura tower and occasional backup from the Tombstones scavenger crew. After four long days the techs were finally ready to flip the switch.

Skyler sat on the bumper of the APC, a half-eaten mango in his hand, the cabin's small red LED providing the only light, since night had fallen an hour earlier. His radio crackled and one of the techs said, "Here we go!"

When the switch was thrown, Skyler thought the lights could probably be seen from space. Every other powered building in Belém was mostly dark, their bulbs burned out or systems simply switched off. Not this one.

As power coursed through its sixty floors, it seemed every single light in the building came on. The place glowed compared to the ghost town around it, and Skyler squinted in the sudden brightness pouring from the lobby.

"Wow," Ana said from her perch on the bumper next to him. Pablo, seated on the ground a few meters away, let out an uncharacteristic hoot and raised one arm in celebration.

"Skyler." Vanessa's voice, on the radio.

He snatched it up and spoke into it. "Are you seeing this? It's amazing."

"You all better get inside," she said. Vanessa had ventured into a building across the street, to relieve herself.

"Why?" he asked. The answer came to him before the word even left his lips. "Oh . . . subs. Yes, you're right."

"They'll come like moths to a flame."

"We'll wait for you," he said. "Hurry."

She did. The woman emerged from the gray building behind a few seconds later. Skyler covered her while Ana and Pablo jogged to the bright lobby. The two of them stopped at the door and took up positions on either side, scanning the avenue in both directions with their rifles.

Within seconds Skyler heard the grunts, the strangely human howls. Then shadows were moving at the edge of the illumination the building provided.

Skyler fired a few warning shots into the murky darkness as he followed Vanessa to the door. The crackle of gunfire echoed off the vacant buildings around them and rolled along the downtown streets like thunder.

Pablo began to fire, and Ana followed suit. Their rifles chattered as if in an argument. Skyler urged Vanessa forward, content to let the others handle any of the creatures that advanced.

He reached the door and immediately took a knee behind Pablo. Between short, rapid breaths he steadied himself and brought his rifle to the ready.

The street outside grew quiet.

Skyler counted three fresh subhuman corpses among the skeletons that already littered the streets. At the edge of his vision, he saw shadows recede into the blackness beyond. However many diseased were out there, they seemed as mesmerized by the lights as Skyler had been, and in no mood to join their pack mates in the dirt.

Ana fired once more. A single, startling round, and when Skyler looked he saw another subhuman, loping on all fours, stagger and crumple into the ragged asphalt wasteland beneath its feet.

Silence followed. Skyler put the radio to his lips and held down the transmit button. "Guys," he said, "see if you can find a master switch for the lighting. A breaker or something, I don't care. Just kill these lights."

"Copy that," the response came.

Almost five minutes passed before the building suddenly plunged back into darkness. Other than a few emergency exit signs, and some accent lighting in the ceiling, the effect was complete.

They waited another ten before relaxing. Pablo agreed to escort the two techs and the aura tower back to camp, and would return at dawn if the others failed to get the aircraft out of the hangar bay.

"Clear us a place to land," Skyler said with a hopeful grin. "Southeast corner is best, I think."

Pablo nodded and they clasped hands. "Adios."

"Adios," Skyler answered.

Neither Ana nor Vanessa wanted to rest, so Skyler led them back to the fifty-ninth floor.

Inside the hangar, the Workman company aircraft looked like it had been staged there for some advertisement photo shoot. Dim red lights inset into the floor lit the plane from beneath, while bright white LEDs along the edge of the ceiling cast the top in a contrasting hue.

A control mechanism for the roof rested inside a metal box on the wall by the door. Skyler popped it open. Inside, a yellow button the size of an orange sat under a clear protective cover. He flipped the cover up and pressed the button once with his palm.

Gnashing of gears and the strains of atrophied equipment followed, died down, and then became a smooth hum as the segmented ceiling panels retracted along rails that were disguised as simple grooves in the wall.

A star-filled sky waited above, the moon hanging directly overhead. On the roof outside, red warning lights lit the edges of the portal in pulses of ruby.

"What now?" Ana asked, unable to keep the anticipation from her voice.

"Preflight," Skyler said, his eyes on the aircraft. "This will take awhile. The bird's been sitting here for almost six years. More, maybe. I want to be doubly sure she's okay to fly."

The two women nodded. He decided now was as good a time as any to walk them through the preparation process. A walk around the vehicle went first, but he'd done that previously and saw nothing to be concerned about. Then he moved in closer and ran a hand over the fuselage. Other than a healthy coat of dust, he found no sign of wear in the panels, no sign of rust or deterioration in the rivets. Indeed, he saw no indication at all that the bird had ever flown. It had, of course, since otherwise it wouldn't be here.

After inspecting the thrust ducts and joints where the flaps attached to the wings, he went to the cabin door and opened it. It took some muscle to overcome the slight pressure difference, and then the interior came into view.

Smells hit him first. Leather and new carpet and industrial adhesives, like a new car. He inhaled a second time and tried to find any hint of rot or mold. Or worse, death. But he came up empty and exhaled with relief.

The inside of the craft was dark, save for light coming in the tinted windows. He fumbled around for a time before finding the stewards panel, and on that a master control for the cabin lights. He flipped it, and warm light filled the cabin.

"Power!" Ana chirped. "After all this time!"

"Indeed," Skyler said. Ultracapacitors drained slowly when unused, and it didn't surprise him that there would be enough residual spool to run the lights. If the cockpit computers worked, though, he'd be shocked.

"I could live here," Vanessa said, strolling down the aisle toward the back of the plane.

Skyler studied the cabin closely for the first time. "Luxury" didn't begin to describe it. There were only six seats, huge cushioned things done in black leather and accented with silver-gray ultrasuede, thick white stitching along every seam. Each seat had a retractable desk of beech wood, a terminal slate, and sensory goggles. A widescreen monitor covered the top half of the back wall. Below it was a recessed wet bar.

Impressive. Skyler couldn't deny it. But his mind shifted quickly to the practical implications. The space was small, smaller than he would have thought. It would not hold much cargo, unless there was more to it than they could see. None of that mattered, though, if the flight systems were shot.

"Who wants to see the cockpit?" he asked.

Ana nodded eagerly. Vanessa ran a hand along the arm of one luxury chair before she finally turned and came to join them. A lawyer, and a senator's daughter, she must have grown up with luxury of this sort, and she still had an affinity for it.

A modest restroom and small serving area separated the cabin from the cockpit. Their contents could be searched later.

Even though he expected it, Skyler swore under his breath when the computers and controls in the cockpit failed to initialize. Not enough power. A systems check would have been preferred before attaching a line to the cap spooler. He shrugged, decided the risk was worth it, and led his crew outside to show them how to open the port and attach the cable. Charging a civilian aircraft like this was only marginally more complicated than spooling a ground car.

Back inside, he tried the computers again and smiled as the screens came to life. The cockpit had few traditional instruments. Instead, shaped displays covered every surface. When off, they looked like part of the walls, ceiling, and dash. One display ran from knee level up to the base of the canopy and clearly contained the most important information: cap levels, range, and a flight planner. Understandably, the ultracapacitor levels were at zero percent, but at least it indicated "charging." The estimated time to completion showed three question marks, so Skyler studied the other screens while he waited.

One display on the wall left of the pilot's seat flashed an overall diagnostic readout, and various entries on it were turning from gray to green even as he watched. Only one line deviated: capacitor levels, which flashed yellow.

"Well?" Vanessa asked.

"Everything looks good. We'll be able to fire up the motors in"—he glanced back at the charging estimate—"two hours." The craft would be at 10 percent charge then, plenty to take it for a test flight and move it to Camp Exodus.

"What do we do in the meantime?" Ana asked.

Skyler turned to her. "We . . ."

She had her hands clasped just in front of her chin, almost as if in prayer, and she bounced gently on her tiptoes. Vanessa leaned against the doorway behind her, exhaustion plain on her face.

"Next," Skyler said, "next we see if there's anything to drink back there."

* * *

A bottle of merlot was uncorked. Two glasses was all it took before Vanessa drifted off in one of the oversized, cushioned passenger chairs.

Ana eased the seat back for her until it became a bed and then found a blanket to cover the woman with. The cabin lights were dimmed, and Skyler led Ana back to the cockpit.

The girl climbed into the co-pilot's seat without a word, and Skyler took his place in the pilot's chair. Despite the exotic, high-end equipment, the position still fit him like an old comfortable shoe. The basic controls were exactly where he would expect, and with a bit of fiddling he even found he could reconfigure the various screens around him. He tried moving some of the information around to more familiar positions, but it was tedious. Then he spotted the option to completely realign the displays to mimic other aircraft.

To his surprise and delight, the database was enormous, and in less than thirty seconds he had the entire cockpit looking exactly like the *Melville*'s. The graphical representation was remarkably accurate.

Another option on the screen was "setup." Skyler tapped it and found where he could set a name for the aircraft. An idea came to him. "Would you like to name her?"

"Name who?" Ana said.

"The bird. This plane."

Her eyes lit up, then her nose wrinkled in concentration. In the soft amber glow of the cockpit lights, she looked rather striking, Skyler thought.

"*La Gaza Ladra*," Ana said.

He loved it simply for the way she said the words. As he tapped in the letters, he asked, "What's it mean?"

"The Thieving Magpie. Something Papa used to play on the guitar."

"Perfect," he said to himself, grinning. "Perfect."

Next to him, Ana beamed. "I've never seen you so happy."

"Doesn't get much better than this," he agreed.

"Hmm." Ana stood. "I forgot something."

"What's that?" he asked, his attention firmly on the readouts that rolled across the screens before him.

His view was suddenly blocked by her hips, her torso, then her face. She slid onto his lap, arms around his neck. Before he could protest her lips met his and she kissed him.

Skyler resisted, but there was nowhere to go. Her fingers tangled in his hair, sending a ripple of electricity down his spine. When her tongue darted in between his lips, Skyler gave in and kissed her back. The world around him melted away, and he put his arm around her waist, pulling her close.

Ana turned and adjusted her legs until she straddled him. The kiss went from gentle, to passionate, to urgent. The warmth of her mouth, her body, drew him in. When her hands began to work at his belt buckle, Skyler pulled away.

"Slow down, slow down," he breathed.

Ana let out a nervous half laugh and swept her hair behind her ears. She bit her lower lip in frustration, then leaned in and kissed him again. A quick, sensuous move that she let linger just long enough to get his pulse racing again.

Then she leaned back. "Sorry. I got carried away."

"No need to apologize."

She stayed where she was, her legs wrapped around his. The position soon became uncomfortable in the narrow pilot's seat.

"Um," Skyler managed.

Ana put a finger to his lips. "Don't say anything. I made the first move; you can retaliate anytime you like."

He grunted a laugh at her choice of words. "It's just . . ."

"Just what?"

"I'm too old for you."

She looked at him with total confusion. Then she shook her head vehemently. "Those rules don't apply anymore, Skyler."

"Don't they?"

"No," she said, her tone flat, very serious. "Not now. Not after everything that's happened in the world. It's like this aircraft, Skyler. *La Gaza Ladra*. If you find something you need, you take it."

"Yeah, but who needs who?"

She glared at him, playful but no less intense. "Are you saying you don't need me?"

A dozen answers flew through his mind, and beyond them

were all the vague warnings of camp politics, impropriety, and his already rocky friendship with Tania Sharma. Vague shapes in the Builders' hazy cloud, one and all.

Skyler pushed the ghosts away and kissed her.

33

DARWIN, AUSTRALIA

25.DEC.2283

"It's freaky how quiet the city is now," Skadz said.

Sam pushed the last remnants of her dinner around the Styrofoam bowl. Rice plus some kind of mystery meat. A freeze-dried, preservative-laden dish of salty mush, made only slightly better with a healthy dash of chili sauce.

They sat side by side on the hangar's roof, under a plastic tarp propped up by two old ladders. A light rain tapped away on the surface and rolled down the sides in tiny streams.

Skadz cleared his throat. "Grillo's really coddled the place, hasn't he?"

She paused mid-bite, the food gone from edible mush to inedible ash. *Coddled doesn't even enter into it.* It had been over a month and she still hadn't been able to speak about what she'd witnessed in Lyons. The topic of Grillo, through her body language alone, had become off-limits around the airport. She'd done her best to avoid the man himself lest he somehow sense a change in the way she looked at him. A hint of disgust or fear she knew he'd find in her eyes.

"You're talkative tonight."

Sam set the bowl aside and filled her cup with runoff water dripping from the side of their makeshift tent. "Going out tomorrow. I'm just thinking through the logistics."

"What's the mission?"

"The mission is fucked-up, that's what," she said. "Grillo always, *always*, has us going for soil and seeds and shit." She took a drink, sloshed the water around her mouth, and spat it out. The salty taste of fake chicken remained, and she repeated the process.

"Charming," he said.

"Bite me."

Winking red light from an approaching aircraft caught both their attention. As they watched, the craft crept up on the airport from the southeast, and soon the howl of its engines could be heard above the rain. The craft slowed until it hovered, and then descended to its designated spot along the row of landing pads that covered the original strip of asphalt.

"This mission, today's," Sam said once the engine noise receded, "is guns. Rifles, handguns, grenades. Body armor, helmets. The works."

Skadz grunted. "Merry fucking Christmas, eh?"

"Hah."

He grew thoughtful. "What's that mean, then? Is Blackfield back in control? Sounds like one of his lists."

"I don't know." The prospect made her shudder. She had other theories but couldn't quite bring herself to voice them. Skadz had resumed his role of friend easily enough, but she'd not gone so far as to consider him a confidant yet. He disappeared for days at a time into the city. With all the Jacobites around, who knew what might be overheard. Skadz had a penchant for gab, a gift for boasting. If she told him about Kelly, or the strange Builder device she'd recovered for Grillo, or the butchery she'd witnessed, word could get around. So she said nothing.

Skadz had yet to try to return to his role as a scavenger, and she suspected he might never.

Sometimes, late at night, she could hear him battling nightmares. Whether or not he was haunted by the girl he'd let die, or something that happened while he was out walking the desolate lands beyond Darwin, she had no idea. He'd avoided the topic and said little of what happened during his walkabout. Despite his nonchalance, Sam only had to look at his eyes to see the pain there. Something had happened out there, something that drove him back.

"So," Skadz asked, "are you going to do it?"

"What?"

"The mission. Guns for Grillo."

"I have to."

He barked a laugh. "Shit . . . have to. Bloody hell, Sammy, you don't have to do anything. Fly out of here and never come back. Who could stop you?"

Lightning danced on the horizon, each brilliant line bringing her visions of Grillo's knife stabbing into that helpless, broken man in the hospital lobby. She saw herself, crouched behind the counter with a book tucked under her arm, a book he'd sent her across the continent to find, a book that everyone *knew* had burned years ago, lost to history.

Sam waited for the thunder to roll by before answering. "Grillo could."

By midafternoon the next day, Samantha found herself falling to Earth. Wind screamed past her ears and rippled the skin on her cheeks as Malaysia raced to meet her.

She guided herself toward the familiar air base and tried to ignore the looming megalopolis of Kuala Lumpur to the south. The massive city stretched from horizon to horizon, and still hid under a cloud of smog five years after SUBS had relieved it of its plague of humans.

The layout of the military compound below her rushed back into her mind and she angled herself toward the large warehouse complex in the southwest quarter. Above her, strung out like climbers on an invisible space elevator, the other four members of today's crew followed her lead. She hoped so, anyway. It wouldn't do to look back.

Sam landed with textbook precision between two huge gray buildings, stark and windowless. Her feet touched ground at a trot, and she let the parachute drift over her and onto the cratered asphalt surface. With little wind to speak of, the giant nylon sheet settled onto the ground with a whisper.

"Clear," she called into her headset. "*Ocean Cloud,* circle with minimal juice until we've secured a landing site."

"Copy that," came the response. The pilot, at least, was one of hers. A pudgy man named Pascal, who'd been flying in and out of Darwin since long before the Elevator arrived. The ground team were all Grillo's men.

Her companions landed in sequence. They were clumsy compared to her, stuck inside environment suits, and lightly armed. Jacobites all, they'd said little on the flight out from Darwin, and though they knew how to strap on a parachute, she could tell none of them had made more than a few training jumps in their day.

Sam ordered them to spread out and hold the area, then she climbed a maintenance ladder on the side of one warehouse and found a place on the roof where she could see most of the base. She scanned the perimeter with a pair of high-power binoculars. As with the first time she'd been here, almost a year ago, the place was quiet. A barbed fence ringed the base, and there was a wall closer in that secured all but the VTOL pads.

Everything seemed to be intact, and she saw no evidence of subhumans inside the wall, other than the corpses of those she'd killed the last time out. They lay where they'd fallen, so many months ago, on the grid of landing pads to the north. She still remembered her argument with Skyler that day. "Land by the fucking warehouses," she'd told him. Just saying it seemed all the reason he needed to do something else. He gave her some bullshit line about how the landing pads were built to handle aircraft, whereas the asphalt wasteland that surrounded the buildings would just crumble under the *Melville's* weight. Even now she felt heat rise in her cheeks at his insistence on always doing things anything but her way. Jackass.

She missed him so badly that tears welled. Sam laughed at her own mopey ridiculousness and drew a sleeve across her eyes. As she climbed back down the flimsy ladder, she wondered for the hundredth time if she'd ever know what happened to him. If he lived or not, where he'd gone. Anything. Most of all: Had it all been worth it?

At her orders, *Ocean Cloud* dropped down from the sky like a rock, blasting her thrusters on full power at the last moment to break the fall. At thirty meters above the ground she settled into a hover, and the pilot lowered the rest of the way with ample caution.

The asphalt held, and soon the engine howl changed to a purr, then a dim whine of electric current.

"Told you, Sky."

She led her companions into the nearest warehouse, the same one she'd looted before. The *Melville*'s cargo bay couldn't hold more than a few crates, and they'd left dozens behind on that mission.

Sam left the three men to search for what they needed and went back outside to guide *Ocean Cloud* to its landing. Pascal set the old hauler down with expert precision, right in between the two warehouses. He waved at her from the cockpit with little enthusiasm. His body language since the moment their Jacobite friends had boarded said what he thought of their sect.

"You and me both," Sam mouthed, and waved back. She offered the words to build camaraderie with the fellow scavenger, but in truth she found it more and more difficult to hate the zealots. Old habits die hard, but her distaste had been eroded now that they'd pacified most of Darwin. The city might be bland and quiet now, but at least one could walk through the Maze without constant fear of a knife in the back.

And their success under Grillo had all but eliminated the need to continually spew sermons from every rank alcove in the city. Success spoke for itself, and across the city people were joining the cult for the protection and privilege it provided. The pattern had been repeated throughout history—join the group in power and receive all the benefits, or refuse and suffer the life of an outcast.

One of the men emerged from the building, boarded *Ocean*, and a minute later drove down the rear cargo deck in a small electric cart. Two steel arms extended from the front of the vehicle, allowing it to lift and move heavy pallets with ease.

Sam followed him inside to help. Her "crew" worked with surprising drive and organization. In just a few minutes, they'd laid out at least fifty small wooden boxes on the floor and were sorting them when she came in.

"I'm going to walk the perimeter," she told them. "Keep an eye out."

"You're supposed to stay with us," one said. None of them stopped their work, and she couldn't tell who had spoken. In their suits they all looked the same. The bulky hoods blocked her view of their faces, making them seem like automatons.

"Just around the building," she added. "Someone should keep a lookout."

One waved at her in acknowledgment.

Sam did a lap around the warehouse, then crossed to the one opposite their target and circled it, too. Halfway around she stopped to study the distant skyline of Kuala Lumpur. From here the skyscrapers looked like jagged teeth, the color of ash. They barely stood out against the dirty sky that loomed over the city. She'd wondered about that sky on the last visit, too. Other cities they'd flown into or over in the *Melville* had cleared up. Five years without people did wonders to a metropolis. Sydney, Tokyo, even Saigon . . . all clear. Kuala Lumpur must have some runaway processers still throwing pollutants up. Factories that ran on autonomous programs. No one had had time to turn off the lights, and ample supplies of raw materials meant the factories could soldier on without the need of human oversight.

That those gray teeth were once gleaming office towers and teeming apartments was hard for her to imagine. Now they were just tombs. She wondered how many millions of corpses lay within those buildings. Twenty million? Thirty? *And so close to Darwin,* she thought. *What a fucking shame.*

She turned back and saw the rear door of the warehouse. On a whim, she tried the handle and found it to be unlocked. A mixture of boredom and curiosity drove her inside.

The layout was identical to the building across the drive. Row after row of metal scaffold shelves, rising up into the darkness. She flipped on a flashlight and swept it across the aisles. At least half the space was empty. In a few places she saw boxes spilled out on the ground, and in one aisle she almost tripped on two skeletons. One wore a Malay army uniform. The other had on ragged civilian clothes. She stepped over them without a second thought.

Farther on she spotted a familiar logo on a series of shoe-box-sized plastic containers. SONTON. Sam grinned. The handgun manufacturer had been the dominant supplier of high-end weapons right up until the apocalypse. She set her flashlight on a nearby shelf and thumbed open one of the boxes. Inside she saw the dark sheen of brushed tungsten. The gun rested in a bed of form-cut packing material and had never been used, as far as she could tell. A tag still hung from the trigger guard. Two clips were nestled into pockets below it, and next to those, a laser sight.

She compared it to her own gun and decided now was a good time to upgrade. It didn't take long to find ammunition of the right caliber, on the next aisle over. Samantha loaded a single magazine and pocketed the leftovers, the extra clip, and the sight. Then she slid the gun into her holster and discarded the old one.

On another aisle she found the grenades.

They were grouped by type and size, most the size of a lemon and of the fragmentation variety. But toward the end she came across smaller versions. These were no bigger than a cigarette lighter. Most were marked in a language she couldn't read, but a few were labeled in English. High-yield antipersonnel. Sonic demobilizers. Sam smiled and, after a quick guilty glance at the door through which she'd entered, she slipped a few of each into her vest pockets.

It hadn't been stated directly, but she knew that her crew of Jacobites were also tasked with keeping an eye on her and wouldn't be too happy if they knew she'd brought such weapons back with her.

Satisfied, and nervous about being gone too long, Sam returned the way she'd come and reentered the first warehouse.

"Find anything?" one of the men asked. "You were gone awhile."

"I had to take a shit," she said casually. "Needed some tissue."

That seemed to settle the matter.

She watched them for a while. They loaded crate after crate of weapons and associated equipment onto the cart, driving four loads out to the waiting aircraft. Sam made a mental tally as they went, and when the men declared their work finished, she realized they'd neglected anything larger than a snub-nosed submachine gun.

"That's it?" she asked.

"Yes."

"It's none of my business," Sam said, "but the stuff you took is all for girls. There's much better weapons in here."

The Jacobite inclined his head. He hesitated before responding. "You're right," he said. "It is none of your business. Let's go."

34

BLACK LEVEL

12.DEC.2284

"To the . . . well, screw it. To the Builders!"

Greg lifted his glass, that ever-present grin on his face somehow even wider.

Marcus echoed the motion, white wine sloshing in his own cup as he raised it. Marcus wore no smile. In fact, Tania had never seen him smile, and it wasn't for a lack of humor. If anything he was an even bigger goof than Greg, and that was saying something.

"To the Builders," Tania said with a shrug. Why not? Like them or not, *understand* them or not, the unseen alien race had certainly had their impact on the world. More so, she thought, than any human ever had, except perhaps through acts largely mythical. She clinked her glass with theirs and looked to Zane Platz and Tim. Tim joined the toast without a word, though she could see the hint of a smile at the corner of his mouth.

Zane, on the other hand, didn't move. His eyes were set on the drink in front of him, the remnants of dinner beside it. He seemed deep in thought, as he had that entire day. The anniversary of the Belém Elevator's arrival, so close upon the date marking his famous brother's death, had really thrown the man off his usual affable manner.

"Zane?" she asked. "You okay?"

Her question took a second to register. Zane jerked slightly, as if he'd been asleep. He turned to her and shrugged, a movement so slight she almost missed it. "Feeling a bit under the weather," he said.

"You look pale."

"Do I? I feel it."

"It's Greg's cooking," Marcus said, deadpan as always. "Only the strong survive."

Greg laughed maniacally. "Fools!" he screeched, like some cartoon villain. "It was poison all along. Soon this station shall be mine!"

Tim laughed and Tania found herself smiling as well. She'd been on Black Level for two weeks, with little to do except enjoy the silly antics of Greg and Marcus. If anything, the time in near isolation aboard the partial space station had only served to increase their penchant for joking around. In two short weeks Tania had laughed more than in the entire year before.

Zane's expression didn't change. He let out a small burp and put a hand over his abdomen. "Ugh . . ."

Tania put a hand on his shoulder. "You should rest."

"Or purge that slop Greg prepared," Marcus said. "Seriously, what did you make that with? Roach droppings?"

"Do roaches poop?" Greg asked.

"Never thought about it until now."

"It's a good question."

"Do they even have an anus? I wonder."

"We'll discuss it later," Greg whispered out the corner of his mouth. "Seconds, anyone?"

Zane groaned again. He clutched at his stomach with one hand now, while his other hand covered his eyes. His chair made a chirp sound as he pushed back from the table with sudden violence.

"My God, Zane," Tania said, taking his forearm to steady him. Tim stood to help.

Suddenly Zane doubled over. His head hit the edge of the

table with a deep thud that rattled the place settings. Tania tried to hold on to him, but he fell limp and weighed too much for her to overcome.

Zane hit the floor with a grunt and went still.

"What's wrong with him?" Tania asked. Panic welled inside her, and her gaze went to his neck, looking for the rash. *Is our Elevator defective, too?* The possibility that what happened in Darwin could also happen here had never occurred to her until now.

But she saw nothing. Nothing except the collapsed, unconscious form of Zane Platz.

Only thirty people lived on Black Level. The station was not equipped for more, being just a single ring that had detached from the much larger Anchor Station. It had no kitchen, no recreation areas, and no medical facility.

The skeleton crew improvised as best they could, Tania thought, but it wasn't enough to help Zane Platz.

At least he's alive, she thought. Unconscious, but a pulse was there and he seemed to be breathing well enough.

She'd spent the night at his side, in the cabin she herself used to occupy. Other than the gentle rise and fall of his chest, he hadn't moved since the collapse at dinner.

A number of video calls were made between Black Level and Melville Station. One of only two medical doctors in the colony did all she could to diagnose the patient remotely, but in the end the process proved too slow and inefficient.

"Move him here," the doctor, Loraine Brooks, said. She'd been a private physician on board Platz Station before the crew fled. Her specialty was children, but like all doctors she had basic training in other areas. "He seems stable enough, and a climber car can't be much worse than that cabin in terms of space and air quality."

"We'll come back right away, then," Tania said.

Tim, listening from the doorway, said, "I'll get some people to help move him."

She nodded at him and took some comfort in the half smile

he offered her. While she fretted and worried he'd taken control of the situation, she reminded herself to thank him for that. His presence, not just here but within the colony in general, was a wonderful piece of luck, she now knew.

In the hallway behind him, she heard Marcus. "The climber will be ready in a few minutes."

"Good," Tim said. Their voices receded down the hall.

The doctor on the screen gave Tania a sympathetic look. "See you soon, Dr. Sharma."

"Thank you, Dr. Brooks." Tania switched off the terminal.

Her old cabin, which appeared to be untouched since she left it almost a year ago, held little sentimental value. All her fond memories, nights spent sipping wine with Natalie over a board game or puzzle, were hidden behind the last days aboard Anchor Station. When she looked about the room now, she saw only a prison cell.

Tania shuddered, then turned her focus to Zane.

"Please stay with us," she whispered. "You've been my rock since we arrived. The only person I can talk to anymore." *It should have been Skyler in that role*. She hated herself for thinking that. She hated herself more for the lame words coming out of her. She'd heard better dialogue in those horrible old romance films the sensory chamber loved to recommend.

The truth was, when Tania looked at Zane she was always trying to find some hint of Neil hiding in there. She had no doubt that if he were here now, the colony would not be fiddling around with pouring concrete and fixing up the nearby dormitory. They would be laser focused on the Builders. Exploring the site in the forest, establishing plans and backup plans for every contingency of what may come next. Already the colony had squandered half the time before the next event, assuming the schedule she'd calculated was accurate.

Everything, she realized, that Skyler had been urging they do. He'd asked a hundred times for permission to find the other missing towers. Permission he didn't need. Especially now that he had an aircraft.

And a lover, a voice in her head said. She pushed that visual aside with a cold shiver. "Will you ever forgive me?" she muttered, holding back tears. Another bad line from a silly romance. Tania felt like slapping herself.

Footsteps outside. "In here," Tim was saying. "Tania, step aside. We're ready to go."

She gave Zane's hand a squeeze and pushed away from the bed to let the others in. They'd brought a folding table to use as a stretcher, but it wouldn't fit through the door. So the group lifted Zane in the blanket upon which he lay, carefully moved him through the narrow entry, and laid him on the table. Someone, not Tania, had the presence of mind to fetch a pillow to put under his head. *Such a simple gesture,* she thought, *and yet more useful and caring than any of my stupid words.*

The climber slipped out of Black Level's meager docking bay ten minutes later and tugged on the cord until it reached a cruising speed of 1,500 kilometers per hour. Even at that blistering pace, it would take more than a day to descend down to Melville.

Once cruising, there was no illusion of gravity to be had. Tania and Tim moved Zane's stretcher to the opposite side of the cabin, so that when they decelerated at the other end he wouldn't be on the "ceiling." After that, there was little to do except wait.

The farm platforms flew by every few hours. They were spaced out along the cord, their altitude determined by the crops grown. The higher up on the Elevator, the more sunlight received during a rotation of the planet below. Unlike Darwin's Elevator, though, there were no other stations to pass. No Hab stations, looking like orbital hotels. No quaint little Midway Station, that smallest of facilities that had been built as an emergency stop-off should anything go wrong. It had rarely been used, as far as Tania knew. She'd certainly never stopped there during her time living above Darwin.

"Should we give him some water?" Tim asked, halfway through the descent.

Tania looked up from the book she'd been reading, a worn paperback she'd found in the climber's "boredom box." "I'm not sure how we would in zero-g, but we can try."

Zane looked peaceful in the absence of gravity. Not that he hadn't before they'd left, but now he seemed younger, more vigorous somehow. His cheeks were fuller, buoyed as he floated against the belts that held him to the table.

His lips, though, were dry and cracked. But try as they might, squeezing water into his mouth from a foil packet did not work. Without gravity, the fluid just dribbled out and floated away in small spheres. Tim waved a hand towel around to capture the liquid before it found its way into anything important.

"Even if it stayed in," Tania said, "he'd still have to swallow it."

They gave up, and waited. And waited.

Finally, hours later, Tania felt the tug of gravity. It woke her from a light nap as the straps of her harness tightened against her shoulders.

Slowing the climber took almost as long as the acceleration process had, the progress display moving with frustrating sloth on the monitor by the airlock. "C'mon, c'mon," Tim muttered.

When the hatch finally opened, Dr. Brooks waited just outside with a team of apparent volunteers. "Take him to the infirmary," she ordered. With a nod at Tania and Tim, the doctor drifted inside and checked Zane's vitals as the others began to wrangle the makeshift stretcher.

"Go with them," Tim said to Tania. "I'll get Karl on the comm and let him know what's happened."

"Thanks."

Tania followed the main group down a spoke to the outer ring, then along a blur of corridors interrupted by the occasional bulkhead.

At Brooks's direction, the team worked with modest efficiency to get Zane transferred to a bed. The doctor hooked up an IV to his arm and began a series of checks. "Our equipment is basic," she explained as she held one of Zane's eyelids open and flashed a light across his pupils. "We may have to move him down to Belém, or move equipment up here."

"Whatever it takes," Tania said. "Just tell me what you want to do."

"For now," she said, "let me work. I'll come get you when I have something."

Despite a desire to stay, Tania read the woman's tone and body language, and departed. The last thing she saw was Brooks pressing her hands against Zane's abdomen.

The doctor looked worried.

When the news came that Zane was in a coma, Tania was not surprised. She couldn't imagine any other explanation for his present condition. The cause, however, remained unknown.

Dr. Brooks provided a list of equipment she needed, either installed on the station or accessible on the ground. "I'm loath to move him, though, and it might not be a bad idea to have the infirmary here more fully provisioned."

Tania agreed and relayed the list to Karl. He said he'd get the scavenger crews on it immediately. With Skyler's newfound aircraft available, they'd search nearby cities as well if the situation required it.

Zane remained stable, and as the days turned into weeks, Tania gradually focused on her duties again. She still visited with him every day. Sometimes once in the evening, other days she would make frequent stops.

Time dragged on with no changes, though. Dr. Brooks began to make more and more frequent mentions of the possibility that he might never wake up. If he'd suffered some kind of embolism, for example.

Skyler's crew suffered a series of failed missions attempting to recover the equipment necessary to do a thorough scan of Zane's internals. Despite herself, Tania began to wonder if there were any alternatives. When a few weeks passed with no results she even began to consider going down to Belém herself and joining the effort. But then Karl and Skyler called her with the first good news in what seemed like an age.

"We found it," Skyler said. "Well, Ana did. She deserves the credit."

"Please thank her for me, Skyler. Tell me what you've got."

"I should have thought of it myself weeks ago. We had a similar problem once, back in Darwin. Someone needed parts for a very specific X-ray machine, and all the crews were searching hospitals without luck. Prumble and I had the idea to look for warehouses or distribution centers used by the manufacturer."

"That's smart," Tania said.

"Yeah, well, if only I'd remembered my own brilliant technique. Luckily Ana thought the same thing and started searching shipping and receiving instead of the surgery wards. Long story short, we've got the equipment you need. Brand-new, factory sealed, never touched."

Tania wanted to hug him through the screen. With that news she felt she could even embrace Ana. "I'd love to thank her in person, next time I'm down there," she said instead.

"Just doing our job," Skyler replied.

"When can you have it delivered?"

Karl spoke up then. "It's a big crate, very heavy, and all the way on the other side of town. But we've got a team on it, and we'll get it on a climber as soon as they bring it to Exodus. You should have it in two or three days, Tania."

Tania's patience was already stretched to the brink, and the wait that still remained felt even worse. But true to Karl's word, two days later the equipment arrived.

Dr. Brooks was unfamiliar with the specific machine they'd fetched, and anyway she'd only been trained how to use such an instrument, not how to install it. Manuals were read; engineers and technicians were pulled off other duties. At one point Dr. Brooks had to ask Tania to leave them alone so they could work.

"I'm fine," Tania said. "I'll help in any way I can."

"You're hovering," the doctor said. "Second-guessing. Pestering."

Tania stared at the woman in surprise. "You . . . you're right. I hadn't thought about it. God. I hate it when people do that to me. Hover, watch over my shoulder."

"Exactly," Brooks said. "Attend to your other duties; we're working on this as fast as we can."

"I know. You're right." She took a moment to walk around and personally apologize to anyone she could find. Then she left and forced herself to find other things to do.

* * *

Another two weeks ground by before Dr. Brooks called a meeting with Tania, Tim, and a few others. Karl was added via the comm.

"It's not good news," she opened with.

Tania's heart sank. Zane had been in a coma so long now, she didn't think there would be much in the way of good news, but to hear it from the doctor served to slam a door shut in her mind.

The woman spoke at length of the scans they'd done, and the diagnosis. Tania listened but heard little of it. Instead she kept replaying Zane's collapse at that dinner. He'd been so vibrant just the day before.

". . . ruptured in his brain, here . . ."

Tania thought back to her childhood. Where Neil had always doted on her like a father, Zane had been more willing to come down to her level. He played with her as if he were the same age, on the occasions that he would visit.

". . . His comatose state may be permanent. . . ."

It was foolish to pretend she'd known the man well. Zane had always been the quiet brother, content to avoid the limelight that Neil loved so much. Except when making some appearance related to a Platz charity, Zane hardly ever had his name in the news.

What impressed Tania the most about Zane Platz was the way he'd risen to the challenge of moving to Belém. Nothing she'd heard about him before that would have led her to think he would even take part in such an endeavor. She would have guessed the man was a pacifist, if anything. But the bond Zane had shared with Neil seemed enough alone to drive him. Tania could relate. *Perhaps that's why he and I have such a natural friendship.*

". . . We may begin to see organ failure. . . ."

Tania held her hand up. "Dr. Brooks, please . . . is there anything we can *do* other than wait?"

The woman looked at her with a sad expression. "There is brain activity," she said. "You can talk to him. Play him the music he loved. Anything like that. But you're a scientist, so I know you prefer facts. The fact is, none of that is proven to help. I fear it is often more to make those who grieve feel . . . useful."

"But it can't hurt," Tim said.

"True enough. Beyond that, it's the mundane things. Keeping

him nourished and hydrated. Moving and massaging his legs, at least until we can get some pressure cuffs brought up. Bathing him. I've been doing this since you brought him in, with the help from a few of the station staff, but help would be appreciated."

"We could have assisted," Tania said. Tim was nodding.

Dr. Brooks waved a hand. "I know, but until we had an idea of what we were dealing with, I wanted to limit contact and keep a close eye on him. Now that he's . . . stable, I would welcome the help."

"We'll set up a rotation," Tania said. "Teach us what to do, and we'll make sure it all happens."

A few more details were discussed, and then the room cleared, leaving only Tim present, and Karl on the comm's screen.

"Zane's insight will be missed," Karl started.

"Don't talk about him like he's dead," Tim shot back.

A silence fell.

Tania cleared her throat. "Go on, Karl."

"I was going to say that, as much as we all want to help, we have other issues that have languished since Zane fell ill. The scavenger crews have spent so much time finding the medical equipment necessary—"

"That stuff will be useful in the future, too. For years," Tim said.

"I know, believe me. I'm just saying, Tania, Tim . . . I'm trying to point out that time is no longer on our side."

"What do you mean?" Tim asked.

Tania knew but let Karl explain.

"The Builders. When we arrived here we knew it would be roughly two years before they returned. Or whatever they're plotting."

"We don't know for sure," Tania said. "But you're close enough. If they keep to the schedule they've used so far, we're now down to just over eight months." *Was it June already?* Tania shook her head in disbelief.

"That's all I wanted to point out," Karl said.

Tim's brow furrowed. "But . . . so what? I mean, what are we supposed to do with that? If there's one thing we've learned about the Builders it's that we have no idea what the heck they're doing."

"I have a few ideas," Tania said.

"Me, too," Karl replied.

Tim looked back and forth between them. "Well?"

"You first," Tania said to Karl.

He took a breath and looked at them both. "I've been wondering if we shouldn't set up a satellite camp. Take a tower and move it out to a safe distance. Just in case."

Tania pretended to consider the idea, but instantly she disliked it.

"What's a safe distance?" Tim asked. "I mean, SUBS spread across the planet almost as fast as the news of it."

"I don't know," he said with a shrug. "One hundred kilometers?"

"How would they acquire provisions?"

"Send one of the new scavenger crews with them. Plus, Skyler could fly supplies and personnel back and forth."

Tania grimaced. "I don't know. . . ."

"It's just an idea," Karl said. "Should anything happen to the camp, it might be good to have a place to run to."

"We have that already," Tim said. He glanced at each of them in turn. "Darwin."

After so much time away, the thought of going back seemed absurd to Tania. "We'd be treated as criminals. Traitors. I don't think that's an option."

"It's an option," Tim said. "I didn't say it was a good one. It's just there. A last resort."

Karl leaned forward. "Look, if something were to happen here that would drive us to flee, it stands to reason the same thing would happen in Darwin. Heck, *they* might even need to flee *here*. Wouldn't that be something."

Tania started to reply, then stopped. A hundred thoughts raced through her mind. Possibilities, reactions, counterreactions. None of it appealed to her. It all seemed to go against the two things she wanted in the world: build a new haven for mankind, and discover what the Builders ultimately wanted.

"See," Tim said. "This is why I don't like guessing games regarding the aliens. We simply have no idea what their purpose is. Or if they even have a purpose."

"I refuse to believe the bastards are doing all this for no reason at all," Karl said.

"Well," Tania said. She slumped back in her chair. "Tim is right. There's still too many unknowns. We have a date this time—March seventh, if the calculations are correct—but that's not enough to take an action that drastic. I'm sorry, Karl, I just don't think dividing our strength is the best idea."

He persisted. "At a minimum, then, we should identify a location. Stock it with minimal supplies." He shut his eyes for a moment and rubbed his neck. Even the slight exposure to SUBS he'd experienced still left him with brutal headaches, and Tania felt a pang of guilt every time she saw him in pain. The disease was in him now, in stasis, getting no worse and no better.

"Okay," Tania said. "Pick the spot and start a list of supplies. We'll wait until, um, 'Builders' Day' is a month or so out before we expend the energy moving supplies there."

"What was your idea, Tania? In terms of preparation."

She clasped her hands in her lap and gave each of them a look she hoped came across as earnest. "As you both recall, just before this Elevator arrived, we were experiencing failures in Darwin's aura. Blips, outages, whatever you want to call it. SUBS got through the protection, and if not for Skyler's actions we might all be dead right now."

Both men gave her blank stares. "Skyler's actions?" Karl asked. "I . . . what do you mean? What actions?"

"He doesn't talk about it much," she said. "Obviously, or you'd both know. Neil sent him to investigate the base of the Darwin Elevator, which contrary to popular belief is quite deep below Nightcliff. Something happened down there, something Skyler doesn't even understand. But somehow, he fixed it, or . . . reset it."

"How?" Tim asked.

"Like I said, he doesn't know. Nor do I, but I suspect his immunity might have had something to do with it."

Tim looked pale. Karl's face tightened. "You're worried the same thing might happen here."

It wasn't a question. "Yes."

Both men were silent for a long time.

"Of course," Tim said with a sober tone, "it's different here. We have the towers. Multiple auras. I guess they could all fail, but that seems counter to their purpose."

"We have no idea what their purpose is," Karl said.

"It's not different, though," Tania said. "Darwin's aura faltered because it was having trouble dealing with a new strain of SUBS. That's the theory, anyway. Skyler was chased down there by one of these 'newsubs,' and my hunch is that he somehow gave the Elevator what it needed to adjust to the new strain."

"This is a lot of guessing," Tim said.

"No other explanation makes sense," Tania replied. "Believe me, I've thought over and discarded a hundred others."

"Okay," Karl said slowly. "The towers might not help. What can we do?"

"My concern," Tania said, "is that we don't have the same access to the true base of the Elevator here in Belém. Skyler was only able to do what he did because researchers had dug down below Nightcliff, back in the early days. Neil guarded this secret well, as the looks on your faces prove."

"So, what are you suggesting? We dig a shaft? How deep are we talking?"

Tania gave a slight shrug. "The true base of Darwin's Elevator is almost a kilometer down."

Tim whistled.

"Equipment isn't the problem here," said Karl. "It's knowledge. You don't just pick a spot on the ground and dig a hole that deep. We need a geologist, and a civil engineer. Or someone like that."

"Hold on. I don't think we need to go that deep," Tania said. "The way Skyler described the cavity, it sounded as if the Builders had done most of the work when they sank this . . . generator . . . down there. Neil's people just had to dig through some initial coverage and then build a stairwell down. We don't need to go that far, though. A simple high-tension cable would do the trick. A way to lower someone down."

"Hell," Karl said. "If what you said is true and a new variant of the subhuman appears, we could just toss one in the pit."

The words, the way he said them, made Tania's stomach tighten. "Perhaps."

"Maybe that's what we're supposed to do with those weird armored versions out at red circle."

"It's . . . possible," Tania allowed. "I'm inclined to avoid dealing with those creatures unless absolutely necessary." She could still see the dark form as it danced among the colonists, killing with wanton ease. The thought of somehow bringing one of them to the Elevator, and dropping it in a pit, seemed ludicrous. Yet she couldn't help but wonder what would happen if they did.

"I think we all agree on that at least," Karl said. "Fine, then. We'll look at digging a tunnel below the camp, and see if we hit a shaft similar to the one in Nightcliff. I'll talk to Skyler, try to get some more detail out of him."

"Thank you, Karl."

"And I'll look into a secondary campsite, as well as a basic list of provisions. Things are starting to settle into a rhythm down here, so it shouldn't take away from anything to start stockpiling supplies. To be honest, with the limited space we're starting to run out of things to do."

"Again, thank you. For everything."

Karl offered a tight smile. "Give Zane a punch in the shoulder for me," he said, and clicked off.

35

GATEWAY STATION

27.MAY.2284

Seen through the lens of spiced rum, Earth looked a bit like Mars.

Russell swirled the liquid in his glass. A few drops spilled onto the plush cream-colored rug, leaving little splotches of red like stains of blood.

The alcohol sloshed back and forth, coloring the planet beyond in alternating waves of blue marble and bloody red mess. A laugh began to rumble deep in his gut. It built and built until he cackled like a little girl.

As quickly as it began, the laugh died. He stared at the planet below with a mixture of anger and longing. A longing to return to how things were, when he ran Nightcliff and was at the top of his game. The anger came from handing all that over to Grillo.

When that word crossed his mind, he wound up and flung the glass at the transparent wall. He gripped the couch in anticipation of a spectacular shatter of crystal slivers. Instead, the glass hit the invisible barrier with a dull thud. It fell to the floor and rolled, trailing rum behind it in a graceful curve along the carpet.

No matter what he did, or how much he drank, all he could think about was Grillo. Goddamned Grillo. His neat suits and pretty-boy hair. His fucking success. Most of all, his endless excuses for delays in delivering the soldiers Russell asked for. Considering how efficiently the man ran the rest of his operations, it sure felt like a convenient comedy of errors when it came to making good on that promise. And deep down, Russell knew he couldn't do anything but shower the man with orders and insults.

Nine months since Grillo had promised soldiers. Nine fucking months.

He heard the doors open behind him, and soft footfalls on the carpet.

Please be a woman, he thought. *Some spectacular, lonely, needy woman who just came to enjoy the view.*

"There you are," said Alex Warthen.

Russell Blackfield shuddered. He suddenly found himself wishing he hadn't thrown the drink. "Can't a guy get some alone time in this tin can?"

Alex came around and sat down on the couch to Russell's right, as if he'd been invited to do so. "We've been turning the station inside out. You missed your climber at eleven hundred hours."

"I needed a drink."

The security chief glanced at the rum that still dripped down the thick glass wall. The liquid gave the abstract impression that Australia bled. "We could have supplied the climber. . . ."

"What's the big fucking deal, Alex? So anxious to be rid of me? Do I need to log my every movement with you?"

Alex held up his hands. "Calm down. We were just worried. You and I both know the importance of keeping a strict climber schedule. When you didn't turn up, well, people don't just miss a climber departure."

"Well, shit, Alex. I'm sorry if I put a wrench in the schedule. What did you think, someone jumped me in a hallway? That the ghost had returned?"

The man took a deliberate look at the glass lying on the floor by the window. "Honestly, we figured you'd passed out somewhere."

Russell got up and strode to the wet bar tucked in the corner of the room. "I'm not that deep into my cups yet, Alex. A bit buzzed, maybe. Give me an hour and you'll find me facedown in some obscure corner of this sodding place." He poured another glass of rum. Russell didn't particularly like rum, but everything else was empty, and anyway alcohol was alcohol when you got down to it. "I would have thought the old man would keep a selection in here worthy of his riches."

"He did. But that was during a time when things like liquor were tacitly allowed through Nightcliff. Not the most important thing to send up. No one was going to suffocate if it didn't make it through. But it made life in these enclosed spaces a bit easier to cope with, so we all used to turn a blind eye. Grillo, on the other hand . . ."

The rum burned pleasantly in Russell's throat and warmed his stomach. He could guess easily enough where this conversation was going, and he didn't think there was enough rum in all the world to suffer through it again. "Go on, say it."

"Grillo didn't get the memo. Or," Alex said somberly, "more likely he did and tore it up. His doctrine doesn't seem to leave room for drink. Or anything else, for that matter."

Another gulp and Russell found enough fortitude to return to the couch. He plopped down with a sigh and put his feet up on the coffee table. He clasped his hands behind his head and stared at Alex for a long moment, trying to see through the man's stoic façade. Not an easy thing to do when sober, and all but impossible now. Russell gave up, spread his hands, and said, "How long until we run out?"

"A month, my guess. Of course we'll still have cider from the farms."

Russell wrinkled his nose. "That shit is vile. Does the job though, I guess."

"Unfortunately," Alex said, "most of the farms with apple crops are still with Tania Sharma."

"Jesus. If I'm not getting it in one end I'm getting it in the other." He leaned forward and rubbed his temples, suddenly wishing he could think clearly. "So are you telling me it's time to relieve Grillo of his duties?"

Alex shrugged. "Rein him in a bit, maybe. He's cooperating on the whole, but you give him too long a leash, Russell. If he turns on us—"

"Goddamn, is this what I've become?"

The comment stopped Alex short. He looked at Russell with confusion.

"Did you and Neil Platz used to sit here and talk about me like this?"

"Well . . ."

"I've become Neil Platz, haven't I? Deposed the fucker just so I could deal with the same shit." He figured he shouldn't say anything else, but the rum let his mouth keep going. "I figured this would be the best bloody job in the world. Top dog, all that shit. Instead it's one long series of headaches."

Alex let the rant fade before he spoke. "I really don't understand you."

"Huh?"

"I mean, deep down . . ." Alex paused. He shifted in his seat, leaned forward. "Deep down, what do you actually want? No, I'm serious. We pulled off our coup. We got rid of Neil, disbanded the council. We had everything, and then out of nowhere you gave half of it to a zealot slumlord."

"Didn't know he was a zealot at the time."

Alex ignored him. "The other half you've shown almost no interest in managing, despite the fact that you continue to insist on being involved in every little decision. It's like you climbed Everest and all you could think to say was, 'Er, bit cold, isn't it?'"

"Bad analogy. Implies there's nowhere to go but down."

Alex spread his hands wide. "Isn't that the truth? You're at the pinnacle of humanity, and you spend the time drunk or disagreeable. Both, more often than not. I mean, what did you hope would happen when we started this endeavor?"

Where's this "we" shit coming from all of a sudden? You were laid up with a broken collarbone the entire time. Russell sighed and turned to the view of Earth again. A sudden melancholy fell over him like a blanket. He took a deep breath, then went to sip his rum, only to realize he'd left the glass on the wet bar. He clenched his fist instead. "What I wanted was to tie everything together, you know? Darwin and orbit in one cohesive whole, instead of the constant pissing match and forced friendship. Both sides reliant on each other and yet reluctant to share, it seemed like a recipe for disaster."

"And you had that," Alex said, "but you broke it apart again when you gave Darwin to Grillo. I don't understand."

Russell shook his head. "No. It broke apart before that. We were close, but then Tania had to go and take all the brightest minds, not to mention our food supply, and bugger off to South America. So you see, we never were whole, Alex."

"That's going to twist in your gut until the bitter end, isn't it? Tania."

"Yeah. Problem?"

Alex sank back in his seat. He closed his eyes for a few seconds, either deep in thought or profoundly tired. Probably both. Russell waited. He looked at his hand again for the liquid confidence, saw it was still empty, and briefly entertained the idea of getting up to fetch it. Given Alex's mood, he decided it could wait.

The man's eyes blinked open again and he met Russell's eyes. "You're a hunter, Blackfield."

"Eh?"

"A hunter. Not an administrator. The role you fought for will never make you happy because you need prey."

"What the fuck are you on about? Are you my shrink now?"

Alex shrugged. "Just telling you what I see."

"Fascinating, *Doctor* Warthen."

"You had drive and ambition in Darwin because you had Neil Platz to plot against. Before that I'm guessing you spent your time scheming to take Arthur Braithwaite's job in Nightcliff."

"That guy was a spineless fop."

"No argument there," Alex said. "Point is, you need an enemy. It's just who you are."

The words somehow broke through Russell's state of intoxication. He could almost taste the truth in them, and it tasted like salty chips. He swallowed with some effort, and for the first time in as long as he could remember, he wanted a glass of water.

Russell Blackfield hated a lot of things, but near the top of the list was being predictable. Being solved. For all his adult life the only prompt he needed to change course was when someone had known the course ahead of time. Knowledge of the future was a powerful thing, and while some people simply found comfort in knowing that what happened today would happen tomorrow, rinse and bloody repeat, others wielded that information like a weapon. They'd be one step ahead, always. Russell's own mother had been the grand master of this. For most of his childhood he'd thought her to be some kind of psychic, a mystical witch of a woman. Try to take money from her purse only to find a mousetrap inside. A little note for him to read through the pulsing pain of fingers nearly broken. "Piss off, get a job and make your own way." He'd sneak in through the back window after a night of drinking and vandalism to find the chair he'd carefully placed before leaving missing a leg, rigged to collapse. The fall to the floor hurt like hell, but worse was the fact that she'd fucking known.

Her lessons were supposed to teach him to be a fine upstanding citizen. It even worked, for a while. But then he realized that if he stole money from her purse on random nights, instead of every Friday, no trap would be set. If he came in through the front door, an hour earlier than usual, she'd miss him. The new tactic worked so well that Russell decided to have the letters VTP tattooed on his right forearm. Initials of some fallen friend, most people assumed. They stood for "Vary The Pattern."

Alex Warthen went on. "You're a mess lately, and I think it's because you're torn between some feeling of obligation to 'run things' while what you really want to do is bring the runaways back into the fold. You're unable to focus. And on top of that is the knowledge that you handed Darwin to someone else, and he's doing a damn fine job."

"I'm only letting you say this shit because I'm too drunk to stand up."

"But it's true, right?"

"Yes it's fucking true!" Russell shouted more than said. "Doesn't mean I have to like hearing it. I still don't understand what the hell you expect me to do. Go down to Darwin with a squadron of thugs and kick Grillo out? Won't be pretty, and like you said, he's the bloody messiah down there."

"What I'm saying," Alex said with pointed patience, "is that you should put all your energy into the runaways, from now until the situation is resolved. And I mean really do it, not just talk."

Russell opened his mouth to speak but Alex's upheld hand stopped him.

"Hear me out. You focus on Tania and the new Elevator. Whatever it takes, just bring them under our umbrella. You know it's what you really want to be doing, anyway. Let myself and a few of the old council members deal with the minutiae of keeping these space stations provisioned."

"And Grillo?"

"I thought I might try handling him."

"Oh? What difference would that make?"

"Your first instinct was to take a squad of thugs down there. I thought I might try a little diplomacy."

Russell rolled his eyes. "Oh God."

"It worked well enough with you for years."

"Now you're just being a prick."

Alex brushed the comment aside. "You tell Grillo I've been placed back in charge of managing shipments on the cord, and I'll take it from there. Once you've got the Brazil situation under control, if I don't have Grillo behaving to our liking then you can turn your guns on him."

The plan had a sobering effect. Alex had him figured perfectly, and he couldn't deny the appeal of putting all his attention into revenge against Tania Sharma. "Grillo promised me fighters. He's been dodging that ever since."

"I'll make it a priority that he deliver."

Russell nodded, then turned to the blue planet out the expansive window. The deal was done. "Neil, Tania, maybe Grillo after that. What happens then?" *What happens when I run out of prey?*

Alex inclined his head slightly. "Well, there's always the Builders."

36

BELÉM, BRAZIL

12.JUL.2284

The thin cord plunged into darkness, well beyond the limit of Skyler's flashlight. Radiance danced along its length, as if a strand of shiny black hair had been stretched right down the middle of the abyss.

He pulled a glow stick from his vest pocket, shook it until his arm hurt, and then cracked it. A green glow built within the childish object.

With his flashlight turned off, the space beneath base camp became pitch-black save for the faint green glow coming from the stick. Skyler held it out over the precipice and dropped it.

It seemed to fall forever, spiraling on the hot air that rose from the power source below. The glowing stick fell until he almost couldn't see it. Finally, the object stopped, as if it had become caught in some invisible field within darkness. Skyler put his binoculars to his eyes and tapped the autofocus until the green glowing stick came into view.

The surface it rested on was another iris, just like he'd seen below Nightcliff. This came as no surprise. Skyler had been down here many times since the tunnel team finished their work, months ago, but he still liked to survey it for any changes. Any hint that it might experience the same failures Darwin's had. The room where he stood, twenty meters beneath the center of camp, had been carved largely by hand after a tunneling machine bored the main access way. Warm air from the alien generator below gave the space a sauna's climate. Moisture dripped down the packed soil walls, traced lines along the rocks too big to remove. Wooden beams were irregularly placed around the circular space, with a simple square formed across the top to presumably hold up the "ceiling."

Something about the pit drew him back, time and time again. It never looked any different, of course. Nothing led him to believe it would, but he still felt the need to check. Part of him wished it would change, that he'd stare down into the hole and see brilliant yellow light emanating from the alien thing, beckoning him to dive in again and become enveloped in the light, in the machine. To feel every memory held within his mind splayed out before him again—

"There you are." It was Karl's voice, from the access way.

Skyler turned from the pit and raised an arm to shield his eyes from the bright light the other man carried. "I usually get some peace and quiet in here."

"Very apt," Karl said, "since peace and quiet is why I came looking for you."

The older man came and stood next to Skyler. He took a pensive glance over the edge, down into the depths, and clicked off his own light.

"How's the headaches?" Skyler asked.

"Under control, thanks to you and a diet of ibuprofen," Karl said.

Skyler said nothing for moment while Karl's eyes adjusted.

"Hell of a long way down," he said once he'd spotted the green light.

"Peace and quiet, you were saying?"

Karl turned his light back on and shot Skyler a sidelong grin. "I've spent the morning on the comm with Tania."

"Oh," Skyler said. *I know that look.* "Some new emergency, and you need me to go fetch something. Let's put off the big issue for a few more days, Skyler. That about right?"

The man's grin shifted to a grimace, and in that instant all the signs of exhaustion and stress returned to his haggard face.

"So what is it this time?" Skyler asked.

A hint of sadness crept into Karl's eyes. He hesitated, studying Skyler as if he'd never seen him before. "This rift between you and Tania, it's pretty deep, isn't it?" Karl gestured at the pit.

"Don't change the subject. Especially not to that subject."

The older man's expression held, though. He looked back and forth at Skyler's eyes, as if seeking his answers there. "You two should hash this out, Skyler. It's unhealthy."

"I'm here if she wants to talk."

"Bullshit," Karl said, his voice even. "Every time she comes down you either have Ana at your side, or me. Plus some excuse locked and loaded in case you might be forced into any conversation other than the business at hand."

"And every time I try to get out of here, to go do the work we all know needs to be done, she finds some critical project that simply must be top priority. Or she simply writes it off as too risky. You all do."

Whatever Karl had been about to say, he swallowed it, and visibly calmed himself. "You're both acting like children."

"I've been cordial. I've done everything asked of me."

"I know," Karl said. "I know. I just wish you two would put that business with Gabriel behind you."

"That's not even the issue anymore. At least it's only part of it. Karl, we've squandered a lot of time. The calendar is no longer on our side. Digging out this room shouldn't even have been on our radar. It's a diversion."

Karl fell silent.

Skyler went on. "I never thought I'd see it happen, but all these scientists, Tania chief among them, seem terrified of risks, of the unknown. The camp needs the tools required for survival, granted, but we've done everything we can without expanding the aura. And all the while the clock ticks."

He took a breath. When Karl said nothing Skyler went on. "Those towers vacated the camp for a reason. We all know it. That thing, whatever the hell it is, out there in the rainforest, is there for some purpose. It must be. Karl, dammit, we need to figure out what the hell is going on here before the Builders throw everything out of whack again. Zane is stable. The camp is operating smoothly. Our last two trades with Blackfield came off without a hitch. And . . ."

". . . time is running out." Karl finished for him.

"Exactly. Yes."

Karl stared into the abyss for a long time. Thick with the smell of soil and rock, the air felt heavy even compared to Belém's humid standards. "Maybe you should just go then," he said, finally. Then he turned toward Skyler and gripped his shoulder. "You're right. Tania will find reasons to keep you here as long as possible, simply because she doesn't want to lose you."

"I'm useful, sure, but not invaluable. We have other immunes now—"

"She doesn't want to lose *you*, Skyler. Don't act like you don't know that. That business with Gabriel, the decisions she was forced to make, devastated her."

"That may be so, but no one forced her to lie to me about it."

Impatience flashed on Karl's face. "Is it so goddamn hard to understand? She was consumed with guilt and saw a way out with just one little white lie. I would have done the same damn thing. But then you caught her in it and had to make a big goddamn stink about it. Did you know she almost quit after that? She wanted to, wanted to run off to Black Level and hide in a cloud of research again."

Skyler hadn't known. "Why didn't she?"

"Talked her out of it. Zane and Tim, I mean, though I would have been happy to help persuade her. Put yourself in her shoes, Skyler. Brilliant scientist, the favorite son—if you'll pardon the expression—of Mr. Platz. She never asked to be the leader, to make decisions that had people's lives hanging in the balance. All she thought she had to do was tell Neil the specifics of the new Builder ship, and then let him take the reins like he always did before. Except it didn't work out that way. Neil finally lost a battle and out of every possible candidate he trusted her with carrying out his plan. I think if Neil Platz earned one thing in his life it's our trust in his judgment of people. He chose you, too, you know. And me."

A picture came to Skyler's mind. The research room on Black Level, where they'd shared a bit of food and drink while they discussed Neil's plan. For all her drive and bravery, he'd seen the terror deep in her eyes. He'd tasted it, when she kissed him moments earlier as thanks for coming to help. He had undertaken that journey with a single-minded sense of purpose, and even left his friends behind in order to seek out Tania. For all the reasons he'd used to justify the race to find her, he knew deep down the truth of it: He'd wanted to be with her. The oldest, dumbest reason in the book. *Who's the liar? What excuse did I give Prumble, or Sam? Something about seeing Neil's plan through, about Tania being the key to it all. Bollocks.*

"Maybe some time away," Karl said, "would do you both some good. Prep your aircraft, get your crew ready, and find out where those towers went. I'll explain to Tania and the others. She's more likely to come around to the idea you're just tracking the other three, instead of tackling those demons in the forest."

Skyler found himself nodding, even though he felt trapped between two choices. Part of him wanted to rush to Tania as he had in Darwin. Apologize, do whatever it took to rewind back to those first days after leaving the city and its Elevator behind.

That was impossible now, though. He knew it. The rift between them had grown too large, and of course there was Ana.

Wild, insatiable Ana.

She'd shared his bed a hundred times now and seemed to grow more eager each time. More than that, she loved him. She'd said it often enough. He'd even repeated the words in the darkness when they lay together, their bodies entwined in the heady sweat of afterglow.

Skyler shook his head to clear the memories. Karl took this as refusal and started to argue, before Skyler silenced him with a raised hand. "We'll take off tomorrow at dawn."

"Okay. Good."

"And Karl? Thanks, friend. For speaking your mind."

Karl clapped him on the shoulder. "I'll talk to Tania after you've left. Find our towers, Skyler."

* * *

La Gaza Ladra's engines roared to life the instant the sun peaked above the canopy east of camp.

Skyler let Ana handle the preflight. He'd walked her through it at least fifteen times already, and on the last flight she'd handled it with only minimal supervision.

He glanced back through the open cockpit door. In the rear compartment, Vanessa and Pablo double-checked the gear. The clean, tasteful interior of the luxury passenger cabin had been abandoned long ago, in the first weeks of recovering the vessel. The cosmetic back wall had been unceremoniously removed, along with the widescreen display and wet bar attached to it, though not until after a raucous movie night. Behind the cabin was a cargo compartment equal in width and with a floor a meter lower. Removable panels within gave access to a crawl space below the passenger cabin, ostensibly for maintenance of the wiring and ventilation systems that supported the area. To Skyler's eye, there was a clear secondary purpose for smuggling.

Two doors on either side of the aircraft's belly provided external access to the cargo space. The design allowed for easy stowage of luggage and small items, but was next to useless for recovery of large items. Skyler felt a bond to the aircraft already, but he knew it would have to be replaced with something more practical at the earliest convenience.

"Tower, this is the Magpie. We're heading out," Ana said into her oversized headset. Though everyone liked the ship's full name, the easier slang version had become more commonly used.

Of course, there were no other planes, no air traffic to manage, but Skyler had insisted the traditions of tower courtesy be maintained, even if informal.

"Magpie, this is the so-called tower. Safe travels, and keep me posted on what you find as long as you can."

"Count on it," Ana said. She flashed Skyler a thumbs-up, an unwitting echo of Angus's signature gesture.

She's older than he was, Skyler realized suddenly, further eroding his initial misgivings about her age.

"The stick is yours," the girl said, which got a quick raise of the eyebrows at the innuendo from Skyler.

"Thanks," he said. "If you're good I'll let you fiddle with it later."

Ana scoffed and rolled her eyes, but not without throwing a small smirk his way.

"Buckle up back there!" Skyler shouted toward the rear.

A few seconds later Pablo called out, "We're ready!"

On the central screen in front of Skyler, a flashing icon reminded him that a flight plan still hadn't been entered. He'd fretted over this choice for months, after carefully entering in the four options now presented to him. Four paths traced out from base camp, carved by the tower groups that went haywire during the fight with Gabriel.

One group, of course, went northeast to encircle the crashed Builder ship. Protecting it, apparently, though Skyler also held the theory that they were protecting everything else from what lay within their ring. He wasn't interested in this group, however. Their location was known, as was the danger they surrounded.

That left three other choices.

One took a path almost to the same location. North by northeast, through the rainforest and then beyond. They'd flown along its trail as far as the coast once, and lost track of it at the waterline. Either the towers had sunk into the ocean, or they'd crossed it. Some of it, anyway. At least the path ran straight, which meant they could follow it on a map.

Yet another group left the camp heading due east. A few weeks ago they'd followed the trail for a hundred kilometers or so before turning back to base. An interesting discovery had been made: The path wasn't straight, as it had appeared from the ground. Looking at it from altitude, they could see that it had a slight curve to it.

The same was true of the last group's route. The group had gone northwest, carving a line right through the city and leaving a path of destruction in its wake, like a tornado with no collateral damage. The curve of its path was almost too subtle to detect; it was only when he'd taken the aircraft up to three thousand meters on a clear day that the gentle arc to the line could be seen.

Curvature worried Skyler. On the surface it would still be fairly trivial to trace on a globe, but they had no evidence that the paths would always follow the same trajectory to their end. What if the curved paths changed directions, or straightened out? What if the one straight path started to curve later along its route? If they could indeed cross water, and the direction change happened out in the ocean, all bets were off.

There was no way to know except to follow one.

"Three paths diverged . . . ," Skyler said to himself.

Ana, he realized, had been watching him as he stared at the choices on the screen, a bemused smirk on her face. "I vote for whichever takes us the farthest away," she said softly.

"No way to know that for sure. How about the one we know hits the ocean?"

She cracked a grin.

Skyler grimaced. He liked the idea, too, but if the path was truly straight it wouldn't cross land again until it reached the Azores, an island group in the North Atlantic. That was near the edge of the Magpie's range. If they couldn't find a place to recharge the caps there, or a replacement aircraft, they could wind up marooned.

He looked at Ana and saw simple determination in her eyes. *Just go for it,* they said. There were worse fates, he decided, than being stuck on an island with her, Vanessa, and Pablo. None, he suspected, would mind terribly.

"It's settled then. North by northeast."

A path of destruction along the ground made the need for navigation pointless at first, but that didn't stop Skyler from keeping Ana busy. He quizzed her on various parts of the instrumentation and had her supply regular updates on their capacitor status, even though the Magpie's computers would alert him to anything that jeopardized the flight plan.

The young woman took to the tasks with some difficulty. It had become obvious to Skyler since they'd first flown the bird on a mission that she learned through example and hands-on activity, not through studying flight manuals or maps as Vanessa did. The older immune was already able to handle the craft with minimal help, and Skyler suspected with only a few more hours of flight time she'd be ready to handle the duty solo. Not so with Ana. He'd given the two women equal time in the pilot's chair—mostly so as not to show favoritism—but Ana simply didn't have the deftness, the patience, that Vanessa did. Still, even if she ended up being unsuitable as a co-pilot, the knowledge she absorbed wouldn't hurt.

The straight gouge left behind by the towers ran for a hundred kilometers through rainforest, a town, a small city, and then still more rainforest. The path ran roughly parallel to the Rio Pará until the mouth of the waterway began to widen. Ahead, the Atlantic Ocean stretched from horizon to horizon, and Skyler began to gain altitude as they crossed over the body of water. According to the flight computer, they would make the Azores island group with just 2 percent charge left in the ultracaps, and Skyler wanted to be able to glide a long way if the need arose. He'd also marked backup landing locations in the system for each leg of the trip. A return to Brazil in the first third, a landing in the Cape Verde islands off Africa's western coast in the middle leg, and beyond that the Azores were their only choice, really.

At cruising altitude, Skyler tapped the comm. "Belém, this is Magpie. We're about to leave radio range. Following the northeastern tower group."

"I hear you, Magpie," Karl said. "Somehow I thought you'd pick that one."

"I'd let you talk me out of it, but then I can see the look on Ana's face."

She stuck her tongue out at him.

"Understood, my friend. Be careful out there. Hey, before we lose you—we've started an effort to install a more robust comm on Black Level. It might take awhile, but feel free to check in now and then and see if you can raise us. The usual channel."

"Will do," Skyler said. Then he nodded at Ana.

She surprised him with a sudden, serious expression, and said the words.

"Magpie, out."

37

DARWIN, AUSTRALIA

13.JUL.2284

Samantha stared at the slip of wrinkled yellow paper pinched between her fingers. She reread the handwritten order from Grillo in mild disbelief, and then looked up at the room of crews and pilots before her. Her gaze drifted to the far end of the hangar, the entrance, where a group of armed guards stood alert.

"I have new orders from Nightcliff," she said. A hush fell over the gathered scavengers. Every seat was full. Some sat on the floor, or stood by the sidewalls. "Um. From now on, no more flights on Sundays. Not even spec missions."

A hundred pairs of eyes all trying to determine if she meant it as a joke. Nightcliff hadn't sent over any flight orders on Sundays in a long time, and the day had become everyone's chance to go out and search on their own. The fact that Sunday had been Nightcliff's day to be silent didn't need explanation, and no one talked about it. Most of the scavengers called it "get shit done day" and took full advantage.

One day of freedom per week had been enough to keep the crews from grumbling too much. Now, though . . .

Woon stood perfectly still behind his improvised bar. He'd

been wiping a mug with a stained cloth, and stopped. Even his expression was blank, as if waiting for a punch line.

"I'm serious," Sam said. " 'No flights on Sundays,' that's what it says. Speculative missions included."

"That's bollocks," a voice near her said. A stocky pilot named Cal. "We get in food and basics these days. None of the barter perks like from before, and now those assholes want to take away our spec jobs?"

"Just find something else to do," Sam said. "It's only Sundays, guys."

Someone off to the side shouted out. "What the fuck are we supposed to do then?"

Sam grimaced. The note offered no advice on that point, but she had a pretty good idea of what Grillo expected, and a *very* good idea of what would happen to anyone who disobeyed him. "I think we're supposed to use it as a day of reflection, or some shit—"

A grunt stood and grabbed his crotch. "Maybe we're supposed to march up to Temple Sulam and say our ascend-ye-fucking-faithfuls."

That got some laughs.

"Brilliant," another added, a woman Sam couldn't see. "Let's confess our sins. Who wants to start?"

More laughter. *Not good,* Sam thought. They didn't know Grillo, not like her. They had no real fear of him yet.

"To hell with that! Let's get rotten!" someone else yelled. A cheer went up.

Half the room was out of their chairs and headed for the bar before she could whistle loud enough to get their attention. "Hang on, for fuck's sake! I wasn't done reading."

Some returned to their chairs; others froze midstride. Sam waited until a few side conversations died out.

She cleared her throat. Her eyes darted to the armed guards by the door. They'd become so much scenery around the airport over the last year, but rarely did they gather in one place like this. If any of the other pilots had noticed, they weren't showing it. That was likely to change in ten seconds.

"There's to be no alcohol served on Sundays, from this point forward. Sorry, Woon."

In the silence that followed, Sam could hear the old cuckoo clock ticking away from the wall behind Woon.

"In here," someone asked, "or anywhere in Darwin?"

Sam shrugged. "Doesn't say."

"Can we drink from our own supplies?"

"Beats me," Sam said. "I guess. It doesn't say."

"Go ask, then, lapdog!" a mechanic shouted. "Or maybe the blokes by the door can shed some light."

In unison, the gathered crowd turned in their seats.

The guards at the door did a pretty good job of hiding whatever intimidation they felt under that collective gaze. One shifted on his feet. Another flexed her fingers on the grip of her weapon. Should it come to blows, the Nightcliff squad was armed but hopelessly outnumbered. It would be ugly. The crackdown that followed would be a bloodbath. She had to do something. Something more than just appearing to be Grillo's goddamn *lapdog*. She'd heard the nickname whispered when people thought she wasn't listening, or grumbled at her back after orders were dished. This was the first time someone had the balls to say it to her face. And who could blame him?

She looked around for Skadz, hoping he'd stick up for her. The crews fucking loved him, of course. Maybe she should abandon everyone for a year and see if it helped her standing.

At least, she thought, *I could pretend to challenge Grillo on this.*

"You know what," she said, then paused. Most of the crowd refocused on her. She waited until she had their attention and wadded up the paper. "Fuck it, you're right. I will go ask. Everyone relax. Get your maintenance done, or line up to tap Woon's thor. Take a day off, if you want. Just stay on the ground until I'm back. Okay?"

She took the grumbles that followed as tacit agreement and headed for the door. The guards filed out with her, as if she were one of them, and she hated them for it. The word *lapdog* rang in her head so loud it might as well have been branded on her cheek.

"I'll get Grillo on the comm for you," one of the guards said.

"No," Sam said. "I'll visit him in person. Get the truck."

"Truck's in use. And you don't tell us what to do."

Sam balled her fists and turned around. The urge to throw a punch boiled just beneath her small reservoir of self-control. Keeping rage like that bottled inside had been almost alien to her in the past, but she'd screwed the cork on tight since that cursed foray into Lyons. Time, and snarky comments from assholes like this, were on the verge of letting some of her anger out, and she found that she liked it. On a whim she shouldered past them and marched toward the airport gate.

"Where are you going?" one asked.

"I'll walk, fuck you very much."

The squad argued behind her, and she felt glad they couldn't see the smile that crept onto her lips. When she ducked under the airport gate, she glanced behind her. Two of the guards had apparently been assigned to follow her and were jogging to catch up.

She announced herself at Nightcliff's gate and the side door swung open. They would have seen her approach across Ryland Square, of course, and since two of their own escorted her, no questions were asked.

Sam recalled Skyler's story, of coming in through the old sewer with a little help from high explosives. *Escape may have been a bitch,* she thought, *but if I ever need to break in, this is the way to do it.*

Kelly's face sprang to mind. If only the woman was still being held here and hadn't foiled Sam's bid to win her some freedom. She wondered if the hard woman was still in that hospital, and what the hell she had going on there that was so important that she'd take the robes, feign a change of heart.

The buzz of activity in Nightcliff's yard stopped her cold. One of the men who'd shadowed her bumped into her and muttered an apology.

"Forget it," Sam said. She started to ask them to explain the view in front of her, then thought better of it and forced herself to walk on.

In Nightcliff's yard, hundreds of Darwin citizens sat on the ground in loose rows facing a wooden stage that had been built near the Elevator tower, just in front of the climber port. As she watched, the row of people closest to the stage stood in unison, at some command she hadn't heard, and began to file up to the lectern at the middle of the platform.

Grillo stood there, flanked by men and women in white robes emblazoned with the Jacobite holy symbol on the chest. The emblem also graced a huge length of cloth behind Grillo. The white sheet had been mounted to a frame made from steel pipes. The cross had been painted in a red so bright it practically glowed, and the ladder that formed the vertical portion of the quasi-Christian symbol had its rungs drawn in black.

The slumlord, if he could still be called that, dressed as always in a neat gray business suit, was not facing the crowd. His attention instead fell on the line of Darwinites who filed up onto the stage. One by one they would kneel in front of Grillo, and he'd trace a few lines on their forehead. She could see his lips moving, but the words were far too quiet to reach her.

"Want to get in line?" one of the guards asked her.

The voice jarred her from a deep trance of morbid fascination, as if she'd been walking past the aftermath of a violent street brawl. "No," she said. "Thanks. Not today."

Her path meandered around the edge of the crowd. She recognized the mess hall and thought of her brief reign as Nightcliff's boxing champ, and her equally brief fling with the guard Vaughn. The thought of asking about him crossed her mind, and then dissolved. She'd used him. He wouldn't be very happy to hear from her.

Past the crowd and the makeshift pulpit, the far side of Nightcliff's vast yard came into view. This side was crowded, too, but not with row after row of ragged citizens.

Sam saw clusters of uniformed soldiers. She knew at a glance they were recruits. The sloppy way they formed their marching lines, the lack of synchronicity in their steps. A shirt untucked here, a hat on backward there. All things that would have been overlooked under Blackfield, but not Grillo.

These fighters were Jacobite, of that she had no doubt. The red emblems stitched or drawn on their cobbled-together uniforms were an unnecessary reinforcement.

She counted at least ten squads, each forty strong by her guess. Four hundred holy warriors each in possession of one of the small, compact weapons Sam had helped recover from Malaysia.

Her escort took her to Grillo's office and left her to sit there, staring at a new Jacobite painting on the wall behind his desk. *This shit is well and truly out of hand,* she was thinking as the door clicked open behind her.

"I give you the day off and you come here," Grillo said from behind her. He walked around and eschewed his chair. Instead he simply leaned on the side of his desk and folded his arms. The confidence in his posture unnerved and deflated her. "I thought you might take the hint and enjoy some well-deserved rest. Which reminds me, I never had the chance to properly thank you for fetching Sister Haley's original work. You've done us all a great service."

She shrugged. "Enjoyable read, was it?"

"I've no idea. Authenticity was verified and now the tome sits in secure storage far below us." He frowned, a sudden contemplative look crossing his face. "Someday, perhaps, things will settle down enough here that the manuscript can be displayed for all to see. In Temple Sulam, perhaps. But not now, not while there's so much work to be done."

Sam withered under his intense gaze and stared at her hands. A feeling of weakness, of the stupidity in coming here with a fire in her belly, coursed through her. "The thing is," she said finally, "none of us want to rest. You never give us missions on Sundays, and that's something the crews have come to rely on. It's their one day to go out and scavenge for themselves. Find parts. Goods they can trade."

"Contraband," Grillo said, one eyebrow ever so slightly arched.

Samantha sighed. "A bit, probably. Nothing compared to the old days. Contraband wasn't even in Blackfield's vocabulary. Unless you were dumb enough to bring something in that might harm the Elevator, no one batted an eye. They got their cut and sent us on our merry way."

"My people are not 'on the take.'"

"Yeah, no, I know," she said lamely. For a second she thought it best to get up and leave, agreeing to implement his orders simply to get out of his presence. But in a strange way she found a bit of strength in knowing that Grillo's people generally behaved well not so much because of high moral caliber as from a strong desire to not be stabbed in the face. "How's Kelly?" she asked, stalling.

"Sister Josephine is very well. A rising star, you might say. I'm sorry, but she seems uninterested in visiting with you again. Now get to the point, Samantha. I have a busy day ahead."

"That is the point. My crews don't have a busy day ahead," she said. "And worse, you're trying to tell them how to conduct themselves. No alcohol? You'll have a riot on your hands."

"Riots I can deal with," he said. There was no emotion in his voice, and yet it had all the authority of a Neil Platz political tirade. "Still, perhaps you're right; perhaps we can make some allowances for services rendered."

"Okay . . . so booze is back on the menu?"

He flashed a sympathetic grin. "Consumed indoors, not at that rank fire hazard you call a tavern. As for speculative missions"—he paused and thought for a moment—"set up a lottery. Any crew that wants to fly puts in their name, and let as many as a quarter of them fly on any given Sunday. Tell them it's less about their freedom and more about taxing Nightcliff's skeleton crew on the holy day."

She knew a final offer when she heard it and considered the allowances good enough for a day's work. "Deal," she said, and that was the end of it. Grillo ushered her from the room, simultaneously inviting a handful of Chinese gangster types in from the small lobby outside his office. He spoke to them in Cantonese with a flawless accent.

They bowed to him as they entered.

38

THE AZORES

14.JUL.2284

"There!" Vanessa said.

Skyler brought the aircraft to a hover. He leaned forward in his seat, straining against the belts, to see where she pointed.

Below, the ocean met a thin line of rocky shore. Cliffs separated the vast sea from a wall of foliage that ran inland to the mountains.

"I see it, too!" Ana called from the rear cabin. She'd traded places with the older woman four hours earlier, and slept most of the time since. Skyler hadn't the heart to wake her when the Azores first came into view. She needed the rest, and with the cap level dwindling he found he wanted Vanessa as his co-pilot, just in case. Ana didn't need to know that part.

He'd been flying parallel to the shore for hours at low speed while the others all looked for signs of where the aura towers might have made landfall. With each passing minute, and the corresponding drop in the Magpie's already limited cap level, he'd been close to giving up hope. The aircraft had not been configured for international trips.

After the long flight over a seemingly endless sea he couldn't imagine how the towers could have made it this far, and he had resigned himself to picturing them resting on the seafloor, surrounded by bioluminescent creatures as alien as the towers themselves.

Yet Vanessa had it right. The path was difficult to see at first. This part of the island had been used for agriculture, and the straight edges of the old fields were still obvious even in the current overgrown state. Trees and plants almost completely obscured the towers' line now, too, after so much time. But it was there. Wider than the roads or the edges of cropland, a laser-straight swath of clear land ran inland until it crested a hill and disappeared over the other side.

"Mark it," Skyler said as he turned the craft to face land. He glanced at the cap level. "Zero-point-five percent. We need to find a place to charge up; this hovering will burn through that in ten minutes. Somewhere other than Lagoa."

The screens in front of Vanessa were configured with maps and the associated tools to manipulate them. She'd become pretty adept at working those views since the aircraft had come into their possession.

Lagoa had been Skyler's first destination when they'd reached the island. The small town was only a short distance from their estimated place of landfall.

From the air, though, it appeared to be dead. Not a single light graced a window or beacon tower there. He had little hope a mini-thor existed in the glorified village, but with dusk rapidly approaching he'd decided to look for the towers' path first. Lights would be easier to spot after dark, anyway.

"Ponta Delgada is the largest nearby," Vanessa said. She tapped a location to the west, just a few kilometers down the beach. Her fingers danced as she zoomed and panned the map. "We could fly along the tower path, to the north side of the island. Ribeira Grande is there. Not as large, but larger than Lagoa."

Skyler could see the first city she mentioned out his window. Or rather, the dark silhouette of it against a rapidly dimming sky. "I don't see any lights in Ponta Delgada." He didn't see any purple glow or mysterious clouds, either. The others had probably noticed this, too, and he knew they'd be thinking the same thing he was: The journey might be far from over.

He felt Vanessa staring at him, waiting for his decision. "North," he said after a few seconds.

When the aircraft crested the island's spine, his heart sank.

The island was utterly, completely dark.

And the tower group's path carved a perfect line through forest and city alike, straight to the north shore until it disappeared over a cliff edge beside the ocean.

"Our trip is just beginning," Skyler muttered.

A scratching sound woke him.

He turned and propped himself on an elbow. The others still slept, and only the barest hint of light filtered in through the window on the cabin door on *La Gaza Ladra*'s starboard side.

His back ached from sleeping on the floor, despite the cushion of a sleeping bag beneath him. Pablo snored softly from his place on the floor at the back of the cabin, while Ana and Vanessa were two unmoving forms in the reclined passenger chairs.

The scratching noise again. Like dead tree branches scraping against a window on a breezy night. It seemed to be coming from the same door where morning light crept in through the porthole window. He staggered to his feet, stifling a yawn and grinding a fist into the small of his back to chase away the pain there.

His view out the small round window was southerly, over the same rise they'd flown across the night before. From this low angle, the tower group's path was easy to spot through the island's dense foliage. Easier still where it reached the edge of the city, carving an avenue-wide line straight through houses and buildings alike.

He'd landed on the rooftop pad at a luxury resort in the hope such a high-end place would have paid the extra cost for a mini-thor, or a stake in one at least. But the place was dead, just like the rest of the island, apparently. He'd kept his fears to himself, that they were stuck here, but Skyler had no doubt that by breakfast time this morning one of the others would voice the concern.

A face appeared outside the window.

Skyler fell back in surprise, stumbled, and landed on his back.

The gaunt face in the round window snarled and Skyler saw thin, ragged fingers clawing at the glass, leaving dirty smears behind. The subhuman had wild beady eyes and rotten teeth. Its brown hair hung in matted clumps around a beard full of unidentifiable bits of dirt and food.

Vanessa stepped between him and the door. In the back of the cabin, Pablo stirred and got to his feet. Ana slept.

"Stay back," Vanessa said, her hand on the cabin door's rotating handle. She gripped it and coiled herself.

"Wait," Skyler said. "There might be more."

"Get your gun, then."

Pablo stepped between them, looking over Vanessa's shoulder at the anguished face outside the window. He had a pistol in his hand and nodded to the woman. "Open it. Cover your ears," he said, his voice a dry rasp from sleep.

Vanessa dug in her feet. "On three. One. Two." She pulled the handle on the third beat until it was upright and threw her shoulder into the loosened door.

Skyler watched through Pablo's legs as the subhuman fell when the door struck it, a motion mirroring Skyler's own stumble. The animal tried to remain upright by running backward in a kind of controlled fall. Pablo gave Vanessa a half second to crouch and cover her ears before he squeezed off two shots into the creature's chest. Little eruptions of blood sprang from each side of the sternum, and then the sub toppled over the edge of the roof, gone as quickly as it had appeared.

The tiny cabin rang in a high-pitched scream. Skyler hadn't thought to cup his own ears. "Close the door!" he shouted, his own voice sounding a kilometer away.

Vanessa reached for the handle, then paused. She said something to Pablo and he replied, but Skyler couldn't hear them. It was like listening to a conversation in an adjacent room through the wall.

The woman stepped out onto the landing pad and stood very still.

Pablo moved to the open doorway and waited, frozen in place.

"What's wrong with you?" Skyler asked.

The tall man turned and pressed a finger to his lips. Skyler climbed to his feet. He glanced back at Ana, half-expecting to find her upright with her hands clasped to stinging ears. The girl had turned over and was still sleeping like a babe.

The bright hum in Skyler's head began to fade. He listened at the door with Pablo while Vanessa stepped farther from the craft. "What is it?" Skyler asked, careful to keep his voice low. "I can't hear anything."

"That's just it," she replied. "Nothing. If the gunshots riled others, they sure are quiet about it. And this one is the first we've seen."

"Weird," Pablo said.

"The population collapsed, maybe," Vanessa said. "It's been almost seven years."

"We shouldn't let our guard down, in any case," Skyler said. The tranquil, dark island had a way of lulling the senses. Until Skyler had seen that twisted face on the other side of the glass, he'd all but forgotten about subhumans.

I'm getting rusty, he thought.

Ana stretched and woke only when there was the smell of food. Preservall bacon and imitation eggs, scrambled over a camp stove on the rooftop by Pablo. Vanessa handled coffee while Skyler stood on top of *La Gaza Ladra*'s fuselage and scanned the city around them with binoculars.

"Good morning," Ana said from below him.

He smiled and waved to her.

"See anything interesting?" she asked a minute later, a steaming mug in her hand.

"I do. Can you look up an address on the terminal for me?"

He rattled off the information as he read it from the side of a long-abandoned utility truck. A logo on the door indicated the local municipal power company, and an address was stenciled below it.

While she searched for the place, he studied the path of the tower group. A perfect line of collapsed buildings and crushed automobiles ran straight through the beach town. He followed it to the water, adjusting his zoom along the way.

The path vanished at the edge of a cliff, at a point where it jutted out from the rest of the shore. In the bright morning, Skyler had to squint as dazzling flashes reflected off the dark blue water. At the base of the cliff, a narrow beach made entirely of rock took the brunt of the ocean's wrath.

There were shapes on the beach, lying in the surf or draped across the larger rocks. Piles of trash, or maybe sea lions? Skyler zoomed farther and focused.

His gut clenched. "Guys," he said, "I found our missing subhumans."

Bodies littered that patch of gravel. Drowned and bloated things once, the subhumans were now so many piles of rancid meat, not even fit for seagulls to pick at. Skyler figured they had tried to congregate around the towers as the group crossed the island, or followed in their wake, blind to the cliff's edge and the vast ocean the towers plowed into. The beings usually had a good sense for self-preservation—Skyler had even seen them swim on a few occasions—but these must have been so enthralled by the activated towers that they simply fell to the rocks below like lemmings, or perhaps the tide was in and they drowned. Hours or days later they washed up onshore by the dozens. In a weird way Skyler admired the efficiency with which the towers had killed the beings.

The address he'd spied turned out to be an office complex, full of dead terminals, decaying bodies, and more mold than he'd ever seen. The windows had been left open to the humid air for six years, and lizards scattered when he stepped inside. Nothing useful would be found there, and more to the point there was no power.

A day passed, then a week, without any more encounters with subhumans. No one spoke of it aloud, but Skyler could see the fear on all their faces of being stuck here. Or rather the acceptance of that possibility. The fear, he thought, might well be his alone. Pablo certainly wouldn't mind spending the rest of his life on a quiet island. Vanessa probably wouldn't, either. Ana, Skyler thought, would just take whatever cards were dealt her, and in her youth probably would think it would be a good life. He knew she was too restless to be happy somewhere like this, though.

Each morning Skyler woke two hours before sunrise and set out to search the surrounding neighborhood for a building with power. Three times he found lights, only to discover the source to be isolated, cap-powered installations. Security floods, a child's night-light, that sort of thing.

Pablo found a few solar panels on a nearby roof and managed to rig them up to charge *La Gaza Ladra*. A well-intentioned project he'd undertaken while everyone else had been out searching, and Skyler took care to praise the effort before letting the man know it would take roughly four years to get a full charge from the source. Still, he didn't disconnect them. If they found nothing else, at least they might get enough of a charge in a few months to be able to fly to one of the other islands in the Azores chain.

One day Vanessa returned from scouting with a slate computer in hand. "Still has a charge," she said as she handed it to Skyler.

"We can't siphon it into the Magpie," he said.

She rolled her eyes. "Don't be thick. Read it."

Intrigued, Skyler glanced at the screen. The island's daily newspaper was on the display. The article in the center of the page caught his eye. "Council upholds policy against thorium reactors," read the headline. His heart sank. He scanned the paragraphs below. Talk of mitigating risk to the island's fragile ecosystem. Sensational and unfounded rants against the possibility of nuclear meltdown.

"We're not going to find any power here, are we?" Vanessa asked.

He sighed, and against his better judgment tapped the option to continue reading. The reporter listed quotes from various islanders about their mistrust of nuclear energy. A holdover, he knew, from fears that began with the earliest forms of the technology, when reactors would fail every few decades, usually due to some act of nature. Once a particularly disgruntled French worker had sabotaged the planet deliberately, leaving an uninhabitable zone in Western Europe that made earlier accidents look like child's play.

"We're going to be here awhile," Vanessa said. "Aren't we?"

Frustration boiled within Skyler. Granted, that old tech was dangerous and irresponsible. But the backlash, if the history books had it right, was beyond ridiculous. A century and a half of willful ignorance toward the best energy source imaginable. The West shot itself in the foot, allowing China to pioneer pebble-bed technology first, then thorium. And finally miniature thorium reactors that could run unsupervised for a thousand years, and power a few modern skyscrapers. While Europe and America struggled to attach a solar panel to every roof and burned every last drop of oil, China and the developing world suddenly had no energy problem to speak of. Then came ultracapacitors, and the ability to store all that power.

By the time the Darwin Elevator touched down, Europe was still in catch-up mode. America was a distant memory. "North Mexico," Skyler's schoolteacher had jokingly called the former superpower. At least Australia hadn't been so closed-minded.

Even here in the Azores, just six short years ago, the local population still mistrusted the technology. *A good thing Belém hadn't been so stubborn,* he thought as he skimmed the rest of the article. *And they had the bloody Amazon to protect. All this place has is a few scraggly hills and a dormant volcano.*

The thought of the volcano brought an image to his mind of the island as viewed from satellite. Gears turned in his head, squeaky things in need of lubrication. He grinned. "Ana?"

She looked up from the dismantled weapon she'd been cleaning.

"Can you pull up the nav maps again?"

Ana frowned. "What are we looking for? We've studied the whole island."

"Not the island," Skyler said. "The ocean. We're looking for giant white propellers. Or . . ." He racked his mind to recall the methods used to harness such energies. "Long tubes floating in the surf. Wind and wave power collectors."

By noon he set out with Ana to the target location, all the way across the island on the western shore. A forty-kilometer hike, one way.

Wave-power generators had been easy to spot, once they knew to look. Long, dark disjointed lines a kilometer offshore. Tracing a simple, straight path to shore revealed the collection station that transmitted the energy out to the rest of the island.

At first they'd all planned to go, until Skyler changed his mind. "This plane is our ticket off this island. Leaving her alone makes me nervous."

They'd seen no other immunes, but the possibility remained that someone might be out there, watching them, waiting for a chance to escape.

"Let's just take the plane over there," Pablo suggested.

"Can't do it," Skyler said with a frown. "We've got enough juice to move her once, if we're lucky. I'd rather save that for when we're sure."

Skyler offered to stay, but the group collectively decided he was the best person to scout the site. This was no time to fool around, and since the handhelds only had a six- or seven-klick range, there'd be no consultation with the others.

Naturally, Ana came along.

She'd been unusually silent after seeing the base of that cliff through his binoculars. She'd seen dead bodies before, they all had, but something about the mass suicide chilled her. Chilled all of them. Maybe it was the manner of death, or the apparent way the towers seemed to power through the crowd with callous indifference. It was easy, Skyler thought, to imagine the subhumans as somehow on the Builders' side, their creations, after what had happened in the rainforest near the Belém Elevator. But this threw that notion back into the fog of confusion that surrounded everything related to the aliens.

Skyler fought to keep the image out of his mind, but like a catchy, horrible song, those corpses seemed to reappear every time he tried to forget them.

"Hey, look," Ana said. She'd stopped in the street. They weren't even at the edge of town yet, still a full day's hike ahead of them.

From the excitement in her voice, he expected to turn and see a light on somewhere. A power source. All he saw, though, was the dark windows of abandoned stores. Ana moved closer to one window, picked up a chunk of broken asphalt from the road, and threw it into the glass pane.

The sound of it shattering echoed along the narrow street.

"What are you—" Skyler started. Then, "Oh . . ."

She'd found a bicycle shop. Touristy things, many with signs hanging from their handlebars indicating daily rental prices. She crawled inside and, after a minute or so, came out the front door with a rugged mountain bike. She laid it against the outside wall and went back in. A moment later, she emerged with a second bike, larger than the first. A man's bike. Expensive looking with huge spring shocks and knobby black tires.

Skyler remained still, listening for any sounds of subhuman presence after the cacophony of breaking glass. He heard nothing, though. After a week he didn't really expect to. It was as if that one pathetic sub scratching at the door of the ship was the poor, lone survivor. When Skyler looked down the empty street he found it easy to imagine that he and his crew were the last souls on the planet.

Ana went inside a third time, and when she came out she carried a kit of some kind as well as a tire pump. She tore it open and produced a small white tube, discarding the rest. Kneeling by the bikes, she began to oil their chains.

They rode in silence. The bikes made the trip much easier, but Skyler insisted they keep a slow pace in case they needed to ditch the transportation in a hurry. Once out of the city, though, that fear diminished. They cruised along an oceanfront road, swerving around derelict cars and the occasional skeleton. Seagulls drifted overhead, calling to one another as they flew in lazy arcs. A perfect, post-apocalyptic day in paradise.

After an hour riding on the bumpy road, Ana called for a break. A small strip of sand on their right marked a break in the otherwise rocky shoreline, and it had caught her attention.

They left their bikes on the roadside and she led the way down steep, weed-choked steps to the beach. Without a word she stripped and trod carefully out into the surf, diving under the first wave that threatened to drench her. When she came up she wrung the water from her hair and motioned for Skyler to join her.

He was one of four people on the entire island, yet still he looked up and down the beach before pulling his clothes off.

They swam together in frigid water under a blazing sun, and made love in that soft place where dwindling waves just managed to kiss their toes and soft sand cradled them like pillows. Then they just lay there, holding hands, staring up at the endless blue sky until the sun and wind dried them.

From when they'd left the road to when they returned, Ana had said nothing. Back on the bikes, she rode a few meters ahead and shot him one quick, simple, wicked grin.

Skyler knew in that moment two things: He loved her. That, and she'd probably be the death of him.

When Skyler saw the red beacon light just above the tree line he almost fell off his bike.

The power station was a squat building tucked back into a thin forest on the inland side of the road, on the edge of a town called Mosteiros.

Ana thrust her arms into the air and shouted something in Spanish. Her bike swerved, forcing her to cut the celebration short and focus on remaining upright.

The coastline on this side of the island consisted of sheer cliffs that rose twenty meters from the turgid water below, only to then level off into a long, gentle grade up to the rim of the old volcano. The fertile land showed all the signs of human agriculture long reclaimed by the wild, with snakelike forests of cryptomeria trees winding their way down the slope. Copses of smaller mahogany dotted the fields of tall grass.

Skyler dismounted a safe distance from the nearly hidden building. Ana followed his example. He followed all the usual precautions of entering a structure that might be a heat source. Subhumans often dwelled within such places, like a cave with a built-in fire to warm their ragged bodies. He kicked in the door and went in with his rifle at the ready. Ana came in at his shoulder, a position and tactic now routine for her. The recklessness she'd exhibited in the past had faded, perhaps for good. More and more Skyler viewed her as a study in contrasts to

Samantha. Where Sam had swagger and strength, Ana displayed cunning and speed.

The windowless building proved devoid of life, save for a few field mice that scurried into the shadows in the presence of two humans. Skyler tried the light switch and laughed aloud when the LEDs mounted on the ceiling beams came to life.

"We did it!" Ana said, giving him a little pat on the behind.

"Let's be doubly sure."

In a basement room they found what they'd come for. A massive cable emerged from the floor of the vast room. There was even a ceremonial red rope around it, with signs in Portuguese that Skyler guessed said something about the wave-generation project's success, and how this cable stretched well out into the ocean. None of that mattered. The lights were on, and in the quiet of that room he could hear the strong hum of electric power flowing through the banks of equipment in the adjoining rooms. High-voltage signs warned against entering, advice he heeded happily.

Skyler inspected the room like some visiting dignitary. Ana mimicked his steps, her eyes boring into him, waiting.

"Let's go back and get the Magpie," he announced.

Three days later *La Gaza Ladra's* ultracapacitors hit full charge, and Skyler told the team to buckle in. On each of their faces he saw relief, but something else, too: wistfulness, like the final day of a grand if exhausting vacation. He felt it, too. A small part of him wished to stay, to spend the rest of his life riding a bike around the beautiful island with Ana alongside and grinning mischievously.

"Next stop," he said as the aircraft lifted off the ground, "Ireland."

39

CAPPAGH, IRELAND

25.JUL.2284

Skyler held at three hundred meters, vertical thrusters wailing to keep the aircraft aloft and stable. He swallowed, his mouth dry as cotton cloth. A light rain dappled the cockpit window, threatening to obscure the view ahead.

No one had spoken since the object came into view. Ana was frozen in her seat next to him. He could feel the presence of Pablo and Vanessa over his shoulder as they crowded the small cockpit to see forward.

Several kilometers in front of them, nestled between two picturesque rolling hills, was a perfect dome. The half sphere was purple in color, opaque, and had a milky pearlescent sheen that rippled and swam across its surface like some shifting reflection of the cloudy sky, banded in ephemeral rainbow hues. It looked like a giant blob of purple liquid held inside a soap bubble shell.

"Land here," Pablo said. The sound of his voice, even with the constant roar of the engines, made Skyler jump.

Ana cleared her throat. "Good idea."

Skyler sat motionless. An answer formed and died on his lips. He couldn't bring himself to look away from the massive purple globe. It had to be at least three hundred meters high, he thought, as the top of it seemed level with *La Gaza Ladra*'s nose. From this distance he couldn't decide if it was solid like steel, or as thin as glass.

"What . . . God, what is that thing?" Vanessa asked.

The scar left by the towers' passage across the landscape led straight into the center of the sphere. On instinct he raised the aircraft another hundred meters, revealing more of the dome's base. Soon the tips of black towers became visible. The objects were spaced evenly at the edge of the dome where it met the ground, their bases half-submerged inside the purple orb.

"No idea," Skyler said, his voice hoarse. He swallowed again and shook his head to clear the cobwebs. "Whatever it is, at least we've found the towers."

"One group, anyway," Ana said.

"What now?" Vanessa asked.

Skyler flexed his fingers on the throttle. "Tania and Karl would want us to turn back, report what we've found." He felt his three crew mates, his friends, staring at him. "I think I want to take a look around."

Ana sighed in relief, and he heard murmured agreement from Pablo and Vanessa.

The sound of engines under strain finally tugged him back to the business at hand. He dipped the nose and turned in a slow circle. The landscape below consisted of rolling golden fields of overgrown weeds, laced with dense forests of impossibly green trees. It reminded him of the Azores, except there was no coastline nearby. The hills seemed to stretch out forever. Here and there he saw signs of small towns and villages peeking above the hills and forests.

Nearby he spotted a wide field more flat than most, with a barn and small house on one corner and a dirt road that led off into the nearby trees. With no better option in sight, Skyler descended and set the aircraft down in tall grass that bent over in rippling circles as the plane neared the ground. He aimed the nose of the plane uphill, took a breath, and killed the engines. The screen before him indicated a capacitor level of 80 percent.

"It's almost dusk," he said to the others. Pablo and Vanessa had not bothered to return to the cabin for landing. "Let's clear that house and barn, and use it for shelter while we're here. Nothing against the Magpie, but I'm getting sick of sleeping in here."

They mumbled agreement, their disappointment clear. As bizarre and terrifying as the alien dome was, they wanted to explore it now.

"We'll hike out to that bubble first thing in the morning," he added. "If there's any of those armored bastards lurking out there, I'd rather face them after some solid sleep and a good meal."

"I could find us some fresh meat," Pablo offered.

"Good, do it. Stay nearby if you don't mind, until we've got a sense of this place. Vanessa? I'd like you to prep our gear for the morning, and make sure the Magpie is locked up tight. Ireland's a big place compared to San Miguel, and I don't want anyone or anything sneaking in here while we're asleep."

"I'll just stay in here," she offered. "I don't mind. Those chairs are as comfortable as any bed when reclined."

"Okay," Skyler said. "Ana, let's check out that cottage."

With dawn came a brief summer shower, before brilliant sunlight banished the clouds.

Skyler woke, stretched, and stood. He and Ana had slept on the floor of the small home's common room. A quaint space with wooden wainscoting and antique furniture.

A pair of corpses lay in an infinite embrace in the one bedroom. Two skeletons under a blanket, their arms about each other and their foreheads touching. Ana had wept at the sight and broke into quiet sobs a few more times throughout the evening. He'd tried to hold her in the darkness that night, but she'd turned away, said it didn't seem right. Skyler had not argued, but after her breathing became deep and even, he reached out and held her hand. The elderly couple in that room affected him only a little. He'd come across similar situations hundreds of times. Well after midnight he realized the scene might have reminded her of the first time they'd seen each other. The courtyard in Belém, where she'd danced with total abandon for the world around her, in front of an audience of two skeletons locked in an embrace, with Skyler hiding in the shadows.

She'd tried to shoot him for that. In the dark Skyler took his earlobe between two fingers and rubbed it where the bullet's wake had tickled the skin. A few more centimeters over and everything would be different now.

When Skyler stepped outside he saw the flicker of firelight coming from the barn. Pablo waved at him when he entered and handed him a plate of roast hen and some potatoes grilled with a heavy dust of garlic powder. Before Skyler could say thanks, a mug of coffee was shoved into his hand and he raised it in cheers. Pablo nodded and returned to the portable stove.

Vanessa emerged from *La Gaza Ladra* a little later, and without being asked she went into the house and woke Ana. Skyler had been caught between his desire to let the girl sleep and his burning interest in the alien dome. Waking Ana was not something he ever looked forward to doing, and when the two women entered the barn he gave Vanessa a quick wink.

As if some pact had been made, no one spoke all morning. Fed and caffeinated, Skyler stood first and went to the aircraft. The others trailed in behind him and began to strap on their gear. Skyler opted for a light, comfortable load: his compact rifle with grenade launcher, a Sonton pistol, and a light backpack stocked with a medical kit and one day's water and food.

The others took their cues from him and equipped similarly.

Ana powered up the cockpit and tried the comm before departing. It had become one of her daily tasks to try to raise the colony as Karl had requested. As of yet, they'd heard nothing, and assumed their transmissions fell on deaf ears in turn. Still, she rattled off a message giving the location of their landing, the presence of the purple bubble, and the fact that the crew was setting off to investigate it now.

"If we run into any of those armored subs," Skyler said as the team set out, "we retreat. Understood? We come back here and bring the big guns with us next time. Today is just a scouting mission, nothing more."

No one debated him. They were all staring at the purple hemisphere on the horizon.

* * *

Up close, the presence of the object made Skyler's breath catch in his throat.

It defied description. He'd look at part of it and imagined it as a diamond-hard mass, as if some alien moon had suddenly winked into existence on this field in Ireland. Then he'd glance at another portion and imagine that he could reach out and pop the thing with his fingernail.

The four immunes stood side by side on the path carved by the purple-lit aura towers, perhaps a hundred meters from the dome.

"What now?" Vanessa asked.

"Let's just," Skyler said, "watch, for a bit."

Pablo took a long draw from his canteen. The pleasant warmth of the day had worn out its welcome after an hour of marching in combat gear. Skyler took a swig of his own and poured a little on his head.

"That thing," Ana said, with a nod toward the dome, as if anyone might doubt what she was looking at, "it's so simple. Beautiful. It terrifies me. I think I'd rather face that fog in Belém, and the dark ones."

Vanessa nodded agreement.

No one spoke for a time. Skyler began to notice flecks of slightly darker areas in the dome's coloration. He leaned to one side and then the other, and decided it wasn't an illusion. The small dark patches were inside the dome, not on its surface.

"Someone else has been here," Pablo said suddenly, in his deadpan way.

Everyone looked at him. Pablo crouched down, focused on the ground in front of him. He pointed. "Campfire."

Skyler crouched next to it and studied the charred wood. The blackened remnants were waterlogged, and crumbled into an ash mulch in his fingers. "It's old," he said. "But not that old. Months old, a year maybe. An immune, then." He felt a tingle along his arms, and felt the queer sensation of being watched.

"Okay," Skyler said. "Let's walk around the perimeter. Maybe there's a . . . door or something."

A bird called overhead. Skyler looked up in time to see the small black creature fly overhead, straight into the side of the dome. He winced, expecting it to crumple and fall down the curved side as if it had hit a plate-glass window. Instead the purple surface dented inward like a balloon. The pearlescent sheen formed a rainbow swirl around the indent.

The indent warped and, with a sudden pop, returned to its original shape. Skyler caught a faint ripple of rainbow light along the surface of the dome, fading as it radiated outward.

The bird vanished inside.

The whole thing had lasted a fraction of a second. Skyler glanced at his companions, only to find them all still focused on the campfire. "Did you see that?" he asked them.

Ana looked up first, a puzzled expression on her face.

"A bird," Skyler said. He chuckled. "It was a magpie, I think. It just flew in. It pushed through and went inside."

"Magpie?" Ana asked. "A good omen."

Skyler walked closer, until he stood five meters from the dome. The others hadn't moved. "Not too close, Sky!" Ana called out.

He leaned, picked up a rock, and tossed it underhand at the milky purple wall in front of him.

The rock clapped against the side as if it had hit solid marble, and fell to the ground with a soft thud.

"What the hell?" Skyler walked closer and reached out his hand.

"Be careful . . . ," Ana said from behind him.

When his fingertips brushed the surface, Skyler felt a tingle of cold rush up his arm, followed instantly by the sensation of heat. The pattern repeated like some resonating frequency, and when taken as a whole felt pleasant. He watched in fascination as the dome's surface bent inward. A growing ring of rainbow refraction stretched outward along the purple face. He tried to pause his hand but couldn't. The current of cold and warm pulses filled his entire body, and his mind seemed to turn to mush. Thoughts mixed, until one was indiscernible from the other. The ring of rainbow light continued to grow as if his finger had touched a star and sent it into a supernova explosion.

I should stop. I should stop. I should stop.

He must have been repeating that thought because it seemed to crop up among all the thousand others that swam through his mind, as milky as the surface of the dome. His brain told him the dome was enveloping him. That he'd already entered the place. That he was still outside. All seemed valid and without contradiction.

Some thoughts began to stretch on and on, played back in some ultra-slow motion. Shapes before his eyes began to hover in place. He tried to look down at his feet and found his head would only move a millimeter at a time.

The slow thoughts began to multiply. They pushed against his mind as if fighting a war against the parts of his mind that wanted to work correctly. The slow thoughts became the norm, the tables turned. Suddenly he found there were corners of his mind working in overdrive, unleashing a dizzying avalanche of ideas, memories, and desires. They raced and raced until they blurred into infinity.

Then all at once everything rushed back into normalcy.

He was inside, and felt as if someone had been spinning him in circles for a week straight, and then rolled him through a pasta press. A wave of nausea drove him to his knees. Cold sweat erupted from every pore on his body. All Skyler could do was stare at the purple-tinged dirt and shiver while the reaction passed.

A minute later he rose to his feet, stumbled, and righted himself. He found it hard to breathe. The air smelled of ozone and felt humid and still around him, like Darwin on the worst of days. He turned and glanced back the way he'd come. Or, the way he thought he'd come. Everything behind him looked the same. A dark, purple wall that ended a few meters away from him, evenly colored. No milky rainbow sheen. No bands of light and dark shades. He could see where it met the soil a few meters away, and yet when he looked straight ahead the purple barrier seemed as far away as the horizon. There was no hint of the outside, no way to see his friends, to see Ana. He waved anyway, in case they could detect some hint of him within the dome.

Skyler looked up. A sensation of vertigo crossed over him as he followed the soaring dome to its zenith. Taking in the entire "sky," he saw that it seemed to pulse. A slow shift from light to dark and back, less than ten seconds for each perfectly rhythmic cycle.

Above him a magpie darted and wheeled. It chittered, as if saying, "We both made it through!" The harsh sound echoed queerly off the interior of the otherwise silent space.

Finally, Skyler looked toward the center of the dome.

He'd expected to find another shell ship on the ground, but if such a thing existed here he couldn't see it. The ground within the dome had been altered. From the edge toward the center, the earth curled upward. Imperceptibly where Skyler stood, the curved floor grew ever steeper until forming a circular pillar in the very center. The pinnacle rose a full hundred meters or more from the floor where Skyler stood, so tall it even began to curve back outward before an abrupt end at a flat surface.

A giant pedestal, he mused, exactly half the height of the dome. The top appeared to be a disk just a few meters in diameter. If something sat atop it, he couldn't see. Certainly the spot was too small to hold a shell ship, but he felt sure something must be there.

The earth that formed the curved floor was uneven and fractured. Large jagged mounds of varying size made a straight path to the center impossible. The mounds were complemented by cavities where chunks of the earth seemed to have just vanished, leaving steep-sided miniature craters of a depth he couldn't discern from his position. He thought they were ponds at first, filled in with rainwater perhaps, but when he looked closer he realized that the surface did not ripple. No, what filled these craters was just like that of the dome itself, as viewed from outside: that same milky, almost oily sheen, although their colors varied from red all the way to a brilliant topaz blue within one small hole near him.

"Bizarre," he whispered aloud. The magpie chirped as if in agreement.

With an effort Skyler shifted his focus away from the multi-hued "ponds" and tried to take in the entire scene again, hoping to spot an easy path to the center. Laced through all the mounds and depressions were cracks of indeterminate depth, akin to earthquake damage. As if in defiance of this tortured landscape, clumps of grass still held on here and there. Wildflowers dotted the mounds and poked up from the crater edges. None, Skyler noted, broke through from below the domelike surfaces within the craters. A squirrel darted across the ground nearby, from one patch of scrub grass to another before disappearing again.

All the while the dome gently pulsed. Light to dark to light, every ten seconds. The pattern lulled him. He shook his head and walked forward.

A strange sound rippled through the domed space. It sounded like an earthquake, except lighter, and came from everywhere at once. The ground did not shake, and as quickly as the crackling sound emerged it receded. Skyler waited until it disappeared completely before he moved on.

The first canyon proved only a meter deep and half that across. He stepped over it and continued. Every few steps he glanced up at that disk at the top of the earthen pillar. Fogged as his mind was, he had no doubt that he must reach that pinnacle and see what the Builders had placed there. The shape could not be an accident.

Part of him wondered why the others had not followed him inside. Another part felt grateful they had not. Crossing through the dome's surface had been the strangest, least pleasant experience in his life. Even worse, he thought, than his fall into that glowing iris so deep below Nightcliff. That had felt like his mind had been laid bare, every neuron exposed. This felt like his memories had been thrown into a blender and run at maximum speed for an hour. His head felt like scrambled eggs.

Another canyon appeared before him. He couldn't remember walking to it, but he felt sure it hadn't just formed in front of him. Indeed, when he took in his surroundings he realized he had indeed moved farther toward the center. As if sensing his confusion, the memory of walking forward emerged.

Again he heard a rattling sound from above, across the entire domed surface. It lasted a few seconds this time and then abruptly ended.

There were other noises, too, he realized. Noises coming from outside. Muffled, scratchy sounds all high-pitched and brief as a drumbeat, at once familiar and alien.

"I need a stiff drink," he said aloud. "No. Coffee."

He had neither on hand, but he did have water. Skyler sat in the dirt and opened his backpack. Normally he carried a canteen at his hip, but today he'd thrown everything in the pack so that he'd be able to shrug it off at a moment's notice. He'd wanted to be able to run away.

Still the sky pulsed, as if a child stood at a sliding dimmer switch, dragging it up and down in even intervals, fascinated by the effect. It was starting to annoy the hell out of him. Sensing a headache coming on, Skyler popped two pills between swigs of cool water.

His aviator's watch showed the wrong time, the wrong date. Every few seconds the numbers would jump ahead by almost an hour, as if the self-correction mechanism couldn't get a fix on one of the satellite time beacons. Crossing through that barrier scrambled the electronics, he decided, and he made a mental note to scavenge a new one. At least the compass on it still worked.

He sat for a few minutes and tried to focus. The pillar loomed ahead of him, insurmountable now that he thought about it. He had no rope, no climbing gear. Skyler was in excellent shape, but he knew his limits. There was no way he could reach that pedestal without some equipment. He wondered if Vanessa had thought to pack any; it had been her job to provision the plane beyond basic necessities.

Reason finally won out over the desire to explore. He stood and pulled his backpack on, then walked back the way he'd come. At the edge of the dome, he paused and took a few long, measured breaths.

Exiting proved much easier. This time he lowered his shoulder and raced through the dome's wall. He felt all the same sensations, only many orders of magnitude faster. He came out the other side confused, shivering. He slipped on muddy ground. Rain pelted him.

This storm must have come out of nowhere, he had time to think before his body hit the soggy ground in a dull splash. Cold shakes began to rattle him. Skyler came to his knees, waited for the maelstrom in his mind to evaporate, and looked for his friends.

They were gone. The sun, so bright and clear when he'd entered, now hid behind a dark gray ceiling of nasty-looking clouds. *What in the hell?*

Off to the side he saw a tent that hadn't been there before. An LED lantern hung from a hook under the awning, casting light around the entrance and half a meter inside. He could see someone sitting within, reading a slate.

Baffled, Skyler began to stumble in the direction of the tent. The person inside looked up. It was Ana, though she looked different. Different clothes, Skyler realized. Hair pulled back in a ponytail. Her face was ashen, as if she'd become sick.

All the color left in that face drained when she saw him. She raced from the tent and threw her arms around him, sobbing.

"Jesus," he said. "Nice to see you, too. Where'd the others go?"

Ana just sobbed. She held him so tightly he thought his arms might fall asleep.

"Okay, okay," he said. "Relax, I'm fine."

For a long time she said nothing. She just held him and wept. At first he found it strangely warming to be missed so, but as the seconds dragged on and she didn't let up, he began to find her reaction almost comical given that they'd only been apart for ten minutes. The grief was genuine, of that he felt sure, but wholly inappropriate.

"We thought you were dead," she said at last.

Skyler almost laughed. The sincerity in her voice stopped him and he returned her hug.

The girl finally pulled back and held him at arm's length, her eyes searching his. "What the . . . Where the hell have you been?"

"Inside, of course. Where'd this storm come from? Sun to downpour in ten minutes flat. That's impressive even by Darwin standards."

"Ten?"

"Good thing you brought a tent. Are the others inside? We need to—"

"Ten minutes?"

When he nodded, her lips pressed together in a tight line.

"Skyler," she said, "you've been gone for over a month."

40

DARWIN, AUSTRALIA

2.SEP.2284

Samantha awoke to a pounding at the door to her room.

"I'm up," she said, her voice the sound of dry brush burning. She fumbled for her canteen and knocked it to the floor. "Shit."

Her watch put the time at one in the morning. The pounding on her door went on, and for a few seconds she wasn't sure if it was real or just the result of a long evening at Woon's.

She rolled onto her side and plucked the steel canteen from the pool of water it had created on the floor. A swallow later she found her voice again. "Go to hell!"

"Grillo is on the comm, Samantha. It's urgent."

One of the Nightcliff goons, she couldn't guess which from the voice. She sat up and swung her feet onto the cold floor. A blistering ache formed somewhere just behind her eyes, and she rubbed her temples with two fingers, to no avail. "What does he want?"

"No idea," the man said. "Not my place to ask."

"Christ," she whispered, not loud enough that he might hear it. These Jacobites were a touchy bunch. She pulled on some socks. "Be there in a sec."

The comm terminal sat on a table in the center of the hangar, where the *Melville* used to rest. Without the presence of the aircraft, the space seemed excessively large, dwarfing the "office" she'd set up in the middle of the floor. A huge board made of cork had been placed next to the main desk, and she'd tacked a map of the local region to it. Colored thumbtacks marked the places scavenged or to be scavenged, a trick she'd learned from Prumble. She'd never seen his map in person, but Skyler had described it, and it beat trying to operate the map screen Skyler had always used to plan their outings.

Grillo watched her approach from his end of the connection. Sam dropped herself heavily on the folding chair in front of the screen and swept her hair back from her face.

"I'm here," she said.

He wasn't in the control room at Nightcliff, or his mansion in Lyons. Behind him, she saw only a concrete wall, with a rusted pipe jutting out of the ceiling and running horizontally behind the man. Grillo looked impeccable, of course. Not a hair out of place. His expression, so often unreadable, right now had a hint of concern. "Rouse as many pilots as you can," he said, "and bring them and their aircraft to the stadium. No other crew aboard."

"What's going on?" Sam asked.

"There's no time, Samantha. Be here in an hour."

"I . . . okay."

"Fly dark, fly low." He cut the link and his image vanished.

Forty minutes later, Sam stood on the tarmac watching her birds take flight.

Nine pilots were available, but only seven planes had their caps charged enough to be useful. Given the short notice, she thought the number impressive, but Grillo had given no hint as to how many he actually needed. It wasn't like him to be vague, or hurried. Something was wrong.

The engines of the sixth craft roared and the shoddy hauler began to climb. That left only the *Ocean Cloud*.

"Sammy!"

She turned at the voice, and saw Skadz standing atop the hangar. He stayed up there sometimes, in a military tent, tending the garden as payment for the rooftop to sleep on. Right now, he gestured urgently toward East Point. She glanced in that direction and saw nothing over the rooftops of the other hangars that lined the old runway. The clouds above, though, were laced with traces of orange and yellow glow.

"What is it?" she shouted back.

"Fire!"

She nodded to him, positive the flames were related to Grillo's urgent call. *Fly dark, fly low.* A knot formed in her gut as she climbed into the idling plane. She thought of that strange alien growth in Old Downtown, the flayed remains of the Jacobite called Faisal, and the strange glowing cube she'd pulled from the crashed ship. She swallowed hard. All of these things she'd deliberately forgotten until now. If something new was happening there, if the thing had suddenly regrown . . .

Pascal looked at her from the cockpit and she made a twirling motion with her hand. *Spin up.*

Gear stowed, Sam moved to the cockpit door and decided to stand there so she could see over the pilot's helmet. The aircraft once ferried wealthy Chinese tourists over the tumultuous waters between the two continents and had cargo capacity enough for two automobiles. "Did the run nonstop when the Elevator came," Pascal had told her the first time she'd rode in the ship. "Twelve years straight, no vacations to speak of, either. Even made two trips when SUBS hit, before it got too crazy up there."

He was a good man, a simple man. Took his orders with no complaints and spent his evenings playing mahjongg with the other veterans outside Kantro's old hangar.

"Running lights off," Sam said as they cleared the airport. "Keep as low as you're comfortable with."

"If you say so," he said.

The fires were behind them, and Sam didn't want to delay for a peek. There'd be time enough for that later.

Darwin passed below in silence. The dark slums of the Maze stretched out to Aura's Edge, and a bit beyond into the no-man's-land that ringed the city. Pascal followed a curved path that kept them just inside the aura, until the stadium came into view. The other aircraft stretched out ahead of them like birds of prey sneaking up on a target. One by one they flipped on their landing lights and descended into the bowl of the arena.

Ocean Cloud cleared the lip last, and Sam sucked in her breath at the sight on the field below. The other aircraft were spread out, and surrounded by Jacobites. The faithful were arrayed like regiments of soldiers, and already she could see them boarding the other aircraft.

A space cleared at one end, and Pascal headed toward it without being told. There was nowhere else to put down. Sam glanced west before the aircraft dropped below the top edge of the stadium's ring. Between here and the coast lay thousands of dark buildings, dappled by the occasional pool of LED or candlelight. She couldn't see the fires Skadz spoke of, but their glow on the cloud layer remained.

Brighter now, she thought.

Thirty Jacobite loyalists piled into *Ocean*'s cargo bay. Men and women alike, lightly armed and stony-faced. Many, she saw, carried coils of rope across their chests like bandoliers.

Grillo came last. He wore a business suit as usual, but to Samantha's surprise it was white, not pin-striped gray. Even the shirt and tie were brilliant white, as if never worn before.

"No time to waste," he said to her. "Have your pilot take the lead. Follow the aura around south to the Gardens."

"What's the mission?"

"I'll explain in the air."

She returned to her spot in the cockpit's doorway and relayed the orders to Pascal. He reacted with calm efficiency, and soon they were over the slums again, heading back the way they came. He acknowledged responses from the other planes as they fell in line behind.

In the back, Grillo moved among the seated warriors. Somehow he managed to keep an air of composure despite the tilting, abrupt movements of the aircraft. His hand would dart to a nylon loop on the wall, or to someone's shoulder, for support, but beyond that he acted as if they weren't moving at all. As she watched, he went to each fighter, men and women alike. He would press his fingers against the center of their foreheads and whisper something. They'd respond with a silent word, and then he would move to the next.

He's gone mental, she thought. The tattered shreds of her theory that it was all an act, for the benefit of their alliance, completely dissolved. They were a cult and he was a personality; a match made in heaven.

Sam almost laughed aloud at the wordplay. If anyone saw her brief smile, she didn't notice it over their general contempt for an outsider.

His rounds finished, Grillo finally came to stand in front of her. He grasped a handhold on the wall without even looking for it, as if he'd flown aboard *Ocean Cloud* a hundred times. With his free hand, he reached inside his coat and pulled a slip of paper from the breast pocket. "Give this to your pilot."

The brittle paper had a drawing on it. Sam couldn't resist, and looked it over. Grillo, or someone under him, had scratched out in pencil a map of a Darwin neighborhood, just north of the Gardens and west of the Narrows. A number of buildings were marked with letters, ranging from A to J.

"Tell him to pick one of the lettered buildings," Grillo added. "And assign other buildings to the remaining aircraft."

"I can hear you," Pascal said from the cockpit. "The paper, Sam?"

She handed it forward and turned back to Grillo. "What's going on?"

"We've reached the tipping point. The last holdouts have banded together, attacked our patrols. They don't want to join in the effort to make Darwin a prosperous, peaceful place."

Maybe they've seen your true freak show nature like I have.

He'd raised his voice, and though he still looked at her she knew he spoke to the Jacobite soldiers behind him.

"For the ladder's sake," he went on, "by dawn this city will be united in singular purpose. Darwin could have been humanity's deathbed, but now . . . *now,* through our work, it will be the seed from which a new world will one day grow."

Bat. Shit. Insane. It was all Sam could think as she looked into the man's glistening eyes. This was no act. Whatever doubts she had, they melted away as she stared into that fervent gaze.

Grillo tilted his head slightly, as if sensing her thoughts. "Once we've solved our basic problems, Samantha, we can turn our attentions to things like the disease, and resistance to it. God willing, people like you may hold the key to our ultimate success, and we're glad to have you with us."

A chill rippled down Sam's spine. The aircraft banked sharply, the motion providing a convenient moment for her to gather her senses as Grillo steadied himself. When the craft leveled again, Samantha managed to meet his eyes. "Great," she said with a half smile. "Um. Go, team."

"That's the spirit," he said. "Let's get ready, everyone. The landing zone might be a bit . . . hot."

Pascal's chosen target building loomed ahead. Twenty stories of concrete grid, with some portions still covered by decorative tile made to look like sandstone. Most of that superfluous surface had been hacked away long ago, along with the windows. A random patchwork filled the spaces where windows once existed. Plastic sheets, tarps of every color, quilts, and even a few ornate Afghan carpets. At least half the window frames had extensions bolted on the outside, extending the living space out on jury-rigged balconies made from every imaginable material. Samantha saw tents on some, but most were covered with buckets to collect rainwater, or potted plants.

The roof was hidden under a dense garden.

A typical Darwin tombstone, in other words. A vertical enclave, with the powerful living at the top.

Only two or three window holes were lit. The flicker of candlelight, or the soft blue-white glow of an LED lantern.

Ocean Cloud approached her target from the south. The fires Skadz had so anxiously pointed out earlier were all north of them, a few blocks away at least. The buildings in this area were so quiet Sam wondered if they'd been abandoned in the face of the attack.

More likely, she thought, their targets represented the enemy's fallback position. A sandwich attack. She leaned forward, squeezing her head into the space between Pascal's seat and the curved glass of the canopy. To the right of their craft, she saw the dark shapes of four other scavenger vehicles as they closed in on other target buildings. Pascal spoke quiet commands into his headset, too soft for her to hear, but the synchronicity of the other planes told the story. If they'd planned the operation for days she doubted they could have achieved any more coordination.

Sam leaned back and turned toward the crowded rear compartment. "Thirty seconds," she said. "What's the plan? Torch and run?"

"Their fighters will be to the north," Grillo said. "Where our ground assault started. Our aim here is to take and hold these buildings, then move on to others as we can. You will take off immediately and return to the stadium for another run, until our faithful have been delivered to all the buildings on the map."

"Copy that," she said, feeling suddenly a thousand kilometers away. *This is war,* she thought. *And by morning, Grillo will own all of Darwin.*

All of it that mattered anyway.

They had made three more trips by the time the sun crested the eastern horizon in a thin red line.

The third trip proved unnecessary, though. Other than a few sporadic gunfights, the war appeared to be over, and for once in her life Samantha did not mind being left out of the action. The dead and wounded loaded into *Ocean Cloud*'s bay for the return flight were proof enough that the operation had been a sloppy, fierce affair. Cries of anguish and muffled grunts of raw pain filled the otherwise quiet cabin as Pascal guided the craft back to Grillo's stadium.

Back in the safety of that concrete bowl, the mood was quite different. Sam sat with Pascal in the open cabin door, their legs hanging over the side. Pascal had brought a zippered bag full of small overripe apples and shared one with her. He ate in silence, which suited Sam just fine.

Across the field Jacobite soldiers celebrated in groups of

ten or twenty. Even in the old stands, where shacks and small tents covered every flat space, the fighters mingled with others, laughing and talking in animated fashion. Battle stories, she knew. The favorite pastime of the newly bloodied.

At least as many groups were huddled in prayer. They knelt in circles, as few as four in number. One such group consisted of at least fifty men and women, and Sam recognized a certain air about them. The hard looks on their faces, the crowd of supporters around them. These were the leaders, she thought, or perhaps the elite fighters. Grillo stood in the center of their ring, speaking quietly with his hands outstretched in piety.

Eventually Grillo made his way back to the aircraft. Pascal saw him coming. "I'll be in the cockpit," he said as he rose from their perch. "Let me know if we're clear to leave."

"Okay," Sam said.

Grillo strode up, a hair slower than he usually walked. He wiped his face with a clean white handkerchief, folded it, and returned it to his breast pocket before speaking. "Thank you for your help tonight," he said.

Sam shrugged. "I hardly did anything."

"You've held up your end of the bargain, Samantha. I may have been too harsh with you before, and I'm sorry if Sister Jo no longer wishes to join you at the airport."

"She can make her own decisions," Sam said. She hoped Kelly wanted her to stay away. *Listen to the ghost.*

"Quite." He clasped his hands behind his back. "Her choice could have eroded your loyalty, however, and I just wanted you to know that I'm grateful you've remained on our little team."

"Not so little anymore," Sam said, casting a glance around the busy arena. Anything to get the focus off herself.

A flash of pride crossed his face. "I'm going to make a small speech soon, and lead a prayer. Would you stay? Stand at my side?"

"At your side? Are you fucking kidding me—I'm sorry. It's late, I . . . at your side? Surely there are others who deserve that kind of honor."

"None more than you. And, truth be told, it might help your . . . status."

"No offense, Grillo, but prayer really isn't my thing. Besides,

I'm exhausted, and our planes need to be recharged and, um . . . cleaned."

He sighed, his mouth curling in an almost imperceptible frown. "Suit yourself," he said.

"Um. What's wrong with my status, anyway? You mean because I'm a—"

"Immune?"

"I was going to say heathen."

"Ah." Grillo took a step to one side and gestured toward the space elevator. The thread was invisible in the hazy morning, but a few climber cars marked it. "We don't care much if one believes in the ladder or not; the proof is right there. It's just a matter of seeing it . . . differently."

Sam pretended to study the length of the alien cable for a moment. "Why'd you think I was going to say 'immune'?" she asked.

He shifted. A brief expression of discomfort passed across his face. She'd seen it once before, and enjoyed it just as much this time. "We don't know what to make of your unique attribute. Some, like me, think you may be the key to our salvation. Others, many, think the opposite."

"Is that why you keep me so close?"

"Partly. You are useful, obviously." He regarded the hull of *Ocean Cloud*. "And if I coddled you, or kept you from harm's way, I would incur not only your wrath but that of the faction skeptical of your nature. If I let you go, or ignored you, I'd go against my own instincts, and the faction that looks at you with awe."

In an instant she went from feeling like a prisoner to feeling like some cherished possession. A tiny voice in Samantha's head, one she usually scoffed at, told her to tread with care. Grillo was all but admitting that she had a lot more power, a lot more leverage, than she'd previously known. "I'm not the only immune," she said.

"I'm afraid all of your old crew are gone now, Samantha. There may be others like you, people who live happily in Darwin without any knowledge of the trait. Unfortunately there's no known test."

He doesn't know about Skadz, then. She hadn't thought to keep his immunity secret before. Certainly everyone at the airport knew he'd returned. That no one had mentioned his condition in the presence of Grillo's overseers was sheer luck, though, and she resolved to put the word out that the topic should be avoided.

"You might be thinking right now," Grillo went on, "that some pendulum of favor has swung to your side. It's true. You've proven yourself to me, Samantha. Despite confiding with Sister Josephine against my explicit instructions, you've continued to follow my orders without hesitation."

Sam spoke before her fear of him could stop the words. "They have a word for what you did; it's called entrapment. Anyway, I keep hoping *Kelly* will change her mind."

"She may. Who can say? In the meantime, consider yourself a part of this . . . this . . ." He couldn't seem to find the right word for the scene around them. He waved a hand at it. Hundreds of Jacobites, many still in combat gear, many more moving about. And beyond, Darwin's skyline.

Grillo's skyline, she corrected herself.

Then she glanced up, following the invisible thread of the Elevator marked by three climber cars below the cloud layer, all the way to the zenith. Somewhere up there were a series of space stations, and Russell Blackfield with all his grunt mercenaries. She wondered what he thought of the transformation Darwin had experienced since he'd left, or if he was even aware.

She didn't think he'd be too happy about it.

41

CAPPAGH, IRELAND

6.SEP.2284

They waited out the storm in Ana's vigil tent.

She'd thought he'd died, and only stubbornness and love kept her camped out at the edge of the dome, waiting. She'd tried to follow him in, of course. They all had. But once Skyler had stepped through, she'd explained, the field became hard as marble. An hour passed, then a day. Weeks. Every day Ana would come sit in front of the dome and try to push her way into it as he had. She'd tried to dig under it. She'd kicked it, punched it, even fired a grenade at it. Nothing helped. At one point she'd seen a bird fly up to the thing and smack against it. The poor creature had fallen to the ground in a lifeless heap, and Ana had cried then. The death of the bird had nearly snuffed out the candle of hope she'd nurtured.

He held her while she wept, a process she needed to work through on her own. He knew that from experience. While she sobbed quietly and buried herself in his arms, his mind grappled with the implications of what had happened.

From his perspective, he'd walked inside that dome, spent ten minutes fumbling about, and then exited. Outside, six weeks had passed. How that could be seemed hardly worth pondering, in Skyler's opinion. The Builders were clearly more technologically advanced than aura towers, interstellar flight, and space elevators. They could mess with time, or at least how the mind experienced it. *The body, too,* he corrected himself. He hadn't walked out of there thirsty or hungry, so the effect couldn't have been just mental.

The part that unnerved him was that it had happened at all. That such a thing was possible. Six weeks gone in ten minutes. That meant a journey taken back in to see what sat atop that pinnacle, even if they worked fast, would last months on the outside. Any delays and he'd come out well past the predicted date of the next Builder event. Whatever that event would entail, Skyler felt damn sure it would be in his best interests to be outside and well clear of the alien bubble at the time.

"Have you heard anything from home?" he asked her after her sobs faded.

She shifted slightly against him. Her hands gripped his shirt just below the collar. "No," she said, her voice muffled by her proximity to his chest. "Well, yes."

"Which?"

"Yes, we heard from them. Two clowns named Greg and Marcus. They started out making polite requests for you to contact them; now they just joke around."

Skyler leaned away and looked at her with skepticism.

"They're so annoying," Ana said, shaking her head. Then she made a face and spoke with a drawl out of some golden age sci-fi film. "'Greetings people of Earth, we have come for your chocolate and your buxom women. We will negotiate only with Skyler Luiken's penis.' Stuff like that. I want to strangle them every time."

Skyler couldn't help but chuckle.

"Don't you start," Ana said with sincere force. "I'll put you on the list, too, dammit. I had to listen to a month of that *mierda* thinking you might be gone forever."

He reasserted his grip around her until the flash of temper melted away. "Sorry," he said. "What did you tell them?"

"Nothing," Ana replied. "Vanessa, Pablo, and I made a pact.

If you were truly gone, we'd just live here and the colony could think we'd all vanished. We left it on for a while, in case anything interesting happened. After a while I stopped paying attention. I think Pablo still checks it now and then."

Six weeks gone. Karl and Tania had probably assumed the worst by now, he thought, but he couldn't begrudge the pact his crew had made.

The storm abated a few hours later, and Skyler helped Ana pack her gear before they set off for the farmhouse. She held his hand as they walked.

Pablo's reaction to Skyler's return was to prepare a dinner worthy of the event.

Wild hare roasted on a spit, with potatoes and carrots found in the nearby fields. Preservall bread dough scavenged in the depths of a looted grocery store a few kilometers away was flash-cooked in *La Gaza Ladra*'s tiny oven. The baguette that resulted tasted pretty good to Skyler. He soaked up the grease from his plate with a hunk of it while he recounted what had happened inside the dome.

"What did it feel like?" Vanessa asked when he'd finished. "Going through, I mean." She'd traded her combat fatigues for a blue dress she'd likely found inside the farmhouse. The change in attire seemed to pull all the hardness from her face, her posture. For the first time since he'd met her, Skyler didn't have to imagine how she'd looked before the world collapsed, before she'd been taken by Gabriel's twisted cult.

"It felt like . . ." Skyler paused. He couldn't find the right words. "It's not fun, I can tell you that. In hindsight, I guess there was a point when part of my brain was inside and part outside, running at different speeds. Everything got out of synch, scrambled."

Pablo dabbed the corners of his mouth with a cloth napkin. A surprising show of table etiquette from the rustic man. "What is this dome, really?"

"I've no idea," Skyler said. "All I can tell you is, for whatever reason, time runs more slowly in there. There's got to be something on top of that pinnacle, and my gut tells me we need to find out what it is before March arrives. That means I need to go back in there right away. Tomorrow, with climbing gear. I'm afraid you'll have to stay here awhile longer. Through winter maybe."

"What?" Ana's question silenced the room. "Tomorrow?"

He tried to take her hand and she snatched it back. "Ana, listen. There's no time to waste—"

"I just got you back, and now you think you're going to leave me alone again? For *months*?"

"There's no other way." He could hear the impotency in his words and tried feebly to say the rest with his eyes.

Ana glared at him. Defiant at first, then simply cold. "There is another way," Ana said. "I'm coming with you."

Vanessa nodded agreement. "Me, too."

Skyler raised his hands in protest. "Look, I appreciate the enthusiasm, but you're forgetting that the dome prevented anyone else from entering last time. Only one of us can go."

"We can try," Ana said emphatically. "There's no harm in it."

Pablo leaned his chair back on two legs and shook his head. "Skyler's right," he said. "But either way, I'm staying. Someone should. Guard the Magpie, keep in contact with the colony."

"It could be months," Skyler said.

The man shrugged. "Farm life suits me, not giant alien domes. . . ."

"Vanessa and I are coming with you, Skyler," Ana said. She hadn't stopped looking at him while Pablo spoke. "We can all try going in at the same time, and see what happens."

Skyler started to protest, but the women's combined gaze felt like having laser beams focused on his forehead, burning into his skull. "Okay," he said. "We'll try."

After the others fell asleep, Skyler pulled a blanket around his shoulders and took the pilot's seat in the Magpie.

He switched on the comm. The link parameters were still set from the transmissions Ana had listened to, and within a second the headset crackled to life and a voice came across, in midsentence.

". . . until our demands are met, and Skyler Luiken is delivered to us—"

"In a pink dress."

"Yes, in a pink dress with a little bow across the chest."

"That's a sash."

"What?"

"A sash goes across the chest. A bow goes in your hair."

"My svelte ass it does. Go look it up."

"You go look it up, and look up 'fashion sense' while you're at it. No one wears a sash."

Skyler fought to hold in laughter. He decided to let them go on a bit longer.

A few seconds of silence passed.

"I wore a sash once, actually," the first speaker said.

"Did you?"

"Yes."

"Did it have words printed on it? Like, maybe, Princess of Anchor Station?"

"It had words, yes. Not those."

"What then?"

"It said 'Marcus is an insufferable prick.'"

Skyler cleared his throat. "Come in, Black Level. This is *La Gaza Ladra*."

A commotion came through the headset. A drink spilled, someone cursed.

"Skyler, hello!" one of them finally said. "This is Marcus."

"And Greg."

"Greg's here, too. Damn, it's great to hear from you."

Skyler smiled to himself. "Thanks. Do, uh, you broadcast like this twenty-four/seven?"

"Three hours every night," Greg said. "I daresay it's become performance art. Half of Black Level and most of Melville Station are probably listening. Hello, everyone."

"I see," Skyler said. "Well, sorry to drop in on your show, but maybe someone can go rouse Tania and switch this to a private channel? It's urgent."

"Sure thing," Marcus said. "Give us a few minutes. Nice to hear from you; we've been . . . well, losing steam."

A series of clicks followed. Five minutes passed and then Tania's voice came through.

"My God, Skyler," she said. "I . . . we'd almost given up hope."

A familiar warmth coursed through him with the sound of her voice. Warmth he hadn't expected, nor the sense of guilt that followed. He suppressed the urge to look over his shoulder, that he might find Ana standing there, as if he were cheating on her. The call could have been made with everyone present, but Skyler had deliberately snuck off after the others slept to make it. For no reason he could put his finger on, he'd decided to keep his tenuous friendship with Tania separate from his relationship with Ana.

"Are you there?" she asked.

"I'm here. Sorry. It's good to hear your voice."

"Yours, too," she said, a note of genuine sadness in her voice. He heard her let out a long breath. "Where are you? Is everyone okay?"

"We're fine. We're in Ireland, and we've found one of the tower groups. I'm sending the coordinates."

The link went quiet, and he knew she was struggling to find a way to ask the next question without it being an accusation.

"Let me explain before you say anything," he said. "The towers surround a dome. A . . . blister on the earth. Strangest thing I've ever seen. It's huge, Tania, and you'll never believe this, but time works differently inside it."

"You went in?"

"We did," he said. He saw no reason to tell her that the rest of the crew had waited outside and ignored the comm for more than a month. "Ten minutes in there and when we came back out six weeks had passed."

"Six," she paused. "Skyler, no offense, but time manipulation is the stuff of fiction. What you're talking about is impossible."

"Well, it happened. I think," he said, working it out as he spoke, "I think it's like the aura. Except instead of putting SUBS into stasis it puts everything into stasis, or nearly so. The air in there, it's humid and has a strange odor. I think there's a chemical component."

"That's . . . Coming from anyone else I'd assume this was

426

a joke. Skyler, you're lucky the air was even breathable. It was suicidal to go in without precautions."

"Chastise me another time. There's more, Tania. Inside there's a, sort of an earthen pinnacle. It's tall and sheer. We had no climbing gear, so we're going back inside tomorrow properly equipped."

"Why? Let's get an observation team up there, study it—"

"Because something must be up there, Tania, and if for some reason it's important there's not a second to lose. Compared to the hell that awaits us within that circle in Belém, this is a much safer crash site to explore. Our only battle here is against the clock."

"I don't like this, Skyler."

"I figured you wouldn't, but we're going. I figure we have an hour to scale it, see what's there, and come back out."

"Why an hour?" she asked. Then, "Oh, I see. Of course."

"We want to be back outside before the Builders return. If they do, I mean."

"There's news on that front," Tania said. Her voice shifted, the tone of sadness and relief replaced by urgency, business. "We've spotted the next ship."

"Already? Did we screw up the date?"

"No," she said. "The date is accurate. March seventh, or thereabouts."

"Then how . . ."

"The ship is *massive,* Skyler."

42

CAPPAGH, IRELAND

7.SEP.2284

At the edge of the murky purple dome, the strategy seemed comical.

Skyler's breath fogged in the crisp morning air, and dark clouds overhead threatened another bout of rain. The two women stood on either side of him. They each held one of his hands, the idea being that if they were physically connected together, it might somehow trick the dome into allowing all three to pass through. Not a bad idea, in Skyler's opinion, but it didn't change the fact that they looked ridiculous.

Luckily only Pablo was there to see them attempt the entry.

"See you in a few months, Pablo," Skyler said over his shoulder.

"Good luck," the tall man said. "I'll be at the farm, napping in a hammock."

"Count of three?" Skyler said to the women. "If only one or two of us get in, turn around and come right back out."

Ana nodded. Vanessa said, "Agreed."

They each wore climbing harnesses and carried gear from the kits Vanessa had so wisely packed before they'd left Belém: climbing rope, crampons, a grappling hook, and even a frog-style ascender. "I grabbed them from that survival store," she'd said.

"I thought we might need to scale a building sometime. I never imagined anything like this."

Though worried about the extra weight, Skyler and Ana also carried small hand axes made for hacking into ice, in case the earthen pillar proved to be more solid than it looked. Only Vanessa, who would spot their climb from the dome floor, carried a gun, on the off chance a subhuman came sniffing after them.

Skyler counted down, and on "three" they stepped forward in unison.

With the benefit of hindsight, he understood now at a basic level what the passage through the dome's wall was doing to his mind. At some point during the transition, part of his mind worked at one time scale, and the rest at a much more accelerated pace. During that brief instant when the bubble enveloped and then closed around his body, every cell, every atom inside him would experience the shift at slightly different moments. That's how he imagined it, anyway. The most impressive aspect to him was the simple fact that the shift didn't tear his body to pieces.

He wondered during the moment of passage what would happen if they spent a year inside the dome. Ten years, even. Would they emerge to a future tens or hundreds of years later? A thousand? He wondered if the Builders could control the time scale within. Crank a dial, have tea inside, and emerge a million years later. The possibilities flittered through his brain like butterflies as he crossed over.

He felt a tug on his left arm and looked that way in a panic, expecting to see only air where Ana had been a second earlier.

She was inside, still next to him, but doubled over and heaving.

Vanessa still held his right hand. He could hear her drawing short, deep breaths. "We made it," she said between gasps.

"Ana," Skyler said, "are you okay?"

The young woman managed to nod and hold a hand up, begging for a few seconds to recover. After a moment she stood and offered him a wan smile.

"Really messes with you, doesn't it?" Skyler asked.

"Even weirder," Vanessa replied from over his shoulder, "is the thought that a few hours have already passed outside."

"That is a good point," Ana said. She shuddered and closed

her eyes for a moment. When they opened, they were clear and bright. "No time to waste. *Vámonos!*"

Skyler gave her a quick kiss on the forehead and turned to face the pinnacle in the center of the domed area. Around them came a flash of sound, like ten thousand fingers tapping against glass.

"What was that?" Vanessa asked.

"I think that was a rainstorm," Skyler said. "Soon you'll notice the dome pulses, dark to light and back. I didn't understand before, but it's days passing outside." Even as he said the words the entire space grew slightly dimmer. They all stood still for a minute, gathering their wits and watching the dome shift in brightness, down and up, down and up. "We've already been in here half a week. C'mon."

He led the way toward the dome's center. The ground curved ever upward, and he had to navigate his way around some of the deeper ravines formed where portions of the uplifted earth had collapsed. All the while the dome pulsed. Dark, then light. Dark, then light. Random phantom noises startled him every few steps. At one point a sound like machine-gun fire made him dive to the ground on instinct, made Vanessa yelp. Ana began to laugh. "Thunderstorm, I'll bet," she said.

Soon the ground became steep enough that Skyler had to lean forward and use his hands for support. The landscape consisted of hard-packed brown dirt and chunks of gray rock, dotted in places with clumps of emerald-green grass. He saw an earthworm wiggle within a centimeter-deep crevice. Above, a pair of magpies wheeled about and called to each other.

When the ground became too steep, Skyler called a halt and let his companions catch their breath. The air inside the dome carried the same ozone smell it had on his last trip. It felt slightly cooler, though, but still warm and humid compared to the cool, crisp morning they'd left outside.

"I'll go first," Skyler said, reiterating the plan they'd agreed to the night before. It had been seven or eight years since he'd scaled a rock, as part of his regular air force combat-readiness training. Rock climbing had been an elective option, and he'd enjoyed the challenge as much as the exercise. The training made him the most experienced of the three. Ana had some skill earned in a summer athletics program, while Vanessa had only tried climbing a few times in the controlled confines of a gym. "It's a lot more fun in the sensory chamber," she'd said with a shrug.

The spire's mass seemed to be formed from the earth itself, as if some force had simply pinched the land here and tugged it straight upward. The material consisted of hard-packed dirt interwoven with decaying roots and other biomass. Strewn throughout were rocks, from scant pebbles to boulders as large as an automobile. Moss grew on everything, and he dreaded the idea of trying to get a solid handhold on the slick growth.

He walked around the circular base and mentally plotted a path to the top. Then, in the interest of time, with one hand he grabbed a root that jutted from the pillar, braced his foot on a thigh-high rock, and began the ascent.

Every five meters he stopped and secured his rope with a crampon. Cost being no concern, Vanessa had chosen the kits with the highest price tags. The devices weighed nearly nothing, so little in fact he found it hard to trust their strength. Skyler tested each link with a strong tug and found them utterly fixed to the surface of the spire.

At thirty meters he reached a large rocky outcropping and paused. Every muscle in his arms burned and his thighs felt like rubber. Below, Ana had begun to climb, following his path exactly. Vanessa waited on the ground below her, spotting her course and shouting advice on where to grab or push off. She stood between two of the pondlike holes in the ground, both deep red in color.

When Ana reached the rock where Skyler waited, she collapsed and splayed herself out against the wall, drawing deep breaths. He gave her a sip of water and kissed her lightly.

"Hey," she said, her eyes closed, "keep going."

For a second he thought she meant to kiss her again, more deeply. The situation, and her exhausted expression, said otherwise. He picked himself up and began to climb again.

Each handhold became a singular effort. The tips of his fingers, though gloved, felt raw and close to bleeding.

"November!" Vanessa shouted from the base.

Fifteen minutes had passed. Two months outside.

Skyler redoubled his effort. Soon the pillar became completely vertical, the rocks smaller and more spread out. His body shook from exertion, as if he hadn't eaten in days.

A few minutes later he found himself faced with the final six-meter span. The portion that went beyond steep and into inverted territory. Standing with one foot on a small jut of rock, one arm looped through an exposed root, Skyler prepared his grappling hook.

He let out six meters of rope and began to swing it back and forth. Ana's pace below almost brought her into a collision with the swaying hook, until he called out to her to halt. Skyler forced his strength into the arc of the grappler, over and over, until finally it almost came in contact with the lip of the pedestal at the top. On the next arc, Skyler put everything he had into the motion and raised his arm as high as he could at the last second. The hook disappeared over the top and he heard the faint sound of metal on stone.

Skyler took a deep breath and began to tug on the line. It pulled smoothly toward him, and he'd resigned himself to watching it fall back over the edge, but then the rope caught and pulled straight.

"Did it catch?" Ana called up.

"I think so," he said to her. "Only one way to know."

Skyler pulled as hard as he could and allowed himself to grin when the rope remained firmly in place. His arm still looped around the root, he cautiously slipped his foot off the rock he'd been perched on. He hung there, his hands in a white-knuckled grip on the grappling rope, his arm strained against the looped vine sticking out from the wall. "It's good!" he called.

The root gave. It pulled out of the earthen wall and suddenly Skyler was dangling, three meters out from the pillar, spinning wildly.

A wave of dizziness and vertigo kept his hands around the rope in a death grip. His eyes were shut equally tight as he waited to see if the grapple would hold. When he opened his eyes, he found himself dangling three meters out from the wall, and six or seven below the pedestal edge at the top. He could see that the blue rope had carved into the dirt and stone making up the lip of the precipice. A few bits of dirt and gravel bounced off his face, punctuating the visual.

He looked back to the wall until he found Ana, staring at him with wide, terrified eyes. Then he glanced down and saw Vanessa standing almost directly below him, her hands clapped over her mouth. Hanging out in space like he was, to him the woman suddenly seemed impossibly far below.

"I'm okay," he called out, loud enough for both of them to hear. "It's holding."

"December!" Vanessa shouted back.

Skyler looked up once more, steeled himself, and began to attach his ascender to the rope. The complicated process was frustrating while hanging free and took more than two precious minutes.

"Here goes," he said to Ana, and then he stood in the foot loops and let the ascender handle glide up the rope. When it bit, he sat again and rocked himself in the next standing motion. With each cycle he gained a half meter, and with the third standing motion his muscle memory kicked in and the process became second nature.

At the lip Skyler rocked himself into a stand one last time, and on the apex he let one hand off the ascender and reached over the ledge to find something to grip. His fingers brushed an exposed rock and he clawed it, then pulled, grunting with the effort.

When he crested the edge, he found himself staring into the bright green eyes of a coiled, snarling subhuman perched on top of a Builder object roughly hourglass in shape. The being clutched the edge of the object with hands that were coated in black to the wrist, as if dipped in oil.

At the sight of Skyler the creature let go of the alien device.

The dome, and everything in it, began to rumble violently.

Far below Skyler, a woman screamed.

43

PLATZ STATION

1.DEC.2284

Alex Warthen circled the table. One hand cupped his chin, his index finger pressed against his lips. He'd said nothing for almost five minutes. He'd just circled, studying the 3-D model of Hab-8.

"Thoughts?" Russell asked. His shallow well of patience had run dry a minute ago, and he'd kept quiet this long only out of his renewed camaraderie with the man.

Since their chat aboard Gateway months ago, Alex had been invigorated, and had pulled in the mousey shrew Sofia Windon to help administrate the stations. The pair were doing a decent job. Better yet, whatever Alex had been saying to Grillo had finally worked. Jacobite cannon fodder were due to arrive within the hour.

"It's a decent plan," Alex said. "I'm worried the loss of life will be substantial, though."

Who gives a bloody shit, Russell thought. *They'll be Grillo's men.* He'd neglected to share that detail with Alex, or anyone else. As far as they knew, Grillo's men were going to fill in on station security duties while Russell headed off to battle. Russell couldn't wait to give them their true orders, make them feel like they were doing the world a favor. "The Fist of God," he'd decided to dub them, sure they wouldn't get the innuendo, or if they did they'd be too embarrassed to say anything. "We'll have surprise on our side," Russell said. "I doubt, after all this time, that Tania and company are maintaining a ready squad to repel such an attack."

"You know this for sure?" Alex asked.

"No," Russell admitted. The informants he'd sent across had been frustratingly, unnervingly quiet. Gone native, maybe, or discovered. A mix of both. "But it makes sense."

"I always plan for the things that don't make sense," Alex said. "Unless, of course, a bloodbath is what you want."

"My men don't mind getting their hands dirty." *Grillo's men, I mean, but you don't need to know that.* Of course Russell would be there, too, and a few handpicked squad leaders from his own pool of mercenaries. They could hang back, though. Give orders. Let the blood flow and clean up the mess afterward, should it even go down like that.

Alex Warthen shrugged. "Seems okay to me, then. I'm sure we can get the rest of the council to buy off on the plan, too."

The comment made Russell want to push his fingers into his ears and press until they punctured his brain. He hoped he kept his disgust hidden as Alex continued to study the projected model on the table. "I look forward to the vote," Russell said, confident he'd imparted minimal sarcasm. Alex expected some, and Russell couldn't disappoint him. That would have been a dead giveaway. "Perhaps we can call it via comm this afternoon? My people will be ready to go by dinner."

"That soon?" Alex asked.

"Yes. If the geeks still on Anchor are right, the Builders will be back in March. Time is running out. I want that shit over there in our hands before the aliens try to rape us again."

Alex, amazingly, nodded. "Okay." He glanced at his slate. "I've got to get down to the port and board my climber. Heading up to Midway Station for a meeting with all the upper-station captains. I'll set the vote for three P.M. if the climber has a comm."

"Perfect," Russell said.

"Nice plan, Blackfield. Good luck."

"Walk you out?"

"I'm fine," Alex said, and departed.

When the door clicked closed behind the security chief, Russell realized his "bloodbath" plan might have won approval simply because he'd be putting himself in harm's way. Alex probably liked the odds that the council's problem child wouldn't return. "On the contrary, asshole," Russell said to the empty room, "I'll have two Elevators, then, and Tania Sharma chained to my bedpost."

Russell tapped the comm on his desk and selected the group contact he'd created, the one marked "the Dog Pound," which would transmit his voice to the cabin of every grunt he commanded on Platz Station.

"Listen up, wags," he said when the connection showed green. "I want each and every one of you in the central dock in twenty minutes. Full gear. Our comrades from the surface, the ones who took over your shitty jobs after you ascended, are coming up to take part in a joint combat operation."

Russell gave a second for the words to settle in.

"I want to show them what a real bunch of hard-ass skull-cracking motherfuckers look like, let you guys boss them around a bit. We'll take them to the gymnasium, where squads will be assigned. . . ." He rattled off a plan from the top of his head. He intended to change it all, anyway, so it didn't matter much. The only part that mattered was getting Grillo's holy warriors into the transport tubs and ushered off to Tania's empire.

Finished, Russell clicked off and jogged to his quarters. Neil Platz's old flat. The place looked like a high-end hotel penthouse, as large and polished as the old goat's ego had been.

Just inside the wide double doors he began to undress, leaving a trail of clothing behind him as he wound through the apartments toward the opulent bathroom. A woman in his bed mumbled something as he passed. He couldn't tell who it was, exactly, with just a creamy thigh and toned calf exposed. He only slowed slightly, enticed by the sight of flesh and enthused by his own state of nudity, but he knew time was running short. The woman would have to wait. He strode on, ignoring her mumbled invitation, and entered the bathroom.

Russell stood under the showerhead, alternating the water from scalding hot to ice cold every few minutes until he felt his mind begin to clear. He kept his eyes open despite the rivulets of water that poured down his face, and stared at an imagined point somewhere far beyond the marble wall of the shower.

Brazil. *Brazil.*

Twenty-five minutes later Russell floated in front of his assembled troops.

"All right, lads, thirty seconds!" he called out.

The lack of significant gravity in the cargo bay made it difficult to put on a suitable show of his military might. His soldiers had been training, though, for a long time, thanks to Grillo's constant delays. Compared to that first time, when they'd entered Gateway like a school of drunken fish, they were as dexterous as gymnasts now. If they had anything to show off compared to Grillo's altar boys, it was that.

Somehow they'd managed to form a line, or rather a ring, around the airlock doors where the Jacobites would exit. He felt a twang of pride. They'd borrowed or improvised magnetic-toed boots in order to keep themselves planted on the deck. The boots didn't have that combat feel, though, and since each commando had to keep one toe pointed down at the floor, in a line together they looked a bit like a chain of Irish dancers. Russell fought to hold in a laugh at that thought and floated into place just in front of the line. An airlock door marked "1" loomed directly in front of him as the clock counted down.

"Take your time guiding them to the outer ring," Russell said, his voice raised for everyone in the expansive bay to hear. "Let 'em flop around a bit, yeah?"

He saw grins behind him. The smiles turned to pure confidence as the timer reached zero. Russell turned to face the door and used a rubber loop on the floor to steady himself. Sometime he'd have to see about a pair of those magnetic-tipped boots.

A series of deep metallic clangs announced the arrival of the climber even before the chime indicated the countdown had ended.

Russell heard a brief hiss as the air inside the climber cars was matched to the pressure within the bay. A light on the airlock door went from red, to yellow, to green. Then it slid up.

He found himself looking down a half-dozen gun barrels.

Shit—

Gunfire cut off the thought. Russell did the only thing he could think to do, and pushed off the floor hard. He hurled toward the ceiling. A searing pain flared from his left calf, and he felt the warm wetness of blood begin to soak his pant leg there. Droplets of red were left in his wake as he vaulted upward.

The deafening chatter of indoor gunfire erupted from all around the bay.

Russell hit the ceiling hard and spun around. Flashes of yellow light pulsed from inside the climber cars. His soldiers were scrambling for cover, to ready their weapons—anything but remain in the line of fire. Already he could see some of his soldiers, the ones who'd been right in front of the doors, swaying from their planted toes like seaweed on the ocean floor.

His troops had been in full gear but had not readied their weapons. That would have been rude. Some had been quicker than others and were beginning to shoot back. A full half of his garrison turned, pushing for the exits. He wanted to scream at them for their cowardice.

A nearby rattling sound forced him to curl into a ball. Sparks flew from all around him as someone below tried to finish him off. The exit suddenly seemed like a damn good idea. Russell pushed toward one and the burning in his leg turned into nuclear fire. He screamed, pulled his handgun, and fired as he rotated around in an uncontrolled spiral. He managed to unload half a clip on the first spin, the other half on the second. Some of his bullets even went into the maw of the nearest climber car airlock.

Below him, battle raged. A rotating blur of gunfire, hand-to-hand combat, and death. Bodies floated all over the bay, some in perfect stillness, some careening around like mannequins with disjointed limbs. Marble-sized globes of blood drifted around the scene as if someone had fired up a macabre bubble machine.

Another spray of gunfire prattled against the ceiling above Russell. He heard the hiss as one round passed within centimeters of his ear, and he tucked into a ball again on pure instinct. His leg burned, each movement as if a knife twisted there. A serrated knife coated with rusty barbed wire heated until it glowed. The pain flooded his mind like an orgasm without the release of pleasure.

Still curled in a ball, Russell collided with something—someone—and then a floor. He opened his eyes and groaned. Soldiers hung on the walls around him, their hands pulling him away from the bay door.

"Seal it," Russell hissed. "Seal that fucking room."

"We still have people in there," someone said against a background of screams and gunshots.

"*I* still have people in there," Russell corrected. "*You* have an order. Fucking do it."

In answer the thick door began to close. Someone on the other side shouted, "Wait!" just before the metallic clang signaled the cargo bay had sealed.

"Vent the air," Russell said. "No one better question that. Vent the air."

"Sir?" someone said.

A question. Russell looked around but found his vision clouded with tears. He squinted.

"Sir," the same voice went on, "comm says they came in through the passenger ports down on A. They're taking prisoners."

"Then seal that level, too," he said. "Vent it."

"There's innocent—"

"Don't start. No room for goddamn debate here. Vent the air. We can't let these bastards gain any more ground."

"Yes, sir."

Russell heard a faint whoosh, and a creaking sound that lasted half a heartbeat. The air, sucked out of the cargo bay into space. A fire prevention technique.

The men and women in the room would be suffocating now. Russell wondered how many had made it into the three exits before the doors were closed, and if any of the survivors were on the enemy side.

The enemy. Grillo, you two-faced cunt, I will cut your heart out for this.

"Someone help me get to station ops," he said. He felt lightheaded. Blood still seeped from his calf in little red spheres.

* * *

The operations room on Platz Station looked just like the other suites of cubicle offices that plagued the complex.

Russell entered on one leg, his arm over the shoulder of a guard who smelled like old socks.

"Report," Russell said as he took a chair. Then he looked at the guard. "Find me a medic. And vodka."

"Mr. Blackfield," said the operations lead on duty, a pouty woman with classic Australian features and drawl. "Level A is at zero atmosphere, and the doors are sealed."

"Good news," he said. "Did they get farther than that?"

"Reports of sporadic fighting on B, but it seems to be under control now."

Russell nodded. The woman seemed remarkably detached from the situation. Cool under fire; he liked that. Rational ideas and prudent tactics fought to gain attention in his mind, all eclipsed by the raw thirst for revenge. *We have to go down to Darwin now, before he entrenches himself further.* He toyed with the idea of rigging a climber to fall uncontrolled on Nightcliff. Fill the thing with fifty tons of old scrap metal and broken parts and it'll take out the entire fortress. He filed the idea for the moment, knowing Grillo spent more than half his time out in Lyons, or at that bloody stadium.

"Hey," he said to the woman. "Your name?"

"Jenny," she said.

"Jenny. Can we do that thing, like Dr. Sharma did? Detach a farm platform?"

"I don't see what that would—"

"Just answer, please."

She grimaced, nodded. "All stations have a separation gap capability, so they can move away from the cord and reposition."

"I love you, Jenny. Pick one and start the process. Someone find me a map of Darwin."

Naked horror flashed across her face as she realized what he intended to do. She visibly gulped, studied her screens for a moment, then set to work.

A nurse came in, dropped a case of supplies on the floor next to

Russell, and began to examine his leg. The man worked quickly, unconcerned if his probing caused pain, or perhaps hoping it would to know where the damage was. He used a pair of scissors to cut the pant leg away, revealing two red holes on either side of the calf muscle.

"Get me Alex Warthen on the comm," Russell said.

Jenny turned to her screen and began to tap in commands. "Um," she said. "Getting a lot of chatter here."

Before Russell could speak, she turned to face him, one finger pressing a headset into her ear. "Reports coming in from the other stations. Anchor Station is overrun. Gateway is under heavy assault."

The rage within Russell Blackfield transformed into a block of ice. He thought back to the day Grillo had offered warriors to aid in his assault on Tania's colony. Months of excuses and delays. Then, suddenly, he had the men, plus the nerve to ask if Jacobite delegations could begin visits to Anchor. Pilgrimages to their holy site, he'd had the gall to say.

"Hab-Six is reporting casualties," Jenny went on. "Hab-Five. Midway."

"Enough," Russell said. *Grillo, you bloody snake.* The nurse sprayed his wound with something that made his leg go cold and numb, then began to wrap gauze around his calf.

"Incoming climbers," another station operator said. A young man with a nasal voice.

"They won't get far," Russell said. "The first wave are still docked."

"From above and below," he added.

Stupid, Russell thought. *They'll just clog the cord waiting for an opening. Unless . . .* "Blockade," Russell said aloud. "They're going to pen us in here. Starve us until we give in."

"I don't think so. They're not slowing."

Everyone went silent. Russell knew they were looking at him. Climbers speeding toward the station meant one thing: total destruction. Plan fucking B for the Jacobites and their holy slumlord.

"How long?" Russell asked.

The young man glanced at his display. "Sixteen minutes."

"Okay," Russell said. "New orders. How long . . . fuck, doesn't even matter how long . . . Detach Platz Station from the cord, right now."

Jenny stared at him, her face a sudden mask. She blinked, as if hearing his command a second time and still not believing it. The other operators were still, too. Even the nurse froze his work at Russell's order.

"Relax, we're not going to go all kamikaze on Darwin. We're going to survive."

"Sir," Jenny said, "it'll take at least an hour to clear everyone from the slice bulkheads. Eight hours to have the station prepped for null gravity, minimum."

Russell shot her a glare that cut off the argument. "How long does it take if you throw every goddamn safety reg out the window? If you wanted, say, to save all our lives."

She swallowed, gave him a terrified nod, and began to enter the instructions. "I need your code to authorize it," she said after a time.

" 'Sex machine.' "

Jenny looked at him, an eyebrow arched.

"Yes, my code is 'sex machine.' Keep staring at me like that, love, and I'll prove it."

Jenny glanced down at her screen and tapped in the code. Warning lights began to spin. Klaxons wailed.

From the hallway outside came the sound of emergency bulkhead doors closing. More noises came from under the floor, inside the walls and ceiling. Water pipes sealing themselves, Russell guessed.

"*Warning,*" a pre-recorded voice said over the station intercom. "*This station is about to experience null gravity. Stow nonsecured objects immediately. All noncritical personnel . . .*"

"Everybody better hang on to something," Jenny said. "Killing spin in five, four, three . . ."

"You," Russell said to nasal-boy. "Count off the minutes till those climbers get here."

He nodded, his face white as a bedsheet. "Uh. Nine minutes."

"Jenny?"

She'd finished her countdown. "We'll clear the cord in . . .

eight," she said. As her words came out the sensation of gravity began to fade.

A mug on the desk next to Russell began to drift upward, as if he were levitating it with his mind. Scissors from the nurse's first aid kit began to float out of their compartment, followed by a stack of bandages that splayed out like a deck of cards.

Across the room, random items began to rise toward the ceiling as if ascending to heaven. Then the station lurched. The walls creaked, and in the same instant there came a chorus of surprised gasps from those in the room, the hall outside. Russell gripped the arms of his chair. Though brief and gentle, the pulse of acceleration still sent every floating item hurling across the room. Flotsam smacked into people's heads and rattled against the wall to Russell's left. A framed picture on the wall shattered when someone's forgotten headset smacked into it, shards of glass expanding into a cloud around the frame.

"Everyone cover yourselves," Jenny said, sounding on the verge of tears. "Reverse thrust coming."

Russell cringed. "Can you cancel that?"

"What? Don't stop?"

The plan formed in Russell's mind like a Darwin thunderstorm. He felt it before he could see it. "Cancel it. How much fuel do we have?"

Jenny glanced at her screen. She tapped a few icons. "Retro-burn canceled; station is adrift."

"Good. How much fuel?"

"Very little. A typical station reposition, if there is such a thing, requires only six brief thrusts. Detach, stop. Reposition, stop. Attach, stop. Of course, I've only done this in simulation, but the reserves allow for maybe seven or eight reposition maneuvers."

Russell tried to think of alternatives, knowing there were none. Grillo had pulled off an incredible coup, if the station reports were accurate. Alex Warthen conveniently left on the last climber before the attack. Russell was alone. He'd lost Darwin willingly, fooled himself into thinking he could get it back. He'd alienated himself from the Orbital Council with such success that Alex Warthen had needed to sit him down like a delinquent schoolboy, for which Russell rewarded him with a reinstatement of sorts.

All he needed to become the true reincarnation of Neil Platz was a bullet between his own eyes. His kingdom had shrunk to this tin can, one marvelous whore in his bedroom, and stubborn delusions of revenge against Tania Sharma.

"Russell?" Jenny asked. "What do we do? Where can we go?"

Vary the pattern.

"The enemy of my enemy is my friend," he said, and glanced at the girl.

She stared at him, a mixture of hope and fear in her wide eyes. Everyone stared at him.

"Save the fuel; we're going to need it," he said. "We go to Brazil. To the colony, and trust in the kindness and mercy of Tania Sharma and Zane Platz."

44

CAPPAGH, IRELAND

DATE IMPRECISE

The dome rattled as if the very planet below it had cracked open.

Fist-sized chunks of earth from the lip of the pinnacle broke away and fell. Skyler's foot slipped in the ascender and he kicked hard to keep his toes within the loop.

Vanessa's scream below turned into battle cry, followed by the rhythmic hammer of gunfire. Her weapon chattered in short bursts. Once, twice, then a third time, each a split second apart.

Ana screamed, her voice a mix of terror and warning.

There came another sound, a new thing that Skyler couldn't comprehend. Below, a swarm of distinct thrumming objects could be heard, emitting an almost electrical hiss, each at its own frequency.

Skyler fought the urge to look down, because the creature in front of him held his gaze with an absolute promise of death in its bloodshot eyes. Tangled strands of greasy gray hair hung across the subhuman's twisted face. Its nostrils flared. Its cracked and blistered lips were slightly parted, revealing a filthy mess of gritted teeth. Soiled clothing still clung to the creature's muscle-corded body. Scrapes and scabs littered its arms.

Its hands and feet were in a perfect row across the front lip of the alien object upon which it perched. Twenty cracked and jagged nails, the middle portion coated black, in an uneven line like some kind of saw blade.

The creature grunted at him. Skyler saw white knuckles on those toes, and the black-covered fingers curled almost imperceptibly as they tightened against the alien object. He saw a slight coiling motion of the body and the lowering of hips, and he did the only thing he could think do to.

He ducked. The subhuman pounced.

Skyler's chin hit the edge of the rocky pinnacle, sending a jolt of pain up through his jaw and into his skull. He tasted blood.

The creature aimed where Skyler's eyes had been. Instead of colliding with Skyler full in the face, it found air and landed with just its knees on the pinnacle. Its abdomen slammed into the top of Skyler's head and, for a split second, he thought it would go over and fall to a quick death. Instead, a hand somehow found Skyler's chin and it clamped down like a vise. Black fingernails dug into his cheek, stinging as if electrically charged, as the weight of the creature went beyond the lip of the pinnacle. The legs went up and over. The other hand found Skyler's shirt and gripped desperately as the subhuman's entire body flipped around.

Skyler grunted with the sudden addition of weight. Just above his waist, the ascender's tension lock gave a little squeak with the extra strain and the rope that ran through it slipped a few centimeters. He tugged the rope near the grapple on pure instinct, a mistake in hindsight. Both of their bodies now pulled on the grapple. The foot he had in the ascender buckled. He yanked his head viciously to the right in an effort to dislodge the fingers that still clawed at his cheek. Pain seared his flesh as the nails were wrenched away by the motion and the creature's hand, now free, fumbled for new purchase as the subhuman swung from the hand that held a fistful of Skyler's shirt. A heartbeat later the free hand clasped onto his leg behind the knee, twisting him awkwardly, one foot still clinging to the ascender for dear life.

The creature roared.

Skyler looked down, arms on fire as he struggled to hold the rope.

In that instant he saw something below that defied explanation. Something so far out of his experience that his mind practically refused to register it.

The red and blue surfaces that had filled the craters on the dome's floor were rising up in amorphous blobs that were somehow solid and as ephemeral as mist simultaneously. Some, those of red hue, had already completely vacated their former holes in the ground and were tearing around the dome's floor with astonishing speed. They *flowed* from one position to the next, surfaces stretched forward in almost smoky tendrils as if they were somehow incompatible with the atmosphere in the dome, and so they couldn't simply move through the air but had to somehow filter through it. Their movements generated the quasi-electrical hum Skyler had heard, and when they came close to one another the noises built rapidly and then discharged as if they repelled one another.

The subhuman still roared, and Skyler's mind snapped back into focus. He saw bared teeth, head and neck coiled back, then snapping forward to bite at his thigh. Skyler reacted on pure instinct and thrust his knee up as the teeth bore down.

His knee met the creature's jaw with a sickening crunch that Skyler felt as much as heard. The sub's jawbone cracked. Its eyes rolled back in abject pain.

Only when Skyler's hands suddenly slipped on the rope did he realize his mistake. The leg he'd thrust to block the attack had been the one in the ascender. Without a foothold, his already burning hands and arms had to support all of his combined weight. Weight he hadn't the strength to bear.

Nor, it turned out, did the grappling hook. He heard it pull free and scrape across the pedestal before he registered the fact that he was falling.

Skyler cried out, held the rope out of sheer survival instinct, as they fell away from the spire toward the humming red forms below and the rattle of Vanessa's weapon.

45

MELVILLE STATION

4.DEC.2284

The hulking form of Platz Station appeared on proximity radar a day earlier, approaching in an orbit equal to what its altitude had been above Darwin.

All attempts at contact failed, though Tim never stopped trying. With a full day to prepare, Tania took the precaution to move all nonessential staff down to Belém, or up to Space-Ag 1. If the incoming station showed signs of altering course, turning itself into a giant battering ram, they'd have plenty of time to evacuate the remaining people.

A larger concern was if the goal was to ram the thin cord of the Elevator itself. The facility was too big and moving too slow to sever the cable like a knife, assuming such an action was even possible. But no one knew what would happen if it simply crashed into the alien cord. The mass of an entire space station pushing against the cable might fold it in half, pull it loose of its anchors, or send reverberations along the entire length that would wreak havoc on everything from Black Level down to the climber port in Belém.

Just in case, Tania had all stations on standing alert to detach and clear. Technically, none of them actually touched the cord. *Attached* was simply the term used when they were positioned with their center ring around the thread. Attaching or detaching required the retraction of special movable bulkheads aligned in a slice along one edge of the station. For most this meant that a gap five meters in width would be created, then closed again once the facility was centered on the Elevator.

Platz Station, like all others, could do this. A key design feature that allowed the stations to be manufactured and assembled in a central location, then moved into place as a whole. Even rearranged later.

Tania sat in front of a widescreen monitor and watched the facility grow ever larger. A half-consumed avocado lay on a dish beside her, along with a cup of water. She sipped the cool liquid and set it back down, her eyes never leaving the screen, even when she wiped sweat from her brow.

"You can hit the showers if you want," Tim said behind her. "I'll monitor this."

Tania turned and smirked at him. She'd come straight from her sparring session, part of the training regimen Karl insisted she begin if she intended to make any more forays outside of Camp Exodus. Her instructor, one of Karl's old "cleaning crew," taught in the Krav Maga style and had no problem pushing her to the limit.

Tim shrank at her look. "Never mind," he said. "No, really, you smell great."

She turned back to the screen and tried to ignore him. Platz Station moved closer with every passing second. She wondered when their location had been discovered, and how. A spy? Some kind of tracking beacon? Both had always been a possibility, and precautions had been taken.

There were lights on in the few porthole windows she could see, and the station spun at its usual speed, which implied it wasn't empty. There'd be no point in spinning up after detachment if it had been vacated. Black Level had been left in null gravity during its entire transit from Darwin to Belém, just to conserve fuel.

Why now? she wondered. The answer seemed obvious. Figuring out the Builders' schedule didn't take much imagination once one had three data points to chart. She thought of the massive ship that grew nearer every day. At six kilometers long, according to visual estimates, the scale simply defied belief. Speculation as to its purpose dominated every conversation from Belém to Black Level, with Greg and Marcus offering some particularly inventive, even hilarious, ideas on their nightly "Broadcast to Skyler." The transmission-turned-show continued despite the successful contact months ago. They'd been inside the dome since, according to the immune Pablo. No sign of them, no way to know if they were okay.

The lights in Platz Station's windows tugged at the corner of her mind. She toyed with the idea that Neil himself had stood at one of those portals. That the rumors of his death were greatly exaggerated, and he'd been hiding out in the bowels of that structure until the moment arrived when he could commandeer it.

Then a different scenario hit her, the one she'd expected since the moment she'd heard of the object's approach. *Blackfield is in there,* she thought. And when the station arrives, climber cars full of soldiers are going to stream out in both directions until the Elevator is in his control. That wouldn't be easy; Tania had seen to that. All the climber controls and dock codes had been changed long ago, just in case. No, the best Blackfield could hope to do is reach the ground, and even then his cars would be suspended well off the ground. The colony would give them ample reason to wish they'd never attempted such an assault.

A change occurred on the screen. Tania squinted and leaned forward, the haze of her daydream fading. "The spin is slowing," she said.

"Hmm?" Tim asked from behind her, in his place at the comm.

"They're drifting now. And—oh, there we go." Plumes of gas erupted from hundreds of ventilation nozzles distributed evenly across one side of the rings. "Braking thrust."

Tim loomed at her shoulder now, watching. "I guess it's going to latch on to the cord."

"Yup."

"What if they packed it with bombs or something?"

A chill shot through Tania. Partly from the picture of that station turning into a small sun and vaporizing the cord, and partly from her lack of imagination for such scenarios.

The comm behind them chimed, an incoming transmission.

"It's them," Tim said. "You want to take it?"

She nodded to him and turned her chair around to face the terminal's screen. "Record it? Thanks." Tania settled herself, took a deep breath, and tapped the icon to answer the call.

Russell Blackfield's face appeared before her. He looked pale, haggard.

"I never thought I'd say this," he said, "but it's good to see you, Tania."

She looked at his face and kept repeating one word in her mind: *liar.* Yet for all her distaste for the man, he sounded sincere. "What is your purpose here, Russell? I must ask that you refrain from connecting to the Elevator, and back off to a distance of one hundred kilometers."

"We can't," he said. "We left in a hurry; air is already scrubbed to the limit."

Tania regarded him with what she hoped looked like cold disbelief. "Again, what are you doing here?"

Russell ran a hand over his face. Something drifted by the camera behind him. A wastebasket, she realized. Seconds later a person drifted into frame, grabbed the basket, and vanished off the other side of the screen. Tania could see other loose items floating around in the background, now that she knew to look for it. They did leave in a hurry. Or it's a clever detail to sell the ruse.

"You know me a little," Russell said. "So I think you'll appreciate how hard this is for me to say. You'll understand how dire the situation is."

She swallowed hard, despite herself.

"Tania Sharma," he said, "I humbly ask for asylum. Sanctuary, for myself and the crew of Platz Station. I . . . ask for mercy. Throw me in a cell if you must, I don't care, just don't tell us to turn around. We can't go back now, any more than you can."

Tim, in the corner of Tania's field of view, shook his head vehemently. If Zane were up and about, he'd be doing the same, she knew. "What's in it for us?" Tania asked.

She'd hoped the question would take Russell off guard. That'd he'd be surprised she'd do anything except agree based on humanitarian reasons. He took the question in stride, though.

"People. You keep asking for people. Well, here's a few thousand, all skilled Orbitals. Plus this station, it's yours. It's the crown jewel of Neil's empire, you know."

"What else?"

Now he showed a flicker of desperation. A quick dart of his eyes to hers, searching some sign of her sincerity. "Um," he said. "Well . . . there's four climbers aboard and twenty or so cars, most of them rated for personnel transport. Soldiers. We lost some in departure, but there's plenty still here. Weapons. Six medical doctors and as many nurses, plus a fully outfitted infirmary."

"Any of our missing friends? Samantha Rinn or Kelly Adelaide, for example? Former council members?"

He shook his head. "We didn't plan to leave. I haven't seen your friends in a long time."

Tania nodded slowly. The station was an incredible addition to the colony, she had no doubt. Everything sounded too good to be true, with the exception of Blackfield's presence. She pondered the idea of sending him back and keeping the rest.

"Please," Russell said. "At least provision us with air and water. Food. Our departure was, well, let's say it was unplanned."

"Something's happened," Tania said. "In Darwin. Something forced you to leave. What was it? Did the aura fail? Did you leave everyone else to die?"

Russell held up his hands. "Whoa, hold on. I'm the victim here, okay?"

Like hell you are.

He went on. "Our station was attacked. They were going to destroy it when their assault failed. We had no choice but to flee."

"Who is 'they'?"

"Grillo," he said. Noting her confusion, he added, "The fucking Jacobites. They run everything now. Darwin. Orbit. All of it. And once they find out there's another Elevator here, there's no telling what they'll do."

She fixed him with a gaze she hoped looked menacing. "They don't know where we are? Where you went?"

He shrugged. "I don't think so, but they have Alex Warthen. He might talk, if Grillo suspects he has information. I doubt it, though; he's honorable to a fault."

Tania's mind raced. Most of it still screamed "trick."

"By letting us stay," Russell said, "you also earn my silence. I could get Nightcliff on the line right now and report our location."

"Fine then," Tania said, harsher than she'd intended. If there was a chance to capture Russell Blackfield, lock him up, and toss the key out an airlock, she had to take it. "Attach and await our instructions."

Against Tim's protests, and her own better judgment, Tania allowed Platz Station to attach to the Elevator.

Within two hours a team of four guards, all volunteers, slid into the station's main cargo bay and took Russell Blackfield into custody. He waited there for them, alone and unarmed as agreed. They reported that the cargo bay showed signs of combat. She had Russell brought down to Melville Station and placed in a cabin under watch. For the moment she thought it best not to meet with him directly.

Instead, Tania boarded a climber herself, along with more guards and her night shift operations team from Melville.

The main cargo bay at the heart of Platz Station indeed appeared to have been the scene of an intense battle. Globules of blood still drifted and pooled near the air vents and exit doors. A shell casing floated past her. Sweeping lines and speckled clusters of bullet impacts decorated the walls, floor, and ceiling. There were no bodies, though. Either the dead had been pushed out an airlock, or they'd been tucked away somewhere within.

A greeting party awaited her. No guards, per the instructions, and no one appeared to be armed. She ordered her people to search them anyway, if anything just to establish authority. Her recent combat and weapons training gave her a confidence she'd not expected, as if she held a secret that would forevermore give her a slight upper hand. No one complained, and no weapons were found. Tania thought she saw relief on their faces. She hoped so, at least. They'd been living under Russell Blackfield's command, and though that had surely generated some bad seeds, Tania decided to make sure the rest saw her as a marked improvement in their lives.

"Who's in charge?" Tania asked.

Most of the group turned to face one woman near the center. She seemed to remember herself, and raised a hand. "Jenny Abrath," she said. "I guess it's me."

"Nice to meet you," Tania said.

"The station is yours, Dr. Sharma."

Goose bumps rose on Tania's arms. "What's your role here, Jenny?"

"I run the operations room," she said. "I could take you there now, if you like."

"Thanks," Tania said, "but no. I want to speak with your doctors first. We have someone in critical condition who could use attention."

The station crew she passed on the journey all had the same look on their faces. Confusion, bewilderment. Hope. Even, she thought, a little respect.

On the way to operations she spied the hallway that led to the apartments Neil Platz used to occupy, as well as the adjacent set where Zane had lived. "Hold on," she said to Jenny. "I want to see something."

Alone, Tania walked down the hall and let a flood of childhood memories fill her mind. She'd run down this hallway many times, intent to share some scholastic achievement or chess victory story with Neil when her own parents were away. Her parents were always away.

Tania opened the door to Neil's apartment and took a few tentative steps inside. The living space appeared used. It made sense that Russell would claim the space, but still it surprised her for some reason. For all Russell's banter against Neil, he sure seemed quick to stand in the man's shoes.

The bedroom door was partly opened and Tania stepped in, not sure exactly what she hoped to find. Neil's scent, or his clothing. Anything to give her a clear and bright memory of him again.

Instead she saw a mess. Clothing strewn about, a towel tossed carelessly on the floor. Two bottles of alcohol sat on the bedside table; a third lay on the ground. *Russell,* she thought. *Of course he'd take this room for himself.*

She retreated into the entrance hall and started back toward the rest of the group. Lush red carpet softened her footfalls.

Halfway back she spied the door to Zane's suite of rooms. She paused there and pushed the door open, half-expecting to find another bedchamber for Russell Blackfield. But the room appeared to be left alone. Debris littered the floor. Pillows from the couch, a slate terminal, a bouquet of fake plastic roses. All, Tania thought, due to the hasty switch to zero-g, not from searchers or looters.

As she pulled the door closed an idea formed. A faint smile crept onto her face as she returned to Jenny and the others.

The infirmary bustled with doctors, nurses, and injured. Half the patients were in beds or on stretchers, wearing bandages with faint splotches of blood seeping through. Bullet wounds, she guessed. The rest of the patients all had minor injuries: bruises, lacerations, the odd broken bone. More evidence that the flight from Darwin had been in haste. A switch to zero-g without preparation would have filled the station with every item not stowed or bolted.

Tania asked to speak to the most senior doctor and pulled the woman aside. She introduced herself as Dr. Volk, and Tania shook her hand. The statuesque woman had elegant dark skin and tightly curled black hair showing a bit of gray at the roots.

"One of our people is in a coma," Tania said to her, and explained the history.

The doctor nodded politely throughout and asked a few questions. "I'm not sure what we can do for him," she said, "after so much time. Keep him comfortable, monitor him, and wait. It sounds like you've got the same equipment we do, more or less, but I'd be happy to compare notes with the doctor on your side."

Tania thanked her and left her to tend to the wounded. She felt as if the doctor could be trusted, something about her manner gave all the right signals, but time would tell. For now, Tania decided she would put Dr. Brooks in charge here, and have Zane Platz transferred back to his old apartment on the station.

Perhaps his own room, his own bed amid familiar smells and noises, would trigger something in his mind.

It can't hurt.

She nodded to Jenny in a way that conveyed "let's go," and fell in with her as they moved through the station's wide hallways toward operations.

Logistics and problem scenarios began to fill Tania's thoughts. The station would have to be searched, weapons confiscated until the inhabitants could be interviewed. Russell's small private army would need to be detained until they could figure out a way to integrate them. Perhaps a heartfelt speech from Russell would do the trick.

Despite the mountain of issues to deal with, her mind kept returning to Zane Platz. She envisioned him resting quietly in his own room, the ghost of his older brother at his side.

Time to come home, Zane.

46

CAPPAGH, IRELAND

DATE IMPRECISE

The safety line swung Skyler and his savage companion into the meat of the earthen spire. Somehow, through luck or subconscious movement, he managed to turn so that the subhuman took the brunt of the impact.

He grunted in unison with the creature, but with far less pain. The being cushioned the impact, went limp as its head was sandwiched between Skyler's leg and the rock-strewn wall. Both of its hands released at once, and it fell away, tumbling down the column and rolling to a stop at its base, lifeless and contorted.

Skyler flailed for a moment. He inhaled a lungful of air and forced himself back from a panic mindset. He released his death grip on the rope, trusting the climbing gear to hold his weight. It did.

He righted himself against the spire's sheer surface and found hand- and footholds with more expertise than he knew he had. Finally stable, he glanced down to assess the situation around him.

His eyes found Ana first, just a few meters away. She stared at him with wide eyes, her face drained of color, mouth agape.

"I'm okay," he said to her.

She blinked in response.

Skyler glanced farther down, to the floor of the dome. Vanessa stood roughly where she'd been when the dome began to vibrate. She was reloading her gun and, as if sensing he was looking at her, glanced up and met his eyes. Her face showed determination and utter, complete confusion.

The red shapes flittered around her, moving between the clumps of rock and around the craters. They were closing in, as if working together like a pack of wolves.

One red shape, just a few meters from Vanessa, had stopped completely. Its edges were somehow stable, and Skyler thought it resembled a human body lying prone.

The vibration of the dome itself suddenly ramped up in intensity. Through his hands and feet, Skyler felt the earthen column shift, and he saw a crack form diagonally along its length.

"Go!" he roared at Ana. "It's shaking apart!"

Above, the pedestal at the top cracked into a hundred pieces and shattered. Chunks of earth fell away, passing just centimeters from Skyler's body. He didn't even have time to cover his head or warn Ana to do so. All he could do was watch, dumbly, and hope he was far enough in under the lip to be protected.

With dreamlike slowness, the hourglass-shaped alien object tumbled past Skyler amid the rest of the fractured debris. He watched it fall to the tapered base of the spire and tumble away into the chaos below.

Then he saw Vanessa, still fumbling to reload, as one of the darting red forms suddenly changed angle and came right at her.

She didn't have time to even raise her weapon as the shape slammed into her.

Vanessa cried out, enveloped in the red field.

It moved through her, and for the briefest of instants Skyler thought he saw another entity within, a humanoid loping on all fours.

And then the red amorphous *stain* moved past her, leaving nothing but empty air behind.

47

PLATZ STATION

20.JAN.2285

Zane Platz opened his eyes after eight months in a coma, sat bolt upright, and laughed.

The laugh faded as he took in his surroundings. His old bed, his room on Platz Station. "It was a dream, then," he said, and passed out again.

Tania had been in the middle of explaining what she'd had for breakfast. She spent an hour here, every morning, recounting the mundane details of the previous day's activity to the comatose man. At first it had been difficult to talk to him, but the comfort of the normal room, and the privacy it afforded, gradually eroded her reluctance.

In all the time she'd been visiting him he'd never done more than breathed in and out. A flicker beneath the eyelids at best.

To see him sit up, to hear him speak, left her slack-jawed.

The man slumped back down into his unconscious state, as if nothing had happened.

"Zane?" she finally asked. "Zane?!"

Tania was half out of her chair, ready to run for the doctor, when Zane stirred. His eyes flickered, then opened. "Tania?" he called, not looking toward her, his voice impossibly hoarse.

"I'm here," she said. She took his hand and gripped it. He still did not move.

"Can you turn the lights on, Tania dear?"

A knot in her gut twisted. "Excuse me, Zane? The lights?"

He blinked, hard. Then his head swiveled toward her. His eyes were open and unseeing. He looked vaguely past her. "I think I'm blind, dear girl. I must have fallen."

"You've . . ." She paused. "I'll go fetch the doctor. Don't move."

Hours later, after the doctors and nurses had come and gone many times, and Zane's visitors stopped in to deliver well wishes, she found herself alone with him again.

Zane could not see. The doctor had said chances were good he'd never regain his vision, news Zane took in stride. He'd said something polite, even pleasant, that Tania had heard but not heard.

They sat in silence for some time. Earlier Tania had explained how he'd come to be back in his room on Platz Station, and she'd given him a high-level summary of everything that had happened during his long slumber.

"Russell is still confined to quarters on Melville," she said. "He hasn't complained once. Everything he's asked for has been related to the safety and comfort of his crew."

"He's saying all the right things," Zane said.

"Exactly." Tania sighed. "At what point does he cross from saying them to meaning them?"

Zane stared in her direction through drooped eyelids, his eyes wandering in unsettling vagueness. "Who says he will? We gain nothing by believing him and letting him out into the colony. Can you imagine him among our people?"

"No, not really," Tania admitted. "Still, it seems untenable to hold him in a single cabin for the rest of his life."

"So . . . have a trial."

"For what crime?" Tania stood and began to pace at the end of Zane's bed. "A coup against Neil after Neil resigned from the council? For the death of Natalie? That was my fault, I'm afraid, and Natalie was arguably on his side anyway." The words tasted like ash. Strangely enough, when she thought about everything that had happened, it was hard to find anything Russell had actually done wrong. A lot of bravado, and certainly some questionable morals, but in the end the man had been trying to put down an uprising and find the information that drove the traitors.

I just called myself a traitor, she realized. *Why am I letting that pervert plant such seeds?* She wondered for the hundredth time what Skyler would have done had he been the one to receive Russell. Shoot him on the spot, probably. *That would have been a crime worth imprisonment,* she thought, and hated herself for it.

"Offer him a job on one of the farm platforms, picking apples. Tell him if he lasts . . . I'm tired, Tania. Let's talk about something else; this is making me agitated."

She ran through all the mundane colony details, with him saying little. She knew she had his full attention, but so many months lying almost motionless had left him atrophied and easily exhausted.

"Keep talking," he said after a period of awkward silence. "It helps to hear you. Hear anything, really."

"I've run out of things to say," she said. "I could read to you, maybe?"

Zane shook his head. "Uh, no, that would only make me feel more like an invalid. Describe the station. This room. I like to think I remember it, but since I can only see it in my mind now . . ."

She nodded, realized he couldn't see that, and said, "Sure. Of course." Tania glanced around. "The carpet is a lush red," she said.

"Neil's fingerprint."

"Yes, he did love his red floors."

Zane chuckled. "Sorry, go on."

"You've two paintings hung on either side of the door. I'm not familiar with either, but they're both lovely. One depicts a mountain pass with a caravan crossing it. Elephants and footmen, that sort of thing. Forgive me, I'm terrible at this."

"No, no. Go on, please."

Sighing, Tania described the second painting, the doors themselves. She avoided the topic of his desk as long as possible, covered in gifts as it was. Eventually it was the only thing left. "A number of people stopped by with well-wishes for you and left tokens on your desk. Flowers, mostly artificial, of course. Someone even left chocolates well within their Preservall date."

"Oh, now we're getting somewhere. Crack them open, will you?"

Tania could imagine the doctor's reaction if she came in to find Zane eating anything, but she found herself moving across the room. The red box of candies was heart-shaped, with some Portuguese written on it that she assumed professed undying love on Valentine's Day. A scavenged object, of course.

Zane's terminal slate lay under the red box. A tiny LED on the surface of it winked on and off, an indication of waiting messages. "Looks like you have electronic well-wishes, too," Tania said as she tucked the red parcel under one arm and picked up the slate.

"Oh?"

"I could read those to you," she said. "Zane the invalid."

He grunted a laugh. "All right then. Bring it over here so I can thumb it."

She set the chocolates on his bedside table and guided his cold hand to the slate, placing his thumb on the small scanner.

Zane waited for the chime and spoke a word, "Byzantine."

The slate unlocked.

"Chocolate first," Zane said.

She opened the box by feel alone as she scanned the message list. At least fifty people had sent get-well messages since the day Platz Station arrived. Mixed with those were hundreds of automated messages the station had filled his inbox with despite his long absence. No one had had time to turn them off. The realization made Tania wonder if Zane's access to the station computers still worked. If so, they could access archived footage from the security cameras and check out Russell's story.

They could go back further than that, she realized, and watch the assault that killed Neil. Or even further, and simply watch the man go about his daily routine.

She handed Zane a chocolate and he popped it into his mouth like an eleven-year-old would. Tania couldn't help but giggle at the expression of pure joy on the man's face as he chewed.

When her attention returned to the screen, the list of messages had scrolled back to the first one in the list, the oldest message there.

From Neil Platz.

Tania sucked in a sharp breath. The tablet dropped from her hands and slapped against Zane's leg.

"What is it, Tania? Is someone here?"

"No," she said, fetching the slate. "It's . . . there's a message from Neil in here."

"From Neil?"

"Dated the same day he . . ."

Zane grew still. "Read it to me, would you?"

Tania swallowed. "The subject is 'A secret I can't take to the grave.' Still want me to—"

"Yes," Zane said. "It's not like I can do it."

He knew as well as she did that the terminal could be set to audio mode, and handle the task and even be controlled by vocal commands. Zane wanted her to hear whatever it said.

Tania cleared her throat, and read.

no time - enemy @ door
builders came before darwin el. sandeep and i found ship 2238.
he destroyed it before we could truly learn. spare tania of that—

She froze, staring at her father's name, the ramifications of the words falling on her like an avalanche. They knew? Neil and her father knew of the Builders and kept it secret?

"Keep reading, dear," Zane said quietly, placing a reaffirming hand on her arm.

His voice broke her trance, and she read on, her hands shaking.

spare tania of that. sandeep had noble intent, died for it.
u need to know: 6 builder events total. incoming is 4, not 3 as others think.
goodbye brother

Tania set the slate down on the bed and wept.

With each racking sob a new revelation hit her like a hammer.

She felt Zane's hand reach for her shoulder, pull her down to lie next to him. He held her as tight as his frail state allowed, and she buried her face against him to cry.

Her mind blotted out the stream of implications that popped like brazen fireworks. She focused on the face of her father, his easy smile and bright eyes. During her childhood he'd been absent more often than not, always off on some mission for the Platz family, for Neil. Despite his frequent and long ventures, however, he never failed to make her feel loved.

She'd been nine years old when the Darwin Elevator arrived. Until now it had never seemed odd that her family lived in the fledgling city at the time, that Neil's vast estate encompassed Nightcliff, where the cord would make landfall. Neil and her father had been working there for years, building an empire together. Desalination plants, aerospace engineering, manufacturing. All the things they shared passion for, all based in Neil's beloved Australia.

Neil used to tell a story in interviews. She remembered the first time she'd heard it. Neil and Sandeep, sitting together, opposite an interviewer. The woman had asked why they chose Darwin to base the massive expansion of Platz Industries, the company Neil's father had built into an empire. "We flipped a coin, actually," Neil had said. "Heads, Australia. Tails, India. I won, obviously, and thought the Northern Territory would be perfect. Close to Malaysia, close to China beyond. We needed materials and brainpower."

"Why not just build in Kuala Lumpur, or Singapore?" the interviewer had asked.

Neil sat forward. Her father, Sandeep, had been uncharacteristically blank during the exchange. She'd always assumed it was because he'd lost the coin flip, the chance to base their family in his homeland.

"Money," Neil had quipped. "You wouldn't believe the tax breaks we were given." Then he'd laughed with the interviewer. Sandeep had only smiled.

He'd only smiled because he knew the real reason Darwin had been chosen.

"All that time," Tania said to the ceiling. "They knew about

Darwin the whole time. Forty years. They must have . . . God, they must have found the Builder ship when they were practically kids. On their first mission together."

Zane said nothing. He'd hardly reacted at all, in fact.

She whirled on him. The vagueness of his gaze still made her uncomfortable. "Did you know about this, Zane?"

"No," he said, numb. "I always chalked it up to incredible luck. Neil had always been lucky. A gene I didn't inherit, or so I thought."

Somewhere deep within Tania a coldness began to grow. She tried to ignore it, then to willingly banish it, but the cold festered and grew. Neil knew all along. "He knew the whole time," Tania said aloud. "Neil. He knew about Darwin, he knew about the disease."

"Hold on—"

"He knew that billions would die and yet he did nothing."

"No," Zane said. "No, I refuse to believe that. Neil was a ruthless entrepreneur, granted, but he could not have stood by and let something like that happen."

Tania barely heard him. "My mother went to India to fight the disease. My father went, too. Neil could have stopped them."

"Stop that, Tania. Stop it now."

"He let them die to protect . . . to protect . . ."

Zane gripped her arm. "We don't know what happened, Tania. We don't know what they knew. You're speculating." He practically spat the last word, and began to cough.

She thought back to her conversations with Neil in the years after the disease. He'd encouraged her to explore the theory of more Builder events to come. In fact, the more she thought about it, all the key ideas on how to approach the problem had come from him, though he'd always voiced them as offhand comments or random musings. He'd left it to her to form the theory to the point where she felt like it had been her own.

Of course. He had to. If he'd admitted to knowing the Builders' timetable, he admitted to prior knowledge of the space elevator in Darwin. Worse—far, far worse—the disease. Without knowing how much Neil knew it would be unfair to assume he could have done anything to save lives. In hindsight he'd clearly known to buy the land in Nightcliff, to form the vast Spaceworks division of Platz Industries. It stood to reason, then, that he'd known something about the disease. And yet Tania couldn't think of anything Neil had done, overt or covert, to save his friends, his family. He'd allowed her mom to go to India to study the illness. And her father . . .

The lack of details around the circumstances of his death hung in her mind like a black hole.

. . . He destroyed it. . . .

He'd gone on a mission to one of the old, pre-Elevator space stations. Emergency repair work in a time when half the world had died or gone mad. And then the station had been destroyed. An explosion, a freak accident. No survivors.

. . . He destroyed it. . . .

Why? Why not tell the world, Father?

Tania could think of only one reason why her father would destroy the first evidence of alien intelligence: guilt. He and Neil had sat on the information for decades, judging by when the Platz operations began to expand into the Northern Territory. They'd profited immensely. They'd hidden the greatest discovery in history from all of mankind.

. . . He destroyed it. . . .

"What are you thinking, dear girl?" Zane asked, his voice a whisper full of gravel.

She squeezed her eyes closed to wring out the last of her tears. The mental hurdle cleared her mind. *I'm thinking what I'd say to Neil, and my father, if they were still here.* She decided Zane didn't need to know that, after all he'd been through. "Six events," she said. "This ship approaching is the fifth. Which means . . ."

Zane gripped her shoulder, then patted it. "One to go."

"One to go," she agreed. Her dreams of late were of skies filled with thousands of Builder shells, encircling the Earth like Jupiter's rings, arriving yearly, then monthly. Daily. Hourly. Long after she'd died of old age they kept coming, until they blotted out the sun.

One to go, she thought. *At least this will all be over soon. A year from now, give or take.*

"You won't," Zane said, then paused. "You won't tell anyone, will you? About Neil, I mean."

"I'm not sure yet," Tania said honestly.

48

CAPPAGH, IRELAND

DATE IMPRECISE

"GO NOW!"

His second shout broke through Ana's daze so completely that he could see the transformation occur. In the time it took to blink her eyes, Ana hardened. A level of concentration, of intent, absent an instant before, flared into her eyes and the set of her jaw. She took one glance down, pivoted, and leapt down to a ledge a meter below her. Then again to another.

Skyler followed, grinding his teeth with each ache and complaint his body threw at him, unable to match Ana's pace. Below, he saw her reach the point of the sloped column base where she could half-run, half-fall the rest of the way, and then she pulled to a halt, suddenly unsure where to focus her wrath. The shifting red shapes reacted to her presence, fanning out again, darting with dizzying speed across her field of view.

The one prone red smear had still not moved since Vanessa fired into it. The object that had snatched up Vanessa, at least the one Skyler guessed had done so—they all looked the same to him—moved differently than the others. Erratic, as if broken or maimed.

Skyler reached the slope and bounded down the incline. He yanked his ice axe from its belt loop and hefted it in his right hand, making a straight line toward the object that had struck Vanessa. In the corner of his eye he saw Ana glance toward him and begin to move his way.

The red object loomed in front of Skyler, still dancing about in impossible, abrupt movements. Suddenly it was right in front of him. He roared and swung down.

Skyler's axe hit the shape with no result at first, as if he'd hit nothing but air. Then a resistance slowed the axe blade, and he felt as if he'd just swung down on a giant pillow. At the point his blade stopped and should have rebounded, Skyler saw the red-hued morass curl and conform around him. With an alien *pop*, the field surrounded and then consumed him, just as the dome had done when he entered.

Just before becoming enveloped, Skyler saw the red shape bulge and something dart out. He saw enough to register Vanessa tumbling away before he was inside.

And then he understood. These were pockets of time, or, rather, fields identical to the dome itself, only much smaller and on a different clock.

A subhuman stood scant centimeters away. Blood trailed from the corner of its mouth, and it held a patch of Vanessa's shirtsleeve in one clenched, black-coated fist. And though his former opponent had just dived aside, the creature already had turned itself toward Skyler, coiled, and swung.

Unfortunately for the creature, it had aimed its attack based on Skyler's speed before he'd entered the faster-moving pocket. Skyler entered to see the fist, black to the wrist, swing wide past his head. The being's upper arm smacked against Skyler's head with no real force behind it.

Their eyes were inches apart. Skyler smelled the foul stench on its breath, saw the individual capillaries in its bloodshot eyes.

Movement behind it caught Skyler's attention. Vanessa, or so he assumed, for the red blob that surrounded him made everything beyond murky. She bounded toward the creature's back in slow motion, constrained by the slower time scale just outside the red pocket that seemed to cling to the subhuman.

"Deaaaattthhhh," the creature hissed, whipping Skyler's attention back.

"You first." He swung up with his axe, intending to spike the sub's abdomen. But it bounded back in the same instant. The head of the axe sailed upward, slicing the creature's chin open in a spray of blood.

The being howled. It swiped one hand in reflexive counterattack while Skyler's arm still extended upward from his swing. The black-coated fist caught him in the side just above the waist, a solid blow that drove Skyler to one knee.

Blood dripping from its chin, the subhuman reeled back and lifted its other arm to swing down on Skyler's head.

Then Vanessa's form pressed into the border of the red aura and she popped through. She came in low, barreled into the back of the creature's legs, and lifted upward all in one motion. The surprised subhuman vaulted into the air and flipped completely over, landing face-first in the churned earth.

Twenty years of jujitsu, Skyler had time to think.

Vanessa wasted no time. She spun and jumped simultaneously, twisting in midair. She landed on the creature's back with both knees and Skyler heard the air rush from the subhuman's lungs just before Vanessa gripped its head with both hands and twisted savagely.

The animal went limp.

"Thanks," Skyler croaked.

"You okay?" Vanessa asked.

"Where's Ana?"

She shook her head, didn't know.

"Where's your gun?"

Vanessa shook her head again, standing up. "Dropped it somewhere."

The ground beneath their feet rumbled. Around them vague shapes moved around the dome floor. Some slow, some at what felt more like real time. All were too obscure to make out from within their own time-shifted pocket. Skyler glanced down at his axe, stood, and hefted it. He looked at Vanessa.

She had no axe, but when she saw him ready his she seemed to suddenly understand the situation they were in. She reached to her calf and unholstered a hunting knife. The carbon-coated blade took on the color of blood inside the red field.

"Find Ana," Skyler said, "and find that Builder object. Then we go."

"Agreed." Then, "Hey. Move with your axe held out before you. Use their speed against them."

He nodded.

Again the floor of the dome trembled. A crack shot across the ground just centimeters from Skyler's feet. He leapt back on instinct as the fracture widened. It went on, the gap as wide as a hand, then almost a full meter in places. Rock and clumps of soil tumbled in.

Skyler felt a pressure against his back and realized too late that he'd come to the edge of the red pocket, which seemed . . .

"The red blob," Skyler blurted. "It's attached to them somehow."

It seemed patently obvious when he said it, but up until that moment he'd hoped that perhaps it would move with him as he went after the others. No such luck.

Vanessa looked down at the creature by her feet, then back at him. He had enough time to see her grin before he popped through the shifting edge of the red space and back into the "normal" time frame of the dome.

His mind scrambled again, but the effect was starting to become something he could manage now, like a pilot learning to handle the press of g-forces. He hunkered, forcing himself to stop and focus on everything and nothing until the neurons in his brain started to fire in synchronicity again.

Ana was nowhere to be seen. All about him the reddish smears of time flowed between the chunks of upthrust earth and rock. He saw one misjudge its path and drop into a crevice formed in the last jolt the dome experienced. There were some purple auras among the red now, moving at a speed closer to reality. In a few places, blue-hued shapes were just starting to lift out of their craters, implying that the color and rate of time's passage were linked. He filed that and swung his attention to the red fields again. A few were close by, and from what he knew of being inside the accelerated pocket, the world outside was not much more clear than shadows and hazy forms. If he stayed far enough away, they'd miss him. That explained, he thought, their erratic movement. They were searching, and as far as he could tell none were moving outside the dome and the aura towers that encircled it.

He heard movement behind and spun about too late. A red was speeding past diagonally to him, and when it came within a few meters the shape's lead tendrils seemed to flow down invisible channels that led straight to Skyler.

Unaware he'd been doing so, he found he held the axe in front of him as Vanessa had suggested. The red blob hit him, enveloped him, forcing his mind to snap once again between two clocks. He shuddered and put all his thought into holding on to the axe as the creature within the ruby cavity slammed into him.

The tactic did not work.

For all Skyler's effort, the subhuman's accelerated viewpoint gave it plenty of time to see his outstretched weapon and shift its position just enough to avoid impaling itself. The sub hit him shoulder to shoulder, a glancing impact that sent them both into a spin. The creature couldn't handle its own momentum and continued past, its body twisting over in midair as it fell away.

Skyler lost his grip on the axe and spun in place, his right leg twisting painfully beneath him. Before he could fall himself the creature moved far enough away that it took its red aura with it, and Skyler found himself thrust back into the slower reality of the dome one more time.

"Stop fucking doing that!" he shouted as he landed painfully on his right knee. He forced himself up in time to see the pocket of red racing toward him again.

And to his left, another came.

Skyler had no time to even look for his axe. He did the only thing he could think of and dove forward into a tucked roll. He felt the painful yet gratifying smack of kneecaps against his back as the charging creature toppled over him, moving too fast within its own frame of reference to stop itself.

Entry into another red aura made Skyler feel more and more like he'd gulped down a bottle of Darwin's worst cider and then twirled in circles for half a goddamn century. He fought to concentrate, felt a momentary panic that he'd *truly* lost track of time. Struggling to his feet, Skyler took an unsteady step toward his enemy if only just to stay within its portable time field. The sub flailed on the ground near him and sprang to its feet just as Skyler approached.

Skyler swung, missed badly. The creature lashed out with a splay of ragged, black-clad fingers and clipped him across the chest.

Something moved to his left and Skyler glanced just in time to see another red shape merging with his. This creature stood smaller than the first, using all fours to run. When it came inside, the two subhumans grunted at each other and fanned out slightly. Sensing the flanking tactic, Skyler stepped back as well, intent to keep both in front of him somehow. He toyed with the idea of running but knew he'd only step outside their time frame and appear as a comically slow jogger from their point of view. They could stroll after him and lick their lips before pouncing.

Terror gripped his heart and squeezed when a third red shape began to push inside the boundary, and Skyler had all but resigned himself to death when he saw—

—*her*.

Ana.

Ana, with a submachine gun that barked thunder and spat fire.

Ana, with two severed black hands tied to her belt, still dripping blood.

Ana, screaming. An incoherent war cry that Skyler felt sure would have given the subhumans pause had they lived to hear it. Her bullets ripped across the chest of the first and the face of the second. Both toppled to the ground before they could even turn to face her.

Ana.

Skyler couldn't take his eyes off the two dismembered hands hanging from her belt. His mouth opened, the question forming and dying, self-evident.

A third creature ventured into the dome within the dome and she shot it, too: a burst that took the being in its heart and sent it toppling backward. The gun clicked, empty.

Then a fourth enemy raced in. In one smooth motion, Ana flipped the gun around in her hands and clubbed the creature so hard in the face that teeth, maybe bone, maybe both, sprayed out.

Lovely Ana. Blood-spattered and full of rage and the best thing Skyler had ever seen.

"Holy *shit*," Skyler managed to say.

"Are you just going to sit there?" she shot back between a quick gasp for air. "Get a pair of hands, they—"

The fifth subhuman to enter blindsided her. It came in fast and low, galloping on hands and feet, and plowed hard into Ana's lower back. She shrieked and went down hard, her face smacking into the ground without the benefit of raised hands to break her fall.

Her attacker rolled past, got up, and turned to finish its work.

"Hey!" Skyler shouted at it. "Over here!"

Ana hadn't moved. The creature decided she was no threat and turned to Skyler. He had no weapon other than a small utility knife in his back pocket, too hard to fish out and deploy. Vanessa's spent rifle lay in the dirt off to Skyler's left where Ana had dropped it. He stepped toward it and the subhuman matched his motion plus a half step forward, closing the gap. It reared up to walk on just its legs now.

"Right," Skyler said, and moved in with clenched fists. He jabbed first with his left then threw a haymaker with his right that caught the being on its ear. It staggered, recovered, stepped in, and shoved unexpectedly with both hands, pushing Skyler back a few steps. He almost fell, one foot brushing the edge of a deep gash in the ground.

Nowhere to retreat, he realized.

Ana still lay prone.

The creature howled and came at him again. Skyler saw movement behind it and knew what to do. *Oldest trick in the book.*

He dropped to his knees and turned.

Vanessa, racing through the edge of the red space and up behind the creature, leapt and kicked with both legs. She hit it perfectly, right between the shoulder blades. With a yelp of surprise and primal understanding the subhuman toppled over Skyler and into the freshly formed ravine behind him. It fell four meters before smashing against the bottom of the cleft, one leg splayed out at an impossible angle. The sub cried out once in pain and then went still.

"Is that all of them?" he asked. He was breathing hard, blood pounding in his ears, the mother of all headaches looming like a storm on the horizon.

"Not even close," Vanessa said. She wiped sweat from her brow and took in the space around them, her breath catching in her throat at the sight of Ana's limp body.

Skyler was already moving. "Cover me."

"Sure."

He slid to his knees at Ana's side and felt for a pulse. He had to press hard on her neck to filter out his own pounding blood and the near-constant vibration of the dome itself, and as he did, Ana groaned slightly. Ever so slightly, but it was enough.

"Skyler," Vanessa said, sounding suddenly far away.

He glanced up. Vanessa stood a few meters off to his side, crouched down and back on her heels. She stared through narrow eyes and Skyler followed the gaze.

The reddish time field associated with the hands Ana had on her belt had faded to almost nothing, dissipating even as Skyler watched until it was gone.

Then he stood as well and took a step back from Ana. Around them loomed the reddish-hued pockets of death of a half-dozen subhumans. As they converged their auras merged like droplets of blood coalescing.

The creature in the middle of the line of enemies was enormous. A head taller than even Samantha and half again as wide. A wall of corded muscle, scars, and filth, all pulled forward by a wide grin of violent ecstasy.

Skyler glanced around. He had no weapon at all, and Ana to protect as much as himself. He looked for anything. A rock, a stick, anything at all, and saw nothing save for the earth at his feet and the edge of the dome itself a few meters away.

The creatures surged forward.

One leapt high, its wild gaze on Ana.

Vanessa screamed, a sub racing at her low.

The monster pack leader roared with bloodlust.

Skyler . . .

The edge of the dome, meters away.

Skyler turned and ran.

* * *

He burst through the edge of the dome and fell into the mud beyond, his mind feeling like so much shredded cheese.

Rain spattered against his face and he let it. He stayed in the mud for a few long minutes and let the water run into his mouth, until he could no longer taste blood.

When his brain seemed to figure out what time meant again, he sat up, pushed himself to his feet, wiped his hands, and took off his climbing harness. He laid the gear on the ground very deliberately.

Then he turned toward the path that led to the farmhouse.

"Right, then," he muttered. "Enough is enough."

Skyler ran as fast as his legs would carry him, which wasn't especially fast at first, but he gained momentum with each step.

At the farmhouse he called out for Pablo, but the man was not around. No matter, Skyler decided, and set to work.

"You motherfuckers want to play with time?" he said to the walls as he dressed a scrape on his arm. "I'll show you how it's done."

Six minutes later he left the cottage again. Relaxed, fed, and bandaged.

And armed to the teeth.

Skyler punched back inside the dome with a submachine gun in each hand.

The scene before him was almost exactly as he'd left it, fifteen minutes earlier. Half a second had passed inside.

He shot the leaping sub first. It hadn't even landed yet from a jump that began fifteen minutes earlier. *Surprise, asshole.* The creature's landing turned into a lifeless belly flop, centimeters from Ana's side.

"Down!" he shouted to Vanessa.

She dropped flat.

Skyler opened fire with both weapons, spraying gunfire indiscriminately before him. The guns pounded back against his palms, sending shock waves of pain up his arms and into his back. He ignored it utterly, held the triggers down. Someone was shouting. Himself, he realized with unexpected glee.

Before him the subhumans fell like cut weeds.

He fired until both guns were spent. Shell casings tumbled in the dirt around him.

When the clips ran dry, Skyler dropped both weapons unceremoniously and whipped around the third from his back.

Only the giant subhuman still stood, standing amid the corpses of its pack. It flexed two mighty arms in a show of rage and howled at Skyler. Then it took a long step forward.

Skyler shook his head. "Enough. Is. *Enough*."

He fired the grenade launcher and the subhuman's head exploded in a shower of bone and blood.

It fell to its knees and collapsed forward in an earth-shaking thud. A sudden, satisfying silence followed.

Vanessa was standing behind him, he realized. "Pistols, at my belt. Take them."

She drew both weapons and stepped to his side. "I had just enough time to think you'd abandoned us before you reappeared," she said breathlessly.

"I felt a little underprepared, decided to change the odds."

She somehow managed a smile. "You look more ridiculous than any of those sensory action heroes."

"You're one to talk," he said. "Twenty years of jujitsu, eh?"

"And finally useful."

"Well, stay sharp. We're not done."

Vanessa's face tightened. She nodded with grim determination. "I'll take Ana outside."

"No," Skyler said, too stern. At Vanessa's surprised look he added, "Time's racing forward out there. If her injury is as bad as I think, every second is going to count. Stay here with her while I finish this."

"Let's just get out of here; there's nothing—"

"Not quite yet. All of this was to protect that damn object, and we're bloody well leaving with it."

Vanessa swallowed. "Okay."

All that remained was details. Skyler found no more red-hued fields whooshing about the dome, only the purples—which he shot—and some blues that moved too slowly to bother with. He simply walked around them.

The dome continued to shake. At the center Skyler saw the earthen pillar crack, then collapse into a small avalanche of debris. When the dust settled, he saw the thing he'd expected to find from the beginning.

Half-buried in the collapsed pillar's base was a Builder ship, nose down, the back half of it splayed open like a charred flower. Skyler gave it a once-over and decided to ignore it. The hourglass-shaped object that had been placed so deliberately upon the peak of the spire was the important part, he knew with instinctual certainty.

He found the object halfway out toward the dome's edge, in a crater that had once presumably contained one of the chromatic time fields. In some delicious irony, the alien object had killed a subhuman when it fell into the depression. The creature lay just beside the thing, its head crushed.

"Get ready, Vanessa!" he shouted over his shoulder. "Coming to you!"

She hollered back in acknowledgment as Skyler lifted, pushed, and pulled the heavy object toward the edge of the dome where Vanessa and Ana waited. He half-hoped to see his young companion sitting up, alert, but she still lay exactly as she had.

"She's got a lot of bruising on her lower back and abdomen," Vanessa said grimly.

Skyler gave a single nod. "We're going to have to move her." He tried to sound strong, and thought he'd failed miserably.

Despite the reluctance in her eyes, Vanessa nodded.

"We'll head straight back to Belém and get her to the doctors. How are we doing on time?"

She glanced at her watch as if she'd forgotten all about it. "February," she said.

The weight of it all suddenly crashed in on Skyler like the collapse of the pillar he'd witnessed. The alien place, the violence, and poor Ana . . . He fought to get his ragged breaths under control. Vanessa placed a calming hand on the center of his back.

"C'mon," he said. "We're almost out of time."

49

DARWIN, AUSTRALIA

24.FEB.2285

The invitation arrived during the night.

Samantha woke to a soft rap at her door. Her head swam from the lingering effects of alcohol and a sudden powerful sensation of déjà vu. An attempt to tell whoever knocked to fuck off came out as a dry croak, and she fumbled about in the dark for her canteen. She found it, drank, and threw it at the door.

"Fuck off!" she said. No one had woken her in the middle of the night like this since Grillo's blitz on the last holdout neighborhood in Darwin. She didn't need another night like that. Not tonight, not ever.

"It's Skadz, Sammy. Open up."

She pinched the bridge of her nose and sat up. Sweat-soaked sheets fell away from her, the result of a blisteringly hot night and her body's attempt to discharge the liquor by any means available. She smelled her armpit and winced. "What the hell do you want?"

"I need you to come with me."

She growled and stumbled to the door of her tiny room. She pulled the door open a crack and looked at her old friend. His eyes were like twin moons against his dark skin, and the dark hangar beyond. "Shouldn't you be as wasted as me? God, I've never seen you drink like you did last night."

It had been a celebration, of sorts. Grillo's position as head of the Jacobite Church cemented, along with official admission of his rule over Darwin and the space elevator. The story went that Platz Station had suffered a full and sudden depressurization and loss of spin. All hands lost, the station scuttled due to damage during the event.

Blackfield, dead.

Sam suspected bullshit from the start but couldn't bring herself to call Grillo out on it. What difference would it make? The man had played his cards and won, and now everyone knew.

The Nightcliff guards stationed at the airport had given everyone a respite from the alcohol ban, and even joined in the forced revelry. The four who shared the hangar with her were all still asleep at the card table below.

Things had gotten . . . a bit wild, even by Sam's lofty standards. She had a vague recollection of diving naked from the catwalk onto a pile of couch cushions below, part of a game to see who could land the farthest from the raised walkway. The loser had to remove an item of clothing. It made sense at the time.

At least she hadn't woken with one of the Nightcliff goons in her bed. Or worse, Skadz.

Sam's head pounded. She felt like she'd been run over by a truck. Skadz, on the other hand, looked alert. Energized. It infuriated her.

"I was drinking water," he said.

"Huh?"

"All night. Water. I tried to tell you to do the same but you had a head start."

She laughed in his face. "Why would I want to drink water?" she asked, and took a sip from her canteen.

"Because we have a meeting to attend. Like I said, I tried to tell you."

"A meeting? Where?"

"In the city."

Samantha laughed again, and tapped her skull. "You go. I'm

still wandering the fun house up here. Besides, I suspect you're just going to try to convince me to bug out with you and leave the city behind." He'd broached the idea a few times since Grillo took the city. Parts of it appealed to her, parts didn't. Mostly, she found that if she ignored anything happening beyond the fence that surrounded the airport, things weren't all bad. The missions were boring, sure, but it beat a life of hiking around and living off the land.

"That's not it at all," he said. "It's about Skyler."

They slipped out through a loose section of the fence on the airport's north side, avoiding the still-guarded main gate.

Skadz ushered her along at a brisk walk. The pace, the fresh air, helped clear Samantha's head enough that soon she didn't need to lean on her friend. Her clothes still clung to her like a clumsy lover, damp with sweat and the hot sticky air of Darwin's slums. She could smell herself and felt vaguely embarrassed at how disgusting she must be, but the worry vanished when Skadz led her into the thick press of the Maze.

The stench of the place hit her like a wall. Shit and piss, incense and hookah, fresh rain and stagnant murky puddles all blended together in the cauldron of a district. Whatever odor she brought to the mix would be a marked improvement.

"I'm gonna be sick," she said just in time to release the meager contents of her stomach onto a brick wall. Skadz held her wet strands of blond hair out of her face, and stood watch while she retched a second time.

Even at this hour, people were wandering by. Not many, though; not like before. The bustle and energy of the Maze seemed gone, and not due to the time of night. The people Sam saw were huddled, dark shapes. Heads down and shoulders slumped, their gaze never wavering from the ground in front of them.

Skadz matched their hunkered, depressed posture and guided her through the twisted mess of alleys. Twice she smacked her forehead on low pipes before she got the hint and bent over.

Three Vietnamese men in soiled clothes came from a doorway and said something to Skadz. A threat of some sort, too quick for

Sam to follow. Skadz didn't break stride. A gun appeared in his hand in response, and they retreated back into the shadow.

"That kinda shit hardly ever happens here anymore," he muttered a few sharp turns later. "The Jakes have this place locked down."

"Don't call them the Jakes," Sam said. She'd heard the slang and chastised Skadz twice already for using it. To Sam it tarnished the memory of her sniper, her friend. The term might be widespread and unstoppable, but that didn't mean she had to hear it from friends.

"Hell. Sorry," Skadz said.

After another dizzying set of turns they stumbled into a wide merger of alleys. Wide by the Maze's standards. Sam recognized it. The café, Clarke's, where Prumble had paid them for the Japan mission, stood at one corner, dark and uninviting.

Skadz walked up to the door and rapped it twice. Seconds later they heard a steel gate behind the door retract. Then the latch made a series of clicks and the door swung open. He said something in a language Sam didn't know, and the old woman within responded in kind with a motherly tone. She ushered the two of them in and pointed at a stairwell half-hidden behind an ornate drape that hung from the wall next to her shop counter.

Skadz went through and Samantha followed him. The stairwell was pitch-black, the narrow steps precarious. At the top a candle lit the hallway. Wood floors creaked under their feet as Skadz strolled calmly to a door. He entered without knocking.

Inside, two men sat on a faded Afghan carpet. One was gaunt, with stringy gray hair and a thin face that seemed stretched across the skull below. He looked vaguely familiar.

The other man was Prumble.

Her hug turned into something of a tackle. Prumble laughed as they fell back against the wall, his girth just enough to save him from toppling over under her affectionate assault.

"Sammy, Sammy," he said, and clapped her on the back.

She released him and put her hands on her hips. "Where the fuck have you been?"

"Right here," he said. "Lying low, gone to ground. The shadow, the snake."

A giggle escaped her lips. "Stealth has never been your strong suit."

"I have a strong suit?"

"You tell me."

Prumble looked up at the ceiling. "Hmm. I have a purple suit with yellow pinstripes. That's pretty strong."

"Seriously, where have you been? You couldn't say hello?"

"Here," he said, the mirth not entirely gone from his pudgy face. "I became an investor in this scraper's rooftop garden, and in the café below. Honestly I haven't left in almost two years, Sam. Haven't spoken to anyone until these two sought me out. I'm still a wanted man, though that particular attribute seems to be waning."

The thin, sickly man next to him shuffled slightly.

"Who's this?" Sam asked.

"Meet Kip Osmak," Prumble said. "Communications officer in Nightcliff Control, former assistant to Russell Blackfield, and longtime supplier of Orbital wish lists to myself."

"Hello," the man said.

Sam looked him up and down, reassessing her opinion. "Nightcliff comm, huh? Must be interesting work."

"I hear many things," Kip said, as if this was a curse. "Interesting things."

"Which brings us," Skadz said, "to the reason for this little reunion. Tell her what you told us, Kip."

Before the slight man could speak, the old woman from downstairs came in with a fresh pot of Darjeeling tea and a plate of pasty white buns dappled with spice. She placed them in the center of the small room and left without a word.

"Many thanks, Renuka," Prumble said as the door clicked closed. "Sit, everyone."

Sam took a cushion near the door, next to Skadz. Prumble sat opposite them, with Kip sandwiched between the giant man and the wall.

"Damn that tea smells good," Skadz said, pouring a cup.

"Good enough to mask my flatulence," Prumble said. He

winked at Samantha. "Kip, speak. I'll sample these buns for dangerous poisons while you tell your tale."

"As Mr. Prumble said," Kip began, "I have a position in the control tower within Nightcliff, and thus access to—"

Prumble held up his hand and Kip went silent. "Christ, man, skip to the good part."

Kip gave a shy nod, his eyes downcast. "Of course. Well, you see, after the schism between Mr. Blackfield and Neil Platz, I—"

"Skyler's alive," Prumble said over the man. "There's a new space elevator over in Brazil, and Skyler's there. They're all there, the runaways, the traitors."

"I . . . holy shit," Sam said. She'd known somehow, but it had always felt more like a childish hope than firm conviction, like a kid who clings to the idea of Santa Claus long after the other children have accepted reality and moved on.

"It gets better," Skadz said. "Well, it gets crazier."

"Oh?"

Kip looked to Prumble, as if seeking permission to speak. This time Prumble nodded at him and sat back.

"Blackfield is there, too," Kip said. "He took Platz Station and joined up with the colony, along with everyone aboard, after the Jakes tried and failed to take over the station."

He let the words sink in for a moment, and Sam felt the reality Grillo and his people had crafted shatter and fall away. For all of Grillo's supposed virtue, he wasn't above a little propaganda to suit his cause. But Skyler and Blackfield, together? On the same side? That she found impossible to believe.

"That ain't the crazy bit," Skadz said.

"It's pretty fucking crazy," Sam said.

"Well, it ain't it."

"In a few days," Kip said, "Grillo and his people will begin something called 'Project Sanctify.'"

Samantha stared at him. "I don't like it already."

"Grillo, his followers, see the Darwin Elevator as a gift from God," Kip said. "They're now aware of the Elevator in Brazil, and as you can probably guess they're not thrilled with the idea."

"Suddenly our Elevator ain't so special," Skadz said. "Bible didn't say 'Jacob's *Ladders*,' yeah?"

Prumble leaned in. "Grillo went to all this trouble to steal the Darwin Elevator from Blackfield, to purify it, you could say, only to find the job's only half-done."

"Fuck," Sam said.

"Indeed."

"So Grillo's going to try to capture that one, as well."

"No," Kip said. "From what I hear, Project Sanctify is about eliminating the colony, and the other Elevator."

"Seems they think it's the devil's work," Skadz said. "Or some shit. The Anti-Elevator."

"Okay," Sam said slowly. "You're right. That's officially crazy."

"Well, Sammy, Kip has even more than that," Skadz said.

An apologetic look crossed the thin man's face when Sam turned her full attention to him.

"Tell her the rest," Prumble said to him.

Kip nodded. "Sanctify is bigger than that. Arrangements are being made to transfer personnel on Darwin's stations down here. Soon only the Jacobite faithful will be allowed in orbit. Anything else is considered blasphemous, apparently." Before Sam could say anything, Kip went on, gaining his voice the more he spoke. "And in the coming weeks, decrees will be announced. Laws to govern Darwin, the city. All of us."

"Jacobite laws," Prumble said. "You can imagine how liberal they are."

Skadz plucked a white bun from the plate. "We're going to go from anarchy to religious fascism. Extreme to bloody fucking extreme, Sammy."

She felt a weight begin to press on her shoulders. A burden of guilt, and unspoken accusation. She'd been complicit in Grillo's rise. She'd helped him deliver on his vision of a prosperous Darwin, and had closed her eyes to what that would mean in the end. Theocracy. Russell Blackfield was no doubt ruthless and dictatorial, but for the most part he'd let people go about their lives. As long as nothing threatened the Elevator, he'd left Darwin to its own devices. It was a shitty way to run the last bastion of humanity, but the idea of living under a totalitarian cult of religious freaks held even less appeal.

The three men were staring at her, waiting. None of them

needed to voice the question; she could see it on all three faces. Kip she couldn't care less about, but to see that accusation on Prumble's face, on Skadz's, cut like a knife.

"I'm on your side," she said. "I've been an idiot, yes, but I'm on your side."

Prumble and Skadz exchanged a glance. "Happy to hear you say that, Sammy," Skadz said.

"So," she said, "I assume we're not just here to gossip. What's the plan? Run for Brazil? Try to stop Grillo?"

"Whoa, now hang on," Skadz said. "Kip isn't done. There's more."

"Goddamn, guys. I don't know if I can handle more," she said.

Now Kip leaned in. His expression changed. He glanced at each of them with sudden familiarity, as if he'd gone from outsider to conspirator. Near enough the truth, Sam realized.

"I still have contact with Platz Station," he said. "A friend there. Our messages are relayed through . . . it doesn't matter, the point is that exchanging information is difficult. Sporadic, terse."

Prumble cut in again. "It's the Builders, Samantha. They're back."

Kip nodded, unfazed at having his big announcement stolen by the big man. "My contact doesn't know much, just that the ship is 'huge,' and almost here."

"Safe to assume," Skadz said, "that Grillo is going to want to be on top of that shit this time around."

Sam found herself nodding. "Equally safe to assume," she said, "that we'd rather it be Skyler, and Tania Sharma? I'm guessing she's with him?"

"She runs things over there," Kip said.

"Wonder if Sky's getting a piece of that action," Skadz mused.

"Mmm," Prumble said. "There's a mental image. Lucky bastard."

"Knock it off, perverts," Sam said.

Prumble mocked surprise. "We meant a piece of the leadership!"

"Right, and I suppose you think he should grab on to that leadership by the ponytail and ride it till sunrise." She let their chuckles fade until the tension rolled back into the room like a dense fog. "So, what are we talking about? The four of us form a ragtag band of freedom fighters to overthrow Grillo and his freak brigade? A plucky group of misfits that stage another coup in Darwin because third time's a charm?"

Prumble shook his head. "I had in mind something more like agents provocateurs," he said. "We can make the man's life very difficult. Very difficult indeed."

Samantha thought of her time aboard Gateway with Kelly. There'd been a visceral satisfaction from playing spoiler there, mucking about behind the scenes. The thought of Kelly filled her with a sudden sorrow. One way or another, rescuing her needed to be part of the plan. Sam filed that for another day.

"In other words," Skadz said soberly, "give Skyler a fighting chance when the shit hits the fan."

"And if we fail?" she asked.

Skadz grinned. "Don't know about you wags, but if the freak train won't stop, I'm getting the bloody hell off."

50

BLACK LEVEL STATION

7.MAR.2285

The Builder ship settled into high geostationary orbit above North Africa, and its size defied imagination.

Even viewed through the remote repair craft, Tania had to rely on radar to confirm the dimensions. She glanced at those numbers every few minutes, hoping they were just confused, hoping the LIDAR readings were somehow being baffled by the surface material of the massive vessel.

The numbers didn't change. Roughly six kilometers from the tapered tip that pointed down toward Earth up to the bulbous end. In shape it resembled a teardrop pointed in the wrong direction—the vessel had flipped around in the last days before arrival—except that the nose of the spherical end did jut out slightly.

There were many protrusions. This surprised Tania, as neither of the previous shell ships had similar features. The extensions were tucked under the main bulb, pointing down toward Earth. Each spike looked small and flimsy compared to the hulking vessel, until Tania estimated the length of the longest among them at half a kilometer. The sizes varied, and if she flipped the image the extensions looked like a cityscape, unlit and dead like the great cities of Earth.

The drone continued to drift in closer. Tim sat in front of Tania in Black Level's control room, operating the automated craft from a touchscreen. He tapped a bright red icon and on the screen Tania could see a puff of exhaust shoot out toward the alien ship. Braking thrust. The craft slowed a bit, now five hundred kilometers away from mass.

"Bring it to a stop at fifty klicks," Tania said.

"Okay."

Off to one side of the room, Greg and Marcus huddled in front of another screen, studying high-resolution shots. They panned and zoomed the images on their monitor, talking quietly between themselves.

A pang of nostalgia warmed Tania. She'd spent many long nights working in this room, studying gamma-ray bursts or impact events on moons in the outer solar system. It felt good to be back here, engaged in science again. She'd grown tired of waiting on pins and needles for word from Skyler. He and his companions were still inside that dome. They'd failed to emerge in time for the event date, and with each additional hour they remained inside, Tania found her hope fading like a dying fire. She'd be stirring embers soon.

It also felt good to be away from Melville and the proximity to Russell Blackfield. Away from Platz Station, too. Zane continued to recover, but their conversations had been awkward since they'd read Neil's final letter.

Tania had left all that behind for now. Everything else could wait.

"Any signs of activity?" she asked Greg and Marcus.

Without looking back, Greg dismissed her with a wave. "All quiet."

"Signs of cratering on the bulbous end," Marcus said.

Greg snorted. "That's what she . . . um, never mind."

Tania sighed in frustration and turned to the main screen again. Cratering? That didn't mesh with the Builders' previous smooth-surfaced arrivals. It made sense, though. If this craft had crossed the vast distance between stars at high speed some erosion was to be expected. Hell, total annihilation was the expected result, without some kind of protective aura.

She smiled privately. Even now, with the auras in Darwin and Belém, plus the miniature versions projected by the towers, she still couldn't put herself in the mindset of what the Builders were technically capable of. Cratering, though, implied they weren't gods. Even such an advanced race couldn't send such a large ship this far completely unscathed. She found a little comfort in that.

The drone continued toward the ship at 500 kilometers per hour. Already the object dominated the screen, and the drone was still an hour away from reaching it.

The lack of activity bothered her. No third Elevator, no stream of packages racing down to the planet below, no sign of the invasion fleet that Neil Platz once predicted. Nothing. *Why so big, then?* Tania still had no idea what the Builders planned to do, but she couldn't imagine sending such a massive object across the vast emptiness for no reason at all.

"Good thing it slowed down," Tim said. "That thing would have demolished the planet if it had kept coming at its initial speed."

"They already demolished the planet," she shot back, followed by a squeeze on his shoulder to assure him she knew what he'd meant.

When first detected, the alien craft had been approaching Earth at incredible speed, already decelerating. They'd not spotted it early enough to know the top speed, but when their scope did find the slowing vessel its velocity was a breathtaking 50,000 kilometers per second. More amazing to Tania was that the method of thrust used to slow the ship, whatever it might have been, produced no visible light. The other detectors were off the charts, but in visible light the gigantic ship had been nearly invisible.

An hour passed. Tania stood, impassive, unable to sit or rest. Part of her wished the tiny station had a gun range. It had been one of the great surprises of her life, days earlier, to find out how mind-clearing target practice could be. Absently she rubbed at her palm, still sore from where the pistol had recoiled against her before she'd learned how to absorb the impact. Karl's instruction had been remarkably good. She had to force herself to blink now and then when her eyes ached from staring at the display. The ship grew and grew until its surface filled the entire screen, and still it was sixty kilometers away from the drone.

Tim hit the braking thrusters again. He'd programmed the sequence, and sat back now as the drone's computer released pulses of exhaust every few seconds, until it came to a stop. A fuel indicator in the corner of the main monitor indicated that just over 80 percent remained. Plenty to circle the vessel a few times before coming back.

"Let's take a look around," she said.

The smooth surface of the Builder ship drifted past the drone as if the tiny craft were floating across a still ocean at night. The sun had dipped below the horizon an hour earlier, plunging the vessel into shadow that would persist until morning. Tim suggested moving in closer and using the drone's searchlight, but that would burn power Tania would rather save, and besides, she still felt uncomfortable with getting too close to the new ship until they knew more about it.

She felt anxious, often pacing the room, her eyes never leaving the screen. She convinced herself that at any moment some calamity would unfold. That those protrusions pointing at Earth were so many gun barrels, and in a sudden bright instant the Builders would pulverize the planet below. Or that they were launch tubes, from which thousands of tiny attack ships would swarm out like wasps and fan across the globe, eradicating the few humans who remained.

When it occurred to her that all the scenarios running through her mind were doomsday ones, she forced herself to stop speculating and focus on the facts in front of her.

"Take a look at this," Marcus said.

Tania broke her gaze away from the main screen and walked over to the two men. Greg moved aside a bit to make room for her.

A close-up image of the pockmarked end of the ship, the end that pointed away from Earth now, filled the screen. Marcus tapped the screen and the image changed. Another portion of the ship, she guessed, with distinctly fewer craters and gouges.

Marcus flipped back to the first image, then bounced between them in rapid succession. After a dozen cycles, Tania realized they were looking at the same section of the ship's surface. Some of the craters were in the same position in both images, only smaller in the second picture.

"It's healing," she said.

"Yup!"

Greg whistled. "Maybe they can do something for your scalp, Marcus."

"Maybe they can do something for your mom's—"

Tania elbowed him. "This is a historic moment, gentlemen. Please, act like it."

Marcus repeated her words under his breath in an exaggerated, mocking tone. He brought up additional pairs of images and began to cycle them. Each showed the same change. Then he tried a pair of images from the tail end of the craft, the end pointing down at the planet. It looked the same, but then, it didn't have the scarring in the first place.

"What about the naughty bits," Greg said. "Er, sorry, Tania. The, um, raised posterior protrusions."

Tania smirked despite herself. Marcus snorted a juvenile laugh and went back to a library view of all the images taken so far. He selected two. No changes between them, but seeing the extensions close-up, Tania realized they had hints of grooves in their surfaces, like the aura towers.

An hour later dawn broke and warm light bathed the alien ship. The drone made another circuit of the huge mass, shifting its path to look up at it from below.

"Guys," Tim said, "I found something." Then, "Wow."

Tania sat with Greg, while Marcus slept in a curled ball on the floor behind them. She looked up, startled, and crossed back to the center of the room. Greg followed her, and Marcus stirred as if sensing the change in mood within the room.

"What is that?" Greg asked.

On the screen, nestled between four of the huge spikes that jutted from the underside of the main bulb, was a hexagonal mark. A portion of the ship's surface was darker than the rest, with five perfectly straight edges forming a rough circle. Inset within the hexagon was another, smaller one. Tim enlarged that portion of the image while simultaneously activating instruction of the remote-controlled vehicle to stop above the shape. Still fifty kilometers distant, the small drone's camera couldn't discern fine detail. "Push in?" Tim asked.

A laugh caught in Greg's throat. He withered under Tania's sidelong glance.

"Yes," she said. "Get to within a kilometer."

Tim turned to her. "Really?"

"Do it, and if we have any other bands, IR or UV, see if you can put them on the side monitor."

"Okay. Right, here goes."

On the screen Greg and Marcus had been huddled in front of, the camera view vanished and a grid of four new images appeared. Infrared, ultraviolet, and two telemetry views. The repair drone wasn't built for this kind of work, but it was pretty good at finding microfractures in a station's hull, or detecting escaping air or water. The tiny craft began a slow approach to the surface of the alien ship. Soon the towers surrounding the hexagonal discoloration filled the edges of the screen, and then even they moved out of view as the little craft drifted closer. Ten kilometers. Five.

When the hexagonal patch on the Builder ship filled the monitor, Tania called a halt.

She stared at it for a long time. One hundred meters across, she guessed. The smaller section within spanned perhaps fifty. Long shadows cast from the surrounding protrusions draped black patches horizontally across the area.

From this distance the drone's camera could pick up some fine details, chief among which was an obvious groove that ran along the edge of the inner hexagon. The outer portion had no such groove, instead appearing to be painted onto the broader surface of the massive ship. Not painted, exactly, but a cosmetic feature, whereas that small inner area was clearly a separate portion of hull. Like a . . .

"Door," she said. "It looks like a door."

Tim took the statement as permission to zoom in on the inset piece. Soon the widescreen display in front of Tania was filled with a simple image of dark gray, with a lighter gray hexagon in the center. It looked in a metaphorical sense like a flag hanging before her in the room, and she wondered then if that was what she was indeed staring at: a ship identifier, like those painted on military boats on Earth for centuries.

"There's something near the center," Marcus said, pointing.

The image only hinted at it, but Marcus had it right. Just below the center of the hexagon Tania could see a bright red dot. She glanced at the smaller monitor off to the side and studied the quadrant devoted to an infrared view. "Look at that," she said.

Everyone turned. On infrared, five such dots glowed bright in a rough ring around the very center of the door. They brightened in unison, then faded. The cycle repeated at a pace that gave Tania the unsettling impression of a beating heart within.

"Zoom in," she said.

"That's max zoom," Tim replied.

"Then go in farther." She answered his next question before he could ask it. "Until we can see those lights close-up."

Tim complied and the remote drone lurched forward in a burst of thrust. Tania's focus alternated between the IR view, the distance-to-contact readout, and the main screen's visible-light presentation.

As the craft moved closer—fifty meters, forty—the pinpoints of light became visible on the main screen. Then they became something more than single points of light, but shapes.

"There's another hexagon in the center of them," Marcus said.

Tania squinted. She couldn't see it at first, but then found what he referred to. This five-sided portion was the same color as the surrounding one, and if not for the five lights around it she would have missed it. The only clue was a thin groove that marked its border with the area around it. The groove caught some of the light coming off the five pulsing beacons.

Five sides. Five lights. Five small shell ships crashed to Earth. She shivered at the thought. But the aura towers dispersed in only four groups. That fact troubled her in a way she couldn't explain.

When the craft loomed just twenty meters from the drone, Tim fired a braking thrust.

Tania stepped forward, studying the screen. The lights were not lights at all, she saw. Not exactly. They were more like portholes. She knew instinctively that the light coming through them was from a single, interior source. She'd had the same impression when she'd seen the pulsing grooves on the aura tower's surface.

Each light was a shape: a circle, a square, a triangle, each with a minor imperfection. The fourth had an oval shape, with one side undulating in an even waveform. The last resembled an hourglass, albeit with small extensions on the top and bottom that reminded Tania of teeth.

No one spoke for a long time. Then Greg asked, "Is it a code?"

"Maybe that's their writing," Tim offered.

Tania nodded. "That's what I was thinking. Like a ship moniker. An identification system."

"Right," Marcus said. "So you don't confuse it with some other behemoth."

"Everyone remember where we parked," Greg said.

The room fell silent again as everyone tried to puzzle out the purpose of the shapes, as if staring at them long enough would somehow unravel the mystery. Tania felt like she'd been given just five characters of Kanji and was expected to learn Japanese from the clues.

"What now?" Tim asked after a minute or two had passed. "We're at fifty percent fuel on the drone. Cap's about the same."

Tania sighed. She wished she was there herself so she could reach out and touch the surface, or peer inside those portholes. Prudence won out. "Bring it back."

Marcus groaned in disappointment.

Tania ignored him. "Everyone get some rest, or study the recordings if you can't sleep. We'll meet in four hours to plan our next move."

Eventually Greg and Marcus departed the room for their cabins, leaving Tania and Tim alone. She hadn't moved from her place in front of the screen, which now replayed the drone's footage in time lapse.

"Tim?"

"Yeah?"

"I want a list of all our vehicles capable of carrying walkers outside."

"Okay. Does that mean we're going to go take a look in person?"

"Someone should," Tania said, knowing she'd go herself.

51

CAPPAGH, IRELAND

DATE IMPRECISE

Vanessa took a cue from Skyler and left the dome to find a cart, or stretcher, anything that would help on their return walk with the unconscious Ana and the heavy alien object.

Skyler had barely drawn a breath when Vanessa reemerged, wheelbarrow rolling in front of her. She had a heavy coat on, and a dust of snow draped her shoulders.

"Good enough," Skyler said. Together they lifted Ana in, resting her on a folded blanket Vanessa had tucked into the bottom. Once the girl was settled, they lifted the alien hourglass and placed it between her legs.

Then they each took one of the two handles and pushed together, the loaded wheelbarrow lurching through the churned and muddy ground.

When the front edge of the wheelbarrow hit the edge of the dome it began to bend the surface outward. As soon as the edge of the matte black hourglass object touched the dome, a brilliant purple-white light exploded across Skyler's field of view. It enveloped him from every direction. He heard a sound like a cannon blast and had a sudden sensation of being underwater, surrounded by buoyant fluid. His vision blurred. He felt like the air was being sucked from his lungs.

Vanessa, next to him, was just a vague form, obscured in a milky purple glow. She screamed.

Then the fluid haze began to shatter and dissolve. Cracks of light appeared everywhere and grew wider. Skyler felt his mind begin to fracture in bizarre combinations of slow and fast, as if his vision had shattered like glass. Some shards presented images of the outside, frozen in time, others the inside of the dome at full speed. The shards jumbled and fractured again. Some combined, snapping together like puzzle pieces. Gradually, over what at once seemed hours and mere fractions of a second, the shards that held the picture of the outside world began to win the titanic struggle, and the images in them began to accelerate in time as the shards themselves grew and fused.

A sound began to build, like an aircraft approaching, the noise amplifying in conjunction with the converging image of the outside world. When the last of the purple vanished from Skyler's view, the sound peaked and vanished in a thundering boom that shook the ground under his feet.

He stumbled to one knee, Vanessa with him.

The purple dome had vanished. Skyler looked up in time to see a curved wall of white racing down toward him.

"Head down!" he shouted to Vanessa, as he threw himself over the wheelbarrow and Ana.

An avalanche of snow crashed around them, from where the dome's edge had been toward the pinnacle at the center.

The dome had vanished, Skyler realized, and the snow that accumulated on top of it fell in one instant, dome-shaped sheet.

Bitter cold swallowed him. Vanessa screamed as ice pummeled the ground around them. Then Skyler felt as if someone had jumped on his back. He groaned under the sudden weight, the sensation of frozen slush on his exposed flesh.

The avalanche ended almost immediately. Skyler's fear of being buried proved exaggerated, as he found himself under just a few centimeters of the white powder. He leapt off the cart and brushed snow from Ana's face and hair.

"It's over," he said to Vanessa, who cowered against the metal side of the wheelbarrow. He staggered to his feet and helped her do the same. "We're out. It's over."

She coughed and looked him over before turning to see the winter world around them. "What happened?"

"When that thing hit the edge, the dome disintegrated."

"It felt like . . ." Vanessa stopped, shivered. "God, I don't know what. A nightmare. A hallucination."

"Yeah," he said. "One time frame collapsing and another rushing in."

"Let's—oh shit."

Skyler barely had time to register the urgency in her voice when Vanessa crouched and drew both pistols he'd given her. He brought his gun to the ready without fully understanding why, simply because the woman had done so. Only when Vanessa started shooting did he understand.

The blue areas within the dome had collapsed as well, and in the snow around them a handful of subhumans were struggling up after being pummeled with the accumulated snow. Vanessa shot three dead before Skyler could manage to find his wits and aim. He put down the last, and then everything went silent.

"Is that the last of them?" Vanessa asked.

A sudden change in the environment around them cut Skyler's reply short. Something that had been there a moment ago vanished, though he couldn't quite figure out what. A sound had gone, like being in a room when the ventilation system suddenly turns off. Vanessa looked around. She'd noticed it, too.

"The towers," she said. "They're dark again."

Skyler looked at the nearest pillar in the circle that now marked where the dome had been. True to Vanessa's word, the trace wave pattern of purple light within it had vanished. Once again it looked like it had before the exodus: black, and dead. The other towers around the perimeter stood dark as well. Skyler shuffled over to the close one, hugging himself against the bite of a frigid breeze, and pushed the massive object.

It didn't budge.

"The hell . . ." He paused. The hum from the towers had begun again. A whisper, but there and building. "Jesus. What now?"

Vanessa grabbed Skyler's arm and pulled. "Let's move away. Something is happening."

Together they pushed the wheelbarrow a dozen meters away from the edge of the circle into a snow-dappled field. By the time they turned to study the circle of aura towers again, the black obelisks had begun to move.

Not all of them, Skyler realized, but exactly half. Every other tower pulled inward, drawn toward the partially buried shell ship in the center. Then with remarkable coordination they began to form into a wedge, the sharp point aimed along the path etched in the ground, toward Belém.

The towers that remained in the circle formation around the crashed ship suddenly parted, and the wedge group began to move.

"They're going back," Vanessa whispered.

"Half, anyway." Skyler tried to imagine some version of reality where this all made sense. He watched the towers pick up speed as they slid along the ground, eerily upright despite the undulations in the ground.

"I call this a success," Vanessa said, a proud grin on her face. "The colony can certainly use them. And if we manage the same result at the other three sites—"

"—there will be a hundred plus in camp again," he said, finishing her thought.

"Maybe we get one of these weird little trophies each time, too."

Skyler found himself nodding, but in his mind the puzzle pieces still refused to fit together. "Right," he muttered. "Let's get back to the Magpie, get Ana home and fixed up. We also need to warn Karl."

"Warn him of what?"

"Those towers," Skyler said. "Nice as it is that they're coming home, if Exodus doesn't start planning to make room for their arrival it's going to be another fiasco."

Wrapped in a musty wool blanket, bandaged hands clutched around a steaming mug of tea, Skyler waited for the comm link to turn green. He'd muttered silent thanks that he'd not turned it on in the middle of another Greg and Marcus broadcast.

It was the last day of February. They'd found Pablo in the barn, cleaning a rabbit carcass for meat. The man looked thin and sported a beard that hadn't been there before. Other than a query about Ana's injury, he said little when the party arrived. Skyler could see the relief in Pablo's eyes, but the man's restrained demeanor gave no more insight into how he'd fared while awaiting their return. Six months alone with only his thoughts. When Skyler asked if he'd heard from the colony he just shrugged. "Once a week. I tell them there's no news; they tell me that they hope we'll hurry. The ship is close now, that doctor says."

With the cold had come subhumans. Pablo figured they sought warmth, and after the first encounter he'd spent most of his time inside the barricaded farmhouse, watching from the second-floor windows for the creatures. He culled the local population by building a bonfire in the adjacent field, picking a few off as they came like moths to the bright blaze. The visits all but stopped after that. He'd either killed them all, or they'd learned to avoid the area.

The link indicator turned green.

"Pablo?"

"It's Skyler, Tania."

He heard a sharp intake of breath. "You're okay," she said. "Oh my God, Skyler, you're alive."

"We all are," he said. "More or less. Tania, we found something—"

She spoke over him. "Skyler, please come back. Today, right now. I . . ." She trailed off. There was desperation in her voice he hadn't heard since the day he found her locked in her cabin on Anchor Station. "So much has happened. Another ship has arrived. And we had another of those vibrations on the Elevator, a discharge of electricity. Something's wrong. I need your wisdom."

"The ship's arrived then?"

"It's enormous, Skyler. Terrifyingly so. Six kilometers long."

Six. Jesus. "Where did it stop?" Part of him, a big part, hoped she'd say Ireland.

"Over Africa. We sent a drone to survey it, Skyler, and found something. There's a door, or airlock, surrounded by these . . .

symbols. Shapes, like writing in a way. Karl and I are planning to—"

"Shapes? What shapes?"

"There's five," she said. "Each is basic, but they all have an imperfection. A circle with a half-circle dent at the top, a square with a notch, a triangle missing one tip. The oval one is wavy on the top half. And the last looks like an hourglass, with little teeth on the top and bottom."

"Tania," he said evenly, "don't do anything. Wait for us to get back."

"Why?"

"We found something in the dome. An object, hourglass-shaped just like you described. And when I entered that cave east of Belém, I saw another. I thought it was a little altar, remember? About the same size as this thing, but circular."

"God, Skyler," she said, then went silent for a few seconds. "I wish I knew what this all meant."

"Me, too, Tania. Me, too."

"Okay. Okay, we'll hold off, but please hurry."

The urgency in her voice came through loud and clear. "Is the ship doing something? Building another Elevator?"

"It's quiet so far. That's not the reason I want you back here."

"Well, regardless, we're leaving immediately. Ana's injured, and I need you to have whatever medics you can muster ready to look at her the moment we arrive. No, more than that, have them contact me as soon as possible. We might be able to diagnose her in flight."

Tania's voice lowered. "Skyler, Blackfield is with us."

The words hung in the air like a bad odor. Skyler tried to digest their meaning, but each thought he had brought with it a hundred questions, none of them good.

Tania spoke before he could. "He came here with Platz Station. There was a battle—"

"Are you okay?" he asked. "Did they win? If you tell me he's in charge—"

"Slow down," Tania said. "The battle was in Darwin, not here. Russell fled and couldn't go anywhere else."

The words settled on him like the lid of a coffin. Everything that had happened, everything else going on, vanished.

"Bullshit," he said. "It's a lie. Put him out an airlock right now, Tania."

"We think he's telling the truth."

"Right. Everything is on the up-and-up, everyone's friends, and yet you want me to rush back there and do what, exactly? Confirm your bad decision to let him in?" He took a deep breath. "Tania, put him out an airlock or I'll do it myself. Nothing that fucker does is truthful, and you know it."

For a long moment she didn't speak.

Skyler closed his eyes. "Please don't tell me he's sitting there with you. That he's joined the colony."

"No," Tania said. "He's confined to quarters here on Melville. The rest of his people are under house arrest on Platz Station until we can figure out what to do."

"There's nothing to figure out," Skyler said. "Put the bastard out an airlock and send the station back to Darwin before it explodes or something. It's a Trojan horse, Tania, it has to be."

"I can't do that. Platz Station is a boon, regardless of who brought it. It doubles our living space and—"

"And you want me to come back and advise you? When will you listen to a word I say? I can't seem to get through anymore." He recognized the flare of temper too late to stop the words, and took a long breath. His ears felt hot and he could feel the pulsing veins in his temples.

"I did what I thought was right," she said. "I know we have had our differences, but I value your judgment. If I made a mistake, fine, come help me fix it, okay? And . . . honestly, I'd feel that much safer with you here."

Further argument wouldn't matter. He knew he had to get back, for Ana's sake more than anything. None of this news changed that.

"Okay," he said. "We're leaving today. Do not . . . *do not* . . . let Blackfield out of his cell."

"We won't, I promise."

Her voice held the hint of a buried apology that he hadn't expected. He tried to see things from her perspective. Blackfield arriving with the crown jewel of Darwin's space stations, and a six-kilometer-long behemoth Builder ship arriving right after that. And now these strange symbols, and matching objects within the crashed shells. She's overwhelmed, beset on all sides with things she can't wrap her mind around. He chastised himself for not seeing it sooner.

"Good," he said with as much warmth and calm as he could muster. "Now, put me through to Karl. There's a bunch of aura towers coming back from here and the camp needs to be ready for them."

52

PLATZ STATION

12.MAR.2285

A woman named Jenny completed the preflight check under Skyler's watchful eye.

He couldn't yet quite bring himself to trust anyone who arrived with Blackfield, but Tania had insisted. Jenny had all the qualifications, and as Tania pointed out, she couldn't really be blamed for doing her duty in the midst of that attack.

She'd been aboard Platz Station when Grillo's forces had attacked, and she'd been the one to handle the station's move to Belém. Tania assured Skyler such an operation was no simple task. Station records confirmed Jenny's story: a transfer to Platz Station from Midway Station after the original crew had evacuated with Zane. So, she wasn't one of Russell's cronies, at least at that time. She claimed to have hated the post and would have preferred to remain on Midway, Darwin's smallest station with a crew of just four. When Skyler asked her what she did to pass the time on Midway, she replied, "Flight sims." Her original post in orbit had been in flying construction craft and loaders in the vast interior bay of Penrith Assembly, and she couldn't shed that itch to fly. Begrudgingly, Skyler decided he liked the woman. She reminded him of Angus.

"EVA suits are here," Tania said from the passenger compartment below the cockpit.

He looked down at his feet, through the hatch in the floor that allowed entry to the cockpit. Tania drifted in the compartment below. "We're about done," he said.

The repair craft had an odd vertical layout, unintuitive at least to Skyler. His mind was hardwired to expect flying craft to be aerodynamic, but of course such considerations didn't matter in space. From the outside it looked like a metal cylinder with six robotic arms of varying size and purpose sticking out from three bulky, square sections. The conical thrusters that guided the craft poked out in clusters of five at seemingly random sections of the hull.

"It's going to be a tight fit down here," Tania said. "I brought six extra air tanks, enough for fifty hours or so round-trip. We should suit up beforehand, I think."

Skyler nodded. The craft had been designed for a two-person crew, one being the pilot, one to venture out and make hull repairs to the station. Apparently Platz had originally intended to provide every station with one, but only three had been manufactured before such pursuits became all but impossible. Belatedly Skyler wondered where he would sit during the journey. The cockpit barely provided room for Jenny. Below, the passenger compartment had been built for one person and welding supplies. Now it held Tania and six air canisters. The hourglass object recovered in Ireland had been packed neatly in an airtight case that originally housed welding gear, and which sat nestled within the craft's robotic arms. Gray nylon straps secured it in place.

"Go get suited," Jenny said. "I can finish this."

Deciding he could trust her, Skyler pulled his legs together and pushed off the ceiling, drifting down to the compartment below. Tania had moved to one side to make room for him. If he positioned himself in the center of the cylinder, he could have easily reached out and touched each side with his fingertips.

A single reddish LED illuminated the cylindrical room and cast Tania in a mixture of warm glow and stark shadow. She smiled meekly at him and looked away an instant after their eyes met. He'd forgotten how effortlessly beautiful she was. Even here, with a sheen of sweat on her brow, her raven hair pulled back in a hasty bun, and an expression equal parts anticipation and exhaustion, she made his breath catch in his throat.

The thought gripped him between two conflicting sensations of guilt. One for the rift that had formed between him and this remarkable woman, and one for the injured young lady he'd left on the ground in Belém. Ana. She'd flown into something approaching a rage when he told her he would be going up the Elevator, and ultimately onto the alien ship. Given her condition, her situation, she'd argued with an almost admirable vehemence. She was still in the infirmary, awake though sedated. Her injuries were extensive: internal bleeding, bruised ribs, and a fractured lower vertebra. Or as Ana growled, "a hell of a backache." When Karl knocked and announced it was time to board the climber, Ana had finally accepted that he was going. She kissed Skyler's forehead and said, "Come back to me, Sky. I miss you already."

Skyler swallowed and forced himself to keep Ana's face in the corner of his mind's eye, like an overlay on a terminal screen. But when Tania glanced back up at him, the terminal in his mind crashed.

"Suits are out on the deck," she said.

"After you," he said, and gestured to the open airlock door.

The white EVA suits were top-of-the-line. Tight auto-fitting elastic garments with heavy black ribbing woven straight into the fabric like mechanical veins. Skyler assumed this was to combat the effects of being in a vacuum, somehow. A few of the station crew waited nearby to help them into the complicated outfits. Tania, either already briefed or just used to wearing such things, shed her own blue jumpsuit without hesitation. Underneath she wore a skintight blue exercise outfit that left so little to the imagination, Skyler found himself glancing away in embarrassment.

"Something wrong?" Tania asked.

"Um, no. You look different, that's all. New exercise routine?"

Tania blushed slightly. "Combat training, per your suggestion. Self-defense, firearms. I'm getting pretty good at Krav Maga."

Skyler studied her anew. He'd tried the Israeli street-fighting technique years before and found it too fast, too brutal. *Fifty hours,* he thought with dread, and tried to conjure his overlay picture of Ana.

He still wore the clothes he'd arrived in. Black cargo pants and a long-sleeved gray shirt. His boots he'd left in a locker on the climber. At the behest of the waiting helpers, Skyler stripped to his underwear and let them guide him into the spacesuit. He felt self-conscious at first, standing there in his briefs, Tania a few meters away. Then he shrugged and grinned at his own childish behavior. Here he was, about to embark on a spacewalk to study an alien ship firsthand, and he was worried Tania might gawk at his bum. A minute earlier he'd gawked at her. He wondered if the only thing that separated him from someone like Blackfield was that he didn't blurt out every primal thought running through his brain.

The process took half an hour. First the skintight suit went on. Despite the rigid wires running under its surface, the suit provided surprising mobility. Next was a hard-shell vest, not unlike body armor but much lighter. One of the helpers explained the suit used counterpressure to combat the effects of vacuum; he hooked up a series of gas lines from the vest's back to connectors above Skyler's elbows and knees.

"What's this bit?" Skyler asked, gesturing to the protrusion on his right forearm. To him it looked like a gun built right into the suit.

"Maneuvering thrust," someone said. "Point in the direction you want to go away from. Yes, away. Sounds weird but it's really intuitive when you're out there."

The comment made him wonder once again just what the hell he was doing here. Certainly there must be five hundred people in the colony better qualified for such an undertaking. If objections had been raised, Tania had settled them all before he'd even made the climb up from Belém. She wanted Skyler on the mission, and that was that.

Finished with her own suit, Tania came to him and tapped a sequence of buttons on the small control pad on his left forearm. Skyler felt each section of the suit tighten to the edge of pain, then relax again, as if the whole outfit were one big blood pressure cuff.

"Time to go," she said when the diagnostic was finished.

On the journey over he told Tania everything that had happened in Ireland.

She asked him countless questions about the dome, and the object they'd found within it. He tried four times to describe the sensations he'd felt when crossing in or out of that purple field. The words didn't seem to do it justice, but Tania accepted them all the same.

She gave him a summary of what they'd learned of the new Builder ship. The unspoken agreement between them that made Ana a taboo subject seemed to extend to Russell Blackfield as well, and Skyler didn't mind. According to Karl the man was still confined to quarters on Melville and had been a model prisoner so far. No decisions had been made on what to do with him in the long term. Plenty of time to have that argument with Tania after the mission, Skyler figured.

A long hour passed in near-total silence, with Skyler doing everything he could think of not to look into Tania's eyes lest he be lost there. He felt very much as he had on a train to Italy as a naïve young man, sharing a compartment with a beautiful stranger. In the span of a few minutes on that journey he'd managed to be caught staring at her legs, and then accidentally insulting her with an observation on the current political climate. The next eight hours had been absolute torture. At least his knowledge of both Italian profanity and politics had improved.

Tania passed some time showing him how to work the arm-mounted thruster and the basics of the helmet's onboard computer. She checked their suits again and spoke with Jenny over the intercom about their approach trajectory. Then, almost casually, Tania brought up the day Russell had ordered Jenny to move Platz Station from Darwin to Belém.

Skyler knew Tania had interviewed the woman already. He'd heard the basics of it himself. Here and now, in a tin can heading to make contact with an alien race that had all but obliterated humanity, Tania struck a friendly tone. Jenny was part of the team now, part of the crew. One of us. Her appointment to pilot this mission suddenly made brilliant, perfect sense to Skyler. She spoke freely.

"Russell had been planning something," Jenny said. "He had his own troops aboard, and all the talk on the station was of what he planned to do with them. They gave up the pretense that you guys were all dead when half the farm platforms came back, so we knew you were out there somewhere. The activity, the soldiers . . . I knew he must have found you."

"So Russell was focused on us," Skyler said. "How'd he miss the climbers full of Jacobite thugs coming up? I mean, he's not stupid. Not intelligent, either, but he's wise."

"Oh, they were expected," Jenny said through the speaker. "We'd been waiting for them for days."

This had been said before, but Skyler thought perhaps it was because no one wanted to admit getting caught with their pants down, least of all Russell.

Jenny went on. "Everyone knew Russell had put Grillo in charge of Darwin. Hell, Russell bragged about it. His vision and leadership laid the groundwork, of course."

"Of course."

"Apparently, Grillo's men were supposed to handle station security while Russell's were over here. I got the sense they expected to arrive at a station empty of guards, but Russell, well, you know how he is."

"Tell me anyway," Skyler said. He glanced at Tania. Blackfield had glossed over these particular details.

"Russell wanted to make a show of authority. I heard the orders he called down to the barracks ring. We hear everything in station ops, you see. 'All combat squads report to the main cargo bay in fifteen minutes,'" she said mimicking him. "'Full gear, dress to impress. Let's make sure this lot knows who their betters are.'"

She went on, fleshing out gaps in a story already told. Skyler and Tania stared at each other in a silent conversation. Russell might have left out details that would make him look bad, but the meat of it he'd told truthfully. Grillo had betrayed him. He'd used the invitation to cover for Russell's security as an opening to flood orbit with his own army. If not for Russell's vain desire to show off his own forces, it would have been a clean coup, Skyler thought. A concentrated force of single-minded purpose, inserted straight into the heart of the station. Which is likely what happened on all the other stations, too.

Skyler reached out and muted the intercom. "None of this translates to 'forgive and forget,' in my book."

Her face, just centimeters from his, showed little insight into her thoughts. Tania's gaze held his, searched his, and Skyler imagined her tabulating some mental scorecard of Russell's virtues or lack thereof.

After a time, Tania nodded once. Her expression changed from solemn to serious. "There's something I need to tell you about, Skyler."

"We're here," Jenny said suddenly. "A thousand klicks and closing."

Tania started to reach for her helmet, but Skyler grasped her wrist. "Tell me what?"

"Later," she said.

Tania closed her eyes just before the cramped compartment depressurized. She listened to her breathing inside the helmet, the soft hum of the air recycler vent near her neck.

When the cabin lost pressure she felt the suit react. Pulses of pressure rippled across her body, from painfully tight to relaxed and gentle, as if she'd received an entire massage in one second.

"Comm test," she said.

"I read you," Skyler replied.

She looked at him and found herself wishing once again she knew him better. He'd said so little since the fiasco with Gabriel, and she found him infuriatingly good at keeping his expression blank and distant. As a punishment for what she'd done, the lie she'd told, she felt it at once deserved and unbearable.

With a wan smile, she turned to the airlock door and pulled the release handle. A puff of condensation burst along its edge and then the door simply swung open. Just like that, Tania found herself looking out at the hexagonal patch of hull on the huge Builder ship.

Up close, the vessel's sheer size took her breath away. Jenny had parked them twenty meters from the surface. All around, massive protrusions extended outward well past their tiny vehicle, blotting out the view of Earth and space almost completely.

A moment of vertigo fell on Tania and she gripped the edges of the airlock with sudden panic. She suddenly felt as if she were looking down, the immense towers like buildings jutting upward past her, and the ancient wiring in her brain screamed "falling!"

Tania willed herself to see the hexagonal patch as being in front of her rather than below, and the sensation faded.

"Here goes nothing," she said, and pulled with both hands on the airlock frame, propelling herself out into open space. By prior agreement, she'd attached a towline to her suit, and once across the gap she'd figure out a way to attach it to the Builder ship.

The hexagonal area of the ship's hull drifted toward her at a leisurely pace. The five illuminated shapes around it all glowed with the same white-yellow hue, the color of the sun. Close up now, she estimated the shapes as being perhaps fifteen centimeters square, a fair amount smaller than the strange object Skyler had recovered from Ireland. The hexagon in the middle spanned maybe four meters on a side.

Tania brought her feet up at the last second and landed on the alien hull. It felt hard as marble under her, despite her boots, which dulled the impact. Her body naturally wanted to bounce away in the lack of gravity, but Tania had expected this and pointed her hand away from the ship. She squeezed her fingers into a ball, then tapped a button on the index finger with her thumb to send out a pulse of thrust. The burst of momentum glued her to the vessel for the moment. "Touchdown," she said.

"Nicely done," Skyler replied. Through the helmet speaker he still sounded right next to her.

Tania removed a line hook from her belt and tried the magnetic attachment first. She placed it just outside the hexagonal patch, on the opposite side of the glowing hourglass shape, for no reason other than it felt like a wise precaution. The magnetic base clapped onto the ship so quickly it almost pulled itself out of her hand. "Connection is solid," she said, "no adhesive required. You're clear to join me."

She glanced back and saw Skyler slip outside, using handholds just outside the door to keep himself glued to the side of the craft. Their cylindrical can of a ship floated against a breathtaking view of Africa beyond. The tan expanse of the Sahara in the center, a hint of Egypt to her right and Morocco to the left, both obscured by the vaulting towers that extended out from the alien ship all around her like vacant, windowless skyscrapers.

"I'm outside, Jenny," Skyler said.

"Copy," the pilot replied. "I'm monitoring your suits from here, and watching on the terminal. Nice view, Tania."

"I agree," Tania said.

Skyler climbed up to the ERV's robotic arms, which cradled the hard black case like a baby. He set to work on the winches that held the case in place, unlatching the one closest to the tiny craft's hull first. Then almost reluctantly he pushed away from the ERV and floated out to the end of the nearest arm.

When Skyler reached out to grab the next handhold, Tania's breath caught in her throat.

The ERV's thrusters bloomed to life.

Exhaust flashed from the array of cones like breath on cold air.

"Shit," Skyler managed to say, probably thinking he'd simply overshot.

"Jenny!" Tania shouted into her headset. "Thruster malfunction!"

Even as she said the word she knew it was wrong. The thrusters had been fired on purpose, at the exact instant Skyler had no hold on the ERV. And in that same moment, the towline had gone slack, released from the other end.

She watched in horror as the vehicle began to accelerate away, the black case that held the Ireland object still firmly clutched in its robotic arms.

Skyler floated free. He cursed into his microphone, sounding more embarrassed than outraged, still not understanding what was happening.

"She's taking it, Skyler!" Tania said.

He seemed to be struggling to right himself.

Tania saw no alternative. She jumped.

She pushed hard with both legs and rocketed across the void of space toward the ERV, gaining quickly on it. The craft's small conical engines fired another pulse, but the craft was not designed to maneuver quickly. Tania held out her arm behind herself and fired one long continuous blast from her own thruster, cruising past Skyler and racing toward the fleeing ship.

She misjudged her speed, slammed into the side of the craft, and bounced off. Gritting her teeth, Tania fired another quick pulse and closed the distance again. This time she managed to get a hand around one of the many rungs protruding from the craft's hull.

Stuck now to the ship, the massive Builder vessel seemed to be the thing moving, getting farther away with each second. Tania weighed her options. Her suit's mask showed a broken link between herself and the craft, so there would be no talking Jenny out of her act of betrayal. On top of that, the woman had closed the craft's door, not that getting back inside would do much.

So Tania did the only thing she could think to do. Pulling herself across the craft's hull, she went to the robotic arms and began to release the holding straps.

The craft accelerated again, but the increase in speed was not enough to throw Tania off. She tried to ignore how far they'd moved from the Builder ship. Getting back might be impossible.

A cold realization began to nag at her as she worked the winches that secured the straps. Getting back *home* might be impossible. Jenny had their air, and was their ride. If she left . . .

Out of nowhere Skyler appeared next to her. He collided with the hard black case and almost knocked it free. She heard him grunt from the impact through her helmet speaker.

"You were right," Tania blurted. "We shouldn't have trusted her."

"I don't think she's one of Russell's," Skyler shot back, working the last strap. "Anyway, she's not getting this goddamn case, agreed?"

"Agreed," Tania said with more conviction than she felt.

Working together they freed the box and drifted away from the ERV a few meters. "Get on that side," Tania instructed, motioning Skyler to move around to the edge of the box that pointed toward the Builder ship. The hexagon on the massive hull looked very small now.

She swallowed, aimed her arm behind herself, and fired. With the added mass of Skyler and the case, she had to maintain her pulse of thrust for what seemed like a minute before they began to move appreciably.

The ERV started to fall away from them, toward Earth.

Perhaps Jenny won't notice we—

No such luck. Tania felt a shiver when the vehicle's thrusters pivoted and fired again, pushing the craft in their direction. It still receded, but not as fast.

Tania forced herself to turn away and focus on the destination, the hexagon. It took a full thirty seconds to cross the distance again, and by the time they neared the door and Tania fired her thruster to slow them, her fuel gauge read just 8 percent.

She glanced back. The ERV was closing on them and showed no sign of slowing. *She's going to ram us.*

Five meters from the hull of the giant ship she heard Skyler suck in a sharp breath.

"Shit," he gasped.

"What?"

"Something's happening," he said.

Tania leaned out to see past him. Of the five shapes that surrounded the hexagonal patch, only one remained illuminated.

The hourglass.

Then a black line began to trace the inner edge of the hexagon. A shadow, she realized. The patch moved inward, then separated into individual sections she hadn't noticed before. These sections pulled outward in a coordinated dance, revealing a tunnel that led into darkness.

They were heading right into it.

Tania whipped around in time to see the ERV less than fifty meters away, racing toward them with suicidal speed. In desperation she pointed her thruster at the ERV and fired. The fuel meter inside her helmet ticked down from eight to zero in a matter of seconds.

Squinting, Tania could just see Jenny's face in the small porthole window at the cockpit. She looked as terrified as

Tania felt, and then she closed her eyes.

"Too fast!" Skyler shouted. His words cut off then. He must have looked back and seen the looming form of the ERV.

And then they crossed through, into the Builder ship.

A second later the ERV slammed into the hull, too big to fit through the newly formed door. The craft crumpled against the edges of the hexagonal opening. Loose bits of material came free.

Air gushed from the broken seal of the aircraft's single door. Tania knew instinctively what this meant. The crew cabin was not pressurized. The cockpit was. In the violence of the impact, both the outer door and inner hatch had ruptured.

She and Skyler kept drifting inward. In all the commotion Tania hadn't even bothered to look where they were going, but it registered with her now that they were moving down a long, straight tunnel. The crumpled remains of the ERV, seen through the receding hexagonal opening, bounced off the hull of the Builder ship and floated away.

Adrift, dead.

Our ride home, Tania thought.

53

THE CORE SHIP

13.MAR.2285

Skyler gathered his wits before she did. He fired his own thruster to stop their progress. They'd traveled a full hundred meters down the corridor.

"What now?" he asked.

Too stunned to speak, Tania just stared at the dark passageway, and the illuminated patch of Earth seen through the now-tiny entrance. "I don't know," she said honestly. "That craft was our way home, Skyler."

"Can we get another one sent out? Can we contact Tim directly?"

"I don't know. . . ." Her own voice sounded strangely distant.

"Try," he said emphatically. "Tania, snap out of it. Try."

She found enough strength in his voice to come back from the shock of seeing the ERV crash. After a calming breath, Tania brought up her suit's menu and tried again to connect via the ERV. The link still showed red. Frowning, she tried a different tactic and activated her emergency beacon. The suit's transmitter would not be powerful enough, but perhaps if they came looking . . .

An idea hit her. Tania jumped back a menu and then entered

the one that listed other comms in her proximity. Skyler's suit showed first.

Just below his entry, she saw the ERV listed. Its entry blinked red. "That's something, at least," Tania said.

"What?"

"The ERV's automatic emergency beacon is transmitting. Maybe Tim and the others will pick that up." She had no doubt they would, in fact. The real question was if they could do anything about it in time.

"How long until we know?"

Tania met his eyes. "Going to be awhile, I'm afraid. We should . . . we need to conserve our air, Skyler."

He nodded grimly. Then he shrugged, as well as he could in the semi-rigid suit. "I say we accept their invitation and go in."

Tania studied him to see if he was joking. He wasn't. "What if this is a launch tube, or the barrel of a gun? We can't just—"

"Sure we can," Skyler said with a shrug. "It's why we're here. I don't want to just sit here, do you?"

Tania turned back and stared at the tiny patch of space at the entrance of the long hall.

"Besides," Skyler said, "who makes a launch tube that opens from the outside?"

His comment struck Tania as trite, yet she couldn't deny the underlying desire to keep going. They were here to explore, to try to discover the purpose of this impossibly large spacecraft parked almost exactly between the two elevators.

Whatever the Builders were up to, she thought, the answer must be within.

One event left, according to Neil's message. Clock's ticking. She reminded herself to tell Skyler about that little bit of news as soon as they departed for home. She'd tried and stopped herself a half-dozen times already, still seeking some way to explain it without making Neil Platz sound like a monster. She owed her old friend that much, at least.

"All right, then," she said. The heads-up display inside her helmet tracked her eye movement, and she used a button woven into her left glove to activate the bright lamps on both sides of her helmet. On a whim, she also accessed the intersuit menu and chose to display Skyler's health vitals just below her own on the main view. Seeing his steady heart rate there, and his aggregated overall anxiety level at well within the norm, gave her a small surge of confidence. She placed his remaining oxygen level next to her own and swallowed. She had six hours; he had seven.

"I'm about out of thrust," Tania said to him.

"No problem," he said. He began to aim his arm in the direction they'd entered, then hesitated, fidgeted.

"You okay?" she asked.

He flashed a thumbs-up. "Wish my brain would stop changing which way is 'down,' but other than that I'll be okay."

She pointed at the side of the hexagon they floated against. "Let's call this down for now, agreed?"

"Sure. Thanks."

She helped him guide the case. Part of her questioned the need to lug the thing around until they knew what it did, or anything about it, really. But it had opened the door, that much was obvious, and somehow it just seemed prudent to keep the object close. She didn't want to let it out of her sight any more than she wanted to let Skyler leave again.

The tunnel, or hallway—whatever it was—stretched on for another hundred meters. The walls reminded her of the shell ships over Darwin and Belém: dark and uninteresting after years of study.

After another sixty meters or so the tunnel ended abruptly at a wall. Tania helped Skyler ease the plastic case to a stop and gave him a questioning look.

"Maybe we missed a junction?" he mused. "Can't imagine how, but—"

A sudden, faint purple light cut his words short. They both turned to face the wall; only it wasn't a wall anymore. The surface retracted like an iris. Multiple plates slid out from a central point, allowing more and more purple-tinged light to flow into the tunnel.

Tania's breath caught in her throat as she took in the room beyond.

There were ten walls, each perhaps ten meters wide and soaring at least a hundred high. Nine walls were black, etched with the same geometric patterns that covered the aura towers in Belém. The last wall glowed with intense, deeply saturated purple light that rippled and shimmered just beneath the surface in waveforms of dizzying complexity.

Bathed in the purple glow, she took in the whole room, looking at it all without looking at anything specific. The ripples of colored light along the glowing wall produced a discernible pattern. The waves, though chaotic and shifting, gravitated upward toward the top of the room. Tania glanced up at what she thought of as the ceiling.

The surface was not flat like the floor. Instead it had deep channels that ran inward to a central, beveled hexagonal mass. At first Tania thought it glowed purple as well, but then she realized the surface was made up of thousands of tiny bumps that caught some of the light coming from the one glowing wall.

Tania stared in total amazement. All the danger of their predicament melted away, and all she could think was how much she wished Tim and the others were seeing this.

Skyler pointed at the lit wall. "Look there," he said.

Exactly halfway up, a circular gap in the light had formed. The circle grew as they watched, forming a dome-shaped indentation perhaps three meters wide and equally deep.

"Help me with this," Skyler said. He gripped the black crate by one handle and undid one of the two heavy latches.

Unsure what he intended, Tania flipped the other latch, and together they carefully opened the lid, not wanting to make any sudden motions that might cause the object within to float free.

She half-expected brilliant purple light to flow out of the case as the lid came up, but nothing happened. In fact, the vaguely hourglass-shaped object within no longer emanated any light at all.

Skyler leaned over the case and pushed his hand in between the object and the foam packing that surrounded it.

"What are you doing?" Tania asked.

"Isn't it obvious?" he replied, and glanced up at the dome-shaped indentation.

Tania didn't think anything here merited the term *obvious*, but she found herself helping Skyler nonetheless. Together they eased the hourglass object from its foam cradle and then pushed off the floor to drift upward with it.

Skyler offered her a thin smile.

"I hope you know what you're doing," she said.

"Last time I knew that," he said, "was when I knocked on your door in Anchor Station."

The offhand comment hit her like a splash of ice-cold water. A sudden avalanche of memories flashed across her mind: the flight from Darwin, the news of Neil's death and the subsequent realization that Zane had survived. The first time she'd walked among the aura towers in Belém. The thrill of defeating Gabriel followed too quickly by the shattering of her friendship with Skyler.

If only she could go back to that moment when he'd knocked on her door. Roll back the clock, make better decisions. If only she could have left her own self-doubt in that cabin and emerged from the beginning as the leader they all wanted her to be.

Tania forced the distraction away and willed herself to focus on the present, and on what little future she feared they had left. The oxygen gauge continued its slow, steady decline, hers faster than his. She needed to relax.

He raised his right arm and nodded at her to do the same. On a three-count that he timed to their arrival at the midway point along the wall, they both pulsed their thrusters to halt their momentum.

"I'm out of fuel," Tania noted.

The concave recession on the purple wall was nearly pitch-black, just like the object they held. Skyler nodded to Tania again and used his own thruster, alone this time, to propel them the rest of the way to the wall.

"What now?" Tania said.

"I think we're supposed to plug it in."

He started to move to push the object into the cavity.

"Wait," Tania said.

Skyler paused. He looked at her with one eyebrow raised.

She thought of what Neil Platz had written about her father. *He destroyed it before we could truly learn.* "We have no idea what this will do," she said. "What if this is some kind of arming switch? A self-destruct mechanism? A trap?"

Skyler glanced at it, his brow furrowed, then back at her. "What if it bakes cookies?" When she frowned he tried again. "What if it activates an aura generator big enough for the entire planet? A ship of this size could do it."

She opened her mouth, then closed it without answering. He was right. Faced with no knowledge, no context, there was no choice but to push forward into the unknown. If one trait defined humanity, surely it was that.

He took her silence as agreement and nudged the hourglass object into the inverted dome.

The hourglass began to glow as it crossed the threshold of the cavity. Faint at first, growing brighter with each centimeter. Then it rotated, pushed by some invisible force, and aligned itself with the room beyond. The edges of the inverted dome began to warp and reshape, taking on the same hourglass form and color. Soon the object and its receptacle glowed as bright as the wall around them. Then brighter, and brighter still.

On instinct, Tania pulsed back from the wall. Skyler followed her lead as the purple light grew to almost blinding intensity. Tania felt a vibration through her spacesuit, as if sound waves buffeted her despite the vacuum. The vibration grew in conjunction with the intense glow, and with it Tania noticed that the wave patterns within the purple glow along the wall became agitated, even violent. Her entire body began to shake, though whether from fear or some external pressure she couldn't tell. "Skyler?!"

"I feel it!"

"What's happening?"

With sudden, blinding ferocity the purple light exploded in a crescendo of energy that pushed her backward to the far wall. She smacked into the surface and felt her skull rattle against the inside of her helmet.

"Erg," Skyler grunted.

Tania tasted blood, and realized she'd bit her tongue. For a moment she drifted, nothing but stars before her eyes and clouds in her mind. Her suit beeped and a mechanical voice said, "Concussion warning." The alert repeated a few times.

Tania forced her eyes closed and held them tight until the residual energy patterns on her eyelids faded.

When she opened her eyes, she found herself at an odd angle, and a wave of disorientation swept over her. Light came from all around now. The purple wall pulsed and roiled, but there were new colors in the cavernous room. Five of the ten walls glowed now, giving the tall space a striped pattern of alternating light and dark. She saw red, green, and yellow, exactly like the other tower groups that had dispersed from Camp Exodus.

There was a fifth color as well, one not seen among the towers from Belém. Pale blue, as bright and pure as glacial ice under a clear summer sky.

She glanced up at the ceiling. The knobby hexagon in the center echoed all the colors from the walls around it simultaneously now. The reflections merged and danced hypnotically. One of the five ribs, the one that extended out to the edge and connected with the purple wall, now glowed with the same color.

"Unbelievable," Skyler whispered.

"It's incredible," Tania agreed. She whispered, too, on pure instinct. She felt like a visitor to some ancient, forbidden temple.

A chime went off in Tania's helmet. Skyler's must have as well, because he glanced sharply at her. The air in her suit had reached 20 percent. Skyler's readout showed just below 40.

"What now?" he asked.

"Nothing to do but wait," she replied.

"I mean after we get rescued and get back home," he said. He'd somehow forced a playful tone into his voice.

"I think it's clear what we have to do next, though for what purpose I still cannot imagine."

"At least we know where the red one is," Skyler said. "The red . . . key."

Tania studied him, a profound sense of dread building within her. He saw it in her eyes.

"Don't worry," he said. "We'll go in with every weapon I can find, and some serious motivation."

She tried to smile and couldn't. Her gaze kept shooting back to the oxygen readout. "There's five colors here, but only four tower groups left the camp. So where's the fifth?"

"I can guess," he said. "The one place an aura tower wouldn't be needed."

After a few seconds she understood. "Darwin."

Skyler nodded, gravely.

"We need to talk to Russell Blackfield," Tania said. The immune's eyes narrowed to thin slits. "When I spoke with him after we fled to Belém, he gloated that our attempt to kill him from orbit failed. He also noted our failure at destroying Nightcliff, said we'd missed."

"We didn't drop anything on . . ." Skyler paused. Then, "Oh . . ."

"Exactly. Russell Blackfield can tell us exactly where the fifth ship crashed."

Skyler frowned, but he was nodding all the same. A few seconds of silence passed, and their attention was drawn back to the light show within the vast room.

"We should wait by the exit," Tania said quietly.

"I kinda like it in here," he replied. "But you're right. Hold on to me, I've still got some fuel left."

He brought them to a stop just at the end of the hexagon tunnel. With nothing else to do, they floated side by side in the opening and watched the planet below as the line between day and night began to creep across the Sahara. The ERV was now a glinting speck in the distance. It would burn up in a few days, Skyler guessed, though Jenny had surely suffocated already.

She must have been one of Grillo's, he realized. Or at least sympathetic to the Jacobites, if not one of them. Perhaps she'd been in contact with them during the flight and reported everything they'd found. He shuddered at the idea.

Skyler twisted to say something to Tania.

"Hold still," she said.

She was working on something on the back of his suit. "What are you doing?"

"Just double-checking the air pack."

He tried to keep from moving, a difficult trick without gravity.

"All set," Tania said, and moved away.

He heard a slight quiver in her voice. A fear that hadn't been there before. "We're going to make it," he said.

She didn't reply. Instead she just looked at the planet below, and took his gloved hand in hers. For a long time neither of them spoke. Skyler kept thinking of things to say, only to find the silence somehow better.

A full half hour passed before his suit began to beep in warning. *Hell. Not yet, surely?* He fumbled through the menu to find his vitals readout, and saw that he had—

"That can't be right."

His oxygen level read almost 50 percent, higher than the last time he'd looked. Some kind of reserve tank they hadn't known about, perhaps. He grinned. *But why is it beeping at me?*

It hit him, then. It wasn't his suit complaining; it was Tania's. In a panic he brought up the display of her vitals, and he froze when he saw the number. One percent. "Oh God, Tania, what did you do?"

She didn't answer. Her hand had gone limp in his.

"Tania!" he shouted at her. He turned and took her faceplate in both hands. She was drifting in and out of consciousness, as if on the verge of sleep. "No, dammit!"

Her lips moved, but no words came through.

"Why?!" he shouted again, fighting tears. The answer, he realized, was obvious.

The speaker in his helmet crackled then. A voice within a harsh cascade of static. ". . . is . . . condition? Repeat . . ."

"Get the fuck over here, now!" Skyler blurted, aware of how shaky he sounded. "She gave me her air. She's almost out!"

". . . Approaching . . . ETA in . . . minutes."

Skyler put his helmet against hers, looking for any sign of life. He held his own breath and waited. Seconds passed. He thought he saw a puff of condensation on the inside of the helmet. A breath. "You hold on, dammit. Hold on, they're close."

Another puff against the glass, weaker than the last.

Then another.

And then nothing.

ACKNOWLEDGMENTS

This novel would not have been possible without the help and support of the following:

My endlessly patient wife, Nancy.

Sara Megibow, my agent and champion.

My editor, Mike Braff, and his colleague, Sarah Peed. Their insights and thoughtfulness constantly amaze me.

All my family and friends. Notably: the Brotherhood and the Cosmonicans.

The tremendously talented Kevin Hearne, my first and biggest fan, and someone I now call a friend.

READ ON FOR AN EXCERPT FROM

THE PLAGUE FORGE

BOOK THREE OF THE DIRE EARTH CYCLE

COMING SOON FROM TITAN BOOKS

1

BELÉM, BRAZIL

20.MAR.2285

Seconds from collision the vehicle lurched.

Mud sprayed from knobby tires as the bulky truck whipped around and slammed back-first into the mouth of the tunnel. Dirt and rock clanged against the roof outside. The whine of electricity bleeding out from the ultracaps below Skyler's feet dropped off to nothing, allowing the clatter of heavy rain on armored body panels to fill the cramped compartment.

"All clear," Pablo said from his perch in the gun turret. "You're up, señor."

Skyler gripped the long chrome handle on the rear door with both hands. The full suit of body armor made him feel like he'd been dipped in concrete. Plates of carbon fiber woven into thick ballistic fabric, even the gloves. He glanced back at Ana. She sat cross-legged in shorts and a T-shirt on the bench that ran the length of the compartment, an improvised explosive in her hands. The thin brick of wrapped plastique sported a hand-built receiver glued to one side. As he watched she stuffed the bundle out a murder hole, then smacked the portal closed with her hand.

The arming beacon lay on the bench beside her, safely in the off position.

"All set," she said. Then she caught Skyler's nod, leaned in, kissed him hard on the lips, and flipped his face mask down for him. "Good luck."

She'd been confined to a bed for the last few weeks after suffering bruised kidneys and some internal bleeding in Ireland. The camp medics, and Skyler, had advised against her going on this mission at all, but when her eyes had flared with dogged determination he'd known the argument was pointless. At least she'd promised to stay inside the vehicle.

He grinned. "You, too."

Ana returned his grin with a half smile of her own, brushed a strand of hair from her face. In that instant she looked as lovely as she ever had, and Skyler glanced away. He couldn't quite explain why, and hoped against hope that Ana hadn't noticed his sudden distance. The truth was, ever since Tania had given him her air aboard that alien ship he had found himself in a strange sort of limbo. He turned back to the task at hand, focused. With both hands he yanked the door handle.

When the door swung open, Skyler found himself staring down the tunnel once again. A steady stream of dirty water ran down the center of the floor where, after all this time, a deep and erratic gouge had been carved. More water dripped and trickled from the curved ceiling and walls, making the inside of the tunnel appear to be engulfed in the same storm that pummeled the rain forest outside.

With all the dexterity his combat armor would allow, Skyler hopped out of the APC and raised his gun. He smacked the weapon's light on, then did the same to the one mounted on his helmet. Already he regretted wearing the heavy suit. Sweat trickled down his back, and his legs felt like lead weights under the bulk.

The gun he'd chosen only made matters worse. The heavy assault rifle fired large-caliber rounds, regular from one magazine and explosive-tipped from a second. He could switch with a flick of his thumb. Mounted halfway down the barrel was a slightly curved steel plate that came up a few centimeters above the body of the weapon, save for a small gap through which he could aim. The bulk of the shield descended down from the barrel, which provided an extra barrier to anything that might seek to hit him in the chest. The protection might come in handy, but it made the weapon unbalanced and difficult to aim. Skyler had almost left it behind in favor of something smaller when Ana pointed out that he only needed it to get to the shell ship. Once he had the relic that lay within, he could ditch the bulky thing and run.

He glanced back one more time, some clever bit of reassurance on his lips. The words were drowned by a thunderous eruption. Pablo, on the roof-mounted rotary cannon. Individual gunshots could not be heard, only the steady hum as the weapon spewed bullets in like a fire hose. It sounded like a pure bass note run through a stack of concert speakers. The vibration shook droplets of water from the circular tunnel around Skyler and made the plates of his combat armor chatter together.

The brutal noise vanished, replaced by the prattle of shell casings tumbling down the side of the APC and into the mud. Pablo fired the weapon for only a few seconds. Whatever had been his target, Skyler imagined it had been reduced to a few shredded bits of meat. He saw none of this, though, as Vanessa had stuffed the vehicle's rear end expertly into the maw of the tunnel, ensuring Skyler would not have to worry about attack from behind.

"Get moving!" Ana shouted at him. She stood crouched in the center of the compartment now, pistols in both hands, ready to move to murder holes on either side of the vehicle should anything get past Pablo's Gatling gun.

The plan required speed, and Skyler had not moved a step yet. He faced the tunnel again and started to jog forward, as if pushed by Ana's gaze at his back.

Skyler's breath fogged the inside of the mask that covered his face. Moisture from the humid air of the tunnel formed droplets on the outside. The thick sheet of clear plastic curved around in front of him, and offered decent enough protection as long as he kept his chin down, visibility be damned.

He walked forward. The mud swallowed and sucked at his boots with each step. He moved farther to the outside of the curved passage, where the mud wasn't as deep, but walking along the steeper part made his footing awkward and forced him to use his left hand to steady himself. This meant he had to carry the heavy rifle and its huge shield with his right. By the time the crashed ship came into view his arm burned, barely able to keep the tip of the barrel from dragging in the rising water. Aim of any effectiveness would be all but impossible.

Pablo's rotary gun hummed again, strangely muted here at the end of the tunnel, as if the sound came rolling down the long tube and then canceled itself out where the space abruptly ended. Beneath the thrum came a rapid series of claps—Ana's pistols. Skyler forced himself to ignore it. They had their job, he had his.

Water pooled in the cavity at the end of the tunnel. Despite the time that had passed since Skyler had first come here, the water had not increased in depth, leaving the scarred vessel resting in waist-deep water. Visibility dropped the closer he came to it, and by the time his boots filled with water Skyler found himself surrounded in humid air that smelled and tasted vaguely of copper.

Movement in front of him.

A black shape, slipping out of the opening on the side of the craft and into the water, so smoothly no splash was generated. Instead a subtle ripple fanned out across the surface.

Skyler braced his feet and raised his weapon with both hands. Between the riot mask in front of his face, the swirling steam in the air, and the plate of shielding mounted halfway down the gun barrel, he could barely see anything. The thing that had slipped into the water had merged with the darkness around it, and his gun's light failed to illuminate anything other than the fine droplets of moisture in the air.

He held his breath and waited, counting silently . . . *four* . . . *five* . . .

Something surged in the water, a bow-shock spray of dark liquid as torso and arms came up and lunged forward.

Skyler recoiled on instinct, felt himself tipping backward under the weight of his gear as the subhuman came fully out of the water, red laser light flaring from its eyes.

Some small corner of Skyler's mind kicked in during the split second it took for the creature to close the distance. He thumbed his weapon's clip selector, switching to explosive-tipped rounds.

He fired.

The bullet hit the creature square in the chest at the same instant its outstretched fingertips brushed Skyler's shield. A deafening crack, a blinding flash of light. Pressure on Skyler's own chest as the blast pushed the two of them apart. He fell backward into the water, had a strange awareness of cold seeping around his combat armor and into his clothing. His ears rang, yet he still heard the subhuman splash back into the pool and writhe there, thrashing in the water like an irritated alligator. Skyler sat up. He raised his gun from the water and aimed toward the splashing chaos a few meters away.

This time he held the trigger down.

A rapid series of small explosions lit the cave, as if someone had thrown a string of lit fireworks into the pool. Some of his rounds hit the back wall; others exploded on impact with the water around the creature, filling the room with a violent spray. Still more found their target, racking the augmented being with brilliant flashes of light, pushing it back.

The subhuman somehow found its footing, tried to dodge first left, then right. Skyler gave it no relief; he kept firing even as he came to his feet. He swept the barrel of the gun in sync with the creature's movements, and sensed the desperation there. It was hard to tell for sure, but Skyler thought he saw one of the creature's arms had been severed just below the elbow.

With a click the magazine of explosive rounds ran dry. The weapon automatically reverted to the main clip, and after only a split second the bark of gunfire filled the space again. Skyler had his legs under himself now, and despite the added weight of water that soaked his clothing, he found himself energized by the sight of a severed arm bobbing in the choppy water nearby. The creature could be hurt.

He focused his armor-piercing rounds on the subhuman's glowing red face, those strange traces of laser light that vaguely marked where its eyes used to be. The creature had backed up all the way to the far wall now and had nowhere else to go. The aggression seemed to drain out of it, and Skyler almost relented when the being took on a sudden, pathetic slouch against the rock and mud, accepting its fate.

Skyler kept firing until the creature slumped and slid down the wall into the water, disappearing below the surface. He fired into the water then, another burst just for good measure.

Then, silence.

Smoke wafted off the barrel of the gun. The water around him sloshed against his legs briefly before settling into an inappropriate serenity.

Skyler waited, breathing the gunpowder-scented air in voracious gulps. He focused on the space where the creature had been, and realized he could just see the top of its head above the water. The black armor had cracked like an eggshell, revealing matted, bloody hair beneath. Jagged bits of the exotic material floated nearby. The sight gave him enough confidence to yank the empty clip of explosive rounds out of his weapon, toss it aside, and slap in his only spare. He flipped the selector back to the more powerful ammunition and willed himself to be calm.

Ten seconds passed. Twenty. Another deep buzz from Pablo's Gatling reminded him of the urgency of their plan.

Emboldened, Skyler waded to the Builder ship. The surface of the hull seemed to drink in the light from his helmet and gun. Geometric grooves along the surface crawled almost imperceptibly as light and shadow played around them. Skyler stepped carefully, unable to see his feet or the tortured lumpy cavern floor below the pool's surface. He moved to the opening on the side of the vessel, gun raised and ready.

Nothing within. No subhumans, at least. Just the pedestal he'd seen before, and on top of it, the object.

Circular, with a single small half-circle notch along the edge. Red light rippled along the straight-edged grooves on its surface. It seemed to brighten as he came closer.

Skyler took one glance around the room, saw nothing moving, and set his rifle on the edge of the opening in the crashed ship. He placed his hands on both sides and hauled his waterlogged and armored self into the cramped space, groaning with the effort. Memories of what had happened in Ireland bloomed to mind, and he wondered for the hundredth time what would happen when he lifted this "key" from its resting place. He'd imagined all sorts of scenarios, the worst being a simple cave-in. Being buried alive was pretty fucking low on his list of preferred ways to die. Standing inside the ship might give him some protection if the cave's roof fell in, and at Ana's insistence he'd packed two days of food and water in his already overloaded kit. "I'll dig you out if I have to, no matter how many of those things try to stop me," she'd said.

The memory of her words urged him into action. Skyler gripped the alien object with both hands, his teeth clenched as he imagined himself being covered with that same black coating the object provided to the subhumans. Nothing happened, though. Perhaps it was his gloves, or his lack of SUBS infection. Either way, the object did not seem to have a taste for him.

He lifted it and braced himself for the worst. An earthquake, a shower of rock . . . anything. Again, nothing happened.

The alien object mercifully weighed less than the one they'd taken from Ireland. He found he could hold it with one arm, like clutching a sleeping child to his side. Skyler left his gun where he'd dropped it and hopped down from the ship.

He was halfway down the tunnel, grinning despite himself, when the rumbling started.

THE DIRE EARTH CYCLE
JASON M. HOUGH

The automated alien ship came and built us a space elevator—an impervious thread connecting Darwin, Australia to the heavens. We took advantage of the Builder's gift and established orbital colonies along the cord. Then, years later, a plague almost completely obliterated the world's population...

BOOK ONE: THE DARWIN ELEVATOR

BOOK THREE: THE PLAGUE FORGE
(September 2013)

THE WITHOUT WARNING TRILOGY
JOHN BIRMINGHAM

WITHOUT WARNING

When a wave of inexplicable energy slams into the United States, America as we know it vanishes. From an engineer in Seattle who becomes his city's only hope, to a war journalist trapped in the Middle East, this is a story of survival, violence, and a new, soul-shattering reality.

AFTER AMERICA

While the United States lies in ruins and a skeleton government tries to rebuild the nation, swarms of pirates and foreign militias plunder the lawless wasteland, where even the president is fair prey.

ANGELS OF VENGEANCE

With a conflicted US president struggling to make momentous decisions in Seattle, and a madman fomenting rebellion in Texas, three women are fighting their own battles—for survival, justice, and revenge.

"A seamless fusion of alternate history, post-apocalyptic fiction, and espionage-fueled thriller... Birmingham's story is tightly woven and deeply considered." *Publishers Weekly*

FOR MORE FANTASTIC FICTION, AUTHOR EVENTS, EXCLUSIVE EXCERPTS,
COMPETITIONS, LIMITED EDITIONS AND MORE

VISIT OUR WEBSITE
titanbooks.com

LIKE US ON FACEBOOK
facebook.com/titanbooks

FOLLOW US ON TWITTER
@TitanBooks

EMAIL US
readerfeedback@titanemail.com